202184082

Rosemary Hennigan is an Irish author who lives in Dublin. She studied Law at Trinity College Dublin and practiced as a solicitor for many years.

She has worked in advocacy for a number of human rights focused NGOs and is a Fulbright Scholar.

She was shortlisted for the Benedict Kiely Short Story Competition and longlisted for the Colm Toibin Short Story Competition. *The Truth Will Out* is her first novel.

THE TRUTH WILL OUT

ROSEMARY HENNIGAN

ORION

An Orion paperback
First published in Great Britain in 2022 by Orion Fiction,
an imprint of The Orion Publishing Group Ltd.,
Carmelite House, 50 Victoria Embankment
London EC4Y 0DZ

An Hachette UK company

1 3 5 7 9 10 8 6 4 2

A CIP catalogue record for this book
is available from the British Library.

ISBN (Mass Market Paperback) 978 1 3987 0481 7
ISBN (eBook) 978 1 3987 0381 0

Typeset by Input Data Services Ltd, Somerset

Printed and bound in Great Britain by Clays Ltd, Elcograf S.p.A.

For my mother, Anne Marie,
and in memory of my father, Brendan,
who showed me beauty, truth, love and mystery.

Prologue

The Past: 15 Years Ago

Bodkin School, Co Clare

In the initial moments after Cillian's death – before the commotion began, before the sirens and the flashing lights – Eabha and Austin stood together at the broken attic window, staring down at his lifeless body on the concrete below. He was wearing his school uniform, his tie as red as the blood pouring out from his broken skull, dead eyes staring back at the de Lacey siblings through the dark fug of night.

Shards of glass still clung to the window frame, teeth poised to bite, flashes of movement revealing the presence of bats, darting silently through the cold air, feasting obliviously on insects. In those first few moments, they were the only people who knew that Cillian was dead. Eabha and Austin, already orphans, already stalked by tragedy, were the only witnesses to what had occurred.

It had happened so quickly. Feet rising from the ground, glass smashing, a gasp of horror, a roar of anger, a rush of wind filling the room as Cillian's body broke against the window. He hadn't even cried out – shock had made him mute – but, in a matter of seconds, he was gone.

The attic was the disused part of the school, mostly forgotten by the teachers, though some of the groundskeepers still used it to store old tools and broken furniture. If these groundskeepers had ever noticed Cillian, Eabha and Austin creeping through the empty corridors to- gether, they never mentioned it, keeping their eyes down and their mouths shut, even when they learned of the tragedy, of Cillian's fall from the window, and the haze of suspicion that settled around the two witnesses to his death.

It took a while for the teachers to find them up there, and longer for the police to climb the stairs and declare the attic a crime scene. Eabha's screams had roused them: strange howls, rising up from her throat, travelling out from the attic, down the corridors of the Bodkin School, to reach the ears of sleeping teachers. Minds addled by the sudden disturbance to sleep, they struggled to find the source of the wailing, walking from dormitory to dormitory, checking every bed, until they found three empty, and no sign of the students who should have been sleeping soundly within them. They didn't think to check the disused wing – the one which was forbidden to students – until Austin came stumbling out of the darkness towards them, out through the door that should have been locked, his face pale as death, his eyes haunted with it.

'It's Cillian,' he said, gasping. 'He's after falling.'

That was when the questions began, questions seemingly without answer, without an end. The teachers asked first, then the paramedics, the police, later the journalists and the public at large. Questions spawning more questions.

How did this happen?

How did Cillian fall?

What did you do?

Over the years, they tried to answer, but they could never quite satisfy anyone. The truth was not clean: it was marred by their uncertainty, by their hesitation, by the shock that made their memories blurred, their thoughts muddled, creating doubt in the minds of those who heard them. This spectral guilt – the faint hint of it – was enough to bleach away their innocence, to lift the last lingering colour of childhood clean away.

From the instant that Cillian's body hit the hard concrete, their lives were changed, no longer their own, futures arrested by a moment in time that now held them captive. The past was a hand around their throats, the fingers pressing down every so often, reminding them of its presence, even as the years stretched, even as the memories paled. The truth fading into story. The truth fading.

Chapter One

The Present: 15 Years Later

Dublin

It was a Wednesday morning in late June when Dara first wandered into Eabha de Lacey's world, entering stage left. A call had come late the night before from a producer at the Abbey Theatre, Miriam Grant, asking Dara if she was free for an audition at short notice. They were casting for a new production of a play that would be staging in the coming months, a revival of *The Truth Will Out*, timed to coincide with the ten-year anniversary of Eabha's original production at the theatre, the production that had carried her straight to stardom. The script – attached to Miriam's email – was one Dara knew well. She had studied it at the Wilde Academy of Drama, this story of ferocious first love, of angst and teenage melodrama, of violent delights and their violent ends.

The controversy generated by the original production of *The Truth Will Out* meant that it was known widely, even by people who had no interest in theatre. As a teenager herself at the time, Dara had badly wanted to see the play, the public anger around it only intensifying her interest in this doomed love story, a young boy tumbling to his death, a mystery still surrounding the circumstances of how it had happened. Her parents hadn't allowed her to see it at the time, so it was only when she reached the Wilde Academy that Eabha's play became real for her.

She had watched her classmates perform it at the Christmas showcase.

Even then, Dara had wondered about Eabha's role in the storytelling, this open pondering on the nature of their guilt or innocence, as if she were speaking hidden thoughts aloud, transmitting them through the actors. There were some who considered it a brave display of honesty, but there were many others who found it shameless, as if she were taunting the audience, unafraid of their judgement – as if she were beyond it.

Scanning through the script Miriam had sent her, a line caught Dara's eye.

> **Eabha:** He still says that he loves me: words of love made rotten by the mouth that forms them. Words of love I once craved to hear, changed now by what Cillian has done to me.

She whispered the line to herself, turning the words over as she tried to get a feel for her character. A revival was either admirably brave or utterly reckless. Ten years on, Eabha was lighting the flames under herself again. Dara wondered at her reasons. The controversy hadn't gone away – Cillian's death still a mystery – and yet Eabha was pushing on at full speed, scratching at scar tissue, ripping old wounds open anew. It was as if she couldn't let it alone, still chasing that first pure hit of success.

She had written a number of other plays – Dara struggled to remember what any of them were about – but none came close to the success of her first. Maybe that was why: maybe a flagging career left her with little choice than to take a risk with a revival.

Miriam's invitation to audition had come as a surprise, though Dara had heard through the whisper network from other actors that they were casting for an upcoming Eabha de Lacey-led production of *The Truth Will Out*. From this scattering of chatter, she knew that the parts of Austin and Cillian had already been cast: Sam Demir would play Austin and Oisín Langford would be Cillian. But the role of Eabha had not yet been filled. This was despite a wide search, despite rounds of auditions with every leading actor in Dublin, and even a few who flew over from London.

If they were contacting Dara, they must have been really struggling with casting. She was under no illusions about the current trajectory of her career: there was only so much rejection that could be dismissed as unlucky. She had yet to successfully land anything more than minor roles in small productions; the role of Eabha was beyond her dreams. Everyone wanted to wear the Bodkin uniform and pout out at an audience from beneath a cloud of long black hair. If Dara's name was on their list, it was at the very bottom.

Only that day, she had been thinking again of quitting, moving from part-time to full-time at the vintage boutique, and earning enough money to rent a place of her own instead of sleeping on her sister's couch. It made Miriam's call feel particularly serendipitous, a tiny burst of hope to light an otherwise gloomy vista. It was highly unlikely that this audition would be different – that she would be chosen out of all the other actors who had auditioned before her – and yet, waiting in the lobby of the Central Hotel on Exchequer Street, Dara wanted it: she really wanted it, hope blooming in her chest.

The stool wobbled slightly under Dara. Across the lobby, another girl sat waiting her turn to be called, flicking through her phone with a composure Dara found lacking in herself.

She had, like everyone else, wondered about Eabha's motivations in writing the play. It would have been so easy to take the truth and twist it to her advantage: Cillian could hardly refute it now. They had put her face on the posters for the original production, the storyteller at the forefront of the story. Eabha was part of the draw, but her prominent positioning at the centre of the story had also provoked a backlash. *The Truth Will Out* was the story of Cillian's death, but by telling it from her own perspective, Eabha had kept the choice of ending for herself. There were plenty who doubted the truth of it.

Dara thought briefly of the boy who had died, his image flashing before her eyes, a boy locked in a perpetual state of adolescence, seventeen years old. Her fingers pulled anxiously on the thin silver hoops hanging from her ears.

What did it matter anyway? Theatre wasn't about truth – at least not in that sense. Theatre was a mirror, a dim reflection of things as they really were, light cast across a stage, into which the actors danced, feet moving with heightened emotion, tongues coated in a thick honey of acceptable deceit. Within the walls of the theatre, a pact existed between the audience and the actors. Once the performance began, they would believe what they were told. Truth was not the activity, not the purpose.

Watching the other actor sitting opposite her, one Birkenstock sandal dangling precariously from her bobbing foot, Dara thought of another line from the script which seemed apt.

> **Eabha:** All I want you to do is listen, Cillian! I'm just asking to be heard!

She had grown up with Eabha's face looking moody on the cover of weekend magazines: a theatre darling, a brooding mystery. What would she be like in person? Would she be as distant as they said? Emotionally detached? Would she still look the same as she had in the poster Dara used to pass on her way to class at the Wilde Academy?

With her dark hair and slightly startled blue-green eyes, Eabha had a mournful bearing to match the past she offered up on stage. Eyes that held a secret, lips that whispered of a world Dara wanted desperately to enter. She just needed a change in her luck, a chance to stand in the aura surrounding Eabha and be coated in the glow of her success.

'Dara? Dara Gaffney?'

She jumped, startled by an impatient voice calling her name. A woman was standing at the door to the casting room, propping it open with her foot, her eyes on a clipboard, strands of hair standing in static disorder around her long face.

'Ah! Dara, there you are. I'm Miriam. Good to meet you in person. Come this way?'

Her script was damp in her hand as Dara followed Miriam into the casting room and stood where she was told, in front of the small table, at which sat a diminutive woman. Bent over the leather notebook in front of her, Dara almost didn't recognise the face from the old posters.

Eabha's short, dark hair sat around her face like an inverted halo, the ends curling around her ears. Full cheeks and naturally red lips set against pale skin made her face seem almost gothically cherubic, helped by the long, dangling earrings hanging from her lobes: two black crosses.

Heart racing, Dara fixed her hair behind her ear while she waited for Eabha to speak.

Eabha de Lacey. Her name kept forming in Dara's mind, the words like a tuneless song she couldn't shift. *Eabha de Lacey.* Both the character she was about to play and the woman who would either cast her that afternoon or, more likely, reject her.

She shook the doubt out through her ears, centring herself on the floor, carefully stretching the muscles in her mouth, willing her body into line, willing her mind into her character.

When, at last, she glanced up from her notes, Eabha's eyes were clear and open. Curiosity sat in them, perhaps mingled with a slight fatigue at the prospect of yet another audition. 'Are you ready?' Eabha said, sitting back in her chair, which gave a small squeak.

'Yes,' Dara replied, scrunching her hands into anxious fists. 'Sorry, I just . . . I mean . . . Yes, I'm ready. Thank you.'

Eabha's eyes flicked down to her notebook again. 'Dara Gaffney. So, you're reading for the part of Eabha, which is to say – me?'

'I am,' Dara said. She wasn't sure if this was an invitation to begin the audition, hesitating as she shifted her weight from one foot to the other.

'You don't look like me,' Eabha remarked, her head cocked at an inquisitive angle. Dara's face was round, her cheeks dimpled, her hair long, blonde and wavy, her lips small and pink, her eyes a hazel green.

'No,' she said. 'I suppose I don't . . . I can dye my hair black? I mean, if you need me to do that.' Her cheeks had grown warm, the air in the room seeming suddenly to empty. She wished someone would open a window.

Eabha had not yet replied. She was sitting back in her chair again, her eyes watching every movement Dara made, every gesture. She seemed in no rush; Dara didn't know if that were a good or a bad sign.

Eabha's face was so familiar and yet entirely unknown – it was unsettling her – and the eyes, the eyes with their silent grief, their secrets. Dara looked away, the gaze unbearable.

Trying to speak, she found her voice absent. Her nerves had sucked the moisture from her vocal cords. Clearing her throat, she tried again. 'Will I . . . will I begin now?'

Eabha leaned forward, a small wrinkle forming between

arched eyebrows. 'Your accent. I know it, but . . .' She waved her hand vaguely. 'I can't quite place it?'

'West Cork,' Dara replied. 'Out on the Beara Peninsula, near Castletownbere. About as west as it gets.'

'Ah,' Eabha said, clicking her fingers. The beads around her wrist gave a little shake. 'That explains it. You sound a little like Cillian – his accent. He was from south Kerry.'

'Oh – I didn't realise that. I always assumed he was from Dublin.'

Eabha was not smiling, but somehow Dara thought she perceived a slight softening of her expression. Her eyes were on the window, on which a pigeon had just landed. It cooed quietly on the whitened sill.

'He was a proud Kerry man – I don't think he'd appreciate me making him seem like a Dub,' she said, almost laughing, 'but I suppose he'd have bigger problems with the way I've written him in the play.'

Something in the way Eabha spoke indicated to Dara that she was supposed to laugh at this, and so she did, contemplating, as she did so, where Eabha's character ended and Eabha really began.

The lack of air in the room and the pressure of Eabha's presence were making Dara's throat run dry again. She stepped towards the table and reached for one of the water bottles in front of Miriam.

'People never really like how they're portrayed in stories,' Dara said, before taking a gulp of water into her mouth; it had warmed slightly in the stuffy room. 'Do you like how you portrayed yourself?'

A flash of surprise crossed Eabha's face, followed by a narrowing of eyes. It was, perhaps, a projection of her hopes, but Dara sensed a deepening of interest. If there was curiosity in those eyes, it was entirely reciprocated. She had never before felt such an intense concentration of energy in a person, poised for a Big Bang.

'Do you know, I've never thought about it,' Eabha replied, after a long pause. 'But I will now . . . Maybe we can discuss it again, if you get the part.' Her smile was somewhat shy, which surprised Dara so much that she managed a smile of her own, her shoulders slowly beginning to fall, her tension easing. 'All right then, Dara Gaffney,' Eabha said, sitting back in her chair again. 'I suppose you had better begin . . . show me what you can do.'

* * *

The audition was long and intense. Eabha had asked her to read a number of different scenes, the air in the room seeming to evaporate further the longer Dara remained. They had read from one of the scenes towards the end, Miriam speaking Cillian's lines in a monotone, while Eabha sat entirely still next to her, her face carefully held, so that no emotion could break through.

> **Cillian:** I don't have any friends here.
> **Eabha:** No — I don't believe that! That can't be true.
> **Cillian:** It is ... Everyone at this school fucking hates me. You're the only one who has ever wanted to get to know me, the only one who wants me around.
> **Eabha:** Lots of people want you around — lots of people love you.
> **Cillian:** No ... no, they don't. It's just you.
> **Eabha:** Your family ... your brother ...

Cillian: Ha! My family?! No ... no, it would
be easier for them if I just disappeared. Why
do you think I'm here, Eabha? In this fucking
prison of a school? They left me here.
Eabha: I'm sure they were doing what they
thought was best for you. And it's not
forever. You'll get out of this place,
Cillian, and when you do, things will get
better ... one day soon.

When she eventually escaped, Dara stood outside the hotel,
filling her lungs with the acrid city air that now seemed almost
fresh compared to the casting room. Body exhausted, her mind
was whirring, her thoughts dragging her back into the room,
combing over Eabha's expressions, interrogating again the rise of
Eabha's eyebrow, the minute twitching of mimetic muscles, the
flickering hints of an emotional reaction across her face while
she listened to Dara speak. Try as she might to analyse these,
Dara couldn't determine what Eabha might think of her. She
gave no indication either way of how the audition had gone and
Dara didn't dare to let her hopes rise too high. If the best actors
in Dublin had failed, who was she to even dream?

* * *

It rained on the cycle home, a bus splashing Dara as she turned
onto Dame Street, so that she was drenched as she climbed the
stairs to the flat, struggling to manoeuvre her bike through the
door and stack it against the wall in the corner. The flat was too
small to contain it, but Dara had lived in Dublin long enough to
know that a bike locked outside would not last long.

Her phone rang in her pocket; she let the bike fall to the
ground in front of her, a little breathless as she answered:

'Hello?'

'Hello – is that Dara?'

'Yes, speaking.'

'Dara, it's Miriam Grant.'

She shut her eyes, willing her heart to calm, willing her hand to stop its trembling.

'Listen, I've got some good news for you . . . you did it, Dara! You really did it! Eabha *loved* your performance. She *raved* about it. I really can't tell you how surprised I was. No offence meant – you understand – but we must have auditioned a hundred girls and she wouldn't even call anyone back for a second audition. But you! She said you were the only actor to understand the fragility of the character. I can't say I'd have picked that out as the deciding factor, but Eabha knows what she wants and, well, eh, it seems she wants you, Dara.' There was a pause. 'Dara? Dara? Are you still there?'

She was on her knees, her hand in front of her mouth, into which her heart had just leaped, breath not quite reaching her lungs. 'Yeah . . . I . . . Oh my god, Miriam, I . . . Thank you. I'm so . . . That's great news . . . I don't know what to say. Thank you!'

'Well, listen, no need to thank me. You were the best. That's all there is to it. We're not the charitable sort! We're not doing you any favours here.'

Miriam gave a simpering laugh at that, as if Dara were naïve to think otherwise. The sound embarrassed her, feeling keenly her youth, her inexperience, and the enormity of the role she was about to take on. Nobody would believe the news when it broke. Nobody would believe that she had been chosen.

'Listen, Dara, I have to run – I'm up to my eyes here – but I'll be in touch with you about rehearsals. OK?'

'That sounds great, Miriam. Yeah, I . . . I can't wait to get started.'

'Oh – one final thing. Eabha wants to do some kind of garden party to introduce you to the rest of the cast. Between you and me, you'll have to get used to all the parties – she likes to surround herself with sycophants, filling the house with people who tell her what she wants to hear.' Miriam paused. 'Just don't tell her I said that, won't you?'

Dara gave a nervous giggle and said: 'No, I . . . Of course not.'

'Good!' Miriam said. 'You'll see for yourself, I suppose . . . the way she gobbles up the attention. But that isn't what I wanted to say. We'll announce your casting soon, but I'm sure you'll understand, given all the *unpleasantness* around the play, you really can't speak to the press without first getting our approval. I know that sounds a bit – I don't know – *paranoid*, but it's just that there has been quite a bit of . . .' She searched for the word. 'Bother.'

Dara's thoughts flashed to her family back in Beara: she could hear the censure already, ears ringing with it.

'You know, there are people who will try to cause trouble, Dara. We just need to manage that as best we can.' Miriam paused again. 'You know what I'm referring to?'

Cillian Butler, the boy who loved a girl who watched him die.

'I do, Miriam. It's not a problem. I understand the need for, eh, discretion.'

'Glad to hear it. I'm sure you'll be a good sport about all this, won't you? Ah, you will. I'm sure you will. Right so, chat soon, Dara. Cheerio! Goodbye!'

* * *

The flat was really only one large room with an unusually high ceiling that the landlord had divided in two with a mezzanine floor, accessed via a set of wooden stairs, jutting out from the wall. On the upper level, Dara's sister Rhona had a bed and a chest of drawers. On the lower level, there was a couch, a compact kitchen in the corner, and a poky bathroom that could fit a toilet, a tiny sink and the narrowest shower unit Dara had ever seen. It was not intended for two, but Dara had needed a place to stay and if they split the rent, she could just about afford it off her salary at the boutique. It was supposed to be temporary, until a change came in her fortune, but that was taking some time.

While she waited for Rhona to return, Dara sat on the couch that was also her bed and wondered – a little giddily – if perhaps this was it. Perhaps, this was the moment when things would really change for her: her big break.

Of course, it hadn't worked that way for the original cast. Theirs was a story told in warning to young actors in need of a dose of reality. An actress named Vanessa Devin had played Eabha in the first run, but, despite largely positive reviews, she had vanished from the scene soon after the run ended. A falling out with Eabha – so they said – after which she had been blackballed by almost every director in the country. The lesson they were supposed to learn from this was simple: *sic transit gloria mundi*. All glory is fleeting.

But, phone in her hand, Dara wondered if there was more to it. Glory might be fleeting, but there was surely more to the story than just a falling out. She typed out Vanessa's name and hit search, looking for evidence of what had really happened, so she could be absolutely sure it wouldn't happen to her.

There was very little online about Vanessa after *The Truth Will Out*, no evidence of recent roles. A photo of the two of them together caught her eye: Vanessa next to Eabha at an after-party at the Gresham Hotel, Eabha's arm wrapped casually around

Vanessa, the way you might with a friend. An equal. Imagine that.

Dara was still engrossed in the photo when Rhona arrived in the door from her shift at a local café, throwing her bag on the kitchen counter as she entered, hands on her hips and eyes turned expectantly towards her sister. There was a large coffee stain on her T-shirt.

'Well?!' she said. 'How was the audition? Tell me everything!'

Dara pulled her legs under her as she turned towards her sister. 'Rhona, you're not going to believe this.' A broad smile filled her face, her cheeks dimpling. 'I got it . . . I *actually* got the role! Can you *fucking* believe it?!'

'Go way, Dara! Did you?' Rhona said with a shriek of joy. 'Jesus Christ, Dara, you're *joking*!'

'No, I'm serious, I got it, Rhona. It's really happening. I can't believe it either!'

Rhona let out another shout of excitement, jumping onto Dara, who groaned as a knee landed into her stomach.

'You're crushing me, Rhona, you clown!' she said. 'Get off me.'

Rhona sat back on the couch and her hair, tucked into a bun on top of her head, bobbed about as if with delight. 'This is huge! We have to celebrate!'

'We can celebrate after rent day,' Dara replied.

'No, I'm sure we have something now!'

Rhona got up and reached into the fridge, her hand emerging with an old can of cheap cider from some now-forgotten party. She opened it, poured the contents into two mugs and handed one to Dara. It was flat and tasted of soured apples.

'You'll be drinking champagne soon enough,' Rhona said, 'but this will do you for now.' She clinked her mug against Dara's and then took a drink, reaching over to squeeze Dara's shoulder. 'I'm so proud of you, little sister.'

A fleeting smile crossed Dara's face before she turned away, her head angled towards the window. A light was shining through the clouds, the grey brightening to white, the sky turning to silver. A new world seemed to paint itself across the blank canvas: Eabha's world.

Chapter Two

An invitation soon arrived for Dara to a garden party at Eabha's home on Leinster Road, at which she would meet the rest of the cast before rehearsals began, just as Miriam said.

All day, a nervous sea was churning in her stomach as she tried to convince herself that she could pass muster as someone who deserved this role, someone who belonged. It still seemed very possible that Eabha might change her mind on a second meeting; no contract had been signed and there was no guarantee of her place in the production beyond a brief phone call from Miriam.

Dara was used to being an imposter – it was her profession – but as she left the flat in denim dungarees and her old Vans with all the holes, she couldn't shake the feeling that a mistake had been made somehow. Who was *she*? Who was she to stand on stage as Eabha de Lacey?

Walking along the narrow footpaths of the Liberties, she pulled at the strap of her dungarees. She was late; her mother had kept her on the phone too long. The news of her casting had spread from Rhona to the Atlantic shore, to the stone house at the end of the grass-eaten lane where Dara had grown up, where her mother sat at the kitchen table, letting her worries mushroom.

'Dara! Your sister is after telling us about the play – so, you got it? You got the part?'

'Yeah, I did . . . sorry, Mam – I should have . . . I mean, I haven't had a chance to tell you yet.' This wasn't quite true: she had been avoiding the conversation, knowing well how it would unfold. And she had been right to worry. She could speak the language of her mother's silences, the tone in her voice both familiar and unwelcome. In the sighs and the hesitations, in the inflections and intonations, sat disapproval. A non-vocalised form of censure.

She could see her mother on the other end of the phone, anxious fingers drumming against the kitchen table, eyes on the thin strip of ocean visible from the window over the sink: 'You know, they never put anyone in jail for the murder of that poor boy, Dara. That's shocking . . . just shocking! Imagine how it must feel for the family! All those years, Dara, left to wonder . . . and then that woman wrote a play about it. A *play*. Why would you get yourself mixed up in something like this?' She didn't pause for Dara to answer. 'Why would you want to get mixed up with . . . with . . . with people like *her*?'

Near Clanbrassil Street, Dara glanced at the time on her phone while a group of kids kicked a ball against the gable wall next to her. She was still running a little behind, picking up her pace as she passed the two women arguing over rolls of fabric propped outside a dressmaker's shop. At the corner of Long Lane, a taxi driver was roaring at a food-delivery cyclist for skipping the lights. The houses were growing larger around her, the bricks older, the gardens more cultivated and the people fewer as Dara crossed the canal at Harold's Cross.

Waiting at the traffic lights, she shut her eyes and thought briefly of that word her mother had said, hanging heavy as honey in Dara's mind. '*Murder.*'

It rippled through her thoughts as she turned onto Leinster Road, a word that didn't fit in this neighbourhood. *Murder* – the word Eabha had brought here when she came. Eabha, who lived in its shadow.

Crossing the road, Dara scanned the doors for numbers, counting down towards 74. A hundred windows were looking back at her, through which she could see snatches of the way other people lived – velvet lampshades, a candelabra, a floral arrangement in a porcelain vase – but the people themselves remained hidden from her casual glance. This was not a part of the city Dara knew well. It belonged to the people who sat in the dark of the auditorium while she entertained them on stage for a fee, people who had pensions and private health insurance, spare rooms and holiday houses that sat empty on the Beara Peninsula for most of the year: a constant reminder for the locals of the wealth of other people, from other places.

Her feet stopped outside number 74. A tall, three-story red-brick with a pale pink front door, above which sat an ornate fanlight in the shape of a rising sun, or was it setting? A mint-green 1964 Ford Cortina was parked outside.

Dara had told her mother that she needed this play, needed the pay cheque, needed the break, the turn in her fortunes – and all of that was true. But, standing for the first time in front of Eabha's home, it felt to Dara that the play meant so much more than any of that. It would create a real future in acting, a life beyond the limits of other people's imaginations and other people's ambitions for her. It meant freedom, in the truest sense of the word: to cast herself out from her own skin and inhabit the skin of another, to be present on a stage and entirely absent, freed from the confines of her own perspective, lost in the words and actions of a character, experiencing life through the prism of the stories she would help to tell, through the people she would make real. Birthed from the page, given life through the movement of her limbs, through her breath, through her voice. And this play meant the creation of Eabha de Lacey herself. Seeing through her eyes, speaking her words . . . Dara's breath caught in her throat as she reached for the doorbell. She couldn't think of a greater thrill than that.

Slowly, the last of her composure was slipping away, dripping through her fingers to form a puddle at her feet. The gleaming window reflected her fear, her skin burning against the denim of her dungarees. Christ – why had she chosen *dungarees*? For a garden party in a house like this? What was she thinking?! She was holding a bottle of cheap white wine in one hand; with the other, she tried to fix her dishevelled hair, hurriedly trying to approximate the image of a person who belonged here.

The front door opened. She jumped slightly; Eabha was before her again. Did she imagine it or was there a shine from Eabha's skin? A glow, like that made when light touches gold?

'Here she is!' Eabha's hands reached for Dara's arms, fingertips pressing down lightly, making the skin briefly white where the blood fled: five round circles on each arm. 'My leading lady! My alter ego! Come in, Dara. Come in, darling. *So* glad you could make it.'

Eabha was wearing a vintage floral tea dress with a broad skirt that drowned her frame and trailed on the floor behind her as she showed Dara into the house. Her feet were bare and both arms were covered in bangles. They tinkled, one against the other, as she walked; melodiously, as if the air around her made music as she passed.

'Everyone's out the back. Is that wine you brought? How nice!' She took the wine from Dara, who released it reluctantly. It was the best she could afford from the Spar near Francis Street and there was a very good chance it was vinegar. 'Come this way! I hope you're hungry. There's *too* much food! I never seem to get the portions right. You'd think I'd learn from the mounds of leftovers, but it seems I'm not for changing.'

Dara followed her down the hallway towards the rear of the house. Her Vans – with the holes – felt heavy on the long Berber rug underfoot. A scent trail of perfumed skin followed in Eabha's wake, drifting into Dara's nasal passages, filling her mind with a pleasant fog.

It felt to Dara as if she were looking at the house through a glass bottle. The light had a golden quality and, with every window open, the air was heavy with the scent of the honey-suckle and the buddleia from the garden. The walls were covered in artwork of wide-eyed women bent into improbable contor-tions, abstract shapes in wild colours, and photographic prints of blurred mountain scenes and haunted people cast in silhouette. Music was playing from some speaker she couldn't see: an in-strumental piece that sounded like The Gloaming.

Dara trailed after Eabha, hesitating for a moment at the open doors, as if waiting to step onto a stage. The drapes stirred next to her. A breeze was rising. Her audience were waiting, the crowd in the garden looking her way as Eabha shouted: 'Our leading lady has arrived, everyone! Right this way, Dara. Help yourself. See – there's oceans of food. I'll never finish it. You all simply must eat up.' She elongated her vowels when she spoke, like the rich kids from South Dublin who would come to Beara every summer, the ones Dara would watch from a distance.

Dara stepped down into the garden, the grass beneath her feet long enough to kiss her ankles, approaching the wooden table with her right arm stretched across her chest, catching her left arm at the elbow.

Eabha took a seat next to Miriam, while across the table sat Sam Demir and someone Dara didn't recognise. He was tall, his limbs long and gathered around him uncomfortably, as if he didn't know how to carry them properly. His hair was gathered into a knot on top of his head. She couldn't see his face; he was concentrating so intently on his plate of couscous and falafel that he had not yet bothered to look up at her.

Her eyes swept past him, towards the end of the garden, where a two-person band was strumming a guitar and a banjo, playing lilting folk songs. A string of pastel-coloured bunting hung along the brick wall behind them, pinned haphazardly. Something about it felt contrived, as if Eabha were trying to impress them, a thought which provided a little comfort to Dara, who was, herself, attempting much the same thing.

Eabha was smiling expectantly at her. 'Take a seat, won't you, Dara? Take the seat next to Sam and Austin. Have you guys met each other yet? Come on, introduce yourselves!'

So it was Austin: the man with the topknot and the long limbs, the man over whom a cloud of suspicion had sat since the day Cillian Butler fell out of an attic window in a boarding school in County Clare.

Her mouth opened, though words didn't immediately come – she had no idea how to greet him – but it didn't matter. Before she could speak, Sam Demir wiped his hand on his napkin and held it out to her, smiling. He had a handsome face, dark skin and dark eyes framed by slightly curly hair. As his hand closed on hers, she thought maybe there was a slight crackle of mutual attraction between them.

'I'm Sam,' he said, his voice deep. He had a way of looking at her as if she held his full attention. It was a quality she had always admired in a person – the ability to make other people feel at ease. It was entirely the opposite of Austin, who was sitting silently next to Sam, making no effort at all to greet her.

'Good to meet you, Sam,' she said, her voice sounding more nervous than she wanted. Austin's presence was unsettling her.

'So you're the one who got the role! You realise you beat every actor in Dublin for this part, right?' Sam said, narrowing his eyes and making a show of looking her over.

She pulled some loose strands of hair out of her face, her laugh shy. 'Oh, well, I mean, I'm as surprised as anyone!'

'Don't be . . . you were obviously the best,' Sam replied.

She laughed again, because she didn't know how else to wear the compliment, but he didn't laugh with her; no comedy was intended.

He was still looking at her – watching, assessing – when, from across the table, Eabha interrupted, calling: 'Austin? Austin, did you say hello to Dara?' She was a little terse and Austin seemed to flinch at the sound of his name, at this requirement to partake in social interaction.

Dara stretched her hand towards him, hoping its shake wouldn't betray her nerves. Austin's hands were very large, enveloping hers entirely. She wondered if they were the hands of a murderer.

'Nice to meet you, Dara.' The sun in his eyes was making Austin squint, his nostrils flaring, his voice limp and resistant to conversation. A thick beard covered the skin around his mouth and chin.

'Nice to meet you too,' she said, taking the empty space Sam had created for her on the bench next to him.

She wondered what her mother would think of all this. The question ran immediately through her mind – the question everyone must have thought when they first met Austin. Did he do it? Did he push his friend from that attic window? She had not expected Austin to be here – *why* was he here?

Her nerve endings hummed, as if a shadow were passing slowly overhead. She glanced at the sky: just a wash of blue.

'So, Eabha,' Sam said, leaning towards her, 'how does it feel to be back at the Abbey?'

'It's been a while since we've hosted you – hasn't it, Eabha?' Miriam said, with a smile which Dara found oddly sharp, the edges of her lips filed to a point. 'You've been concentrating on *smaller* productions, haven't you? More your style, perhaps?'

Eabha's fingers were plucking at a loose thread dangling from the cuff of her sleeve. 'I go where I'm wanted, Miriam.'

'Oh, well, of *course* you're wanted at the Abbey,' Miriam replied, with her simpering laugh. 'We're very excited to have you back . . .' She threw a sideways glance at Austin. 'Maybe with less of the fireworks this time.'

'So, it didn't put you off then?' Sam asked blithely. 'All the, eh, "fireworks", as you call it?' Dara felt a slight tightening in her throat. Fireworks seemed like a mild description of the controversy that had engulfed the play's first run at the Abbey. She had heard some of the story, but she would need to know more if they were to avoid repeating mistakes, creating wild explosions of light and sound.

'We'll manage all that,' Miriam said, with a tight smile. 'It's tricky – you know what people are like, but, I'll tell you one thing, it won't be any harm to seat sales.'

With a sip of his wine, Sam shuffled forward slightly on the bench, turning to Eabha. 'And how are you feeling about it? Nervous? Excited?'

'Oh, god . . . I don't know really . . . excited, I suppose . . . maybe a little daunted. It's been ten years since I told this story for myself and, you know, it's a . . . it's a difficult story to tell. It wakes the ghosts again and makes them shriek.'

They were silent for a moment, heads bowed respectfully, as if the ghost of Cillian had appeared next to Eabha, summoned to her side by this sombre invocation.

Next to Sam, Austin rose abruptly to his feet, saying something about hearing the doorbell. He walked up the steps and into the living room, where he disappeared from view, his movements heavy and lumbering, each step a struggle.

Eabha rose too, the cheerfulness drained from her now, as if Cillian had sucked it dry. 'Excuse me a minute,' she said. 'I'm just going to ask the band to play another song.'

Dara watched her move ponderously through the garden, lost in her thoughts, running her hand along the lavender bush and then cupping it to her nose and breathing it deep. The garden was cultivated but utterly wild. *Sprezzatura*, the Italians called it. Wisteria tumbled from the back wall into the honeysuckle. A bank of marigolds was in full bloom next to a collection of wildflowers: vibrant poppies, cornflowers of electric blue, bashful roses with blushing petals, and there – at the foot of the angelica – some tiny strawberries for the taking.

When Austin returned to the garden, Oisín Langford was following behind him.

'The bollocks himself!' Sam called over, bringing a smile to Oisín's face.

At the Wilde Academy, Dara had barely been noticed, too shy to make waves in a sea of extroverts, and she doubted Oisín would recognise her now. He, on the other hand, had been something of a minor celebrity amongst the drama students. This was mostly due to a small, recurring role on a Netflix show about Vikings. The role had involved a particularly moving (Dara thought hammy) death scene, which, years on, still remained the high point of his audition reel. But the reputation which preceded Oisín included his deep and messy romantic entanglements with other actors and, seeing the playful smile slapped across his face as he looked at her for the first time, Dara thought she could see why.

As his eyes latched onto hers, Dara wondered if she would be the exception or the next in line. He was looking directly at her, blue eyes waiting expectantly for her to greet him, so she rose to her feet, holding out her hand.

He didn't take it, instead pulling her into an embrace. He had somehow managed to gather her to him so tightly that her whole body was pressed against his, her leg between his legs. This happened in such a curiously smooth movement that it seemed practised. Certainly, it didn't seem accidental, and Dara was relieved when he pulled away from her again, warm air filling the space between them.

'I've been looking forward to meeting you, Dara,' Oisín said. 'The woman I'm supposed to love.'

'I'm not sure if I would describe myself that way,' she replied, sitting down on the bench again hastily; next to Sam, where it was safe.

'Sorry, was that weird? I didn't mean it to be weird,' Oisín said, laughing as he reached for the bottle of wine on the table and poured some into an empty glass. 'I was trying to sound—'

'Like a creep?' Sam offered, provoking a chuckle from Miriam.

'I was going to say debonair, but yeah . . . sure,' Oisín replied, with a smirk.

Dara could see immediately why Eabha had chosen Oisín to play Cillian. He spoke with an almost teenage bravado – though she knew they were both twenty-four – and he had the air of someone desperate for attention, for love. This was something

Dara had often sensed in other actors and she wondered briefly if other people could sense it in her too. An awful ache, a driving need to be adored.

Oisín took Eabha's now empty seat next to Miriam, immediately knocking back some of his wine, splashing some onto the fabric of his shirt. He was wearing a short-sleeved white shirt with a pattern of tiny gold lightning bolts. 'So, what have I missed? What are you talking about? You all look so . . .' He looked at each of them in turn. 'Serious.'

'I'd like to get to know our protagonist here a little,' Sam said, nodding towards Austin, who was now chewing on some flatbread.

'You mean antagonist, surely?' Oisín replied, reaching for a handful of olives, which he let drop into his mouth one by one, chewing them all simultaneously so that some juice dribbled from the side of his mouth. 'I mean, he's the antagonist from Cillian's point of view at least.'

Dara looked to Austin who was shaking his head. 'You're describing a character . . . it's not me. You know that, right?'

'Yeah, of course,' Oisín said, 'but it's based on you. It's not completely made up.'

Austin's eyes travelled out towards his sister, standing alone in the centre of the garden, swaying to the Sufjan Stevens cover coming from the two musicians in the corner. Somehow she still held their attention, still central to proceedings, though she had absented herself. 'I think Eabha would agree she used a fair bit of artistic licence,' Austin said.

'Isn't that what they say about the ending?' Oisín replied, then laughed quickly, before Austin could react, and added: 'I'm joking! Just winding you up, Austin. Relax!'

Austin's teeth moved back and forth over the dry skin of his lips, as if baring them to Oisín. 'Are we going to have a problem with you?' he said. His voice was low and deep and seemed to barrel Dara in the chest. She glanced at Oisín, who showed no sign of fear.

'Not at all,' he answered, grinning at Austin. 'I'll behave myself.' He turned to Miriam, giving her a quick nudge with his elbow. 'Do you reckon there will be protests this time? Will we all be in the papers?'

Miriam wrinkled her nose. 'Why don't you ask Austin?' She shifted in her chair, her chin in the air. 'He would know more about that than me.'

Austin was picking at the food in his teeth with his tongue. 'I remember it well: it nearly fucking killed me.'

This declaration and the seriousness with which he had delivered it was not at all what Dara had been expecting.

'You serious?' Oisín said to Austin, who pushed his empty plate away, resting his arms on the table in front of him.

'Deadly serious,' he replied. 'That fucking play put me in the hospital.' He glanced down the grass towards his sister, then raised a finger to his lips. 'Don't tell her I told you that . . . she wants to keep it secret.'

Discomfort spread, like a glaze, across their skin. Sam coughed. Miriam reached for her phone, fingers tapping as she typed rapidly. Dara kept her eyes fixed on Eabha.

Shifting in his seat, Oisín shook his head. 'Shit man,' he said, laughing nervously. 'What the fuck happened?'

'Can't say. Sworn to secrecy.' Austin reached for his glass of water and took a sip.

Drops of condensation were sliding down the bottle of rosé. Dara reached for it, filling up her glass. The silence at the table was growing as long as the shadows stalking across the lawn towards Eabha.

'Do you think we could make some requests? Something a

little . . . livelier? This music is putting me to sleep,' Sam commented, sitting forward in his chair in a brave attempt to shift the conversation.

Grateful for the chance to escape Austin's grim aura, Oisín hopped out of his seat, kicking his shoes off. 'I'll talk to the guitarist,' he said, running off across the grass, his feet bare and the bottoms of his jeans rolled up to mid-calf. He didn't make it all the way to the musicians, stopping to greet Eabha, who took his hands so they could dance together.

Sam leaned back towards Dara and she caught the scent of his shampoo – or maybe his cologne – something like almonds and sandalwood. Watching Eabha and Oisín dance, something in the way they moved together surprised her, a synchronicity of movement, a familiarity of form.

She looked over her shoulder at Sam, his breath on her cheek. 'Do they know each other already?'

'A little,' he replied. 'Eabha used to direct these short character pieces at Smock Alley Theatre – she called them her "dramatic bursts". A lot of actors got their start through her – myself and Oisín included. She made an army of devotees that way.'

'Sycophants,' Miriam muttered.

'Your word, Miriam,' Sam replied with a tight smile.

Across the grass, Oisín had pulled Eabha close to him, her head now on his shoulder, the last of the sunlight glinting into the garden through the trees behind them, casting them in silhouette. Sam was swaying slightly to the music and Dara felt herself begin to sway with him. The wine was making her skin feel warm, sending her thoughts into retreat, her mind aglow.

She was enjoying the moment – the dancers on the grass, the soft, lyrical twang of the guitars, the sun on her face, the hum of nearby honeybees – so that when Austin abruptly stood up again, he startled Dara. As he rose, his knee banged against the table, sending the glass bottle of San Pellegrino tumbling over, water drenching the basket of sourdough in the middle of the table.

'Are you all right?' Dara said, on her feet, reaching instinctively for a napkin to mop the water.

Austin was staring out at the grass – at his sister, at Oisín. For a moment, she thought he might explain himself, might explain the anger she could see blazing now in his eyes and in the blood-drenched capillaries of his cheeks.

'She just wants a fucking audience,' he said. 'That's all this fucking is, that's why we're here. That's all it ever fucking is with her.'

'That's all *what* is?' Dara asked, pulling at the strap on her dungarees. Water was dripping over the edge of the table; she placed a napkin over it and let the paper drink it deep.

'It's the fucking Eabha show again,' Austin said. 'Ah fuck this anyway.'

They watched him disappear into the house, from where they could hear doors banging, something ceramic falling onto something hard, and the sound of thick leather boots against the wooden floorboards. It was the last they saw of him that evening.

'What was that all about?' Dara said quietly to Sam, who just shrugged, and said: 'Weird guy.' As if that settled the matter.

Dara looked into the house. The drapes danced gently next to the door. All was calm now that Austin was gone.

'He creeps me out.' She felt a slight shiver come over her. 'I can't help wondering about . . . well, you know . . .'

Sam met her eye, a small curl to his lip. 'If he murdered Cillian? We're all wondering that.'

There it was again, that word: murder.

'It's a cruel artistic choice, isn't it?' Miriam said. Her eyes were still on her phone, but she was not, it seemed, entirely ignoring their conversation. 'Making a play out of our curiosity, nurturing the voyeur in us. Titillating us all with the truth, almost showing us what happened, then draping the crucial moment in darkness.' She lifted her sunglasses off her face and propped them on top of her head, where they settled into the thick waves of her greying hair. 'I'll tell you what, though. People love it. It fills theatres like nothing else. People always want to solve the mystery. They think they can figure it out, wrap the story up with a nice bow on top. All neat and tidy, so they can sleep better at night.'

'That must lead to a lot of disappointed audiences,' Sam remarked, bringing his foot to rest on the bench next to Dara. His ankles were bare, the hair on his leg thick and dark. She leaned closer to him again, just slightly. 'The play doesn't exactly solve the mystery for them.'

'No,' Miriam said, her eyes roving towards Eabha. 'Nobody knows what really happened that night, but everyone has a theory. Everyone thinks they can figure it out, and she just keeps us guessing, dangling the truth in front of our eyes, never quite revealing it.'

Watching Oisín twirl Eabha on the grass, Dara began to wonder if the ugliness of the world could ever really be held at bay, the truth ever kept hidden. And she wondered how she would describe any of this to Rhona when she got home later that night. The pretensions, the falsity, and the aching wealth of it all. The secrets and the unease that Eabha could not quite obscure, despite her best efforts at sensory distraction.

Still, there was a heady pull to it, and as she watched Oisín and Eabha move together – blurred slightly by the cloud of midges gathering around them as the sun began its slow task of setting

– Dara felt her critical faculties slip away, lulled into dormancy. Lungs heavy with pollen, she let the harsh edge of reality grow blunted, let the tension leak from her shoulders, allowing herself to forget that she didn't belong, that she was other, wearing her old dungarees and Vans with the holes.

Chapter Three

Their first table read together took place in the attic of the house on Leinster Road. Eabha had converted the attic into a rehearsal room of sorts, a smell of fresh paint greeting them as they entered.

They had arrived early that morning, each of them taking one of the oversized cushions Eabha had thrown around the floor. She, herself, sat on the fraying settee which stood against the white wall opposite. Next to it stood a tall lamp with a mustard yellow lampshade, but the rest of the room was unfurnished. On the windowsill, incense was burning, and through the smoke, occasional sounds of birdsong and passing cars floated in, disturbing their progress.

'I know, I know, it's unorthodox to rehearse at my house,' Eabha said before they started. 'But you need to *feel* what it was like – hidden away in that attic together, the way it was for us at school. Nobody knew we were there, nobody ever interfered . . . it was just us, locking ourselves away from everyone else for hours at a time.' There was a pause. 'Cillian kept these weird little objects up there. Animal skulls he found, a dozen wooden figures he carved with his penknife . . . creepy little things . . . faceless people. I don't know what happened to them after he died – they must have been thrown away – but I took the goat skull with me that night. I wanted to keep it safe for him. Sounds silly now, of course ... but, at the time, it seemed to matter.' Her voice drifted towards silence, one thought dimming as another rose. 'It's hard to explain unless you experience it, but it did something to us ... that time together. You need to understand that feeling.'

They began the table read together, starting out buoyant and hopeful, if a little shaky with nerves. But Eabha's presence in the room quickly put Dara off. Almost immediately, she began tripping over her lines, marbles in her mouth. It felt bizarre to play a younger, lightly fictionalised version of Eabha while she sat inches away from Dara, her body curled over the threadbare antique settee. Dara couldn't stop glancing over at her, waiting for a reaction, though Eabha didn't give any. She could see Oisín and Sam exchanging quizzical glances while she read, doubt visible in the arch of their eyebrows, in the tight seal of their lips. Her skin burned with each new mistake, provoking the obvious question: why exactly had Eabha chosen *her*?

The heart of the play – indeed much of the reason for its success – was the soul-baring nakedness of Eabha's depiction of herself. But Dara felt utterly inhibited as she read her lines and, by the time they reached the ending, she was deflated, out of her depth and drowning in her own lack of talent.

When they had finished the first full reading, Oisín – body stretched out on the floor at Eabha's feet – dropped his script onto the carpet next to him and said: 'Right. Well, think we can all agree that's going to need a bit of work.' He rolled onto his back. 'Will we start again?' Eabha, seemingly unaware the question was posed to her, didn't reply. 'Eabha? ... Hello? M a d a m   D i r e c t o r?'

This slow enunciation of her role in the morning's proceedings brought her attention back into the room. She looked over at

Oisín, blinking rapidly, then stretched her arms into the air with a long yawn, and said: 'We need coffee.'

Dara was in a state of mortified disarray, muscles contracting and organs twisting as her body cringed into itself, as if trying to fold her away like a piece of paper made small enough to shove deep into the bottom of a pocket. Her eyes rambled repeatedly Sam's way. This was why it would be a mistake to pursue that interest, to indulge that flutter she had felt when he'd greeted her with a kiss to the cheek that morning and said he liked her T-shirt. She needed to embarrass herself professionally in peace, without also wondering if Sam would fancy her less.

Eabha's hand was reaching towards her. 'Why the long face?' she asked, pulling Dara onto her feet; stronger than she looked. Sam and Oisín had already disappeared down the stairs, leaving them alone together in the attic.

'I was awful,' Dara said emphatically. What was the point in hiding it? She might, at least, get credit for a little self-awareness.

'Don't be silly. You couldn't possibly know your character yet,' Eabha said, her fingers pressing gently against Dara's right shoulder blade. 'We've only just met.' She was so slight – just five feet tall – and her skin was so pale that she did not seem entirely corporeal, as if she were made of glass: opaque and frosted.

Together, they descended the two flights of stairs to the kitchen, with Eabha's arm locked around Dara's body. The walls were painted a pale pink, as if the house were blushing: Dara could relate.

As they entered the kitchen, Eabha's hand – fingers heavy with a jumble of rings, each with a different gemstone of amber, amethyst and opal – lifted from Dara's shoulder. 'Oisín, will you make the coffee? In the big cafetière, please.'

It was surprisingly airy for a basement kitchen, light pouring in through the long glass doors which led out to a small, sunken patio, where a round, wrought-iron table sat with four chairs.

It didn't seem like Oisín's first time in the kitchen; this Dara noted immediately. He knew his way around, taking the cafetière from the press and sourcing the ground coffee without the need to consult Eabha. With a touch of jealousy, she wondered at the familiarity, how it had happened so quickly.

He was whistling a song while he filled the kettle and measured out the coffee, entirely at ease, running his hand repeatedly through his sandy brown hair, fluffing it absently with restless fingers. There was a small gold piercing in his right earlobe and Dara could see the presence of a chain through the thin cotton of his T-shirt, on which the name of a band was printed – Fontaines DC – along with an old black and white photograph of a young boy puffing on a cigarette.

Were there other rooms that Oisín knew? Other places opened to him? Other intimacies shared? She thought of the way Eabha's forehead had come to rest against Oisín's chin while they danced together on the grass, just as Austin rose abruptly to his feet, while the blood rushed to his face and the anger spat out from his tongue.

On the patio, Sam was fishing some cigarettes out of his pocket, lighting one up, rocking his chair precariously on two legs, his foot balanced on the edge of the small brick wall around Eabha's kitchen garden. The herbaceous scent of thyme and rosemary mixed with the cigarette smoke. Next to him, Eabha sat resplendent in the sunshine, smiling at Oisín as he appeared a few moments later with the freshly brewed coffee.

'So,' she said brightly. 'I thought perhaps we could take this chance to talk.' She poured some coffee for each of them. 'You know, if this performance is to come together, we need to build some trust between us.' Her eyes swept over them, a smile flickering across her lips. 'I'm sure you've all read some horror story or other about me and my brother by now. Some of you might even agree with what they say about us . . .'

Eabha paused briefly, taking a delicate sip from her coffee, as if to give them a moment to reconsider that idea, to see her seated here, the picture of genteel graciousness, and to square that picture with the audacious stories told about her. Murder? Pah!

'All I can do is try to be open with you all.' Her eyes, blue-green orbs, were shining with moisture now. 'You're free to ask me anything – all the questions in your hearts.' Briefly, she reached for Dara's hand to her right, clasping Sam's to her left. Oisín was sitting opposite, out of reach, so she held him with her gaze instead. 'Radical honesty between us is the only way. So, please. I mean it. Ask me anything.'

It was a generous move, a confident move – but did she mean it? Eabha had been young when she made her life public property: only twenty-one when her debut landed into the world, toppling her life as it had been and creating another from the rubble. It seemed a high price for success. Back in Beara, if Dara so much as sneezed, the entire townland knew. The idea of willingly surrendering her privacy to a theatre of strangers, night after night, seemed hideous to her. But she couldn't exactly put that in a question.

A wind was rising, the venetian blinds knocking against the glass, and somewhere a lawnmower was chewing grass. At the patio table, there was stillness. Sam glanced at Oisín and Dara, neither of whom seemed inclined to speak, and then – impatient – reached for his coffee with the hand not holding his cigarette. 'All right, well, I have a question.'

'Great! Ask me anything, Sam.'

'In the garden the other day, your brother told us the first production nearly killed him. Is that . . . is that true?'

'Oh, goodness, Sam, really?' She sounded irritated, impatient even. Dara supposed it must become quite grating, Eabha's brother so often eclipsing her art.

'Yes, really. I've been wondering what he really meant by that. He said he meant it.'

'He said he was deadly serious,' Oisín added quietly, biting at the skin of his thumb.

Eabha was coquettish again – girlish, as if to render herself harmless and unthreatening to them. 'Oh, no – he was exaggerating! Austin can be a little dramatic about the past.' Her cup rattled against the porcelain saucer as she reached for it again. 'He felt the pressure more than the rest of us, of course – I suppose that won't come as a surprise. He's the one they blame.' She looked up through the long lashes that fanned out from her eyelids. 'But you don't need to worry about any of that. It'll be different this time. We've learned from all that – *I've* learned. I'm older now, more experienced. And Cillian's been dead fifteen years. What harm can he do us now? Fifteen years in the cold earth: dead almost as long as he was alive. Maybe now he'll rest.'

Sam pulled more smoke into his lungs, letting it circulate. 'Surely the best way to avoid more scrutiny is to avoid another production?'

Eabha gave a surprised laugh. 'Well, if you think that, why did you take the part?'

Sam's thumb ran over his lip, his eyes on his Stan Smith trainers. 'I am but a humble jobbing actor, while you, Eabha, are a theatrical legend. You don't need this.'

'Is that what you think?'

'Is that not the truth?'

Eabha took a breath, leaving this last question unanswered. The breeze was brisk now, the crumbling petals on the old rose bush behind her head fluttering limply in the heat. 'People talk about that night as if they were there, as if they could possibly know what passed between the three of us. They focus on Cillian's death as if that's all that matters – but it's not. Everything leading to that point in time is just as worthy of our attention, our scrutiny. Death devours life because it is the ultimate mystery, but a person's life should never be supplanted by their death. That's what a tragic death does – it overshadows a person. Our fear of death makes us forget that it's only one small part of a person's story.' She pulled her knee towards her chest, the heel of her bare foot balancing at the edge of her chair. Her toenails were painted a dull red. Dara looked at Oisín, uncharacteristically silent. He seemed to be soaking in every word Eabha said but his expression gave nothing of his own reaction away.

'So you're saying you welcome the scrutiny? You actually want it?' Sam asked. His jaw was well-defined, not quite square, and it was solidly set now while he waited for Eabha to answer.

'I want people to connect with the work,' Eabha replied, 'to *understand*.'

'But you can't select your audience or control them. You can't keep them focused only on the parts of the story you like.'

'No, of course not. I can only hope that every so often, maybe every couple of nights, there's someone in the auditorium who *gets* it.' She sat up straighter on her chair, adjusting her white linen dress, the tassels at her neck dancing at the disturbance.

Dara felt an urge to reach out and grab Eabha's face between her two hands and say: *I get it! I do! I know how it feels! That hunger for understanding – that's inside me too!* Her performance that morning returned to her mind, the memory racing through her, like acid rising from her stomach. There would be no connection, no recognition, no moment of shared consciousness between the audience and the players if Dara couldn't inhabit her character. She glanced at Oisín again and wondered if his silence was born out of a similar fear.

Her eyes turned next to Eabha, who was looking directly at her, as if reading Dara's mind. 'The only way I can be understood is through all of you, through the story you tell on the stage. You're my voice. You understand?'

Dara felt as if her stomach had been squeezed inside her, as if it were held in a vice grip by Eabha's small hand. She couldn't fail her: she wouldn't.

'So, let's try another reading, will we? You can ask questions as we move through the scenes.'

Reluctantly, Dara pulled her script out of her pocket, the pages already battered from anxious fingers thumbing through them. 'Which scene will we read?'

'Oisín, why don't you pick?' Eabha said, her head turned to the side. "You've gone all quiet on us." She sniffed. "You remind me of my brother already."

He gave a half-smile. 'Just taking it all in," he replied, sitting up straighter and clearing his throat. "All right, let's do the scene when Cillian starts opening up to you. The first time you sneak out together.'

'All right then,' Eabha said. 'Ready, Sam? Ready, Dara . . . or should I call you, Eabha? Act one, scene four.'

SCENE: *Night-time, a half-moon overhead, a deserted landscape across which the shadows dance. On the horizon, windblown hawthorns look like long-limbed spectres. A stone wall, covered in moss, stands next to a grove of trees.*

Enter **AUSTIN**, **EABHA** *and* **CILLIAN** *wearing the uniform of the Bodkin School.*

Austin: So this is what you do for fun? There's nothing here ... it's just rocks and hills and—

Eabha: —Emptiness.

Cillian: What did you expect? A fucking fun fair?

Austin: When you said we were sneaking out, I had something a little livelier in mind ...

Eabha: I heard some girls in my class talking about some pub in the town that might serve us?

Cillian (*irritably*): No — they won't. They can spot a Bodkin kid a mile off.

Eabha: Surely we could *try*? Austin and I are new — they wouldn't recognise us?

Cillian (*temper rising*): If you have a better offer, Eabha — be my guest, go down to the town with whoever you want ... don't let me stop you!

Eabha (*a little taken aback, walks towards him*): No, I ... I want to hang out with you, Cillian. (*Looks around again, as if looking for points of interest in the dark and barren landscape*) Do you come out here alone? Usually?

Cillian (*Kicking at the loose earth at his foot*): Yeah ... like, who would I be out here with?

Eabha: Your friends?

Cillian *looks up at her, checking to see*

if, as he expects, she is mocking him, but
Eabha's *expression is earnest.*
Cillian: No, I ... I come here alone.

Oisín lowered his script. 'Can we pause there? I need to ask you about Cillian.'

Dara caught the brief grimace that flashed across Eabha's face. She felt it herself, the humbling nature of context: the boy who had died, his ghost sitting in the sun next to them.

'Did the poor fucker really not have any friends?'

Eabha ran her hand through her hair, pensive for a moment. 'No, the other kids were cruel to him. They were these rich kids of diplomats and lawyers and CEOs – and, for them, the Bodkin was all part of a master plan for life, you know? It was a gateway for their choice of the best universities, the best careers. But it was different for Cillian ... it was different for us too. I guess that's why we were drawn to him.' Dara watched the way the light fell across Eabha's face as she spoke, the way her skin shone in the sunlight until it was as white as her dress. 'His family just dumped him at that school and he could never understand why. He felt betrayed, terribly betrayed.'

'Why would they do that to him?' Oisín asked. Dara wondered too: her mother had begged her not to move away to Dublin, ringing her every night for the first six months to check that she was in one piece. It had annoyed her at the time, but now the memory of those phone calls was maturing into something like gratitude. There was no version of life she could imagine where her parents would leave her rotting in a boarding school.

'His mother was an alcoholic,' Eabha replied, eyes on the shining obsidian surface of her coffee. 'She spent her time in and out of institutions and clinics. Drink destroyed her and he spent his childhood in the shadow of it. Then his father stuck him in boarding school to get him out of the way – I'm sure he thought he was doing the right thing, but Cillian couldn't understand it. As far as he was concerned, everything was about his mother – her addiction, her treatment, her attempts at recovery. And it just ... broke him to be left behind. Even if he had lived, I don't think he would have recovered from that abandonment.' She paused, swallowed, and said again: 'Even if he had lived.'

Again, he seemed to hover near her shoulder, summoned by her sadness, by the regret in her voice, by the compressed mess of emotion she kept in her ribcage, packed into the narrow space around her heart.

'Cillian was always alone when we first met him,' she continued, her voice quieter when she spoke again. 'That was why he came into our lives in the first place – Austin walked into his first class and just took the empty seat next to Cillian, not really thinking about who he was sitting beside.' She shook her head, her hand resting against her face, palm cupping her nose and mouth so that they could hear her only faintly. 'But Cillian was so grateful ... as if Austin had chosen him or something, plucked him out over the others. We didn't know then ... how could we have known? How could we have known how it would end?'

Next to Dara, a crunch of foliage sounded as a sparrow took flight from the magnolia tree. It looked naked and bereft now without its petals, without the pale pink lanterns perched on the woody fingertips of each branch.

When she looked back at Eabha again, her gaze was long and vacant. Lifting her script, gently Dara said: 'Will we continue?'

'Yes,' Eabha replied, gathering her mind back into her body. 'Let's continue.'

Eabha: Well, you have us now, Cillian ...
(*Her hand is still on his shoulder as she
smiles at him, but* **Cillian** *doesn't smile back.
He looks unsure of himself*)
Austin: So what's there to do out here?
Cillian: It depends ... sometimes I just
wander around and see what I find. Sometimes,
if my brother Fergal has brought any of his
poitín for me, I might drink some of that
... or sometimes I go looking for
mushrooms ...
Eabha: Mushrooms?
Cillian: Yeah ... the magic ones. You can
find them between the rocks, if you know what
you're looking for. That's always a treat,
if I can find them. (*He spreads his arms,
his back to the audience, as if to open
himself instead to the trees behind him*) They
transform this place, just like they say ...
like magic. It's like I can see the world
better, you know? Like I detach from my body
and lose myself. I'm not here anymore ...
(*His head rolls back on his neck, eyes staring
upward as the dark night stares back at him*)
Like I don't exist.
Eabha (*unsure*): But is that ... a good
thing?!
Cillian: It's the best I can hope for right
now.

'Sorry, I need to stop again—' Oisín's face was twisted in confusion, his eyes, nose and mouth coalescing in the centre of his face. 'I just need to understand him – was he depressed? I mean, did Cillian *want* to die? Maybe not overtly, but on some level?' Dara watched him run his hand repeatedly through his hair, agitation in each sweep of his fingers. 'Because there are people that interpret the ending that way.'

'There are people who think that's what really happened,' Sam added. He hadn't spoken for a while, but now he was leaning forward towards Eabha, deeply interested in what her answer might be. 'There are people who think Cillian jumped out that window and you lied to protect his family from the truth.'

Eabha sat back in her chair and let her eyes drift over their heads and towards the garden once more. 'I wish it were so simple, Sam. But if there were a way to vindicate my brother like that . . . if there were a way to shut people up once and for all – with their whispers about us and their conspiracy theories – I would sing it from the rooftops.'

Sam sat back again, but he didn't seem satisfied by the answer. He lifted his right leg onto his left knee, the foot twitching from the ankle. They were each, it seemed, as jittery as the other.

Eabha turned to Oisín again. 'You need to know what Cillian was like, beyond just the play – I understand that. But I don't know where to start, really. Cillian was . . . he was . . . It's so hard to put him into words . . . Cillian understood how it felt to be alone in the world, the dizzying feeling of that lost security, the absence of home.'

Dara studied the movement of emotion across her features while Eabha spoke, while memories breached from the murky depths and were submerged again. She wanted to capture each one, to douse them in formaldehyde and stick them in a jar, ready to be used for future performances.

Wriggling again in her seat, Eabha pulled on the tassels of her dress and said: 'See, unlike Cillian, we chose the Bodkin School.' She pushed her hair out of her face, took a sip of her coffee. 'It was my mother who died first. It was very advanced when we discovered it – the cancer. She didn't live very long. A matter of weeks. My father died a month after she did. An aneurysm, one morning after breakfast. It was as if he didn't want to live without her.'

She had written her grief into the play – a silent presence in the back of every scene, death humming in the gap between words – but, still, Dara felt an inward convulsion as Eabha spoke. It felt like an intrusion, as if they were passively feasting on Eabha's misfortune, chewing on her troubles like meat from a bone, a bone they would soon pick clean.

'At the time, it felt as if they had abandoned us, left us bruised and battered, battling on in a new life we never wanted.' Eabha sighed then, kicking her dress outward from her body, as if the material were too tight on her skin. 'We were lucky they chose Aunt Celia as our guardian. She let us make our own choices – that helped. But our choices were few. We chose the Bodkin so we could escape into the isolation of it, the vast empty skies, stretching for miles.'

'And is that why you chose Cillian?' Oisín asked, pulling at the silver chain around his neck. 'Abandonment issues?' His tone struck Dara as strangely combative.

'I suppose you could call it that . . .' Eabha replied slowly. She seemed to shrink into her chair as she spoke, reduced suddenly, flattened out.

Oisín had been tense since this dissection of Cillian began, as if it were his skin the scalpel sliced open. Dara watched as he exhaled long and hard, eyes cast up to the rooftop as a spotted starling disappeared into a nest hidden in the pointed apex of the dormer window. 'My mam walked out on us,' Oisín said, looking over at Eabha again, his expression uncharacteristically serious. 'I was seven, so . . . I get how it feels.'

'Oh,' Eabha said quietly.

'Yeah, like, I get why it . . . why it's easier.' He was struggling to articulate. 'I just mean, I get why you would find it easier being around Cillian.'

'Yeah, no, you're right – it was easier,' Eabha said, nodding. 'It was a comfort. He understood, instinctively. And I liked that he liked me. It made me feel tethered to something, to someone, at a time when everything was bewildering and just . . . just so endlessly *grim* for us. You probably think that makes me shallow.' She looked at Sam. 'Maybe it does. But it's an amazing feeling . . . to be loved like that, more than you should be . . . more than is reasonable . . . unconditionally, even madly. I mattered so deeply to Cillian that he would do anything for me, even . . . even die for me. That's what he said.' She stopped abruptly and then she was gone again, her mind wandering off somewhere, hand in hand with Cillian's ghost.

'Maybe we should take a break there?' Dara suggested, looking around at them.

'Sure,' Eabha said, her attention returning briefly to the present. 'But the scene was better this time, right?'

'It was definitely better this time,' Oisín agreed, his hand reaching across the table to take Eabha's. Dara watched him squeeze her hand in his and felt sure that he was lying. They were still so stilted, so nervous with each other, unsure of their characters' motivations, trying to fit inside the minds of three traumatised teenagers. And all the while, their suspicion was dancing in the air around them.

* * *

When Rhona asked her later that evening how the first re-hearsal had gone, Dara wasn't quite sure how to answer. She could describe Oisín's open fascination with Eabha, his eager-ness to please, the latent attraction evident whenever he turned his eyes to his director. Or she could speak of the undercurrent of attraction between her and Sam, his distrust towards Eabha, there in the curl of his lips and the whorl of his cigarette smoke. She could confess that she felt a fraud, an actor acting the role of an actor acting the role of a character. Or she could tell Rhona of the way Eabha strained against her memories, slipping in and out of the past, as if gliding through a still body of water, towards an ending only she knew.

They hadn't discussed it yet – the ending, the moment of Cillian's death – and it felt as if they were dancing around it still, the mystery of it hanging over them, just as it did in real life. But Dara would not tell Rhona the question which kept her from sleep that night, while she lay flat on the couch in the dark, staring at the black mirror of the blank television screen. They were part of the play now. Did that make them part of the problem?

Did that make them complicit?

Chapter Four

A feeling of complicity lingered throughout the first week of rehearsals and, by the time Friday came, there was a bitter taste in Dara's mouth: fruit turning bad while she ate it. An air of secrecy hung over each day, Eabha's evasiveness fuelling their doubt, sending their thoughts inevitably out of the moment and towards the past, to the moment of Cillian's death, where they stood on the concrete next to him, looking up at Eabha in the attic window, begging her to tell them what really happened.

On Friday evening, before parting ways at the junction of Leinster and Rathmines Road, Sam looked from Dara to Oisín, their faces drawn, moods low, and said: 'Anyone for a cheeky drink? I don't think we should leave things like this. I'm not going home this depressed.'

'I'd love to,' Dara said at once. Between juggling rehearsals each day and working every spare moment she could at the boutique, she was wound up tight and needed to unclench some of the tension seizing her limbs. Payment for rehearsals had not yet been discussed and she still owed Rhona rent from the previous month, even as the next rent day approached.

'I'll come for a bit,' Oisín said, 'but I'm meeting a friend in an hour, so we better be quick about it.'

'Grand,' Sam said, leading the way towards O'Connell's Pub, a short walk from Portobello Bridge, where the six o'clock news was playing on the television in the corner and a couple of men sat at the bar making vague denunciations about 'that shower in government' to nobody in particular.

They trooped in, past the barman, who glanced sceptically at them from behind the taps, and chose a table down the back of the pub in a quiet corner where they wouldn't be overheard.

Oisín ordered for them at the bar, while Dara plonked herself on a stool, feeling the weight of the day as if it were moving from the roots of her hair, through her scalp, and descending downward into her bones. She stretched out her back, relieved to be somewhere other than Rhona's flat. The thought of it seemed unbearably small after spending so much time at the house on Leinster Road.

'So,' Sam said, folding his arms onto the table in front of him. 'We did it, Dara. We survived the first week!'

'Barely – I felt like it would never end.' She grimaced, sighing into her hand, then peeking out at him through her fingers. 'I promise I'll improve.'

'What are you talking about? It's just early days,' Sam replied. 'You know, you're doing better than you think.' He was looking at her again with the same intense interest, something warm and searching in his gaze, as if he wanted to know everything about her.

The interest was mutual. All week, she had watched him at rehearsal, so conscientious about his work, so serious, until a sudden smile would burst from his face when his eyes met hers, sending a sudden thrill bolting through her.

'Liar,' she said with a grin. 'I just can't seem to get the words out right. It's like my limbs are wooden and my voice – *God*! I sound like a five-year-old. All squeaky and . . . and compressed.'

Sam, a quizzical look on his face, gave a small laugh. 'Jesus, Dara. Are you always this hard on yourself?'

She laughed, dislodging some of the tension in her chest. 'Yes. Absolutely. Always have been. Can't seem to help it!'

'Why? Something to prove?'

'What do you mean?'

Sam smiled again. 'Well, people who demand so much of themselves usually have something to prove.' He paused. 'Who hurt you? Want me to slap him for you?'

She thought briefly of a boyfriend she had once, back home in Beara, only she was the one who had hurt him – fleeing, just as soon as she could, to Dublin. There hadn't been any boyfriends since. The occasional date, the occasional late-night mistake, but nobody who held her attention. Until, that is, the afternoon in Eabha's garden.

'No, it's just—' Dara's eyes were on the knot in the wooden table in front of her, an elongated oval shape which made her think of an open-mouthed scream. 'It's just that, where I come from isn't like here. My family are practical people. When I told them I wanted to study drama – I'm not joking with you – my parents acted like I'd told them I was dying. Like, honestly, you're laughing but they're just waiting for me to fail at all this . . . and it's not them being mean or trying to undermine me on purpose or anything like that. They just don't understand . . . like they can't really imagine what it would be like for me to succeed at acting. It's not something that's possible in the world they've always known.' Her expression was wan, but Sam was still watching her with rapt attention. She drummed her fingers against her collarbone. 'It just makes me *really* not want to fail at this, you know?'

'You're not going to fail,' Sam said firmly. 'You're talented,

Dara – plus, Eabha de Lacey is a pretty big deal in this town, so if she's backing you, other directors will take notice.'

'Is she still a big deal? Like, to other directors?'

'Yeah, well, she has never had the same commercial success since *The Truth Will Out*, but she's very highly regarded as a playwright. The critics adore her.'

Dara blinked. 'I just . . . I just can't understand why she chose me.'

He reached across the table, holding her hand briefly, so that her skin seemed to radiate heat. 'Because you were the best, Dara. It's that simple.'

It would have been so easy to believe him, to let his confidence fill her. She could surrender control, reach towards him, kiss him, as she thought maybe – just maybe – he wanted her to, letting him hold her, while he broke through the layers of her self-doubt, freeing her from them once and for all.

She pushed her hair behind her ears, watching Oisín carrying three pints of Guinness, carefully balanced in his hands, with two packets of crisps clenched between his teeth. It would be a mistake – not only to further erode any professionalism existing around rehearsals, but to make Sam's interest in her the foundation for a new confidence. She glanced at him quickly and then looked away again: no, she was sure of it. It would be a mistake to pursue anything with Sam.

'You need any help?' Sam said to Oisín, who shook his head, throwing his leg over a stool, while Sam took the crisps from his mouth and opened them up on the table. Oisín pulled his stool closer to them, raising his pint to his lips. He took a sip, a foam moustache appearing on his upper lip.

'Fucking delicious,' he said, running a hand over his mouth. 'I've been dying for that.' He looked at each of them in turn. 'So, how are we all feeling?'

'Not sure, if I'm honest,' Sam said. 'A bit shook. I was warned about Eabha de Lacey, but, Jesus ... it's all very intense, isn't it?'

'What do you mean *warned*?!' Dara said, spluttering on her pint. 'Warned about what? Nobody bloody warned me!'

Sam tucked his hands under his armpits. 'Ah, you know, just the whole big mess ...' He waved one hand in the air vaguely, then tucked it away again. 'You know, what happened with Cillian Butler and all the stuff after it.'

'The stuff after it?' Dara said, reaching for a handful of crisps.

'Yeah, like, you know, the Garda investigation, Austin's lawyers getting him off on a technicality,' Oisín said.

Dara's nose wrinkled, looking from Sam to Oisín and back again. 'You're not seriously talking about that conspiracy shite people go on with? Where are your tinfoil hats, lads?'

'Look, of course some of it has been *exaggerated*,' Sam said, his arms folded on the table in front of him, 'but some things are just fact: the police didn't believe their story – you know, Cillian just *falling* out the window. And even though they couldn't find enough evidence, there are plenty of people who still think Austin pushed him and Eabha covered for him – or the two of them are in on it together.'

Some lines from the play rose up to tickle Dara's thoughts.

Cillian: Stop looking at me like that.
Austin: Like what?
Cillian: Like you want to kill me.

'That's ... that's just people spreading rumours,' Dara said, shifting on her stool. 'I mean, it's so *implausible*. They were kids – like, Austin was only seventeen! Why would they do something like that?'

'A crime of passion is always like that, Dara,' Sam said, 'and who better than a teenager to take things too far?'

Oisín took a large gulp of his drink. 'I think we all know how that could feel,' he said, pulling his chain free from beneath his shirt, playing with it in his mouth.

'Look, the way I remember it,' Sam continued, 'there was a big controversy when Cillian died because his family didn't believe it was an accident – that got people speculating about it, you know? There was all that stuff they found in the attic . . . the drugs and the drink and the weird animal bones and shit . . . it all made him seem unstable, so another theory is that maybe he killed himself – like he jumped from the attic in some moment of mania – but the Butler family rejected that as well. Austin and Cillian had been fighting the week he died, fighting about Eabha. He beat the shit out of Cillian, really laying into him. There were witnesses – lots of them – and they told the police that two teachers had to physically pull Austin away from Cillian, while he howled like an animal. Then Cillian dies a few days later in strange circumstances? It all starts to sound a bit coincidental. It wasn't long before that rumour began to spread.'

Dara could picture the scene easily; Eabha had described it clearly in the script. Austin's anger, Cillian's fear.

Austin (roaring): What did you do to my sister? What did you *fucking* do to my sister?!

She looked down at her arms, the sleeves pushed up to her elbows, imagining bruises appearing slowly across her skin. Bruises in the form of fingerprints. Bruises that had once marked Eabha's arms.

Cillian: It was an accident, I swear, Austin! Just an accident! Get off me! Please, you're hurting me!

Austin strikes again until **Cillian** *is on the ground, then seizes him by the shirt, his fist landing another blow, sending blood splattering across the concrete path outside the school, beneath the attic of the western turret.*

'The Butler family showed up at the Bodkin School then,' Sam continued, 'sniffing around, asking questions, and next thing you know, a lot of witnesses are making statements to the police.'

'So, there it was: evidence mounting against Austin. A motive of some kind,' Oisín added.

Dara felt her face grow hot again, as if the sun had burrowed under her skin that afternoon and trapped itself there. She checked her nose for evidence of sunburn, tapping the skin lightly. 'So, they arrested him?'

'Well, that's the thing – they didn't get that far,' Oisín replied. 'They invited him to the police station and questioned him for a few hours.'

'Without a lawyer or a guardian, without a caution,' Sam added. 'He was still underage at the time, so that was a big no-no.'

'That was their big mistake.'

'And then the rich family lawyers rowed in and that was that,' Sam concluded.

'They let him go?' Dara said.

'They had to. They fucked up.'

Dara frowned, trying to connect the story she had just heard with Eabha, the person whose company she had shared all week. 'None of that is in the old news reports online,' she said slowly. 'Where are you guys hearing this stuff?'

'People started telling me bits and pieces when they heard I got the part,' Oisín said. 'The theatre world is fascinated by her: their little murderess.'

'Stop,' Dara said, rolling her eyes, but Oisín didn't seem to be joking.

'It's true,' Sam said. 'They talk about her *constantly* behind her back – they'd tell you all sorts – but she's still theirs, you know? They protect her. Always have, always will.'

'Even if they think she's guilty?' Dara asked.

'I guess so, if her talent is worth it . . .' Sam raised his pint to his lips. 'I don't think they *really* believe she's guilty. But, if you ask me, people are a little too ambivalent about it. They're invested in the story of Eabha de Lacey, either way,' he said. 'Fascinated.'

'My mam is worried I'll get, like, mixed up in something serious,' Dara admitted. 'She thinks Cillian was murdered.'

'Most people do,' Sam said. 'The weird thing for me is why Eabha would write a *play* about it. She could have just slipped away into obscurity. Nobody would remember her now. She'd get away with it. But, instead, she threw gunpowder on it.'

'But,' Dara reached into the packet for more crisps, which crumpled in her hand, 'Cillian was their only friend at the Bodkin. Sure, what he did to her was fucked up, but *murder*? I don't know . . . I just can't see it!' She leaned her head back and poured the crumbs directly into her mouth. 'If you ask me, people just want a salacious story.'

'Of course they do,' Oisín said, 'and that's why we all have jobs. Drama, isn't it?'

The men at the bar were roaring at the television again, this time a football match receiving their ire, a free kick under dispute, one man writhing on the grass, another pleading with a harried referee.

'But the controversy doesn't do Eabha any harm, does it?' Oisín leaned over his pint. 'The play was a sensation because she sold it as the truth of what happened that night. Everyone went to see it. That's why anyone even knows her name.'

Sam looked up, eyebrows rising with his gaze. 'It's a shame it's so self-serving – it could have been a decent play if she had the guts to actually tell the truth.'

'You don't think it's the truth?' Dara said. She wasn't sure that she did either, but the conversation was rattling her, making her feel as if she were the one accused of deceit. She found herself defensive about the alleged crime of another.

'I mean, you've met them now,' Sam replied. 'Would it really surprise you to learn that Cillian didn't just fall out that window?' He scratched at the stubble on his chin. 'There's something about Austin . . . I wouldn't like to meet him on an empty road on a dark night, you know what I mean?'

Oisín laughed, but Dara looked down at the screaming knot on the table again. 'He's intense, but that doesn't make him a killer,' she muttered. 'If you'd been through what he has, you'd probably be a little weird too.'

'So, you're *sure* nothing happened in that attic?' Sam pressed. 'You're positive Cillian was just some kind of klutz?'

He seemed to find the conversation amusing, which was starting to irritate Dara. If what he was saying were true, surely that meant they were involved in a cover-up? Perpetuating a lie, helping a killer. There it was again, that nagging feeling: complicity. She shook her hair out with her hands, but the feeling wouldn't dislodge itself from the tips.

'I don't know . . . I really don't know what to believe,' she said, realising as she spoke that this was the truth of it. All week, she had been hoping that Eabha might knock the doubt out of her, but Eabha seemed oblivious to her need, drifting around the place in silk kimonos and velvet capes, as if eccentricity and otherworldliness placed her above such mundane things as fact and accuracy, guilt and innocence.

'Of course, the other possibility is that Cillian did it on purpose,' Sam continued. 'He might have jumped.'

'That sounds more likely to me,' Dara said quickly.

Did it?! Or was it just the more convenient explanation, the more forgiving? She scratched at her hair, unable to make up her mind one way or another.

'It's not impossible,' Sam said thoughtfully. 'The post-mortem found drugs in his system when he died, right? So, maybe it was genuinely an accident. Or maybe something went haywire in his mind and he didn't know what he was doing? It's all in the play – the clues are all there and they all fit, depending on the outcome you want to reach.'

Dara took another sip of her pint, growing more uncomfortable by the minute. Beneath the surface of Eabha's pale face lay a swamp of dark secrets, into which they were sinking.

'What else should I know about the de Laceys then?' Her laugh was nervous.

'Ah, you're in deep now, Dara. I just assumed you knew what you were getting yourself in for.' Oisín was grinning at her; she wished he'd stop.

'Can I ask you something?' Sam said, his chin in his hand. 'Do you guys think Eabha is genuine? All that *enthusiasm*, all those dreamy looks . . . it seems forced to me. Like a character she inhabits. You can almost see the moment she flicks the switch on.'

Dara watched him lick his finger and dab at the crumbs clinging to the greasy packet of crisps. He seemed so suspicious of Eabha, perhaps even more so than Austin, which confused her.

'Aren't we all performing parts for each other? When it comes down to it,' she said. 'Isn't that just what people do?' She looked over at Oisín, who was chewing on his chain again. 'It is weird though, isn't it? Playing the part of real people, while they watch us pretend to be them.'

'But we're only playing versions of real people. We're playing the versions Eabha wants to show the world,' Sam replied. 'That's what's so messed up about it all.'

'She who holds the pen, holds the power,' Dara said, taking another sip of her pint. There was a text on her phone from Rhona, who wanted to know where she was. Again, the thought of the small flat made Dara cringe: the water stains on the ceiling, the electrical wires hanging loose along the walls, the threadbare carpet.

'We staying for another?' Sam said hopefully, his eyes passing from Dara to Oisín, who banged his empty glass on the table in front of him, the foam residue dispersing slowly across it.

'Can't, sorry. I'm going to have to take off. Need to get down to South William Street for seven thirty,' Oisín said.

'One of your women, is it?' Sam said, smirking. 'Who is it this time?'

'Why don't you mind your own business, Sam?' Oisín replied, middle finger raised, before turning to Dara with a smile. 'Can we do this again another time? I don't think I'll survive this play without you two keeping me sane.'

'I'm making no promises on the sanity, but yeah . . . we should do it again.' She turned to Sam, regretting each word as she spoke it. 'I better go too. I have the early shift at the boutique tomorrow.' Small as it was, the flat ate up most of her wages and she couldn't be sure she had the price of another round in her bank account anyway.

'Where do you work?' Sam asked. Was she imagining it, or did he sound disappointed that she wasn't staying?

'Oh, just this little boutique on Drury Street – vintage stuff mostly. You know how it is . . . bills to pay.'

'Don't I know.' Sam exhaled out through his nose a little bitterly. 'And people think we're just indulging our hobbies.'

'If this play goes well, it could be a decent payday for us,' Oisín said, on his feet again, fixing his chain under his T-shirt.

Dara wondered briefly when she should expect to get paid for the play, but it didn't seem like the moment to ask. 'I wouldn't say no to a national tour,' she said instead.

'We might get to the West End,' Sam suggested, 'if we're lucky.'

'Why stop there?' Oisín said, grinning. 'I'm thinking Broadway, baby!'

Sam's smile was wry. 'You're a dreamer.'

Dara smiled. 'But it's the only way to be.'

* * *

They remained on her mind all weekend. In moments of reverie, as she restocked the shelves in the boutique, she found her thoughts meandering back to them. Flashes of Eabha gazing out the attic window, or a chain between Oisín's teeth, or Sam's dark eyes meeting hers through the branches of buddleia. Lines from her script rose and fell from her lips, as if occupying the space between thoughts.

Eabha: We could run away, the two of us . . . we could live like this forever!

Cillian: Your brother would come looking for
you. Wherever we go, Austin would find us ...
(*He pauses*) Who would you choose? If you had
to? Me or him?
Eabha: Stop it, Cillian. Don't ask me that.
Don't ever ask me that!

On Sunday morning, there was a piece announcing her casting in the newspaper. In the Culture section, next to a photo of Eabha, was her name.

Always one to surprise us, Eabha de Lacey has cast newcomer, Dara Gaffney, in her hotly anticipated new production of ***The Truth Will Out***. De Lacey's upcoming revival of her notorious play will mark Gaffney's first major role on an Irish stage. A baptism of fire and huge pressure for any actor, but especially one so young and un-tested. How she'll handle the public attention off-stage will be as important as her acting performance. An association with Eabha de Lacey – infamous for the murky death of Cillian Butler – will be make or break for Gaffney.

Dara had a shift at the boutique, her phone buzzing in her pocket throughout the day with messages from friends, family, other actors she knew, even a few casting directors who had roundly rejected her previously. Mostly, the messages were congratula-tory; a few more prying, seeking to satisfy a curious thirst. Her mother rang, with a voice damp with worry, to say that it was never too late to change her mind and come home. But then, that was her mother's answer to everything.

When her shift finished, Dara wandered the canal before heading home, thinking of Leinster Road. Her mind pulled her back to Eabha, to Sam, to Oisín, as if there were a cord tied around it, tugging her back to that house, where the world was cast in a golden hue and even the dust hanging limp in the air seemed to glow.

Rhona was waiting when she arrived at the flat, the newspaper in her hand. 'Here she is! The star of the show!'

Cringing, Dara reached for the paper, crumpling it as she tried to snatch it from her sister. 'Put it away! I don't want to see it again!'

'Why? This is huge, Dara! It's what you've been waiting for!'

Dara sat down on the couch next to Rhona, shifting the cushion behind her back. 'Yeah, but did they really have to bring Cillian Butler into it?!'

'Dara . . . like, what did you expect?' Rhona adjusted her position so that her back was supported by the arm of the couch and her socked feet were pressing against Dara. 'You're going to have to get used to that kind of attention, do you know what I mean?'

Dara, swatting at Rhona's feet until she moved them again, said: 'I looked at the comments on that article, Rhona. Ten of them in a row, just the word "*killers*", over and over again. Do I have to get used to that?'

'No, I mean, obviously that's not OK.' Rhona frowned, watching the tension running through her sister. 'Here, don't get upset, Dara – it's just weirdos on the internet.'

'No, don't . . . don't do that, Rhona, OK?' Dara said, sitting up straight so suddenly that Rhona jumped slightly.

'What do you mean? Don't do what?'

'Don't undermine me like that! I already have Mam telling me to quit the play and go home to Beara. I need you on my side.'

'Ah, Dara, of course I'm on your side,' Rhona said, surprised at the strength of Dara's reaction. 'I'm your biggest fan – I swear I am. Sure, you were the best Annie ever seen on the Beara Peninsula.'

Dara threw a cushion at her.

'What?' Rhona said, laughing. 'That curly head on you.'

'You're a wagon.'

'Give us a song, go on.'

'Oh, shut up!'

The thought of the production of *Annie* – one of those mildly mortifying fiascos involving the local musical society, a perpetually off-key piano and a dodgy ginger wig – was dislodging some of the tension in Dara. She gave a sharp laugh.

'You know, that would have been around the same time Eabha was debuting *The Truth Will Out* at the Abbey – bit of a difference.'

'Hard to believe that little Annie has finally made it,' Rhona said. She looked at her sister again. 'But, come here, Dara, I don't want you thinking I'm like Mam and Dad. Seriously, don't ever think that. I support you completely.' She pulled the sleeves of her hoody around her hands. 'And, sure, if it's any consolation, they think I'm wasting my life too. I don't know . . . maybe they're right.'

Dara caught the look on her face before Rhona turned away. 'Have you been thinking any more about that nursing course?' she asked.

'I have, yeah . . . I'd have to move back to Beara for a while and save on rent,' Rhona said, 'which I'm not mad about. I fought fecking hard to get out of that house, you know?'

'I know . . . but it'll just be temporary? A means to an end?'

'These things always start out temporary, don't they?' She rubbed her nose, then sighed. 'What would you do?" Her expression was suddenly very serious. "If I had to move out? It's a small space to share with a stranger.'

'Jesus, I couldn't,' Dara said. 'I'd have to find somewhere else. But don't worry about that. I'd manage. I'll stay with friends.'

'All your friends are as broke as you are,' Rhona said.

'Well, you never know,' Dara replied, 'if this play goes well, it could be the start of something, Rhona. My career could really take off.'

'I've no doubt,' Rhona said. 'Mam and Dad will like that – get your face on a billboard and they'll die.'

Dara shook her head. 'I think Mam half expects me to end up in jail. She rang me earlier. Aunty Sheila is after telling her I'm "aiding and abetting a murderer".'

Rhona snorted. 'Aunty Sheila is a dose.'

'I know, but Mam listens to her.' Dara fell silent briefly. 'And I know I'm being stupid, Rhona, but I can't help wondering if she's right?'

'She's not. Don't let them ruin this for you.'

Dara wasn't listening anymore, her attention on her phone, the screen lit up with a text message from an unknown number.

Linda O'Rowe Dara, it's Linda O'Rowe from the Irish Independent here. Saw the announcement in *The Times* this morning.

Without another word to Rhona, Dara rose to her feet, locking herself in the bathroom where she couldn't be observed. Fear was galloping through her as she read the rest of the text message.

Would you be free for a chat at some stage? I have some questions for you about Eabha de Lacey and the revival of *The Truth Will Out*. This is your chance to be heard. We should talk.

She wouldn't answer Linda – she was under strict instructions to run every media query past the production team – but after her conversation with Sam and Oisín, Dara didn't feel inclined to tell Eabha about it either.

What harm was there in one little secret? She could hold this back – just this message – in case her mother was right and she was hurtling towards trouble.

In case she needed an escape plan.

Chapter Five

'I have some news.'

Eabha was standing at the door of the rehearsal room, wearing a white shirt with very red lipstick. Her smile was strained and she was unable to stand still, her hands fidgeting by her sides, her weight shifting between her feet as if perpetual motion would ward off whatever was agitating her.

Dara was sitting cross-legged on one of the cushions. She hadn't slept the night before, the text from Linda unsettling her. 'What's happening?' she asked, rubbing at the corner of her eye where sleep still lingered.

'It's the Abbey,' Eabha said, her chin at a defiant angle. 'I had to part ways with Miriam over the weekend.' Her fingers fiddled with the long chains around her neck, from which hung three lockets.

'So, wait, did we lose the theatre?!' Sam said, perching slowly on the very edge of the settee, as if to steady himself. 'I don't understand – what happened?'

'Well, don't look so upset, Sam! It's good news for us, really, because—' Eabha paused. 'I've accepted an offer to take a slot in the Gate Theatre.'

'The Gate?'

'Yes . . . the director, Geoffrey Goode, is an old pal of mine and he has offered us an impossibly good deal. Artistic licence to do what we like – and we're opening the new season!'

Sam's hand was in front of his mouth; he removed it slowly. 'I thought it was supposed to be back to the original theatre – wasn't that the plan?'

'Well, yes, but there was a disagreement with the Abbey. Look, it's not a big deal . . . it's just that Miriam wanted to have final say on anything I might say to the media. She said the theatre are very nervous after what happened the last time – the controversy. And about Austin too.' She looked down at her hands, her nails painted as red as her lips. 'She was treating me like some sort of liability, like a risk to be managed. And she talked about Austin like he was . . . like he was deranged.'

'That's poor form,' Oisín said, his hands in his pockets. He was standing next to the window, his face caught in a pocket of sunlight. 'You could hardly let Miriam treat you like that.'

'Exactly, Oisín,' Eabha replied.

He seemed to glow beneath her gaze. He wasn't even trying to hide his attraction, but Dara couldn't quite work out if it was mutual: Eabha flirted with everyone.

'So you pulled out from the Abbey?' Dara said, dragging Eabha's attention back to her. 'That's it? What about Miriam?'

'What about her?' Eabha said with a small laugh. 'I've had my doubts about her for a while. She's washed up, clinging on at the Abbey only because she knows everyone. We're better off without her.'

Dara blinked several times, biting the inside of her lip, trying to keep the doubt from colouring her expression. Miriam was a highly respected producer. It seemed childish to suggest otherwise.

Eabha flicked her hair back from her face. 'A part of me feels Miriam was deliberately trying to sabotage me this whole time. I know that sounds – I don't know – melodramatic, but I just . . . I *must* be able to rely on my team, so, naturally, I had to part ways with Miriam and the Abbey. At least Geoffrey understands me. He knows I need good people around me.' She looked up, giving a shaky laugh. 'There must be trust between us. Always trust.'

This seemed pointed and, to Dara's surprise, Eabha was looking directly at her as she spoke. She looked away, thinking of the text from Linda O'Rowe on her phone, that one small secret that now seemed as if it were burned into the skin of her brow.

'You said we're opening the new season at the Gate, right?' Sam said, drawing Eabha's attention his way as he tried to get his head around what was happening. 'So, what does that mean? When exactly would we be staging the play?'

Eabha took a breath, excitement in her eyes. 'Five weeks from today.'

'*Five* weeks?!' Sam said, on his feet now.

'Yes – five weeks.' She looked from one of them to the next, her eyes sweeping over them slowly. When they landed on Dara, they made her think of sea-worn stone.

She watched the way the light reflected in Eabha's eyes, the way the sharp line of her jaw caused a shadow to fall over her neck and shoulder, the way her fingers swept her hair back behind her ear, from which a pearl hung, quivering. The idea of pulling off a convincing depiction of Eabha in such a short timeframe seemed beyond her ability.

'That's . . . that doesn't give us much time,' Sam stammered. His eyes were darting between Oisín and Dara, waiting for them to back him up, to express misgivings or fears. But Oisín was staring down at the wooden floorboards, his hand running back and forth through the dishevelled mop of hair on his head. Dara's face was deliberately blank: she needed time to decide how she felt. It would be rushed, of course, but then what was she really waiting for? This play was going to launch her into a better life. Hadn't she waited long enough for that?

Sam, impatient, paced from the window to the door and then back again as he said: 'But how can we do this?! How can we pull this together? There's no time! Have you even thought this through?'

'There will be time,' Eabha said. She had turned suddenly rigid, the nervous energy leaving her body. 'Sam, you must think I'm some kind of amateur. Do I look like someone who acts impulsively? Do I look like someone who doesn't take my career seriously? Is that why you're questioning me, Sam? Do you think I'm an idiot? Genuinely, do tell me.'

Her voice was quiet, her tone soft, but her words were like cold air moving through the room, a chill setting in, despite the heat of the day. Dara's nerve endings hummed, as if she had been swept up with Sam into a current of Eabha's disapproval.

'No, Eabha, of course not. I ... I'm just a bit—' The quiet severity of Eabha's response had thrown his legs from under him. 'I didn't mean to say ... I mean, I didn't mean to imply ... I would *never* imply ...'

His words trailed away as Eabha walked to the window and leaned against the window ledge, her body motionless as her eyes drifted down to her garden, lush with summer. She waited while Sam tried and failed to recover the situation, letting the silence expand slowly, filling the room with unspoken words.

Dara's eyes unconsciously travelled to the door, thinking of escape.

Instead, she said: 'What happens next? What do we need to do?'

Eabha turned around, a pleasant expression fixed on her face once again. 'Well, the lead-in time has obviously shortened, so I'm going to need you all here for session days from now on

– that means you'll be here first thing every day until last thing every night. You'll take your meals here, bathe here, wash your clothes here, live every spare moment *here*, so we can use every ounce of energy you have for the performance. This is going to be your lives from now on – and it's going to be worth it.'

Dara nodded, letting this sink in slowly. Maybe an immersion in the play was what she needed. Maybe it would allow her to really live the role, to inhabit Eabha fully. She would worry about the rest later – her job at the boutique, the rent. Surely they would be paid soon anyway? It felt as if she was scurrying to make her life fit with Eabha's demands, but she would make it work. It was the play that mattered. Her future depended on this performance.

Sam cleared his throat. 'And how are we going to get a production together in five weeks? Are we starting from scratch?'

Dara wondered where he got his courage. He was standing slightly apart from them now, by the door. Isolated.

Eabha inhaled slowly, moving to the settee as Oisín followed. He sat down next to her and she draped an arm around his shoulder, leaning towards him until her head was lightly touching his chest and shoulder. Her movements reminded Dara of a cat, her body slinking towards Oisín to demand his attention.

Eabha didn't look at Sam as she answered him, restrained emotion tightening her vocal chords. 'I understand you're nervous, Sam, but we'll do it because it *has* to be done. We already have a production plan – I'm just going to hand it over to the Gate's team to implement now instead of Miriam. The stage build is pretty minimal for this production anyway. It's mostly lighting and the construction of the attic turret. That won't take long and the Gate are giving me their full team. The only urgency is on marketing and publicity. We need to sell seats.'

The mention of publicity sent a bolt of nerves running through

Dara's body, her mind jumping again to the text on her phone. *This is your chance to be heard.*

'We don't have time for glitzy marketing,' Eabha was saying, 'so we're going to lean into the barren, empty mood of the play and shoot you right here, in front of the attic window.' Eabha paused, her eyes sweeping over them again. Only Oisín was enthusiastic, both Sam and Dara antsy. 'Look, I really need you all behind me on this from now on. We rise or fall together.'

Dara's heart rate was already elevated, but it took another jump as Eabha stood up from the settee again and walked towards her.

'You look so frightened, Dara, but there's no need to worry. We had more time for the first run, but that also left more time for problems.' Her hands were on Dara's shoulders. 'Will you trust me?'

Her eyes round, her breathing a little unsteady, Dara nodded. 'Of course.'

She knew, even then, that this was more aspiration than truth. Somewhere in the back of her mind, she had comforted herself with the idea that there was still time to figure things out, to get her head straight before they launched into full production mode. But that was clearly at an end now. She was committed – to the play, to Eabha, even to Austin. It was as Eabha said: they would rise or fall together. Her stomach gurgled, fear mixing with acid.

Eabha turned to Sam next, reaching for his hand. 'And you? Do you think you could give me the benefit of the doubt?'

Sam's eyes were firmly on his scuffed Stan Smiths, but he nodded his head and muttered some words of affirmation.

'There's going to be a lot of public attention from now on,' Eabha said, her hands gripping her hips. 'We have interview requests rolling in and we haven't even made an announcement about the Gate yet.' She seemed almost breathless, two small round spots of pink forming on her cheeks. They clashed with the red of her lips. 'I need you to tell me if you're approached by any journalists. The lies they told the last time still haunt me and my brother. The scrutiny made it difficult for the cast to trust each other – to trust me.'

In her pocket, Dara's hand fidgeted with her phone. Had she abused that trust already? Maybe she should mention the text from Linda O'Rowe now.

Maybe . . .

She was dithering, words not coming, her voice hiding somewhere in the dark tunnel of her windpipe.

'Are you expecting similar trouble from the media this time?' Oisín asked.

'More than likely. They can't help themselves. But the truth is, we need the coverage.' Eabha's shoulders rose and fell limply. 'Believe me, I know what they're like. They'll try to turn you against each other – against me. That's what they did the last time. They will call me a liar, a killer. They'll say you're all part of it now. I need you to be prepared for this. I need you to know that they're wrong.'

Sam looked as if he wanted to leave the room and never return. Dara felt it too, an itch under her skin, fear running through her blood, adrenaline flowing, whispering to her of danger.

Eabha was working hard to give an impression of ease, a smile firmly fixed to her face. Dara swallowed, forcing a matching smile of her own. They mirrored each other; one smile as fake as its reflection.

* * *

The day's rehearsal was long, their interactions strained by the anxious air wafting between them. There was no time now for slow, ponderous discovery, no time to allow the characters to gain form gradually through repetition. Eabha's eye had taken on an acutely critical edge and her frequent interjections made progress stilted, numerous interruptions littering the day. It was a day of muted sighs, muscles tensing, shoulders slumping, fingers fidgeting.

'Not like that – I need to hear your desperation, Oisín. Let me hear your obsession.'

'No, Dara, you *want* his attention – you *need* it. But it's too much. You can't control it. Show me. Let us *see* it.'

'You've got to hold the feeling inside you, Sam. It's beneath the surface, just under the skin. Subtle – it's always subtle with Austin.'

On and on, she pushed them through the afternoon, probing and prodding until they were wet with sweat, the windows thrown open to the birdsong outside, the hum of cars, the bark of a dog in the middle distance.

Eabha wanted to work on the scene of the first kiss, the moment she first connected with Cillian, which meant Dara would need to connect with Oisín.

Eabha *walks to the centre of the stage, a spotlight casting her in light, while* **Austin** *and* **Cillian** *freeze in place, in shadow.*

Eabha *(to the audience):* I found a note. It was tucked into a nook in the trunk of one of the birch trees on the school grounds, where I would sit alone and think of my family and the home we had lost. But I hadn't been alone. He had been there, watching me, all that time. *(She turns and looks at* **Cillian***, who is briefly lit to the audience, his eyes* *tracking her as she moves closer to him*) At the corner of my vision, there was a flash of white, like a flag waving to me. So I reached my hand into the nook and found this. (*Takes the note from the front pocket of her shirt. She unfolds the note and reads*)

Dear E,

I've been too nervous to tell you to your face, but I need you to know how much I like you.

C x

I left him a reply, tucked it into the nook of the tree where I knew he'd find it. I knew he would be watching me. Always watching.

Dear C,

Tell me to my face.

E x

*The spotlight drops and **Eabha** returns to her position on the stage between **Cillian** and **Austin**.*

'Dara, Oisín – you're sitting there like strangers! You need to loosen up.' The more Eabha pointed it out, the more awkward Dara began to feel, as if she didn't properly fit inside her skin. 'Look at you! I can sense it from here – you're both wound so tight!'

Dara looked to Sam again, partly to avoid looking at Oisín. He made a face, sympathising with her.

Since their first rehearsal, the boundaries between the professional and personal world had been gossamer-thin. Eabha's methods were unusual, but Dara hadn't expected to feel quite so exposed. Maybe it was because Sam was watching her, or maybe it was the way Eabha was staring at her with such fixed interest.

Oisín shuffled closer to her on the settee.

'Ready?' he said, leaning towards her.

She nodded, glancing again at Sam, who was now bent over, rolling a cigarette, his expression deeply serious, as if it required his full concentration. She looked again at Oisín.

'Can we . . .' Dara's lips were dry. 'Can we just read a couple of lines before? You know, just to . . . just to ease into it?'

Cillian: I found your note
Eabha: Of course you did . . . (*moves closer to him, feigning a confidence she doesn't quite feel*) So? Are you going to tell me in person?

*Cillian reaches over and kisses **Eabha**, his hand cupping her cheek.*

Unconsciously, Dara's eyes rolled toward Sam as she kissed Oisín. He was looking down at his script, his expression blank as a clouded day, but when her eyes fell on Eabha, she found her smiling. She didn't know whether to smile in return, the awkwardness of the situation making her body recoil. She would have liked the presence of someone else – Miriam, even – who could police the boundaries between them, the boundaries Eabha seemed so keen to destroy.

Oisín moved to the next line.

Cillian: I can't stop thinking about you. It's like you've crawled inside me, like . . . like . . . you're wandering through my mind, through my dreams . . .
Eabha (*shy, suddenly*): Really? You really mean that?
Cillian: I do . . . Eabha, you're at the end of

every thought, every sentence, dangling there
before my eyes all the time.
Eabha: But you ... you didn't say anything
... I was starting to think you had changed
your mind about me.
Cillian: Never.

Cillian leans in and kisses her again.

Cillian: I had to play it cool — you know
what Austin is like. He's *always* around you.
It's hard to get you alone.
Eabha: I'm sure Austin wouldn't mind if we
spent some time together.
Cillian: He would ... you know he would. He
wants you all to himself.

Cillian reaches over and kisses **Eabha** *a third
time. His arm slowly, tentatively, draws her
closer. They sit together for a moment, her
forehead leaning against his.*

Dara looked at her castmates, unsure what to say. She ran her
tongue over her dry lips. It was strange kissing Oisín, as if he
wasn't quite there with her, his mind on something or someone
else.

Sam was watching her. 'Should we take a quick break?'

'We don't have time,' Eabha said, her hands travelling over
Oisín's body, massaging his shoulders, loosening his hips. 'When
you kiss her, you need to hold her as if she's a bird, as if you don't
want to frighten her away.'

She took Dara in her arms next, her touch strong but light,
as if she were offering Dara a place of safety, a nest in which she
could feel at ease. Eabha's breath was on her face, stirring the

strands of her blonde hair. There was something in the way she was looking at her, a glint to her eye, hinting at some hidden thought.

'You try now,' Eabha said, releasing Dara from her arms suddenly.

Dara stepped back, fixed her T-shirt, glancing at Oisín. He seemed annoyed at her as he took Eabha's place and Dara wondered briefly if Eabha were aware of the effect she had on them, this competition brewing between them for her attention, this jealousy.

She stiffened immediately as Oisín hands closed around her, his fingers a little rough on her back, his lips dead as he placed them against hers again. But they practised together until, gradually, Oisín relaxed into his character, until Dara found that her face fit well in the dip of his neck, until she was used to inhaling the deep, sweet and musty mix of his deodorant and his sweat, until she forgot that Sam and Eabha were watching. Alone with Cillian, on a rocky hillside in Clare.

* * *

'You did well today, Dara,' Eabha said, tidying the cushions onto the settee while Dara gathered her belongings and pulled her arms through the sleeves of her denim jacket. Sam and Oisín had already left, both relieved to make an escape, each muttering about needing a pint. Dara let them leave without her, lingering behind, sipping from her water bottle, stretching out her arms, then pulling her hair into a tight bun at the back of her head, hoping for a quiet word with Eabha – alone.

'Really?' she said, unconvinced. 'I'm not sure it's as smooth as it could be with Oisín yet.' She sighed, pulling at the dry skin on her lower lip. 'Is there anything else I could be doing? Is there something I'm missing?'

'Don't worry about Oisín,' Eabha replied, turning to face Dara. 'I'll take care of that. You just keep doing what you're doing.' She smiled: the lipstick had faded from her lips, only a faint line remaining around the edges. 'You have this strange contradiction in you. You seem utterly unsure of yourself, but that's not the case, is it?'

'How do you mean?' Dara said, pulling at one of her silver hoops, her earlobe briefly elongating as she did so.

A warm smile spread across Eabha's face as she filled the distance between them, placing a hand on Dara's shoulder. 'You know you can do it. Otherwise you wouldn't be here. You chose acting. You chose theatre . . . you're not the wilting flower you pretend to be.'

'I don't know what you mean,' Dara replied. From this proximity, Eabha's eyes seemed to cut through her. Their colour was oceanic. She felt a wave of some unfamiliar emotion wash over her, an urge to reach out and run her fingers slowly across Eabha's face, to see her eyes close and her lips part at Dara's touch. She was standing so close – was it deliberate provocation? Or was it a tease?

'Yes, you do,' Eabha said. 'I can see it in you. You know you can do it, but you're frightened of the opinions of others. You want to shine, but you're scared. You're used to people doubting you – I'm right, aren't I? I can tell from your reaction. You've gone quite red! You're really blushing.'

Dara turned away, looking towards the window again, the sky a blank grey. Her hands sat firmly by her sides where they could make no trouble.

'Don't worry,' Eabha continued, reaching for the loose strands of hair framing Dara's face and lifting them out of her eyes. 'There's nothing to be embarrassed about. I know that feeling. I used to feel it too.' Dara's breath was coming a little quicker, the blood racing into the vessels of her dimpled cheeks. 'I had a choice. I could play the role of orphan. I could be the girl who was there the night Cillian Butler fell out a window and died. Or I could tell my own story. Make my own identity.' Eabha's nose was now inches from Dara's face. 'I stopped listening to my doubts and fears. I made a new life for myself, Dara – the life I wanted. And you can too.'

With a smile, Eabha pulled Dara into a hug, resting her head on Dara's shoulder, and then, to her surprise, she reached up to kiss Dara's cheek. The intimacy of the gesture startled her. She watched Eabha, as if frightened of what she might do next, gazing at her lips, red and full. They seemed to open slowly, as if she were about to speak, to breathe some secret. Instead, she gave a small sigh and pulled away.

'That's enough about that for tonight,' Eabha said, moving towards the door, the moment suddenly broken, the intimacy evaporated, almost as if it had never been, as if Dara had imagined it. The sweat on her skin felt suddenly cold.

Dara took her backpack from the floor, letting the last of the water in her bottle trickle down her dry throat. As she walked down the stairs, she tried to make sense of what had happened. On the one hand, she felt suddenly visible, as if Eabha had recognised her somehow, in a way the people closest to her often couldn't. On the other, she felt oddly used, as if Eabha had been testing her reactions in some way. Had she done the same to Oisín? Had she tested him too? Did he pass? His obvious interest in her reciprocated somehow?

On the street outside, Dara turned left towards Harold's Cross but didn't make it further than the bridge, reluctant to return to the confines of the flat just yet. Pausing on the bridge, she watched the dance of street lights reflected in the gently flowing water of the canal.

Eabha was right about her. She had chosen acting against the odds, in the face of a body of opinion that made her feel ridiculous for daring to dream. If she could free herself from hesitation and inhibition, if she could stop holding herself back, the possibilities stretched and stretched before her. All she had to do was trust in Eabha's vision. All she had to do was find a way to trust in Eabha.

Chapter Six

Dara was hanging some silk slips on a rail in the boutique when Sam arrived, spotting her through the shop window. Sunday mornings were slow, only the occasional browser stopping in, so Dara would spend the shift alone, mostly restocking the shop floor and rearranging the window display. Sometimes she would surreptitiously close the shop and step out to buy a coffee from the café next door, watching the city slowly come to life around her. A dog barking at the seagulls pecking at a rubbish bag outside Grogan's. Tourists wandering sunken-eyed in search of salty cures for excessive levity on the cobblestones of Temple Bar the night before. Mass-goers streaming out from the church on Clarendon Street, their souls newly cleansed and ready for another week of sinning.

When Sam texted that morning to see if she was around, Dara had nearly said no. The long days of rehearsals meant that they were almost constantly together, and whether it was the heat filling the enclosed attic, or the tension rising from their scripts like a vapour, it was becoming more difficult to avoid the pull of his brown eyes.

The first week had been eye-opening, the dynamics between them already settling into a pattern. They had split themselves inadvertently into two camps, arranging themselves by some spontaneous order: Oisín and Eabha drawn together, while Sam gravitated always to Dara's side. In the garden, he might pluck a blade of grass and drag it slowly up her arm, or lean his head on her bare thigh and turn his face up towards the sun that barrelled down on them from the duck-egg sky. And she would fight the urge to run her fingers through his thick hair with the curled ends and draw a smile to his face as he looked up at her.

Dara only had to watch Eabha and Oisín together to know that keeping Sam at a distance was wise. It was as if Oisín burned when he was around Eabha and she seemed to enjoy stoking the fire in him, a bellows in her hand, pumping with gusto as she fed the flames.

Now, there were just five short weeks to get this performance right: Dara couldn't risk further destabilising the complex mix of chemical compounds filling the air around them. But despite misgivings, when Sam asked if he could see her, she couldn't bring herself to say no, telling him to drop into the boutique at some point that day.

He arrived shortly before midday, his arms pulling her immediately to his chest as he greeted her. His skin carried the usual scent of almonds, of sandalwood. She inhaled and let it fill her, growing very fond of his presence.

'Am I distracting you from your work or can you chat for a minute?' he asked.

Her eyes flashed to the security camera in the corner.

'Yeah,' she said. 'Just come over to the counter so it looks like you're browsing the jewellery.'

'Right,' Sam replied, with a small laugh. 'Always acting, aren't you, Dara?' He said it lightly, but there was a truth to the jest that didn't go unnoticed. 'I almost didn't recognise you when I saw you in the window,' he added. 'Nice dress. Is it new?'

She was wearing a deep crimson lace dress with a frilled neck that sat just below her chin. 'You like it?' she asked, twirling on the ball of her foot.

'You look like Eabha dressed like that,' Sam replied, a whisper of criticism in his voice.

'That's sort of the idea,' she said, pulling nervously on her hair. 'I thought I might stay in character – you know, walk around in her skin.' She looked down at the blonde strands of hair between her fingers. 'I still need to do something about this.' She gathered her hair into her hands, holding it just below her chin, and then gazed at him over her shoulder, eyelashes batting, summoning the most provocative Eabha expression she could to her face.

Leaning on the counter, Sam's eyes narrowed momentarily, as if to better examine her. 'Don't do that – I prefer you as you are.'

'Really? Don't you find Eabha fascinating? Everyone else does.'

'Well, I don't.' His voice was stern, his face turned away from her.

With a pang of embarrassment, Dara realised he was un-amused. She let her hair tumble down her back again. Reaching for the stack of knit jumpers sitting on the counter next to her, she began folding them; left arm first, then right, her face now as red as her dress. 'So, what did you want to talk to me about anyway?'

'I wanted to see how you're feeling about this fucking play,' Sam said. 'I feel like I'm losing my mind. We're all acting as if opening in a few weeks is totally grand – am I the only one who thinks it's a fucking disaster?'

'I guess it makes things a little more stressful,' Dara said cautiously.

'Are you going to be able to keep this job?' Sam asked, looking around at the displays. 'I've had to pull out of a string of voice-over slots already. Eabha said she can't spare me.'

'Oh shit, sorry Sam,' Dara replied. 'That's a pain . . .'

'Yeah, well, I didn't expect this play to open so soon – I had three voiceovers booked this week. But Eabha didn't exactly check with us, did she? Just marched ahead and suited herself.'

Dara shook her head, eyes on her work, the jumper in her hand a fluffy neon pink, with jagged black lightning bolts across it. 'Sam, you really need to give Eabha a break . . . I don't think she's *trying* to mess things up for you.'

Her words set his eyes alight. 'Dara, come on!' His full weight was on the glass counter as he leaned closer to her. 'She's impossible – don't you think so?'

'Not particularly, Sam, no. She's the first director who has cast me in a role like this and she has been nothing but nice to me – nothing but supportive.'

Sam turned away so that his back was to her now, his eyes on the empty street outside. 'Give her time. I've heard things about her, Dara.'

Dara stopped her folding, her elbows on the counter. 'What's that supposed to mean? What don't I know?'

Sam turned towards her again. 'I bumped into Miriam last night at the Project Arts Centre.'

'Right, and I'm sure she had a lot of nice things to say about Eabha?'

'That's the thing – Miriam is able to talk now, the way she couldn't when she was working with Eabha. She said Eabha unilaterally pulled out from the Abbey . . . out of the blue, no reason given.'

Dara's eyes flicked upwards. 'No – Eabha said there was a falling out? They were trying to control her.'

'Come on – we both know Eabha lied.'

Dara scratched at her arm, nervous suddenly. 'Why would Eabha lie?'

'I have no idea,' Sam replied. 'Miriam said that Eabha was being really huffy with the Abbey since day one. She kept making little digs about not being invited back to direct at the Abbey, then went full diva whenever they tried to broach how they might handle any negative media attention.'

'I'm not sure that's fair,' Dara said quietly. 'It can't be easy for her.'

'Well, Miriam's pretty sure Eabha bolted because she's fucking paranoid about disloyalty. I mean, that's pretty obvious from how much she talks about *trusting her.*'

It was true: Eabha seemed to parse every reaction they had for signs of dissent, but she could understand why. 'Sounds like she was right not to trust Miriam.'

Sam's laugh was harsh. 'That's what happens when you cut people loose – Miriam was singing like a canary. Told me all kinds of shit.'

Dara's lips tightened, her hands still, the jumper bunching in her anxious grip. 'What did she say?!'

'Well, she told me that Austin had a full-on mental breakdown the first time they staged this play. That's what he meant when he said it put him in hospital.'

'Jesus! Are you serious?'

'I couldn't believe it either – frankly, I'm a little impressed they managed to keep it so hush-hush all these years,' Sam said, rubbing the stubble on his chin.

'Did she tell you what happened to him?'

'They found him wandering backstage, out of his mind, on opening night ten years ago. He had a full-on psychotic episode . . . he didn't know where he was, couldn't tell the past from the present, as if he were living through the night Cillian died all over again.' Sam shook his head. 'It's fucked up, Dara.'

Her thoughts flashed to an image of a teenage Austin,

constructed from Eabha's storytelling, pieces of him littered through the script. Seventeen, just a shadow of stubble across his face, his hair shorn tightly against his scalp, wearing a school uniform, standing by the rocky seashore near the Bodkin School, staring out at the angry waves.

'Shit, Sam,' Dara said. 'I feel kind of sorry for him.'

'For Austin?!'

'Yeah . . . I don't know. It just . . . it just makes sense of him. No wonder he's a little strange. You know? Like, *Jesus* – he lost his mind the last time it was staged.'

'They're keeping secrets from us,' Sam said. She watched him pace the floor, moving from the shelves of frilled blouses to the wide-leg jumpsuits. 'Eabha said she would be honest with us. She said we should be open with her. She said it was the only way the performance would work – but she's hiding *so* much from us.'

Dara couldn't disagree, her eyes on the door, through which a customer had just entered. An automatic smile jumped onto her face and a greeting came from her mouth, convincingly light and carefree. 'Hi there. Let me know if I can be of assistance.'

Sam watched the transformation with a shake of his head but said nothing, pretending to browse through the sunglasses stand while the customer riffled briefly through a box of old scarves.

'Give her time,' Dara whispered to Sam, her eyes darting skittishly between him and the customer. 'I hear what you're saying and you're right to feel upset, but it's not easy for her either.'

Sam let out another sigh, rooting in his pocket for his cigarettes. 'I can't decide if you're too trusting, or if I'm paranoid.'

She smiled weakly. 'I guess we're going to find out.'

Sam nodded, a deep discomfort shaping his features. He stuck an unlit cigarette between his teeth. She could feel a distance between them suddenly, cooling the warmth in his eyes when he looked at her. She would have liked to pull him towards her, to bury her face on his shoulder, and tell him it would be OK. It would be OK because they had each other. Instead, she held the jumper in her anxious hands still, hesitating so long that the moment wilted and was gone.

'I'll see you later,' Sam said, his voice gruff, and then walked out of the boutique without looking back, leaving her to stand behind the counter, gazing vacuously at her only customer, another fake smile pasted across her worried face.

* * *

Her conversation with Sam was still playing on her mind as Dara walked down Leinster Road that afternoon, trepidation filling each step. She had been invited for Sunday lunch with Eabha, Austin and their grand-aunt Celia, a personal invitation not extended to Sam or Oisín. She wasn't quite sure how she would manage without either of them to hide behind, especially in Austin's company for an entire afternoon. The wine she carried – a biodynamic red she couldn't afford, from a new wine bar recommended by Sam – was sloshing in her hand, keeping rhythm with the nerves in her stomach.

On arrival, Dara was given a flute of champagne and introduced to Celia, their former guardian, who managed to make this fact known almost immediately, as if it were very important that Dara understood her significance in their lives. 'They were wonderful kids, the two of them,' she said airily, focusing on the space over Dara's head. 'I was very glad I could be there for them, of course, when Máire and Eamonn died. Awful thing to happen.'

'I'm sure they were very lucky to have you, Celia,' Dara said, unsure why she was pursuing this line of conversation. She sipped her champagne, bubbles dispersing across her tongue.

Was it something that happened when your private life became subject to a public controversy? This need to seize control of the record, to set it straight? She hoped never to find out.

'We were *very* lucky,' Eabha said, perhaps a little too loudly, as if a stenographer was sitting in the corner, typing notes on the public record. 'We still are!'

She was dressed in a midnight blue satin dress; it rustled when she moved, which was often. She seemed fretful, steering the conversation quickly towards easier topics than their childhood: plans for the garden, the possibility of a short trip to Venice for the Biennale next year.

'My first trip to the Biennale was when I was very young. My father had a piece exhibited that year, so we had the VIP treatment – as you can imagine, it was all very exciting,' Celia said, face lit with a faint glow of nostalgia.

Dara smiled and nodded as she listened, swirling the champagne around her glass, unable to relate. Her own childhood holidays had comprised a ferry to France and a campsite in Brittany for two weeks in the summer, days spent building sandcastles on the nearby beach, nights spent using buttons to bet on games of rummy around the small table in the caravan. She smiled at the thought, at the starkness of the contrast; Gaffney family holidays sounded a lot more fun.

Austin was mostly mute, contributing little, only speaking when required. He was hovering next to the bookshelf, on which stood a bust of Artemis – goddess of wild things – a glass of sparkling water fizzing in his hand. He sipped it mechanically every so often, his other hand in his pocket, maintaining an almost pointed silence until they had finished their aperitifs and taken their places at the table.

Beneath the chandelier, long, taper candles drooled wax. The table was dressed in crisp, white linen. As she placed her napkin on her lap, Dara sat very straight in her chair, hoping she wouldn't spill anything. Sitting opposite her, Austin's attention was fixed on a painting hanging behind her head. She had noticed it immediately on entering the room: an abstract oil painting of three white figures against a dark backdrop, one with their back to the viewer, a second staring directly out from the painting and a third bent towards the ground, as if in agony.

The food had been catered again: this time, lamb shank with dauphinoise potatoes and a variety of roasted vegetable. 'Do pass the bowls around, will you Dara?' Eabha said, spooning some potatoes onto Celia's plate and then her own.

Dara reached for the carrots, wondering if the awkward atmosphere around the table was typical, or if there was something in particular provoking it. She glanced at Austin, still staring at the painting behind her.

'Carrots?' she said with a smile, holding them out for him, but he didn't seem to hear.

'Is that . . . one of Grandad's paintings?' he asked, looking first at Eabha, and then Celia. 'I don't recognise it.'

Eabha stiffened immediately, looking from the painting over Dara's head to the glower on Austin's face. 'Yes, it is,' she said calmly, reaching for the porcelain gravy boat.

Dara set the unwanted carrots down again, slowly cutting through her lamb, eyes firmly on her plate.

'What happened to the last painting? The seascape?' He sounded upset already, hostility radiating from him suddenly, poking at his topknot with angry fingers. 'Have you been selling them again? Have you been selling Grandad's paintings?'

Eabha coughed curtly to clear her throat, avoiding the harsh edge in Austin's eye. 'You know I have.' She rearranged the napkin on her lap. 'How do you think I pay for this house? For your lifestyle? For Celia's?'

Austin swallowed, blinking rapidly. His eyes seemed to burn with a thought unshared, silent again for a moment, as if he were gathering his strength for a fight. 'We've . . . we've talked about this, Eabha. You said you'd tell me the next time. We agreed that we'd discuss which paintings are sold and which we keep.' He was physically so large that, even from across the table, Dara could feel the strength with which his heel struck the leg of his chair. There was anger in it, restrained for now – but only just.

'We can't afford to keep them anymore.' Eabha's knife ran cleanly through her meat. She raised a small piece of pink lamb to her mouth and chewed with deliberateness. 'Can we talk about this later, Austin? I don't want to bore Dara.' The look in Eabha's eye as she glanced Dara's way contained an unspoken apology.

'I'm sure Dara won't mind us sorting this out now,' Austin snapped, turning to Celia. 'Did you know about this?'

Celia nodded. 'I did, of course. I had to sign something. Eabha's right – we don't have the luxury of keeping the last of the collection, Austin.'

The food now sat in a semicircle on the table in front of Austin, waiting for him to fill his plate. Brusquely, he took a portion of each and then pushed them away again, into the middle of the table, next to the candles.

'There won't be any paintings left at this rate. We're already down to the last few. What do we do when we've sold them all?' He shook his head, irritated. 'There has to be another way.'

'Why do you think Eabha's doing this play again?' Celia said. 'The debt has to be paid, Austin. We either sell the paintings or we sell my house. I know which I'd prefer.' She sounded jaded, as if this was an old argument, recurring frequently. Watching the tiredness on her face – the resignation – Dara felt sympathy stir for the old woman. It could not have been an easy lot in life, taking on parental responsibility for Eabha and Austin, only to have Cillian Butler fall from a window to his death.

Eabha was looking at her again, laughing nervously. 'I'm sorry about this, Dara. You're getting caught up in some family stuff.'

'You might as well explain it to her,' Austin barked from across the table. 'You're the one who wanted her here – the least you can do is fill her in.'

Eabha inhaled, her hands clasped in her lap. There was an amber ring on her right index finger; she twisted it slowly. 'Our grandfather – Arthur – was an artist and there's a small market of collectors who buy his paintings from us from time to time.'

'We sell them for a song,' Austin said bitterly, 'and I don't see any of it. Not a penny.'

'What Austin isn't saying is that we're in a lot of debt and I have no choice but to do what I can to keep us in our homes.'

Austin made a sound that was something like a snort. 'There's nothing you wouldn't sell – is there, Eabha? You've sold our lives to the highest bidder.'

The air in the room felt elasticated, as if at any moment, it would snap.

Dara's mind was racing through possible excuses, possible reasons to leave, but she couldn't seem to voice any, unwilling to draw Austin's attention back to her. Rooted to the spot, she sat and watched a drop of gravy sliding slowly down the lip of the jug. She could have reached out and caught it with her finger before it stained the white tablecloth; instead, she sat very still and let her food grow cold.

'I suppose everyone saw that article in the newspaper this morning?' Austin said, sniffing loudly, his eyes moving from one of them to next.

Dara knew the article he was talking about. Her mother had sent it to her this morning, the headline blaring out from the screen of her phone: *Eabha de Lacey is Back! But will the Truth Actually Come Out this Time?*

Linda O'Rowe had prepared a detailed explainer of the controversy surrounding Cillian's death and the botched investigation into Austin. It was designed to get anyone new to the story up to speed fast, just in case the passage of time had blunted their memories. All the gory details, made fresh again.

'Austin, please let's not talk about that—' Eabha said, but her brother ignored her.

'Dara? Come on, you must have seen it? A nice family history there for you.'

Dara coughed, reaching for her water. 'I mean, they'll try anything to sell papers these days, won't they?' she said, her laugh nervous. He seemed to be looking for a confrontation.

'Quite right,' Celia said. 'It's appalling what they've done to this family.'

'They wouldn't be writing about us if Eabha could find a way to exist without the limelight.'

'Please, Austin – *please* don't be like this.' Eabha's jaw was tight and Dara could feel the coldness seeping out of her again. 'Dara doesn't want to hear it.'

'I bet she does,' Austin said, a horrible grin on his face, his chin jutting outward defiantly. 'I bet Dara is just *itching* to know all our family secrets.'

Eabha's fork clattered onto the plate, her eyes flashing furiously to her brother. 'Austin, don't,' she snapped. Her breathing was fast, but she modulated her tone before she spoke again. 'Please, don't cause a scene . . . I'm sorry about the painting. But please . . . let's talk about it later?'

Austin chewed his food thoughtfully, as if considering this

suggestion sincerely, before turning to Dara. 'Do you know we're not actually related? Me and Eabha?'

Dara was so surprised she almost choked on her water, coughing to clear her throat before she could answer. 'You're . . . you're not? But you look so alike!'

'We do. It's quite a coincidence, isn't it?' He smiled. 'But no . . . I'm adopted. Celia and Eabha are family, but we just pretend I am too. We have these nice lunches and we pretend I'm one of them. Just a happy little family.'

'I wish you wouldn't say that, Austin,' Eabha said, as gently as she could manage. 'There's more to family than blood, right?'

Austin was gazing silently at Eabha. 'It's easy for you to say that, isn't it? Mum and Dad only adopted me because they thought they couldn't have a child of their own.' He pushed his chair back from the table slightly. 'And then you came along . . . their miracle child.'

'Stop it,' Eabha said, exasperated. 'Please, stop it. That's just not true. You were just as much their child. They loved us equally.'

Celia gave an uncharacteristically coarse grunt. 'Eabha's right. Blood relationships are not all they're cracked up to be, Austin. Look at my family. They don't go away, do they? A bad rash, if you ask me.'

'Our father's family don't approve of us,' Eabha said for Dara's benefit. 'They're all doctors and scientists. They find us deeply silly.'

'Ah,' Dara said, feeling the need to say something. 'Now, that's something I can relate to.'

'It's not unusual, I suppose,' Eabha acknowledged, with a slight shrug.

'They don't just find us "silly", do they, Eabha?' Austin looked at Dara again. 'They think we're killers, Dara. Our extended family think I pushed Cillian to his death.'

'Austin!' It was the same quiet, icy tone Eabha had used on Sam a few days before at rehearsals. It seemed to work as effectively on her brother: he held Eabha's furious gaze for several silent moments before returning his attention to his plate.

Dara bit the inside of her lip, thinking of the veiled accusations in Linda's article. *Will we ever really know the full story of what happened the night Cillian died? Will the truth ever really out?* She looked at Austin again, his back hunched over his plate, as if all the anger and resentment were held in his shoulders. Her eyes fell to his hands: they were so large that it would be the work of a moment to reach a hand towards her, seize her by the throat and squeeze the life from her.

Dara thought of a stage direction from the very end of the play.

Cillian lies dead on the ground in a pool of blood.

So easily, her mind produced a picture for her: Austin – younger, yes, but with the same scorching resentment in him – pushing a boy to his death. It made her feel breathless, the room suddenly too hot. She shouldn't have come, her presence a mistake. The meal was a performance for her benefit, the table laid with theatrical props, but Austin had changed the script and Eabha was losing her directorial control.

Austin pushed his chair back so quickly that it toppled over, lying on the parquet floor with its legs in the air. 'I'm not fucking doing this,' he said, his voice a growl. 'I'm not going along with your little happy family game anymore!'

With that, he walked around the table, reaching over Dara's head to pull the painting from the wall. She ducked away from him, her hand instinctively protecting her neck, though she was not his target.

'Austin!' Eabha cried again, on her feet now as she watched him wrench the painting off the wall so angrily that he almost took the nail with him. 'Austin, where are you going?! Stop! Come back!' Eabha's napkin was in her hand, her face a picture of shock, her mouth open, forming a perfect dark circle.

Austin was already gone, the front door flapping open behind him, a gust of wind catching the stack of newspapers sitting on top of the cabinet in the hallway, sending the pages dancing along the monochrome tiles. From the window, in a state of mutual surprise, they watched him march down the stone steps towards Leinster Road with Arthur de Lacey's painting tucked neatly under his arm.

When she described the scene to Sam and Oisín later, Dara said it was as if they had sucked her into the heart of an argument already raging, like wildfire blazing through gorse. The curtain might be drawn, the audience gone, but the drama was never really over. The de Laceys were locked in a performance that never ended.

Chapter Seven

It seemed that Eabha was as embarrassed as Dara about the scene Austin had caused at Sunday lunch. Shortly after six the following morning, she sent Dara a grovelling text, asking if they could meet for breakfast. Dara agreed, meeting her at the house shortly after eight. They walked together to Rathmines village, Eabha's arm hooked around Dara's elbow.

'I have to apologise, Dara. I didn't know I was bringing you into a family squabble. It's just . . . seeing that article in the newspaper touched a raw nerve for Austin,' Eabha began, 'and he's very touchy about my grandfather's paintings. I should have known it would happen. He's all wound up about the play already . . .'

'Why do it then?' Dara said, words escaping her mouth of their own volition, impatience flaring. 'If it upsets Austin so much, why restage the play at all? Is it really about the money?' She could feel the rigidity in her bones, as if the marrow had undergone some change: heat applied, soft tissue turned to metal. If Eabha was going to drag her into this mayhem, the least she could do was explain it.

'Yes,' Eabha replied immediately. 'I'm doing all I can to support the three of us, but it's not exactly easy. None of my work has had the same impact as my debut. Celia can't manage her money and Austin is basically unemployable.'

'How do you mean? Why can't he work?'

Eabha gripped Dara's arm a little tighter. 'He has tried from time to time, but he isn't able to hold down a job for long. He never went back to school after Cillian died – just ran away and tried to forget all that had happened. He only came back to us when the play opened and, even then, I think it was only because he had no other choice. Rock bottom: drugs, drink – god knows what else. He never tells me about that time in his life.'

Dara watched the flock of pigeons gathered outside the public library opposite them. Someone had showered the path with crumbs and they were pecking at the concrete with abandon, feathers ruffled in the fight for breakfast.

'He's been living with Celia since his recovery. Technically, he's her carer, but Celia says he's not much use at that.' Eabha gave a sad little laugh. 'So, it's all on me, really. And the best thing I have to offer is this . . . this play.'

The clock tower in the village showed it was just before nine. On the street below, office workers with shirtsleeves pushed up past their elbows were carrying takeaway coffees back to their desks. Women with spongy mats rolled up under their arms made their way into a yoga studio on the corner. A harried-looking mother, pushing a pram, was leading a toddler on a scooter towards the supermarket across the road.

'Do you ever regret it? Writing the play? Telling your story?' Dara asked, looking down at Eabha next to her. Her eyes were hidden behind round sunglasses, a mustard-yellow tunic hanging like a sack from her narrow shoulders.

'No. Not for a moment,' she replied. 'I can't imagine still living with all of it kept inside of me. It was intolerable. Sometimes you just have to speak and take the consequences as they come. There will be people who don't listen and other people who hate what you say, but you can't let them dictate how you live. It's your voice, your life.'

Dara's heart rate was increasing, but she felt compelled to ask the question that had been pestering her. 'Even if you hurt Austin in the process?'

'Even then,' Eabha said at once. 'If I don't tell our story, who will? The past is not a fixed thing. It's shaped by us every time we bring it into the present, every time the story is told. And I won't let someone else tell our story, Dara.' She stopped outside the bakery on the corner, using her sunglasses to pin her dark hair out of her face.

Her eyes were blue and green and fiercely bright in the morning sun. 'There are things you need to understand, Dara. It's not . . . it's not the way they make it seem – the media, Cillian's family, all the people who *twist* things.' She sighed, her eyes closing briefly while her fingers traced her eyebrows. 'Everyone at the Bodkin turned on us – the teachers, the students, even the people we had liked and trusted. They told the police that Austin had already tried to kill Cillian – as if that stupid fight between them was more than a few punches and a black eye.' Her eyes looked skyward, towards the clock tower again. 'Austin only punched him because Cillian was violent with me. But nobody wanted to know about that. They just made Austin into a villain. And the police – if they hadn't fucked up the questioning – they would have tried to do him for murder. *Murder.* My brother?! I know he seems . . . I mean, I *know* how he comes across – but he is soft inside. That's his problem. He's terrified. He lashes out because he's afraid.'

Dara didn't know what to say. It all felt horribly real when Eabha talked about it like this – not a few lines on a page, not a series of images constructed from descriptions in stage directions, but a real event. A real death. The horror of it echoing out from that point in time, that moment when one life ended and two were forever changed.

'You look shocked,' Eabha said, watching her. 'I'm sorry if I said too much – I just felt, after yesterday, that you should know.'

'No, it's . . . I'm not shocked.' Dara pulled her jacket tighter around her, feeling suddenly cold in the shade beneath the bakery's awning. 'I've heard it before . . . it's just different, hearing you speak about it like that.'

Eabha gave a nod. 'I'm sorry if you find it upsetting.'

'No, I'd rather you talked to me about it. I'd like if things were out in the open.'

'I'm not always sure what I can say and who I can say it to . . . Over the years, you start to lose an instinct for who you can trust.'

'You can trust me,' Dara said and realised that, at least in that particular moment, she really meant it.

Eabha was smiling again, her arms reaching forward to embrace Dara. 'I thought so,' she said, then took a step back, straightening her tunic again. 'Come on, let's get some coffee. We need to get back before Sam and Oisín arrive.'

They joined the queue at the counter inside, behind an elderly man with a spaniel at his feet and a newspaper rolled up under his armpit. Dara wondered briefly if he had seen Linda O'Rowe's piece the day before, if he had sat with his pastry and his coffee dispassionately reading the tragic backstory of the woman next to him in the queue.

'You know, I'm so pleased I cast you, Dara. I saw the potential in you from the start,' Eabha said, while Dara looked down at the spaniel on its leash and felt a little foolish that Eabha's words were making her feel proud. 'I needed to cast someone I could trust and you seemed . . .' She searched for the word. 'Honest.'

Dara watched the man tug on the leash so that the spaniel's

head jerked forward as he led her towards the door; Eabha's arm was firmly hooked around her own again.

'I'm glad,' she said. There was a subtle pressure behind Eabha's words, a challenge in her choice of adjective: honest. Was she imagining it or had Eabha's grip tightened on her arm?

Her turn came to order and Eabha stepped forward, freeing Dara's arm from her grip at last while she examined the pastries behind the glass counter. Her arm now her own again, Dara looked down at the bare skin, speckled red where Eabha had been holding her, so tightly, as if she were afraid Dara might run away.

She took a breath, reminding herself that this was what she wanted, that it would be worth it, that Eabha would not let her down. And, in return, all she had to do was earn her trust and not let Eabha down either. What could be simpler?

* * *

They spent Monday morning deepening their work on Cillian's motivations, exploring the early days of Eabha and Cillian's relationship – before the stalking began, before the jealousy and the accusations. The early days had been exciting, first love blooming.

'And I did love him,' Eabha said, as if knowing they would doubt her. 'In my own way.'

'Why was Cillian so jealous?' Sam asked, frowning down at his script. 'I mean, he's even jealous of your brother – but where was it coming from?'

Dara rubbed the back of her neck. She knew the lines Sam was referring to, the words rising in her mind. They had taken on a different meaning now that she knew Austin and Eabha weren't biologically related – was that something Cillian had known or was it just something that he sensed?

Eabha (*laughing uneasily*): I don't understand
... what's your problem with Austin? You know
we're very close. We always have been.
Cillian: I know that ... but ... it's like
he's competing with me for your attention,
for your love. He wants you all to himself,
Eabha. He'll never let you go.
Eabha: You need to understand his side. I'm
all he has left, Cillian!
Cillian: Yeah ... and that's the problem.

'The jealousy started when I tried to put some distance between us,' Eabha explained. 'Cillian sensed my doubt, even before I was fully aware of it myself. And his reaction was to cling to me even more, which only scared me further away ... I don't think he wanted to acknowledge his own behaviour. He had convinced himself that I was his and that we had this great love ... perfect and pure.' She shook her head, her dark hair unmoving. 'He thought that, if anything broke us apart, it would be some enemy outside of us, some external force. He couldn't accept that I would choose to leave him.'

Oisín blew the air out of his lungs. 'I know how it feels to have a crush,' he said, 'but Cillian really took it to an extreme.'

'He felt things so deeply,' Eabha said, 'and he needed help learning to process his emotions, to understand them. He couldn't always contain how he felt.'

'I can't decide if I should feel sorry for him or angry at him for what he did to you,' Dara mumbled, catching Eabha's eye as she looked up.

'You can feel both,' Eabha said gently. 'I do.'

* * *

After rehearsal that evening, Dara stood with a box of hair dye, in Rhona's small bathroom, reading the instructions again to make sure she got it right. The shelves next to the shower were cluttered with half-finished shampoo bottles, an array of make-up palettes and brushes, a radioactive-looking bottle of tan; an orange handprint on the tiles suggested it had been recently used by Rhona.

Dara had taken a fresh towel from the hot press and placed it on the floor next to the bathtub, before leaning her head over the side and brushing dye across her blonde hair until each and every strand was covered: root to tip.

Stepping into the bath, she washed the dye out again, watching the black water stream down her skin, circling into the drain, which gurgled and belched back at her. When the water ran clear, she switched the shower off and stood at the mirror again, gazing at the dark hair hanging limply against her pale face.

A photographer was coming to shoot her for the posters on Wednesday. They would soon festoon the walls of the city, announcing to the world that it was really happening again, that this time, the truth would out. Only it wouldn't be Eabha staring out from the posters at passers-by: it would be Dara. She would be the face of the play, which also meant she would be the face of the backlash.

She had been trying to prepare herself for the inevitable resurgence of the controversy which had dogged the last production. Her internet search history was littered with questions about the de Laceys, Cillian Butler, the investigation, the Bodkin School, and the first production of *The Truth Will Out*. She had scoured news reports from ten years before, seen countless tabloid photos of a younger Austin all over the internet. His coat collar pulled up to his chin, a series of hats obscuring his face, his palm held out to block the lens of numerous cameras, his every move stalked. There were photos of Eabha too, but she had never bothered to hide from the attention, striding confidently in and out of the Abbey Theatre, like a woman ready to ascend her throne.

Despite her best efforts, none of Dara's research made her feel any better prepared for what lay ahead. But while she waited for her hair to dry, she took a seat on the couch, reaching for her laptop and scrolling through the photos again, a compulsion pressing her to search deeper and deeper for answers. It was only when she heard Rhona's heavy footsteps on the staircase outside that she rubbed her tired eyes, closed her laptop and set it down on the couch next to her.

A key turned in the lock of the front door. 'I'm home,' Rhona called, as she stepped inside. A loud inhalation of breath sounded as her eyes fell on her sister. 'Dara! Your *hair*! What did you do?!'

Dara's hands flew instinctively to her head. 'Oh . . .' she said dully. 'Yeah . . . I . . . I dyed it.'

'Oh my god!' Rhona sat on the couch next to her. 'I hardly recognised you! You look . . .' She reached for Dara's hair and let it fall again. '*So* different.'

'It's just for the play. They're taking photos this week,' Dara explained, yawning as she pulled the duvet from its spot in the corner. 'The character needs dark hair, you know? I can't see myself as Eabha without it.'

'It's so strange looking at you like that. I can't get used to it,' Rhona said, rising to hang her jacket on the hook next to the door. 'It's like you're someone else.'

Dara let out another long yawn but didn't respond, reaching for her pillow which she threw onto the couch. Being someone else was the goal. A full transfiguration, from Dara to Eabha.

She sat down on the couch again, pulling the duvet up to her chin.

'How was your night out?' she asked, tying her dark hair into a bun with the elastic around her wrist, where it would not provoke further comment.

'Ah, the usual,' Rhona said, waving her hand. 'I told them all I'll be leaving for Cork soon.'

'So you've made a decision? You're definitely leaving?' They had been talking about it for days: the pros and cons of a career in nursing.

Rhona's eyes briefly shut, her finger tapping her temple, where a headache was already beginning to form, a foreshadowing of the hangover to come. 'I don't see another way, to be honest with you. I'm not making any money up here and it's starting to feel like I'm drifting. I can't keep delaying the inevitable.'

She sounded so bitter about it that Dara wondered briefly if she should try to convince her otherwise, convince her to stay. But they had been here before and Rhona seemed to have made up her mind this time, a certainty in her now that had been missing before. So, instead, Dara said: 'It'll be all right. You might like the nursing course?'

'I won't.'

'But it'll be nice to be back in Cork? You've loads of friends down there.'

'Most of them have moved away.'

'Then you'll make new friends.'

'Maybe.'

'And you'll like the money . . . the security.'

'Stop, Dara. Please . . . it's not like I have a choice. Dreams don't always come true.' Rhona sat down on the couch, angling her face so she could look at her sister. 'What are you going to do when I leave Dublin? Like, where are you going to live?'

Dara bit her lip unconsciously, her thoughts tumbling towards anxiety. They could just not pay this final month's rent and forfeit the deposit from the landlord. He'd give her two weeks' notice on the arrears promptly enough – the tight bastard – and then . . .

She stopped the thought dead in its tracks before it gained momentum. 'I don't know yet, but I'll figure it out. I'm sure a friend will have a couch I can borrow.'

Even as she said it, she knew that this wasn't a real prospect. Most of her Dublin friends still lived at home where they didn't have to pay rent, and her friends from outside of Dublin were overcrowded enough already. They could give her a couple of nights on the floor, but it was not a viable prospect for longer than that. She didn't know anyone in Dublin with a salary and a spare room.

'I feel awful, Dara. Your selfish prick of a sister is abandoning you.'

'You're not selfish,' Dara said. She smiled and added: 'Just a prick.'

Rhona pushed her hair off her face. 'I'm leaving you high and dry.'

'You've got to do what's right for you.'

Rhona snorted. 'You sound like . . . I don't know . . . a motivational poster.'

Dara giggled. 'Follow your heart.'

'Jesus . . . if only.'

Dara rubbed her face slowly with her hand. Her phone had just vibrated next to her.

Oisín Langford (23.20pm): Are you out tonight? Eabha is opening some champagne and invited me over.

She tossed her phone aside, fighting the flicker of jealousy rising at the thought of them together, and conceded this round to Oisín. Nice of him to let her know she was falling behind in the race for Eabha's affections.

She turned back to Rhona with a shake of her head. 'I don't get it. Eabha told me her family is in a load of debt, but now she's drinking champagne with Oisín tonight. Some people have no idea how it feels to be properly broke.'

Rhona nodded solemnly. 'Rich people are an odd breed, Dara. You can't trust them.'

'I just don't understand,' Dara said, exasperated. 'She makes this show of hosting people with fancy meals in her big house. Like, why all the pretending? What's she trying to achieve?'

'Is she lying to everyone else or just to herself?'

'I don't know, really,' Dara said. 'Maybe both . . . Sam and Oisín told me about the parties she has. Everyone shows up. Baths full of champagne. Dancing until dawn. A breakfast bonfire on the lawn. The only rule is you have to wear white. Anything else goes.' She scratched at her hair. 'I think she does it to convince the world she's still relevant . . . still exciting.'

None of the stories seemed to feature Eabha herself. She would throw her home open to the world, invite them inside and then retreat from them herself. What did Eabha get out of it? Dara thought of Miriam's description of her, a woman surrounding herself with a membrane of fans, stans and sycophants – protection against a world that must have terrified her, a world which believed she was a killer.

Rhona's eyes were closed, her head resting on Dara's shoulder. 'Sounds to me like she's trying too fucking hard,' she said, drifting towards sleep. 'Hiding herself in plain sight . . . maybe all that champagne in the bath is why she's broke. Imagine what Mam would say if she heard about that!'

Dara grinned, then assumed her mother's usual, mithered

expression. 'Would she not *drink* it, at least? All that champagne *literally* down the drain – the *notions!*'

Rhona laughed, then yawned, arms outstretched to the ceiling. 'Here, I need to go to bed.'

'Yeah,' Dara said. 'Me too.' Another yawn escaped, matching that of her sister's. Her mind jumped ahead, though she wished it wouldn't. It was after midnight, which meant they were another day closer to opening night.

'The lesson in all this,' Rhona said, making her way up the stairs to her bedroom, 'is we should simply eat the rich.'

Dara laughed, fixing the pillow beneath her head. 'All right, Ms Marx. Wake me up when the revolution comes.'

Rhona waved sleepily as Dara reached for her phone again, scrolling past Oisín's text until she found the latest message from Linda O'Rowe at the *Irish Independent*. It had arrived while she was dyeing her hair.

Linda O'Rowe (21.03pm): Dara, it's Linda again. I've been in touch with the family of Cillian Butler. His father wants to speak with Eabha de Lacey but she's refusing. The family are launching a campaign to get the play cancelled. Any comment you'd like to make? Last chance to get ahead of this. My deadline is tomorrow at 5. I'm publishing on Wednesday. Call me. It's in your interest.

A campaign against the play would galvanise the controversy, helping vague misgivings bloom into legitimate fears.

Dara put her phone down again, thinking of her mother, her father, her Aunty Sheila – everyone she knew back in Beara. What would they think of her?

Sam had sent her a photo that was circulating online of Richard Butler, Cillian's father. He was holding an image of Cillian in his school uniform. She had seen it before during her internet scrolling. His grin was lopsided, his hair gelled down over his eyes, his eyebrow pierced. Always seventeen, frozen in time.

Somehow Dara had found herself on the opposite side of a grieving father and a dead boy. The enforced silence and the complicity it implied was weighing on her. If she could speak freely, she would have told Richard Butler she was sorry for his loss, for his pain that grew with the years and his grief that fed on it.

But she would also ask Richard why he blamed Eabha, why he overlooked Cillian's treatment of her, why he heaped his pain onto the de Laceys, why he ignored the consequences of his own actions, why he left Cillian to his lonely fate, where he grew sick on his feelings of abandonment: all those years, alone at the Bodkin School.

She left Linda's text unanswered; there was nothing she could say. She couldn't speak, couldn't voice these thoughts, couldn't say how she felt because she had promised Eabha her silence.

Dara turned over on the couch, her face pressed against the pillow, and tried to shut the vision of Cillian's face out of her mind. But he was there when she closed her eyes and he was there as she gradually fell asleep. She had chosen her side and now she had to live with it.

Chapter Eight

Linda O'Rowe's article landed in the newspaper midweek, news of the Butler family's campaign hitting just as the photographer was finishing up with Dara. She had been posing for his camera all morning in the rehearsal room. She sat on a stool next to the attic window, so that the light caught her profile, with the window in shot, glass shining and ready to be broken.

The photographer was busy packing his equipment away when the news bulletin sounded on the radio.

The family of a schoolboy who died tragically fifteen years ago at the prestigious Bodkin School in County Clare are calling on the public to support their campaign to stop a controversial play restaging in Dublin next month . . .

'Wow, that's . . . that's this play, isn't it?' the photographer said, glancing up from the tripod he was folding and repacking into a black case.

'The very one,' Dara replied, eyes on the mirror in her hand, scrubbing at the make-up on her lips and eyes, wiping Eabha's face away and restoring her own.

His hands stilled. 'And . . . like, I mean, are they going to cancel it?!'

Dara stared fixedly at her own face in the mirror, ignoring his eyes – the scrutiny in them, the judgement she knew would be there and didn't care to see.

'No idea,' she said, her eyes travelling towards the window. 'I guess we'll have to wait and see.'

'But what about you . . . like, are you not worried about it?'

Her eyes drifted to his. 'You know what they say.' She gave a limp smile, flicking her hair off her shoulder. 'On with the show and all that.'

* * *

Eabha barely acknowledged news of the public campaign against her, saying firmly that rehearsals would be a controversy-free zone. 'Let's just leave it all at the door, OK? It will only suck our creative energy and I bet that's *exactly* what they want.'

It had hardened quickly into a rule – the Butler family protest was not to be discussed – and they were unwilling to create a confrontation over it. Nobody wanted to give Eabha the impression of disloyalty, not while the strain she was under showed itself more and more with each passing day. It was there in the short temper, the tiredness around her eyes, a propensity to distraction, to melancholy, while the dwindling days carried them mercilessly forward towards opening night.

Despite the pressure of rehearsals, it was the protest that occupied Dara, Sam and Oisín's minds. After the day's rehearsal they arranged to go for a drink in the bar on the corner of Rathmines Road, somewhere they could speak freely.

They sat in the back, their faces cast in shadow by the dancing candlelight in front of them. Dara watched the other people around them – wearing suits, with ties loosened at the neck, a gym bag at their feet, probably someone waiting at home for them – and felt entirely alien. What would they say – these normal people – if they knew the three sitting in the corner had been declared *personae non gratae* on the lunchtime news?

Under the table, Sam pressed his leg against hers, breaking her spiralling thoughts, drawing her attention back to him. Closing her eyes briefly, she could feel the thump of her heart, like a fist pummelling her chest. She caught his eye, looked away, looked back. He was smiling.

Despite herself, she laughed, as if her body were forcing out through her mouth some of the muddled feelings Sam stirred in her, producing a vaguely happy, vaguely nervous sound of reluctant laughter.

Oisín looked up from his pint, catching the silent exchange between them, a flurry of communication in a language of gesture and glance.

'What's so funny?' he said, his shoulders hunching forward slightly.

Dara shook her head, gathering her dark hair into her hand. 'Nothing,' she said, but the smile lingered on her face.

Oisín watched her, disgruntled now. 'Have I missed something here? Is there something I should know about . . .' He waved an accusing finger between Dara and Sam. 'This?'

'No—' she said casually, reaching for her glass and taking an artful sip of her gin. 'Why are you being all paranoid, Oisín?' She turned to Sam, who was still silent. 'Get a load of Austin over here. Very on character.'

'Don't be smart, Dara,' Oisín bit back. 'It doesn't suit you.'

'All right, Oisín,' Sam said, raising his hand, fingers spread. 'No need for that. It's been a long week for all of us. We're all a little tense. Let's not start a row.'

Dara folded her arms carefully, watching Oisín with a sense of curiosity more than annoyance. She knew she shouldn't say it, but the gin had made quick work of her tongue, loosening it from the controlling influence of her mind. 'You can hardly talk anyway, Oisín. What's going on with you and Eabha?'

To her surprise, a playful smile spread across his face, displacing the scowl. He leaned forward on the table. 'Wouldn't *you* like to know,' he said, staring very pointedly back at her.

Brow wrinkling, she shook her head. 'But I already do, Oisín – it's obvious. Everywhere Eabha turns, there you are.'

'She needs my support.' Oisín sat back on his chair again, turning his glass in his hand. 'She can't just walk away from it at the end of the day like we can. It's her life – her real life. Not just a few weeks spent pretending. It's a struggle for her.'

Sam's dark eyes rolled. 'Ah, come on. Eabha knew the controversy would happen again – and she chose to go through with the restaging anyway. It's almost like she's punishing herself. I just can't get my head around *why* she's doing this, especially to her brother.'

'She needs the money,' Dara replied. 'She told me they're in debt – it seems quite bad.'

'Is that so?' Sam said coldly. 'I suppose it's not surprising at the rate Eabha spends it.'

'She has been selling her grandfather's paintings to try make a bit of money.'

'I'd say they get a few quid for an Arthur de Lacey original,' Oisín said, a thoughtful expression on his face as he played with his chain.

'Austin was furious about it,' Dara added. 'They had a huge row. He took a painting off Eabha's wall and stormed out with it. I thought, for a second, he was going to destroy it. The look on his face—' She gave a shudder. 'He's just . . . filled with such *anger*.'

'When was this?' Oisín asked. 'Why weren't we there?!'

'It was at Sunday lunch last week.' Her eyelashes batted slowly, triumph hiding in Dara's dimples. 'Eabha invited me over.' She watched – with some small satisfaction – Oisín deflate at the news that he, the favourite, had not been invited, had not been wanted.

'They don't seem to get along, do they?' Sam said. 'I suppose it's not surprising, really. Imagine your sister setting you up as public villain number one like that.'

'That's not how Eabha sees it,' Dara said, playing with the wax dripping down the red candles in front of them. 'She thinks she's setting the record straight about what happened.'

'Well, she's not doing a good job.' Sam laughed, though Dara didn't know why.

'Why do you hate her so much?' she said, the question blunt.

Oisín leaned forward on the table. 'Yeah, I've been wondering that myself, Sam. What's your problem with Eabha?'

'I don't have a problem with her. She just annoys me,' Sam replied, a little defensively. 'She makes it seem so easy. I've been working my arse off for years, getting by on fucking scraps, and she got to the top with one play. Doesn't that bother you too?'

'I wouldn't trade places with her, if that's what you mean,' Dara said.

Oisín was shaking his head. 'You're jealous, Sam.'

'It's not about jealousy. It's about unearned privilege. You think a guy like me gets the breaks she does? Do you think she would have been this successful if they hadn't put her face all over the posters? Her big blue eyes gazing out like fucking Bambi?'

Oisín's eyes rose briefly to the ceiling as he got to his feet. 'Is it heavy, Sam?' he said. 'That big chip on your shoulder?'

He didn't wait for a reply, wandering away from the table in the direction of the toilets. He stopped on his way, throwing an arm around a girl he must have known – tall and willowy with auburn hair, she looked nothing at all like Eabha.

Dara turned back towards Sam, whose face was thunder, his leg no longer pressing against hers. He was leaning over his pint, staring into it silently.

'Don't mind him,' she said. 'Oisín's just being a prick tonight.'

'She's making a fool of him. He thinks he gets Eabha more than we do.'

'Why do you think that is?'

Sam raised his pint to his lips. 'I don't know . . . he's been relating to it all a bit too much from the start. Don't you think?' He wiped the foam from around his mouth. 'I don't know if it's something to do with his mother walking out on him? Maybe not . . . what do I know?' He shook his head. 'It just feels like he has invested a lot of himself into this play – into *her*.'

Frowning now, Dara ran her finger over the rim of her glass, thinking of her work with Oisín, those moments in rehearsals when he would look at her in character as Cillian, speaking Cillian's lines, Eabha's words. 'I know what you mean. He loses himself sometimes.' She knew that feeling; there were moments, brief snatches of time during rehearsals, when she had felt the same.

Her eyes glazed, attention drifting from Sam, retreating from the present. She was thinking of a monologue in the script. It had been on her mind a lot lately.

Eabha (*to audience*)**:** Did I take advantage of Cillian's interest in me? In a way, I suppose I did — but then he took advantage of me too. Isn't that what love is? A selfish act by two people profoundly afraid of loneliness. What's

love without obsession? Without a need that
rips through you, that breaks you? What's
love without that pain? Love is a response to
fear. It's an act of self-preservation. Love
means standing hand in hand, beating back
the darkness together, fighting the emptiness,
the gnawing sense in the pit of your soul
that you don't matter. Because at least to
this other person, the one who says they love
you, at least for the brief time you spend
together ... you matter. Cillian made me feel
that I mattered.

'Do you think he loves her? Oisín?' Dara asked, eyes coming into focus again on Sam's face.

He looked surprised. 'Eabha?! No ... I mean, he's fucking ob*sess*ed, but it's not the same thing.'

Dara looked over at Oisín, laughing with the auburn-haired girl and her friends. He seemed relaxed, his earlier hostility melted away, or was it just that he reserved it for them? Was Cillian biding his time, waiting to co-opt Oisín again when he could wreak most havoc?

Dara shifted in her seat, looking again at Sam. 'You know, Austin told me he's adopted.' This new information had been on her mind for the past few days. She couldn't decide whether it was significant, or where it fit in the puzzle, but her mind kept bringing her back to the fact of the adoption: the implications, the possibilities. 'I think he told me to hurt Eabha – she seemed very upset by it.'

There was a new interest springing from Sam's eyes. 'Well, isn't that something ...'

Dara was, again, very aware of Sam's leg pressed against hers.

Was she imagining it or was he pressing a little harder now? She shut her eyes briefly, feeling the heat of this small scrap of his body against hers. Her hand – curled around her glass – itched with a restlessness. She could reach out, with just the very tips of her fingers, and trace them slowly along his thigh.

'It makes sense of a few things for me,' Sam said after a moment's silence, his face and tone passive, betraying nothing of what was or was not happening beneath the table. 'I mean, I've always wondered why he clings to her the way he does. It's not like she has treated him well – I mean, just look at the play. It's a monstrosity for Austin. It literally broke him. I've never understood why he lets her tell that story again and again. It's never made sense to me . . . now it does.'

'What do you mean?' Dara said, one elbow leaning on the table in front of her. 'How does it make sense?'

'Think about it,' Sam said. 'Eabha is all Austin has in the world and even that relationship feels insecure to him. He's at sea, just as Cillian was, and he's clinging to her, just as Cillian did. Maybe there's even . . . well . . . an attraction there – I don't know.'

Dara was staring at the candle in front of her, watching the shape the red wax made on the table. It didn't seem completely outlandish to her and that surprised her thoroughly. 'There's something between them,' she said, 'something they keep hidden.'

Sam shrugged. 'Maybe it's a conspiracy to murder.'

Dara felt a mild annoyance at his flippancy. She was thinking of Cillian's father, Richard Butler, holding a photograph of his son, begging for his death to be acknowledged, taken seriously. A long, deep sigh sounded from her mouth. She lifted her leg away from Sam, crossing it over her knee.

'If they did it,' she said, her eyes on the faces of the strangers scattered around the bar, with their ordinary conversations and their ordinary laugher – none of them speaking credibly of the possibility of murder. 'Sam, if they're guilty . . . what does that make us?'

To her surprise, Sam reached for hand. She looked down at his fingers, the nails neatly cut, the half-moons white. 'It makes us optimists,' he replied. 'That's all.' He squeezed her fingers with his. 'Don't take on responsibility for this, Dara. It's not your burden to bear.'

She smiled and held his hand and tried to accept what he said, but her anxious mind was now quivering. It had only been a few short weeks, but, already, Dara could feel a distance growing between her past and present self, as if time itself were stretching her, pulling her into a new and contorted future. There was a pressure in her chest again, a tightness across her ribs and there, pooling in her stomach, an unshakeable force.

Guilt.

* * *

With four weeks left before opening night and the days racing past, Eabha drew her brother closer. It came as a surprise to Dara; Austin was so antagonistic towards the play, towards Eabha – what good could come of involving him in the production? She put the question to Eabha, who stared out at the garden from the attic window, as if from a prison she had imposed on herself.

'Austin knows these characters. I think he'll really help us to pull it together. So, I've . . . I've asked him to help us with the rehearsals.'

Dara didn't feel she was in a position to object – it was Eabha's decision to make – but her explanation felt lacking. The push and the pull of their relationship confused Dara; they were tied to each other, though it only seemed to cause them pain. It seemed, to Dara, an act motivated by a guilt that dripped from Eabha, like fat from meat. Maybe she was involving Austin to give him some control over the play, ceding some power to him, letting his perspective on the story colour it. Observing Eabha now – with the light from the world outside pressing against her as it passed through the small window – it was as if a low rumble surrounded her, echoing up from deeper currents and radiating out through her skin, a tumult of emotion, a great gale roiling the open ocean.

Dara shut her eyes and tried to calm a rising panic. Twenty eight days left and Eabha was starting to make mistakes. Twenty eight days left and it was far from clear Eabha knew what she was doing.

* * *

On the morning Austin was due at Leinster Road for his first rehearsal, a nervousness infested the attic. Oisín, in particular, was tense. Dara and Sam were waiting in the rehearsal room while Eabha took a call downstairs, watching Oisín's long strides from the window to the door and back again. As he paced, he shook out his hands every so often, as if the tension might leak out through his fingertips if he could only shake them hard enough.

'What's wrong with you?' Sam asked, irritated. 'You're fucking hyper over there. Sit down, will you?'

'Is something on your mind?' Dara asked, lying on her stomach on one of the oversized cushions on the floor. 'Oisín? What is it?'

'I'm fine, I just . . .' He stopped, looking from Sam to Dara, his hands now clenched into fists. 'It's just . . . why is she bringing him here?'

'We've all been wondering that . . .' Dara muttered, watching the door.

Sam, who had been leaning against the wall opposite him, stepped forward. 'Why do you care so much? Are you afraid of him?'

'No, I . . .' Oisín hesitated, considering his words, reluctant to reveal them, then saw that he had no option. 'I went to see Austin during the week . . .'

Dara's eyes met Sam's. 'You did what?!'

Oisín's face wore an expression of misery. 'Eabha doesn't know about it, OK? And now I'm worried he's going to say something about it when he's here.'

'*Why* would you do that, Oisín?' Sam said, words manifesting into a groan. 'That's so fucking dumb. Austin's a total liability! The less we have to do with him, the better.'

Oisín's pace increased, the wooden boards creaking under his feet noisily as he walked. 'I know, but I wanted to talk to him about Cillian. You know, to try to understand his character.'

'Why didn't you just tell Eabha about this?' Dara asked, glancing nervously at Sam.

'I didn't want to involve her,' Oisín replied. 'She has been strange with me and . . .' He let the sentence die. 'This character is . . . I can't get into his head. There isn't time and – I don't know, I just . . . I thought Austin could help me with it . . .'

'Jesus, Oisín,' Sam said. 'You really think *Austin* can help you with that?'

'I just wanted to talk to him about it all,' Oisín replied, looking miserable. 'He's the centre of this story . . . he's the missing part in all this. And I wanted to hear what he had to say about it.' His eyes flashed from Sam to Dara. 'Should I just tell her? Will I tell her now that I went to see him?'

'Just . . . just relax, Oisín,' Sam said, a hand on Oisín's

shoulder. 'You spoke to her brother – that's all. It's not like you betrayed her.'

Oisín shook his head, pacing again, out of Sam's reach. 'She won't see it like that. You don't know her like I do.'

'Was it worth it?' Dara asked, kneeling up on her cushion. 'Did speaking to Austin help you?'

'Not really.' Oisín stopped moving briefly, crossing his arms in front of his chest. 'He just offered me drugs.'

'Really . . . why would he do that?!' Dara said, eyebrows rising skyward. 'Eabha said he's been clean for a decade – since the play's debut.'

'Well then, Eabha doesn't know her brother as well as she thinks,' Oisín remarked. 'He uses hallucinogens. He says it's for meditative practice.'

'Right,' Sam said, his laugh severe. 'Of course he does.'

'No, man, I'm serious,' Oisín insisted. 'He's really into this Eastern-thought shit. He said it saved his life . . . his sanity.' He ran his hands through his hair compulsively, a habit that usually meant a spike in stress hormones.

'I don't understand,' Dara said. 'Why did he offer you drugs?' Dimly, they could hear Eabha's voice downstairs, a strained laugh.

'Austin said Eabha leaves a lot of stuff about Cillian out of the play, stuff you need to know to make sense of him,' Oisín replied, pulling on the chain around his neck. 'He used to take whatever he could get his hands on – you know that already. But Austin said he always thought Cillian wanted to get caught. The school would tell his family when they found him at it, but the Butlers did nothing – of course they didn't – and that only made him worse. He was heading for expulsion when he died . . . that's not something you'll read in the papers.' Oisín reached into the pocket of his beige trousers and pulled out a small, clear bag, lifting it to eye level so they could see the brown mush-rooms through the plastic. 'Austin said Cillian was doing magic mushrooms the night he died. They were in his system when they did the post-mortem.'

'Put them away, Oisín,' Dara snapped, her eyes on the door, through which Eabha could appear at any moment.

'It was Austin's idea,' Oisín said, sticking the bag into his pocket again. 'He said the mushrooms would let me see the world the way Cillian did.'

Sam's dark eyes were deeply sceptical. 'So, what's your plan? You're going to take magic mushrooms so you can play Cillian, is it? A little trip into his dearly departed soul?'

'No, I mean . . . well, maybe. I don't know . . . Austin said it was a bad trip the night he died – I'm not going to do *that*.' He shrugged. 'I don't know . . . I just thought it might help me understand his frame of mind better. Just micro-dosing them, you know. It's safe.'

A quick exchange passed between Sam and Dara, a ripple of nerves.

'Maybe it would be better if you told Eabha about this,' Dara suggested.

'Absolutely not,' Oisín said immediately, 'and you're not going to tell her either, OK? Austin made me promise I wouldn't tell anyone about the mushrooms.'

Dara sighed into her hands. 'Jesus, Oisín, and doesn't that worry you? Hiding things from Eabha? Keeping secrets with Austin? You can't trust him – he's . . . he's not right.'

'Just keep it to yourselves, OK? That's all I'm asking.' Oisín gazed sternly at Dara until she nodded her head, though it made her feel deeply uneasy. More secrets; when would they spill out?

It was a mistake to involve Austin in any of this. She had seen how quickly his anger leapt through him, flooding him in a matter of moments. There wasn't time to manage his emotions, the days already slipping by in a whirl of panic and distraction. But nobody had asked her opinion. She was swept up in the choices of others – the mistakes – a current of them carrying her now: she wondered where they would take her.

Downstairs, a knock sounded on the front door.

Chapter Nine

Austin made his presence felt immediately at the house on Leinster Road. He had the same blue-green eyes as Eabha, but he towered over her, reducing her, making her seem almost elven next to him. Even Sam, the tallest of them, only came to his shoulder.

But it wasn't just his sheer physical size that made Dara nervous of Austin, it was the way he wielded it: large hands quick to form fists, shoulders hunching, the muscles tensed and ready for use.

He was wearing a collarless white linen shirt – untucked at the back – and a pair of brown corduroy trousers. His long, dark hair was tied into a small bun at the back of his head, though this seemed less like a deliberate fashion choice than genuine apathy towards his appearance.

They decamped to the garden to make the most of the sunshine, the rehearsal room too cramped on these warm days, when it was easy to grow lethargic in the heat. On the lawn, Dara lay on her back, watching the sun wink through the leaves of the apple tree at the end of the garden, the grass whispered at her ear, while she squinted occasionally down at her lines.

Austin stretched one languid leg out in front of him, leaning back on his hands. He looked bored already; Dara wondered if it was the sort of boredom that might escalate into outright conflict, or if he would content himself with an afternoon of quiet resentment.

Eabha had brought a chair from the patio onto the grass and sat next to Oisín, arranging her tulle skirt around her knees. Dusty pink, like a cloud at dusk.

'Thank you for coming today, Austin. I was hoping you could give the cast another perspective on the play – I guess it has been feeling quite myopic lately, so we're hoping you'll bring fresh eyes to it.'

'What do you want me to do exactly?' He sounded irritated, though they hadn't yet begun. 'You want me to watch the rehearsal and answer some questions. Is that it?'

'If that's all right?' Eabha replied. She was nervous around him, hyper-attuned to every minor fluctuation in his emotional state.

'All right then,' Austin muttered, with all the enthusiasm of a child at bedtime.

It was strange to watch this effect Austin had on his sister and she on him. They behaved sometimes like old friends grown distant over some now forgotten slight. Shy and polite, but with an undercurrent of tension always humming.

'Should we start the rehearsal then?' Sam asked, leaning back on his elbows.

Austin made a sort of grunting sound. 'Yeah, can we get this started?' He glanced at his watch. 'I've got to head off again in about half an hour.'

Dara wondered mildly what it was Austin did with his time – he didn't seem like someone with hobbies – but then it wasn't their use of his time that seemed to be the problem. It was the play: its existence, theirs.

An almost imperceptible movement of Eabha's eyebrows indicated annoyance. 'Well then, we better get started,' she said, turning the pages of her script brusquely. 'Which scene will we read?'

'Don't care.' Austin pulled his boots off, throwing them onto the grass next to him. A musty smell spread from his feet as he stretched his legs out again, putting his hands under his head. Dara's nose wrinkled with distaste.

'Let's pick it up from the scene at the lake,' Eabha said. 'The first time Cillian hurt me.'

Austin breathed in heavily. 'Ah yes,' he said. 'I just love reliving fond memories.'

SCENE: Daytime, a clearing in the woods where **Austin** is gathering firewood. A cold wind sweeps through the trees as **Eabha** and **Cillian**, wrapped in towels, stand drying themselves after a swim, laughing together while **Austin** broods and tries his best to ignore them.

Eabha: I feel like I will never be warm again!
Cillian: Baltic. Absolutely Baltic!
Eabha: I feel like my blood is ice.
Cillian: How's that fire coming, Austin?
Austin (struggling with matches): I'm just ... trying to get the wood to light.
Cillian: You need some sort of lighter fluid on that. (**Cillian** kneels down next to him, a bottle of vodka in his hand, and douses the sticks. He takes the lighter from **Austin's** hand and places the flame in proximity to the

kindling, which roars into a blaze. They step
back, Cillian laughing proudly.)

'Dara, show us how cold you are,' Eabha said, interrupting.
'Kneel down by the fire. Dry your hair with the towel. Make us
feel the cold too.'

Cillian spots something at the edge of the
clearing, white and shaped differently to the
other rocks on the shoreline.

Eabha: Where are you going? Cillian ...?
Cillian, come back!
Cillian: I think I ... I think I see
something ...

They watch him clambering through the
clearing until, after some moments, Cillian
returns, brandishing the skull of a wild goat.

Cillian (*triumphant*): Look at this!

'Alas, poor Yorick,' Sam muttered, slipping briefly out of
character.

Cillian hands the skull to Eabha, who takes
it reluctantly and then passes it quickly to
Austin instead. He inspects it, turning it
over.

Austin: What is this?
Cillian: What does it look like? It's the
skull of one of the wild goats of the
Burren. Some people say they're just goats
that wandered off from the flock and got lost
out on the rocks. But others say they're

shapeshifters. *Púca*, they call them. Legend says the *púca* invade the goats after they die out here and give them a second life roaming the land. Give it here!

*Austin tosses the skull back to **Cillian**, who waves it in Eabha's face, running the curled horn along her cheek. She recoils, but he doesn't stop, enjoying her discomfort.*

Eabha: Stop, Cillian! Stop that!
Austin (*peevish*): Leave her alone, Cillian.
Cillian: Ah fuck off, Austin. I'm just having a laugh.

Oisín lowered his script. 'Did he really believe this shit? You know, all the superstition about the goat?'

'I think he did,' Eabha replied.

'It was just the drugs—' Austin interjected. 'They did weird things to him. Fucked with his head. He would see things, alone on the Burren at night. Creepy things. And he'd bring shit like the goat skull back to the attic so he could scare people with it.'

'It wasn't his fault,' Eabha said. 'His mind was this . . . it was this hive of anxiety. He lived at the edge of his emotions, experiencing the world at an elevated pitch.' She smiled, as if at a fond memory, though when Dara glanced at Austin, his face was stony. 'Cillian was just like them really – a wild goat, in human form.' She licked her finger, then turned the page of her script. 'Next line, Dara.'

Eabha: How long have we left before we're due back at school?
Austin (*checking his watch*): About another three hours.

Eabha: I wish we could just stay. I don't want to go back there ... I'm so sick of it ... sick of their stupid rules and the endless routines!

Cillian pulls a bag of hallucinogenic mushrooms from his pocket.

Cillian: We have enough time for these ... if you still want to try them?
Austin: So he came through for you? Your brother?
Cillian: Course he did. The only visitor I ever get is the black sheep of the Butler family. And the only care package Fergal ever brings is vodka and drugs.

Sam lowered his script. 'Was that true? His family never visited? Just his brother?'

Austin gave a slight shrug. 'That's what Cillian said. I only met Richard Butler after his son was already dead.' He pulled at some blades of grass. 'Fergal would come round every few weeks and take Cillian off for the day. When he got back to school, he'd be half-cut on something or another. I helped him hide from the teachers if I could, but I think they mostly pretended not to notice. It wasn't worth their while phoning the Butlers about it – they weren't coming to get him.' The grass trickled from his fingers. 'Cillian didn't really cause any trouble for the school, not until the very end. He'd just take himself off to the attic, or go wandering across the hills. He always came back, so they didn't ask too many questions.' Austin was squinting, sunlight breaking through the branches of the apple tree, the light catching on his face. 'Has Eabha ever shown you the goat skull?'

'Please don't go on about that thing . . .' Eabha's hand was gripping the lockets around her neck, her lips straining against her teeth. 'Can we please just continue?' She looked up at Dara. 'It's your line.'

Dara wasn't listening, her hungry eyes staring at Austin's face.

'Dara?' Eabha said again. 'Are you there?'

She snapped back into focus. 'Yes – sorry. I'm ready.'

'I need you to look at Sam. I mean, *really* look at him. You don't want to disappoint your brother. You want his approval. But you also desperately want to escape this place. You want an adventure with Cillian. You want to feel free, unbounded . . . and you want Austin to *let* you be free – to give you permission.'

Dara swallowed, cleared her throat, letting her eyes focus on Sam's face. He held her gaze, his eyes warm, the whisper of a smile at the corner of his lips: she wanted to reach out and touch him, to run her fingers along his lips, to press them open with her tongue, to feel him give way to her.

When would it fade? This need? She was not prepared for it to last like this – her romantic interests were reliably temporary, fickle and quick to fade away again. Her last boyfriend – a friend of a friend who she met at a Halloween party in a house near the Coombe – stuck around for nearly three months before the very tepid nature of her interest in him became impossible to ignore. That was two years ago now.

The problem was that she liked the initial rush of enthusiasm so much more than the rest – the first spark, like an explosion of colour, though it never lasted long, diluting with time and distraction, into nothingness, like ink dissolving into water. Yet here was Sam, like a tune she couldn't get out of her head, sustaining her attention, despite all expectation – why was that?

She closed her eyes, bit the inside of her lip, and tried to focus. He was not Sam: she was not Dara. Limestone rock was beneath her feet, the wind lashing at her face. Opening her eyes again, she looked at Sam and tried to see Austin in him.

```
Cillian (looking at Eabha and Austin
expectantly): Well? Are we going to try them?
Eabha: Austin ...?
Austin (reluctant): I can't tell you what to
do, Eabha ... but I don't think this is a
good idea.
Cillian (pushes him): Relax, Austin, would
you? It'll be grand. I've tried them before
plenty of times. It's not a big deal. Trust
me.
Eabha (excited): I think I want to try them
... Austin, do you mind if I try them?
```

'You're upset now, Sam,' Eabha said. 'You want to keep your sister safe and here is Cillian putting her in danger. Your grief for your mother and father makes you afraid you'll lose her too. You feel like she's slipping away from you.'

Sam hesitated, his eyes on Austin. 'Is that right, Austin? Is that how you were feeling?'

Dara watched Eabha for a reaction, but her expression was inscrutable.

Austin gave a snort. 'I don't remember,' he said, scratching at his ribs through his shirt. 'Probably? I don't know . . . I thought it was a stupid fucking idea. Cillian was liable to drown himself in the lake by accident, or walk off a mountainside – and that was sober. I didn't know what he'd do on mushrooms. So, no . . . I wasn't exactly over the moon about the idea.'

Sam's gaze returned to his script, reading his next line.

```
Austin: If this is something you want to do,
```

then go ahead ... but I'm going to sit this
one out.

Dara tilted her head as she gave Sam a searching look. The angle posed a question, a mannerism she had learned from her study of Eabha.

Cillian: You sure, man? (*Cillian takes two
mushrooms from the bag and places them on the
palm of his hands.*) You're going to miss out
on all the fun!
Austin: Yeah, you're grand. I'll make sure you
don't drown yourselves or something.
Eabha (*quietly*): You sure, Austin? I don't
have to try them.
Austin: No, it's grand ... go ahead. If you
want to try them, you should. I'll be here
... you know, so it's safe.
Cillian (*holding up a mushroom*): Now, Eabha,
you have to really chew it, OK? Don't swallow
until you've chewed.

*Eabha takes the mushroom from him, placing it
on her tongue. She chews vigorously. Cillian
does the same while Eabha laughs excitedly.*

Austin (*quietly*): I'm going to find some more
kindling. Don't kill yourselves while I'm
gone.

Sam lowered his script again. 'I don't understand why you let her do this?' he said to Austin. 'It seems really out of character to me. Like, why didn't you just tell her not to? It reads to me like she *wanted* you to stop her?'

Dara's eyes flashed to Eabha, who was staring pointedly at her feet.

Oisín, annoyed by another interruption to the scene, let out a sigh, which Sam heard but chose to ignore. He was looking fixedly at Austin, who, with another passive shrug of his shoulders, said: 'Honestly, I really don't remember. She made her own decisions.'

'Did she though?' Sam said, stubbornness in the set of his jaw. 'Because the rest of the play gives a different impression.'

'Why do you think he let me take them, Sam?' Eabha asked, leaning forward.

'I've no idea,' Sam replied, arms folded, sitting cross-legged next to Oisín.

Eabha held his gaze a moment, then angled her head towards Dara instead. 'And, Dara? What do you think?'

She cleared her throat, glancing nervously at Austin, who was looking down at the grass, a heap of torn blades now sitting next to him. She could see in his resolute silence a familiar anger rising.

'I think Austin recognises that Cillian has a hold on her – on you.' Dara sat up. 'He can't break that through brute force or brotherly protectiveness. So, I think he's hoping that I – that *you* – would recognise the danger of the situation without him pointing it out to you. He hopes that you would see Cillian as he does and make the right choice for yourself.'

Eabha's eyes were still on Sam. 'Does that make sense to you, Sam?'

Sam was watching Austin, who hadn't reacted and showed no intention of offering an opinion. A little sullen now, he nodded, eyes dropping to his script again.

'Can we keep going?' Oisín said, petulantly pulling on his chain. 'It's hard to get a good run at this when we keep stopping . . . we're running out of time.'

'Yes, we'll keep going,' Eabha said, 'but I think these questions are productive.' Dara watched Eabha's eyes bounce uncertainly from her script to her brother's face. He was staring down at the grass, affecting a nonchalance that Dara doubted he really felt.

Eabha appears in a bright light, *Cillian* fading into the darkness of the stage. She dances, arms waving, the psychedelic effects making her feel light, as if her bones have emptied of their marrow, turning her skin to feathers, her body weightless. A rock hits the ground near her. She stares at the spot where it lands. Another follows it, striking her upper thigh. She cries out in pain. The third rock hits her forehead, just above her eye. Blood trickles from the wound.

Eabha: What are you doing?! Cillian ...?

From the darkness, Cillian takes a step forward into the light. He raises his arm, another rock in his hand, ready to fling her way. In his left hand, he still holds the skull of the wild goat, raising it now so that it sits against his forehead, staring with empty eyes at Eabha.

Eabha (*terrified*): Please ... (*She raises her hands in a defensive gesture*) Please — stop this, Cillian. Don't hurt me!

The script was scrunched up in Dara's hot hand. 'I can't believe Cillian did this to you,' she muttered.

Eabha's fingers were clutching at her skirt so hard that it looked as if she might rip the tulle.

On the grass, Austin made a sound like a grunt, lifting their attention from their scripts to the scornful look on his face.

'You're still angry at him,' Dara said, her eyes on Austin again, studying him. 'Even after all this time?'

Austin shifted on the grass again. 'Yes . . . even after all this time.' The anger in his voice had a destabilising effect on her, as if he had reached into her inner ear and adjusted the fluids.

'What happened that day at the lake?' Oisín asked. 'I'm not talking about the play. I mean, what *really* happened? What was going on in Cillian's head when he attacked you?'

'He said it was the mushrooms,' Eabha replied. A breeze was tousling her hair; she pushed it out of her eyes. 'He said afterwards that he thought I was this shrieking banshee creature, coming for him.'

'So . . .' Oisín pulled on his chain again. 'You're saying it was just a bad trip?'

Scepticism sat in Eabha's eyes. She exchanged a look with her brother, choosing her words carefully. 'That's what he said.'

'But what do you really think?' Sam asked, his voice containing an entreaty, challenging her to be open with them. Would she rise to it?

Eabha fidgeted with the tulle again. 'I think Cillian was a troubled boy. I think he felt a violent impulse towards me and acted on it in the moment.' She took a breath, eyes briefly closing. 'He wanted me to *prove* to him that I loved him, but no matter what I said, I couldn't ever satisfy him. It was never enough. And I think it was in him that day . . . simmering . . . a resentment towards me, somewhere at the back of his mind.'

'And you?' Dara said, eyes on Austin. 'Why do you think he did it?'

Austin exhaled heavily through his nose. 'He was using Eabha as a lifeline – clinging to her.' He lay back on the grass again, his hands over his eyes, blocking out the sun. 'It was all the product of manipulation. I had told him things I couldn't tell anyone else and he used it to manipulate Eabha. I told him about my parents, my relationship with my sister, my grief – and he used it all to win her over, pulling her strings like she was some kind of puppet. He made her feel that he was the only one who understood her, who loved her. And, in return, she was supposed to guarantee his happiness. That's what abusers do – they find decent, caring people and they take advantage.'

'There was a side to him you never saw, Austin,' Eabha said quietly. 'He was living through tragedy, watching his mother kill herself in slow motion, his entire family life devoured by her addiction. That's not the typical experience of a seventeen-year-old. It made him act in ways he shouldn't have, but it's not as simple as you make out.'

Dara watched her look away, watched her fingers playing with her chapped lips as if they were keys on a piano. She seemed intent on defending Cillian, as if her guilt required it.

'You make him seem like a better person than he was,' Austin replied. 'He doesn't deserve it.' His voice was sharp, cutting the air between them.

'That's not true – I've never hidden what he did to me – it's all in the play.' Eabha paused, trying to calm her breathing. 'I just . . . It's important to me that he isn't a caricature. He deserves that.' She swallowed, her eyes on a seagull, cawing at them from the roof. 'Cillian once told me about being at home for Christmas, his mother slumped into a chair, not even hiding her drinking from him anymore. He couldn't even think of her ~~~~ing the smell that clung to her – a heavy per- ~~~tting alcohol and vomit.' Austin adjusted his position on the grass, maintaining a wordless scepticism. Eabha's eyes had glazed over. 'He was very lost. Pitiful, really.'

'He used you,' Austin muttered.

'He needed me,' Eabha snapped back, 'and he loved me. He just . . . he didn't know how to show it. How could he?'

Austin gave an incomprehensible grunt, the sound of derision. For a moment, he was silent, lulled – or so it seemed – into a state of accord, the conflict fizzling from him, rising into the warm air which carried it away. But then Eabha let out the smallest sigh, her eyes settling on Oisín, and Austin saw something in the way she held herself, and in the soft smile lifting the edges of her lips, something he didn't like.

Turning to Dara, Sam and Oisín, as the anger returned in one sudden gust, Austin said: 'So, do you want to see it? The goat skull?'

'They don't,' Eabha said quickly, blood filling her cheeks.

'You still have it?' Oisín asked. '*Why* would you keep that thing?!'

'I didn't,' Austin replied. '*She* did.' His finger jabbed at Eabha; it was stubby, the nails bitten to the quick. Dara could imagine him doing it, teeth gnawing at keratin until it hurt. 'She took it from the attic with her, kept it all this time. She even used it during the first play. It wasn't a prop – it was the real thing.' He turned to his sister, fire in his eyes. 'Ask her why, Oisín. Go on – ask her.'

Dara's eyes flicked to Eabha, fury in the cold stare and in the crush of her script, held tightly in a fist. 'Why are you doing this, Austin?'

'Will I go get it?' Austin said, white teeth visible in his beard. He looked at Dara, then Oisín and Sam. 'She keeps the thing in her bedroom. She keeps it to remind herself isn't it?'

'Enough, Austin! Jesus, will you stop? Nobody cares about the skull.'

Dara glanced at Sam, who looked as if he cared quite a bit, but it was Austin who rose to his feet suddenly, his large hands shoved into his pockets, the outline of his knuckles visible through the corduroy.

'It's not in the script, but you should know I had to drag them back to the school – the two of them were still tripping and we were miles from the school. It took us hours. There was blood streaming from a wound in Eabha's head and, honestly, I thought she might die there on the rocks. It was so dark – not a car passing, not a light from a house in the distance – all I had was the moon to guide us back to the road. Cillian was blubbering, but Eabha was so silent it terrified me.'

Dara watched him warily, her eyes always returning to his hands. What had they done? What were they capable of now?

'The teachers weren't even angry when we got back,' Austin continued. 'They were just relieved there weren't three dead students lost somewhere on the Burren.' He pulled on the end of his beard, rocking back and forth on his heels. 'And you know what he did? When we got back to the school, they took Eabha down to the sickbay and brought me and Cillian down to the canteen to get something to eat. And he sat there opposite me, eating a bowl of cornflakes, not a care in the world and a big shit-eating grin on his face, with that stupid fucking skull next to him. "That was a bit of fun," he says, as if it had all been nothing but a joke to him. He didn't feel any guilt for what he had done.' Austin sniffed, running an angry hand under his nostrils. His eyes seemed to pierce the air as he looked at his sister, his voice – to Dara's surprise – breaking slightly as he spoke again: 'Why didn't you listen to me, Eabha? Why did you let him into our lives?' His ribcage was heaving, his hand jumping to his chest. Dara watched the shake of his body, his face contorting.

'What's happening?' she asked, watching Austin trying to gulp down some air, even as his lungs resisted, even as his body rebelled against him.

'He's fine,' Eabha said calmly. 'He just needs space.'

She reached towards her brother, but he flinched at her touch, like a wild animal suddenly spooked, pushing her away from him so forcefully that she lost her footing and stumbled backwards.

'Leave me alone,' he roared, staggering towards the house, with Eabha following at a short distance behind him, repeating himself again as he noticed she was trailing him. 'Leave me alone!'

There was an edge to his voice now, but Eabha didn't hesitate, her skirt rippling around her as she walked calmly in the shadow of his footsteps, as if this were a daily duty.

'Should we help her?' Dara said, her voice low as they watched Austin and Eabha disappear into the house again, exiting the stage. Inside, they could hear them arguing, Austin shouting, Eabha imploring. A banging of doors signalled that they had moved further into the house, the racket dulling, though not gone. Dara watched the empty windows, thinking of the power in Austin's large hands. 'I think we should help her.' She was climbing to her feet when Sam's hand reached towards her.

'No,' he said, a firm grip on her arm. 'No, whatever is happening, it's between them.'

A silence developed between the three still in the garden, in which the tension of fifteen years seemed to spread like a horrible glue, coating their skin, their hair, their eyelashes. They listened and waited for signs of life, but neither Eabha nor Austin reappeared in the garden. They didn't know whether to leave or wait, no direction coming, no willingness to think for themselves. So they sat in a state of indecision and felt the dread settle over them, dread of what was happening now and of what could happen yet.

Dara lay back on the grass once more and turned her eyes to the sky, across which two crows passed – streaks of black against the blue – and she wondered what she was doing, right there in the middle of someone else's trauma, experiencing it vicariously, through the layers of Eabha's skin, as if she had been there all along, living it with her. Was Eabha living it still?

She rolled over and let her eyes settle on Sam's face, then reached her hand slowly through the blades of grass until her fingers touched Sam's. She felt him jump slightly, startled by her, but only briefly, his hand closing around hers, his eyes watching Oisín, though Oisín didn't seem to notice, and silently Dara sat and clung to Sam, and gratefully she let him hold her firmly to the ground, lest she float into the air, lest she disappear into the vast and empty sky.

Chapter Ten

Sam met Dara on her lunch break the following day, loitering at the door of the boutique, hands in his pockets, eyes scanning up and down the road while he waited for her. He was on edge, though she didn't know why, uneasy in himself as they walked the short distance to Powerscourt House. The stone steps, once leading to the townhouse of a Viscount, now led to a series of shops and cafés, from which poured a steady stream of people who sat on the stones next to Dara and Sam: a couple with a dachshund dressed in a green knitted jumper; two women in near-identical office wear, long lanyards hanging from their necks.

Dara stretched her legs out in front of her, skin dotted with bruises accumulated from minor mishaps during rehearsals. That morning, she had paid Rhona her half of the final month's rent, depleting her bank account again, which was causing her not inconsiderable stress. The search for a new place to live was not going well. So far, the only affordable accommodation she had found was a studio with a bunk bed she would have to share with another girl, in a house with several other people on the North Circular Road. It seemed too grim to contemplate, so Dara had spent much of the morning running through a list of friends who might let her sleep on their floor for a few days. The list was short.

'You OK?' Sam asked, eyebrow rising quizzically at the expression on her face as she stared down at her dispiriting lunch: a plain cheese sandwich on white bread that she had made before leaving for work that morning.

'Yeah . . . just so sick of being broke,' Dara replied, taking a bite, the tanginess of the cheddar making her mouth feel immediately dry.

'I know the feeling,' Sam said, sucking air in through his teeth. 'I'll be forty by the time I get out of my parents' house at this rate.' He was eating a chicken fillet roll, from which mayonnaise was dripping, a white rivulet snaking down his hands and landing on the stone steps between his feet.

'Do you know when Eabha will start paying us?' Dara asked. 'My sister's going home to Cork and I can't afford to cover rent on my own. I need to give up my job at the boutique – I can't keep doing it all. I'm exhausted.' Her mother had texted her that morning, a seemingly innocent reminder that she was always welcome at home. It just so happened to contain another subtler message – unspoken, yet undeniable to Dara – that she should not bother to ask for help with rent: not again, not for this play.

She shut her eyes briefly. It was not the life she wanted, but sometimes, in moments of weakness, it seemed so much easier to stop fighting the inevitability of her failure and do what her mother wanted, a return to the stone house at the end of the boreen.

'We should really be paid by now,' Sam said. 'You could ask Eabha about it – it's not an unreasonable question.' He wiped the mayonnaise from his mouth with a thin napkin. 'It wouldn't surprise me if she's holding back payment to see if the seats sell.'

'Do you think so?! I really need to be paid, Sam. Rents are insane right now. The only place I can afford is Leitrim.'

'Yeah, I know. It's depressing. I still live with my folks, which makes things a bit easier. But they've started talking about moving back to Turkey when they retire. Think I'm the only thing holding them back.'

She watched him while she took another bite of her unwanted sandwich. He was opening up to her about his personal life. The thought brought a small smile to her face; immediately, she tried to hide it from him.

'Really? They'd move to Turkey?' she said, as if to coax more from him. The sun was catching the sharp profile of his face; she wanted to trace it with her finger.

'Yeah, well, Dad moved over here when they married, opened a kebab shop, made a life here. But I think he's always has missed home. We visit when we can, but it's not as often as he'd like. And Mam would like the sun. I think she figures she owes my dad a few years in Turkey after a couple of decades of Irish rain.'

Dara laughed. A seagull had landed on the steps next to her, lured by the crumbs from her sandwich. She kicked at it with her foot.

When she looked back, Sam's steady gaze was on her. 'It can be hard to keep your chin up when you're starting out,' he said. 'I'm beginning to get some regular work, but I had to claw my way here and it's still very uncertain, even now . . . I know what you're going through.'

Dara rested her head on her knees, watching as more seagulls gathered ominously on the step at their feet. 'Is that why Eabha's success gets to you so much? She looks the part, she acts the part . . . she gets the breaks?'

'Maybe . . . I don't know.' Sam rubbed at his mouth with his napkin again. There was the shadow of a moustache under his nose. He threw another glance at the women eating lunch on the steps behind them, lanyards thrown over their backs to stop them trailing into their Caesar salads. 'I guess she just seems so oblivious to how hard it can be to get anywhere in this business, you know? All the doors just open to her, and she swans in. Some of us clawed at the door for years.'

'I think she's making a mistake involving Austin,' Dara admitted. 'You saw him yesterday – it's obviously too much for him.' She flicked a crust in the direction of the gulls, causing a flurry of violence as beaks snapped at the staling bread. 'What if it happens again, Sam? What if Austin has another breakdown?'

Sam ran a hand over his face. 'I don't know, Dara. I presume they've thought about this possibility. They must have. Eabha wouldn't be including him if there was a danger, right?'

'I honestly don't know, Sam. I don't know if I trust her to think about that.' Her neck bent forward, sending her head into her hands. 'Jesus, this is such a mess.'

Sam let out a long sigh, his hand reaching towards Dara, pulling her into a hug. She breathed out slowly, glad of his presence, the strength of his arms around her, closing her eyes and letting him calm her. His heartbeat was steady against her chest and, gradually, she felt hers begin to slow, as if following his lead.

'It'll be all right,' he said, his voice at her ear, his fingers fanning through her hair. 'We'll get through this together.'

He sounded so convincing that, for just a brief moment, she allowed herself to believe him, letting the worry sink into the deepest, darkest pockets of her mind where it would stay hidden, at least until Sam left again, and she was alone with her thoughts. Then, the worry could come scuttling out again.

There were twenty-seven days to opening night.

* * *

When Eabha invited her over for a drink that evening, Dara hesitated. It was the end of a long day at the boutique, interrupted by a distressed phone call from her mother: an interview with Richard Butler had aired on a local radio station in Cork.

'They interviewed the boy's father, Dara, and he said he's been trying to contact your Eabha, but she won't meet with him. Would she not *talk* to the poor man?'

'I don't know, Mam,' Dara had replied. 'I don't ask her about all of that.'

'Maybe you should, Dara. You're wrapped up in this now. You need to protect yourself, love. Nobody else will.'

Her words were still ringing in Dara's ear when the invitation came from Eabha. But though she hesitated, Dara didn't say no. What her mother said was true. Each day brought more attention her way: a request for comment, or her name circulating on a thread online discussing the moral implications of Eabha telling Cillian's story, or her social media accounts being tagged in photos of Cillian on some memorial page or other – why did people do that? What did they want her to say or do?

So far, she had kept silent – following orders from her director – but it wasn't making the attention fade. If anything, the vacuum their silence created made space for a host of theories and speculations – a rumour that the investigation was about to be reopened, a theory that Eabha was revisiting the play in an attempt to distract Austin from an imminent confession – and Dara found herself determined to understand why. It wasn't enough anymore to acquiesce in the silence, not when she was now implicated alongside Eabha and Austin. And so, with a burning need to know racing through her, she left the flat, carried her bike down the creaking stairs, and cycled the short distance back to Leinster Road. Back to Eabha.

* * *

It was just after eight when she arrived at the house. Eabha was already wearing pyjamas: green silk, with a pattern of black and white snakes.

'I'm having a spritz,' she said, leading the way into the living room. 'What will you have, Dara dear?'

'A spritz sounds good,' Dara said, unbuttoning her jacket and hanging it on the hatstand as she walked past. On the wall, the de Lacey family smiled at her from a series of framed photographs, a gallery of eyes staring out as she passed. There was something odd about the display, as if the photographs were there to make a point: to reassure the casual observer that this collection of people was, indeed, a family.

Dara wandered into the living room, where Eabha was standing at the bar cart in the corner. It was a vintage gold wheeled object on which sat a collection of almost empty alcohol bottles, with peeling labels that were sticky at the edges from spilled liquor.

'I'm glad you could come over,' Eabha said. 'I'm having a miserable day and drinking alone is too sad.'

'Anything happen?' Dara asked, hands in her pockets while she watched Eabha open a new bottle of Aperol.

'Just the usual,' she replied, filling two glasses with ice and adding some segments of orange. 'There's so much to do with the Gate. We're getting there, but the timing really is tight.' She glanced at Dara over her shoulder, hesitating for a second before she continued: 'And . . . I had a letter from Richard Butler this morning. He has formally asked me to cancel the play. Can you believe that?'

Eabha was shaking her head, measuring prosecco into the glasses, then adding a splash of sparkling water. She handed one to Dara.

'Ever since Cillian's mother died, Richard has focused all his energy on Cillian's death. He's fixating on it . . . as if there is anything me and my brother could ever say or do to make him feel better.' She sniffed, then took a sip of her drink. 'I don't know why everyone wants us to be these . . . these killers. It's like they won't stop until we say we did it.'

Eabha took a seat on the couch, patting the velvet cushion next to her until Dara sat down beside her. She crossed her legs one way, then swapped them, unable to find a comfortable position.

'Grief does funny things to people,' Dara ventured, unsure what to say or how to offer any comfort. 'And when the world feels shaky underfoot, people search for things that bring some stability to their lives again.' Her mind flashed quickly to Sam, thinking of his hand on hers, the steadiness of his presence. It was easier when Sam was nearby, as if Dara were better able to remember herself in Eabha's company when he was next to her.

'That's true,' Eabha said, nodding her head sincerely. 'People want easy stories – things they can instinctively understand – so they go grasping wildly about the place for simple explanations in the face of extraordinary circumstances. That's what he's doing.' She gulped her drink, glancing sideways at Dara. 'Richard Butler has gone hunting for a villain.'

When Dara didn't reply, Eabha raised her glass to her lips again. 'Why is that, Dara? Why do people *want* the worst possible explanation to be true? They want to believe that we pushed Cillian out that window. Two kids, killing their friend – I can't think of anything worse.' Frustration rippled across her forehead. 'It's like they *want* us to be evil. Nobody likes the sheer fucking chaos of life, the random accidents. They won't accept that sometimes death is meaningless, so they tell these stories about evil people, like me and Austin. They make up conspiracies instead of accepting that sometimes death is mundane and sometimes it's unlikely.'

She fell silent, staring at the dark window, through which they could see nothing but the coming night, as if it were an abyss bearing down on them from the outside world.

A sigh escaped Eabha's lips. 'I don't know . . . Richard seems to need his crusade.'

There were faint freckles across her cheeks and the bridge of her nose. Dara could see them now that Eabha's face was bare of make-up. They made her seem younger. 'How is Austin doing?' she said gently. 'How is he coping?'

Eabha's attention moved from the window back to Dara, an insincere smile rising to her face. 'He's coping: that's enough.' She reached for Dara's hand, which had been resting on her leg, holding it just as Sam had – but how different it felt. 'You haven't seen Austin at his best . . . and I know he can be difficult . . . but he loves me and he has always protected me.' She paused, the light from the lamp next to her reflected in the moisture now filling her eyes. 'The trouble is, I can't give him what he's looking for, what he needs.'

'What's that?' Dara asked, watching as Eabha's lip began to shake.

'Redemption,' she replied, her eyes full as she looked at Dara.

Dara held Eabha's hand firmly in her own, her grip unmoving. 'Is that why you wrote the play? Is that what this is all about?'

'What was I supposed to do? You use the tools available to you,' Eabha said, her voice suddenly dead. 'I mean, how could they resist a story like mine? I knew it would sell. And I knew that would give me a chance to . . . to be someone.'

Pulling her hand free from Dara, she set her drink down again, spilling some on the table, a ring forming around the glass, soaking into the wood.

'So, it's deliberately provocative?' Dara said. 'The play?'

'I guess,' Eabha replied, not looking at her. 'It had to succeed so I could escape.'

'Escape what?' Dara asked, pushing Eabha now, reaching for that elusive 'radical honesty' that had been promised. If she was going to be sucked into this world, she could at least understand it.

'The dreariness of grief, I suppose,' Eabha said, her body angled towards Dara. 'You can't imagine how it felt back then. One death after another. Three people I had loved, gone from me – my mother, my father, then Cillian.' She sniffed again, pulling her legs up to her chest. 'Austin left me too, for a while. He took off once the investigation ended, trying to forget himself. I suppose you've heard about all of that?'

'A little,' Dara said. 'He went off the rails?' She could remember vaguely something she had read about it online, presented to the reader as irrefutable proof of Austin's guilty mind. It had disturbed her to see how easily facts could be made to suit the desired narrative, truth a sideshow. But then, wasn't that their project too?

'Is that how they describe it?' Eabha said, with a rueful laugh. 'Austin fell in with a crowd of people who had lives that were as chaotic as his own, and some bad habits that helped them cope. I suppose he blended in with them, didn't have to explain himself, or be judged – that's one way to manage trauma.' She pushed her hair back behind her ears. 'But it wasn't for me. Sometimes it's easier to stay silent and be forgotten, but if I don't tell this story, who will? If I don't speak, someone else will own the past, someone else will control it. And it's a lonely life, to carry a trauma that's unacknowledged. I didn't want that ... I wanted to be heard, Dara.' She looked Dara dead in the eye. 'And it was obvious how I could make that happen.' There was a horrible smile on Eabha's face as she waved her arms around her theatrically, her voice bitter. 'And look at me now . . . a shining success.'

Dara didn't laugh. 'Despite what it does to Austin?'

'God, is everything always about Austin?' Eabha's body seemed to sink into itself at the question, as if she had shrunk into her pyjamas. 'Look, I thought this time would be easier for him – I mean, Cillian's dead fifteen years, for Christ's sake. I really didn't think people would react like this again. But Richard Butler has whipped it all up.' She met Dara's eye again. 'Austin thinks they're following him now . . . photographers. He said there were two men in a car driving behind him the other day and, honestly, I . . . I don't know if, if I believe him. It happened this way before . . . he started seeing things.'

She fell silent for a moment, her lips parting as if to speak, before she snatched the words back into her mouth again, the sounds sitting unformed in her throat.

Abruptly, she rose to her feet, nodding towards Dara's glass, which was still almost full. 'Do you want another?'

'I'm fine,' Dara replied, watching while Eabha went to fix herself a second. She was so tightly wound that Dara could almost see the fibres fraying in her. 'Eabha, is . . . is Austin getting any professional help?'

'Oh, yes, heaps of it,' she replied, free pouring into her glass. 'He has doctors and therapists and all sorts of medications. He's fine, really, I'm sure. I mean, maybe there *were* two men following him. Maybe I'm the one who is paranoid!'

A humourless laugh sounded from her, ice clinking in her glass as she carried it back to the couch, sitting down heavily next to Dara.

'So,' she said, slapping Dara on the knee convivially. 'Tell me, have you had any luck finding somewhere to live?'

'Not yet,' Dara said, the reminder unwelcome, the sudden change in tone jarring. She ran a hand through her hair, thinking of all the rental ads she had emailed that day and how few had replied. 'But it's OK. There's still time.'

Eabha's smile was making Dara a little nervous. There was something too enthusiastic about it. It was as Sam had described: a switch flicking, a light coming on beneath the surface of her skin, a performance beginning.

'You know, I've been thinking about your situation,' she said, 'and, really, the answer is staring us in the face.' Eabha's hand clasped Dara's hand again. 'You could stay here! With me! I mean, if you'd like that? I have more space than I need and, this way, you could really immerse yourself in the work for the next few weeks. You'll have the shortest commute to rehearsal – just straight up the stairs to the attic.' She was beaming at Dara, who felt obliged to smile back.

Her heart was beating fast, her mouth dry now, her thoughts exploding with possibility, pouring in a thousand different directions. Eabha was waiting for an answer, but she didn't have one to give. Thinking purely practically, it made sense. More than that, it was a godsend. Her current alternative was a dank bedsit in some corner of the city she didn't know. The idea of living in this beautiful house – on this tree-lined road with its perfectly manicured hedges – felt nothing short of a dream. She could live with Eabha de Lacey, see her every day, watch how she changed with the hours, dawn to dusk, the currents of her emotions washing this way and that, as close as she could to the source of her new life, her good fortune.

As her eyes met Eabha's – glinting as if with gold – Dara's thoughts coagulated together again, descending from the air overhead, her rational mind taking the reins once more from her soaring heart. She was thinking of Sam. He would say it was another ploy, another attempt to draw Dara closer, as if Eabha had tied twine around her and was slowly, gradually winding it around her.

'That's so kind of you,' Dara said, her voice flat as she spoke, 'but I can't . . . I really don't want to be a burden.'

'What do you mean? You wouldn't be a burden! Not at all! Not even a little. You can choose your own room upstairs – I'll get the windows open and the beds aired right now. I can give you keys so you can come and go when you choose—'

'Really, thank you, but—'

'Oh no, Dara, don't say no. Not yet! Just think about it, OK? I'd really like it if you'd think about it.'

Dara could see that this was true. She watched the flickering emotions crossing Eabha's face: it wasn't just a favour, or some act of charity. It really felt as if Eabha wanted her company. She stopped the thought. Was this more of it? More of the game Eabha played with them, slowly sapping them of agency until they didn't know their own minds.

Dara took a breath. 'Look . . . I'll think about it. And thank you, Eabha. I mean it. It's very generous.'

On the couch next to them, Eabha's phone lit up, Dara's eyes flashing instinctively to the screen. It was a text from Oisín. She took another large gulp of her drink, watching Eabha's attention immediately drawn away from her, towards her phone.

Dara placed her glass down on the table. 'I better head off,' she said, rising to her feet. She did not want to be there when Oisín inevitably arrived. 'It's getting late.'

Eabha looked up, distracted. 'All right. Well, I'm glad you came over. You'll think about my offer?'

'I will,' Dara replied, making her way to the hallway.

Taking her jacket from the hatstand, she glanced at the framed photographs again, pausing at one of Eabha on a beach with her long dark hair, and next to her, a teenage Austin. The two adults standing behind them must have been their parents: Eamonn and Máire. She could see a whisper of Eabha in her mother, but there was nothing of Austin in either of them, not even the blue-green eyes. There were no other photos of Austin, all photographic evidence of his existence seeming to end at seventeen, at Cillian's death. His absence from the family photos told a story of its own.

Dara headed for the door.

Eabha wanted her close, and there were few people who could say that. Not even her brother.

* * *

On the cycle home to the flat, Dara thought of nothing but Eabha's offer, examining it from all angles while she tried to visualise herself living in number 74 Leinster Road. She thought about it while she lay on the couch trying in vain to sleep and thought about it some more while she ate a bowl of cereal over the sink the following morning.

By the time Rhona came downstairs for breakfast, rubbing sleep from her eyes, her hair a mess across her face, Dara couldn't hold the thought any longer. 'Eabha offered to let me stay with her,' she said, the words escaping in one long exhalation of breath, 'and I think I'm going to accept.'

Rhona's eyes opened a little wider, a look of confusion briefly crossing her face. 'Wow, I—' She reached for the kettle, filling it with water, then poured two spoonfuls of instant coffee into a mug. 'That's huge, Dara! Inviting you into her home like that? She must really like you.'

'I don't know about that,' Dara said. 'She probably feels sorry for me.'

'Nah, rich people don't think like that. God only knows what she sees in you' – Dara raised her middle finger – 'but you've obviously won her over.' Rhona leaned back against the kitchen counter. 'Seriously, you should take this opportunity.'

'I mean, it's daft. I barely know her! But then . . . you know . . . am I really going to say no to her, to an opportunity like this?'

'You'd be mad to say no,' Rhona said, her mouth pulled into a yawn. 'A big step up from that bloody couch.'

'I know . . . I just—' She watched Rhona slot two pieces of sliced pan into the toaster, scratching at the lines across her face left by her pillow. 'It feels like I'm playing into her hands. I mean, she likes to keep us close to her . . . maybe too close.' Doubts lingered. Was she walking into danger? Running towards the storm instead of away from it? 'You know Mam would say I shouldn't.'

'Yeah, but Mam wants you back home and married to your old boyfriend – what was his name?' Rhona replied.

'Kevin.'

'Yeah – *boring* Kevin.' The kettle boiled, switching itself off. Rhona reached for it, submerging the granules in hot water until the mug was steaming with black coffee. 'Don't think twice about Mam. She means well but she hasn't a clue.'

Rhona was saying exactly what Dara wanted to hear, which made Dara doubt her. 'Really? You *really* think this is a good idea?'

Rhona sipped her coffee, placing the mug down on the counter again, her hand on her hip. 'Dara, love,' she said. 'What choice have you?'

There was something about the casualness of Rhona's shrug, the way her attention had already returned to her breakfast, which made Dara feel as if she was creating a fuss about nothing. Rhona was right: there was no real alternative. And if she went into it with her eyes open, surely she could maintain some control over the situation.

Despite the great encroachment of Eabha de Lacey into her life, Dara could still set boundaries – hadn't she proved that with Sam? It was only for a few weeks – until the seats were sold and she was paid, until opening night came and, with it, her first taste of success. She was up to her eyes in Eabha's world already. She might as well enjoy a little of the reflected glory.

Chapter Eleven

Leaving the flat was simpler than she expected. She rang Eabha after breakfast and arranged to move in that evening. Why wait, when time was not on their side? Better to press on, through the rising waters.

There wasn't much to pack in the end, Dara's existence minimalist by necessity, having no part of the world that she could call her own. It sometimes felt as if she had been issued a bare licence to exist, while, all around her, there were people with economic value in the world: feudal lords of the modern age within the autonomous zone of their homes and gardens. Without these things, her life was precarious. She had felt it living on the couch in Rhona's flat and she felt it again as she wheeled her suitcase up Leinster Road, climbing the steps to Eabha's front door.

'Come in, come in, Dara!' Eabha said breezily. She was wearing a pale pink silk robe, with trailing sleeves that hung at her sides, the cuffs of which were lined with matching pink feathers. When she smiled, Dara spotted the tell-tale sign of strain, front teeth pressed against each other so tightly that she could practically hear the crunch of enamel. 'You must be Dara's sister?' Eabha turned to Rhona, who pulled her hand out of the pocket of her zip-up top and gave a casual wave.

'Yeah . . . how's it going? I'm Rhona.'

Eabha descended the steps – squeezing around Dara's suitcase – and thrust her hand into Rhona's. 'It's so lovely to finally meet you. I've heard *so* much about you.'

'Yeah, same. Dara never stops talking about you!' Rhona said.

Eabha's smile rose and then slackened again quickly. The stress she was under was visible in her body, though she tried to hide it. Dara wondered, as she always did, which worries, in particular, were snaking through Eabha's mind. Was it all the thousands of things that needed to be done before opening night? Or was it the increasing volume of public noise and disquiet coming Eabha's way now that the Butlers' campaign against the play was growing legs? A petition was circulating online, seeking signatures from sympathetic internet scrollers. When Dara last checked, there were 8,567 signatures on the '*Stop the Lies and Cancel Eabha de Lacey at the Gate Theatre*' petition page.

'Won't you come in, Rhona?' Eabha asked, trying to relax her shoulders.

'No, thanks – I really can't stay,' Rhona replied. 'I'm just moving this one in and then I'll be off.'

'Oh no, you *have* to stay and celebrate Dara moving in! You'll stay for a drink, won't you? Do you like margaritas?' Eabha said, helping Dara to lift the suitcase up the stone steps, over the threshold, and onto the oak floors.

'She does,' Dara said quickly, meeting Rhona's narrowed eyes with a smile. 'She'd love to stay for a drink.'

Rhona looked at her little sister, assessed her level of need, and then relented. 'Sure, all right then . . . when do I ever turn down a drink?'

'Wonderful,' Eabha said, clapping her hands several times with a manic energy before shutting the door behind them.

The air inside felt warm and just a little oxygen-depleted, as if the breeze outside were giving the house a wide berth, circumnavigating number 74 and its occupants.

'Come down to the kitchen,' Eabha said over her shoulder, moving around them in a flurry of feathers and a blur of pink. 'Oisín's making margaritas. I hope you like them strong!'

Mention of Oisín hit Dara square in the stomach.

'Oisín's here?!' she said, surprise in her voice as she followed Eabha down the stairs to the basement kitchen.

'Yes,' Eabha replied, glancing back at her briefly. 'You don't mind?'

'Of course not!' Dara smiled through the lie. They were still locked in a contest for Eabha's affection: Oisín in the lead for obvious reasons, but Dara now following swiftly behind. He was cold with her when he heard the news that she was moving in, nose clearly out of joint, and his presence that evening seemed like an attempt to claim his territory.

By contrast, Sam hadn't replied to her texts all day, not since she had told him she would be moving into Eabha's home. His silence was pointed and deliberate and, though he hadn't said it directly, she could feel, in the absence of words, a sincere disapproval. It was probably – no, definitely – for the best from a career perspective not to pursue anything with Sam, but the idea of a growing distance from him made her stomach lurch.

In the kitchen, Oisín was at the blender, creating some kind of concoction approximating a margarita. He was drunk – she could tell immediately from the sloppy smile on his face – and seemed determined to pretend that he was happy to see her and Rhona.

'Look who it is! Leinster Road's newest resident,' he shouted, lifting her off her feet as she entered the room, trying too hard to compensate for his clear jealousy that he was not the only one with access to Eabha. He needn't have worried: she had no intention of usurping him, just learning from Eabha what she could.

Her hands were against his chest and she was about to push him away from her when Oisín leaned forward to kiss her, missing most of her cheek and catching the corner of her mouth.

'Jesus, what is in those margaritas?' She gave an embarrassed laugh, wiping her lips with the back of her hand. It was accidental – wasn't it?

She glanced at Eabha, who was taking a seat at the kitchen island, and found her staring straight back at her, her expression disconcertingly blank. Dara looked away again, both unnerved and unable to shake the sense that, on some level, Oisín was trying to mess with her.

Austin's voice rose in her mind, something he had said about Cillian, about the look on his face when they returned to the Bodkin after he attacked Eabha at the lake. A mischief that was dark and fundamentally apathetic.

'You want a drink?' Oisín asked her, his eyes pointedly meeting hers, before a clumsy hand reached over to mess with her hair. She shrank from what, she supposed, was intended as a playful gesture, her temper immediately flaring.

'Would you stop it, Oisín?' she said, pushing him away. 'Yes, go make me a drink, OK?'

'Make us all a drink,' Eabha said, slapping the marble countertop with impatience as Oisín wandered back to the blender. 'Hurry up, bartender!'

He offered Rhona the first taste of the bright green mixture he had made, her lips disappearing into her mouth as she declared Oisín's margaritas 'pure lethal'. But that didn't stop her accepting a glassful, and then another. They were on their third cocktail when Eabha suggested that Rhona should stay the night. Rhona agreed, but on condition that she would bunk in with Dara, something Eabha said was 'quaint'.

On cocktail four, Oisín demanded to know Rhona's 'most embarrassing story about Dara' and then laughed until he snorted at her description of Dara's starring role as Annie.

Watching him, Dara wondered if he had been taking the mushrooms Austin had given him. He was relaxed, enjoying himself, all signs of the jealousy that Dara had been anticipating now gone. His focus was on Eabha, his eyes returning frequently to her face, every movement she made causing a reaction in him, as if they were connected by string: one pull from Eabha and Oisín's limbs would jerk in response.

It was obvious why he had been cast. He had a raw energy and the same untamed, chaotic disquiet as Cillian: maybe that's where Eabha's interest lay. Oisín took life as it came. No grand plan, no thoughts of the ideal circumstances in which his future self might live, no contemplation of things like job security or a pension.

But watching him now, Dara felt a tug of pity. He was out of his depth, Eabha's gravitational pull gradually distorting him. And the thought made her squirm in her seat: was it just Oisín or would it distort her too? She looked down at her hands, her vision damp with the margaritas she had consumed, and wondered if it had happened already, if it was happening now, if she was changing, shifting, twisting. Slowly, her hand reached for her dyed hair, twirling the dark strands between finger and thumb.

She looked up. Again, Eabha was gazing at her, calmly now, all sign of distress gone from her, as if appraising the scene, her work well done, the pieces falling gradually into place, the actors primed and ready, the scene set: everything happening exactly as planned.

* * *

When Oisín started singing rebel songs, Dara declared it time for bed, heading upstairs with Rhona, while Eabha stayed in the kitchen and tried to convince him to drink some water and sober up.

'So, are the two of them together or what?' Rhona asked when she thought they were out of earshot.

Dragging her suitcase up the stairs behind her, Dara nodded. 'Yeah. Like, they haven't actually said anything, but it's obvious.' She wondered if Oisín would stay the night.

'But they're so different,' Rhona continued. 'Like, what do they talk about?!'

'I'm not sure they do much talking,' Dara said, struggling with the suitcase as she climbed the last few stairs.

Rhona laughed at that. 'Is it not awkward for the rest of you?'

'A bit,' Dara admitted, leading the way to her new bedroom. 'Sam and I just ignore it, but it happened the last time as well – the last production. Apparently, the actor who played her brother was wild about her. Oliver, his name was.'

Rhona made a grunting sound. 'Does everyone fall in love with Eabha?'

Dara didn't reply. Eabha did have a powerful effect on people: an intoxicant, senses dulling, reason lulled into dormancy, an aura of promise around her, a hopefulness when she spoke, as if great things were just about to happen. Dara had felt it herself: wasn't she feeling it still?

In her bedroom, a candle was burning next to the bed, the smell of lavender wafting over her as she took in the clean, spacious space, with its high ceilings, deep-set windows and king-size bed, instead of an old couch.

'Rhona,' she said as they stood together in the middle of the room. 'What is my life?'

Rhona put an arm around her sister and squeezed her shoulder. 'Enjoy it. Soak it all in while you can.' She rested her head against Dara's briefly. 'I'm proud of you, you know that?'

'Oh Christ,' Dara moaned. 'I can't cope with you being sincere! You'll make me cry.'

Rhona laughed, caught Dara by the neck and pulled her into a headlock. 'You prefer this do you?' she said, tickling her with her free hand while Dara swatted her away.

'Stop it,' she said, trying to pull her head free. 'Get off me! Say nice things again!'

Rhona released her and Dara pulled her head free, sitting down on the bed while she caught her breath. Rhona lay down next to her, her socked feet dangling off the end. It felt – all of a sudden – too much, as if she were standing still while, all around her, the world were gaining speed, whooshing past her ears. Her breathing was audible and a little laboured.

'You all right, Dara?'

'Yeah,' she said, unconvincingly. 'It's going to be OK, isn't it, Rhona?'

Rhona's eyes were on her sister's back, down which her dark hair flowed.

'Yeah,' she said. 'It's all going to be OK, Dara.'

* * *

Rhona left first thing the following morning while the house was still sleeping, with the dawn chorus in full swing in the apple tree and the day whitening the sky at the bottom of the garden. Dara listened to the front door close behind her sister, then turned her face back into the pillow and let sleep pull her under again for a few hours.

When she came downstairs for breakfast shortly after eight, to Dara's great relief, there was no sign of Oisín. In the kitchen,

Eabha was sitting alone, three newspapers spread in front of her on the marble countertop, each of them open at an article about the play. She was cutting them out with scissors, the ink rubbing off on her fingers, a black smudge across her cheek.

'Morning,' Dara said, pouring some coffee from the cafetière next to Eabha. 'Did Oisín stay last night?'

'No, I sent him home in a taxi,' she replied, not looking up from her newspapers. 'I didn't want to deal with his hangover this morning.' There was a severity in her face, a harshness to her voice. 'There's too much work to do.'

Dara drank some of her coffee, her arms sliding across the polished marble so that it pulled against her skin, her eyes on the cuttings in front of Eabha. 'Anything I should know about in there?'

'Just the usual shite,' Eabha muttered. 'Richard Butler has the local politicians in Clare condemning me now.'

'For a play?'

'For having a voice,' Eabha replied. She reached for her phone, opening up her inbox and summoning an email to the screen. 'Take a look at this,' she said, handing the phone to Dara.

It was an email from the *Clare Star* with a series of questions for Eabha. They were about to run a story about the campaign against her. Dara's eyes scanned the first question.

Do you feel any responsibility to the family of Cillian Butler for profiting off his death with your play?

'"Profiting off his death" – that's a bit strong, isn't it?'
Eabha didn't look up, but her jaw tensed. 'There's more.'

Do you support a full public inquiry into the circumstances surrounding the death of Cillian Butler and the involvement of you and your brother, Austin de Lacey?

The final question was perhaps the most pointed.

Will you apologise to Richard Butler for the heartbreak your play has caused the Butler family?

Dara slid the phone back along the countertop to Eabha. 'What are you going to say?'

'What I always say,' Eabha replied. 'Watch the play – that's my comment.'

She pulled her clippings into a pile, then tossed the rest of the papers into the recycling bin. Dara glanced at the stack while Eabha doused her hands under the tap. The article sitting on top was a think-piece from an *Irish Times* columnist Dara didn't recognise. She reached for it.

Her Truth, Your Truth, My Truth?
Does the controversy around Eabha de Lacey's The Truth Will Out show that we've lost our ability to tell fact from fiction?

The photo accompanying the piece was a recent shot of Eabha, standing outside the Gate Theatre. She recognised the mustard-yellow tunic dress.

'Where did that photo come from?' Dara asked, squinting down at the article in her hands. 'Are there photographers following you now?' Austin's paranoia was beginning to feel more rational.

At the sink, Eabha switched the tap off, drying her hands on a tea towel. 'I don't know. They must have been waiting outside the Gate. I didn't even see them.'

Dara sat down on one of the stools, grappling with the idea that her face might appear in some newspaper or other one of these days, next to an article lambasting Eabha. She was thinking of the comments it would generate, the people from home who would see her public dressing-down by association.

Though Eabha was entirely unfazed by the idea of photographers following her through the city, the questions she had received from a small, local paper seemed to have touched a nerve. 'You know, it was the *Clare Star* that broke the news Austin was being investigated for Cillian's death.'

Her voice sliced through Dara's thoughts. She knew the article Eabha was referring to – she had found it in one of her internet trawls.

A student at the prestigious Bodkin School is being questioned by local police in connection with the untimely death of Cillian Butler (17).

'It was front page of the newspaper,' Eabha continued. 'The other kids stuck it up all over the school so Austin would see it wherever he went. They were taunting him, calling him a killer. They even scratched it into the wooden door of Austin's cubicle – Cillian's name. They weren't doing it for Cillian. It wasn't about him. They just took joy in Austin's pain. They had made him into a monster in their minds and that meant they could be as cruel as they wanted to be.' Her eyes were staring into nothing, into the past, the memories sketching themselves across her face, visible in the furrowing of her brow, in the way her lip trembled. 'He came to find me that morning and his *face* – I'll, I'll never forget it, Dara.' She blinked several times. 'I had to call Celia to come and take us home. Austin never went back to school after that. He couldn't.'

Dara watched Eabha reach for the stack of articles, a heaviness in her shoulders.

'And now the *Clare Star* has the gall to ask me for a comment? They want *me* to apologise to Cillian's absentee, dickhead Dad?' She walked towards the door. 'All I did was witness a tragedy and tell people about it.'

'Was it worth it?' Dara asked, the question bursting from her mouth, as if it had been waiting, poised to spring. Maybe it had, from the moment she first stepped into the casting room.

At the door, Eabha paused, her hand resting against the wooden door frame.

Dara swallowed: 'Writing the play? Eabha, do you regret it?'

Her voice was quiet when she spoke, stripped bare of defences. 'You're asking why I put myself through all this,' Eabha said. 'The previous cast used to ask me that too – especially Oliver. He thought it was too much for me to handle. But, you see, it's the opposite. My only other option was to make myself very small and unobtrusive – unseen, unheard, and what's the point in that? They're still listening to me, Dara. Even after all these years, they care what I do.' She headed towards the stairs. 'They don't come to see other things I create.' Her head bowed briefly, as if to acknowledge a fleeting moment of modesty. 'But this awful little origin story can still fill an auditorium.'

A final time, she glanced back into the kitchen.

'So, yes. The answer is yes, Dara. Whatever the cost, it's worth it in the end.'

* * *

Taking her coffee upstairs with her, Dara sat on her bed and opened her laptop. She glanced at her watch; there were twenty minutes left before rehearsals would begin – enough time to look again for information on the previous production. Now that her face was on the posters, there was no hiding from it.

But her trawls through the search results never seemed to answer her questions. Information on the previous cast was scant, though there was a little more material about Vanessa Devin than the rest. She had an American smile, white and sparkling out from her black and white headshot. Physically, she had a shallow resemblance to Eabha, but she carried herself differently. A camera seemed to draw her out of herself, more life in her face, more movement rippling through the muscles. By contrast, Eabha demurred, casting her gaze upwards through her eyelashes, as if their furious flicking might offer some protection from the relentless scrutiny of the world.

Dara's fingers flew across her keyboard, searching the online world for whispers of Nick O'Mahony. He had played Cillian in the original play, making him the old Oisín. But she could find very little about him, his career apparently stalling since *The Truth Will Out*, though there was nothing she could find hinting at a reason.

Next she searched for the previous Austin, played by Oliver Fiennes, finding more information on him, even a few photographs. She spotted Eabha hovering in the background of one. It looked like it was from the afterparty at the Gresham Hotel on the first opening night, ten years ago. That would have been the night of Austin's breakdown, a thought which sent a bolt of apprehension through Dara as their own opening night drew closer. She ran a hand through her hair, as if to shake loose encroaching anxiety, and focused instead on the photograph again.

Oliver was standing next to Vanessa and Nick – all three of them with bright, joyful smiles on their faces – and, in the background behind them, stood Eabha. Dara zoomed in on her face. Eabha's eyes, made red by the flash of the camera, gazed back at her.

There was one other image that stood out, hidden on the third page of the search results. Eabha and Oliver standing together at some other event, a red carpet under their feet. His arm was around her, slung low on her waist, his hand on her hip with a casualness that only came from intimacy. Their faces were close together, almost cheek to cheek. Dara read the caption on the photo.

Eabha de Lacey, darling of the theatre scene, with current squeeze, Oliver Fiennes. Oliver played Eabha's murderous brother in her debut play but that hasn't stopped this pair of lovebirds!

The existence of this other cast disturbed her, as if they were encroaching somehow into the world that she, Sam and Oisín were building together, as if the past were trying to compete.

Closing her laptop again, Dara threw it down on the bed and walked to the window. Eabha was in the garden, pulling at weeds, a pile of discarded, unwanted plants sitting next to her on the grass. She was singing – to the flowers or to herself, Dara couldn't tell – her voice entering through the open window.

Where were they now? Her first trio of co-conspirators – Vanessa, Oliver and Nick – who had helped her climb out of the cold and into the heat of the limelight. Had she drawn them as close to her, fixed string to their limbs, and made marionettes of them too? Or had they seen in Eabha something that even Sam had missed? Beneath the glow, when the lights went off, some malevolence lurking in the darkness.

Chapter Twelve

Dara had been living with Eabha for a few days when she met Oisín on the stairs one morning. He paused only briefly on his way towards the front door, just flashed her a smile and said: 'How's it going, Dara?' She barely had a chance to reply before he was out the door and down the steps, pacing along Leinster Road with an inculpatory spring in his step.

When Eabha came downstairs to the kitchen, Dara was standing at the counter, her knife piercing the shining skin of some strawberries, slicing the flesh into quarters, before she added them to her bowl of granola. They greeted each other briefly while Eabha wandered to the cafetière and poured herself some coffee. Watching her sip carefully at the edge of the ceramic cup, Dara laid her knife down on the chopping board. She took a breath, a dribble of pale pink strawberry juice snaking down her arm and into her sleeve. 'So, Oisín stayed over last night?'

Eabha looked up. There were dark circles under her eyes, the skin a little puffy. 'He did,' she said, shutting down further comment, taking a banana from the fruit bowl on the kitchen island. 'I'm going to take this outside. Join me?'

Dara grabbed her bowl of granola and followed Eabha out to the patio, taking the seat next to her. The morning air was a little cold, the sun flickering in and out of view as a bank of clouds tumbled by overhead.

'Miriam is coming over today,' Eabha said. 'We need to talk about a few things and, honestly, I think it will be a little tense.' She ran the back of her hand across her brow. 'Unfortunately, that means we'll have to finish rehearsals early today. And you might want to make yourself scarce for a few hours.' Eabha seemed faintly embarrassed by this and it struck Dara as likely the first time she had shown a capacity for such mortal things as embarrassment. 'We didn't exactly part ways on good terms and I think Miriam might be trying to get some money out of me . . . she seems to think I have some.'

Next to her, peacock butterflies were ransacking the buddleia plant. Eabha reached her hand towards them but they didn't flinch or move away.

Dara took a bite of her granola. 'I don't understand – why would you pay Miriam any money?'

Eabha's eyebrow arched. 'Well, she says she's going to sue me . . . for breach of contract or something silly like that.'

'You could defend yourself? Say it was a mutual breakdown in the business relationship?' Dara suggested.

Eabha was still watching the butterflies. 'It's just easier to pay her off. We don't need her bothering us.'

'But can you afford it?' Dara replied. She was in no mood to let Eabha drift through this conversation in her usual, airy way. The question of pay had still not been answered and Dara was beginning to wonder if Eabha had any plan to pay them for their long days of rehearsals. If she could pay Miriam, surely she could pay her actors?

'Who knows?!' Eabha let out a loud, dramatic groan. 'Probably not.'

Dara squinted in the sunlight, confused. 'Eabha, I don't

understand. What are you saying? Are we in trouble? Like, financially?'

Eabha sat back in her chair, turning her face towards the sunlight so that it caught on her sharp features. 'It'll be fine – don't worry. I just need to sort some things out with Austin and sell a few more of my grandfather's paintings.' She cast a sidelong glance at Dara. 'It's mainly a cash-flow thing. You know how it is: everything's tied up.' Her hand waved dismissively, as if to indicate that these financial dealings were not worth her time.

Dara felt a quiver of irritation run through her: did Eabha think the cast could live on dust, air and promises? In the absence of home ownership and a famous artist for a grandfather, Dara felt quite entitled to worry.

Noticing her discontent at last, Eabha sat up a little straighter in her chair. 'Look, the play will pay off, Dara. Trust me! But these things take time to come through.' She ran her finger down her slender nose and let it rest on her lips for a moment while she considered her next words. 'It's been difficult lately . . . the money thing. I'm not the shiny young star anymore. No matter how good the work is, people aren't that interested. I suppose I've been slow to accept that.' She looked up, forcing a smile onto her face. 'This revival was a gamble, but despite Richard Butler's best efforts, people want to see this play. Seats are selling, Dara. It's going to work out – believe me.'

Dara laid her spoon down on the table next to the bowl. At last check, the signatures on the petition to cancel the show were at 9,874. Even if Eabha could withstand that pressure, could the theatre? Could Dara?

Goosebumps were spreading across her bare legs, exposed in her cotton pyjama shorts, despite the heat of the morning. She was living in a mirage, the wealth performative, a thin façade over a crumbling structure. At least she wasn't alone: they were occupying a shared illusion, the four of them locked away in the rehearsal room, pretending to be on a desolate outcrop at the edge of the Atlantic.

Thinking of delusions, Dara said: 'Austin hasn't been around for a while. How is he doing now?'

'Not great,' Eabha replied, closing her eyes again.

Dara watched the sunlight glint from the thin gold chain around her neck. With her head back, the white expanse of her chest was open and unguarded. It made her seem to Dara suddenly vulnerable, as if inviting some passing predator to come bounding through the quiet garden and rip at her throat. Sometimes it felt as if they were always prowling – just beyond the garden wall, just on the other side of the gate.

'You've seen the *Justice for Cillian* campaign online?' Eabha asked, running her hand through her unwashed hair. Tousled, it floated back into place around her face.

Dara nodded. 'Their petition is about to hit 10,000 signatures.'

'Yes, I saw.' She let out a loud yawn, as if to prove how unfussed it made her. 'They're more organised this time around – I'll give them that. *Write to your local TD and tell them to lock up Eabha and Austin de Lacey, noted menaces to society . . .*' She rolled her eyes. 'I think Richard is linking in with some activist types online. Real conspiracy shit-stirrers.' With a shrug, she reached for her coffee, eyes on the black liquid, in which her face was reflected. 'I can't say they bother me, but it's getting to Austin. He's following it all compulsively – keeps sending me screenshots of things people are posting.' Her eyes flicked upward. 'He's right about the photographers . . . they are following us.'

'So they're not in his head? I suppose, in a way, that's a relief?'

'In a way . . .' She took a long, slow sip of coffee. 'I caught another one outside the Gate yesterday. Geoffrey says he told the staff to keep them off the property, but there's nothing he can do when they're on the public street.'

Dara rubbed her arms for warmth, though it was far from cold. 'And have you seen any outside the house?'

'Not yet.'

Dara's heart sank at her choice of words – *yet* – but Eabha remained entirely unruffled, folding her arms across her body, her clavicle prominent through her skin.

'The campaign is smart – the whole *Justice for Cillian* thing. Richard's no fool. It gives the press something new to talk about and people can't help but pity the grieving family.' Dara watched the light play in the blue-green of her eyes. 'Cillian would hate it – his brother Fergal was the only one who gave a shit about him. Fergal, me and Austin. But that's not how Richard wants the world to see it.'

'You talk about him sometimes as if he's still alive for you,' Dara said. 'You think about Cillian's reactions to things happening now.'

'Do I?'

'Yes . . . you do. Eabha, is it possible . . . I mean, do you still love Cillian?' She wasn't sure where the question came from, but it was something about the way Eabha spoke about Cillian, a softness she seemed not to feel towards anyone else, except occasionally Oisín, and even less frequently, Dara.

Eabha's face changed as a passing cloud obstructed the sun again. She wrapped her gown tightly around her body. 'What is love, Dara?' A hollow laugh sounded from her mouth; an awful sound.

The words of Eabha's monologue rose in Dara's mind. '*Love is a selfish act by two people profoundly afraid of loneliness,*' she said.

'Very clever,' Eabha replied, pulling the belt of her gown through her fingers absently. 'Someone knows her lines.' She sighed. 'Love isn't always worth it, because it is always followed by loss, by death – just as pain always follows pleasure. It's the simple truth of our condition. It's childish to behave otherwise. You need to protect yourself from the inevitability of heartbreak. Otherwise it will destroy you.'

Dara sat back slowly in her chair, feeling as if she were seeing Eabha clearly for the first time. The gloss gone, the gold faded, the darkness in her sneaking out, the truth revealing itself with an almost casual swagger. 'And Oisín?' she said, thinking of his face on the stairs that morning.

Eabha's smile was ugly. 'I'm sure you'll understand that's between me and Oisín.' There was a warning in her voice.

Dara reached again for her breakfast. She had learned when to back away. While she ate, the silence between them lengthened and deepened, filled only with the sound of granola crunching between her teeth.

Eabha was looking down at her gown, lacing the belt through her fingers, the movement rhythmic, her expression thoughtful. When she broke the silence again, she was more distant.

'Dara, I need to know – why were you so reluctant to stay with me? When I first offered? It's just that you were in such a bad situation and yet you resisted my offer . . . I keep wondering why.'

'I didn't want you to feel like you *had* to offer,' Dara said slowly. 'I didn't want to put you in that position.' Her mind was sifting through different combinations of words, searching for a way to spare Eabha's blushes by withholding the full truth – that Dara didn't quite trust her motives – while avoiding outright lies and falsehoods. There were far too many of those as it was.

Her initial offering did not entirely satisfy Eabha. 'But . . . but I would never feel obliged to do something like that.'

'Yeah . . . that's what Rhona said too. I guess I understand that better now.'

Eabha remained unconvinced. 'Was that all?' She leaned forward. 'Or was there another reason?'

Dara pushed her chair back and walked into the direct sunlight where it was warmer, the current of moving air she created briefly disturbing the butterflies from their work at the buddleia. She watched them for a moment, the bright blue eyes on their wings seeming to wink at her as they perched on the long purple flower cones, harvesting pollen. 'Eabha, I was embarrassed. I didn't want you to feel sorry for me.' This was true, if incomplete.

'Feel sorry for you? But you aren't deserving of my pity!' Eabha sat back in her chair, her mouth wide open, laughing suddenly.

Nonplussed, Dara scratched at her nose, the red and flaky skin a tell-tale sign of her carelessness with sun cream. 'What's so funny?'

'Dara, the fact that you lack some financial security is not something I would ever pity. You have a family who love you, a sister you adore. How could I ever feel *sorry* for you?'

There was a sharpness in her voice that came as a surprise. Dara had never imagined Eabha looking at her life and feeling anything like envy. But there it was, clear as day.

Unsure what to say, Dara gave a nervous laugh, tucking her hair behind her ear. 'Oh . . . I . . . I see.'

'I worried that maybe you were . . . *afraid* to stay with me. You know . . . because of everything they say about us.' The humour had dissolved from her expression. 'Maybe you think we're monsters?'

Dara reached over and took Eabha's hand in hers again, lacing her fingers through Eabha's. 'I don't believe what they say.' As she squeezed Eabha's hand, Dara tried to convince herself that this was not entirely a lie. 'You're a good person, Eabha. You took a chance casting me, now you've given me a home too. You changed my life. I'm so grateful.'

Eabha pulled her hand free, a tight smile on her face now. 'Please, Dara. You don't need to thank me. It just makes sense.' She took another sip of her coffee, her stiff manner contrasting with Dara's effusiveness. 'So, you're OK to give me and Miriam some space today?'

Dara, feeling silly again, said: 'Of course. I'll make myself scarce.'

She watched Eabha's face slowly darken further, her mood curdling. 'Miriam's been hinting at something . . . not exactly making threats, but suggesting she might know something. I'm afraid she's going to try to blackmail me.'

'Sam bumped into her at an event a while ago,' Dara said, before she could stop herself. 'Miriam told him about Austin's hospitalisation – he said she was speaking very freely. Do you think she's been talking to the press?' The possibility frightened her. If Miriam could hurt Eabha, she could hurt all of them.

'Maybe.' Eabha pinched the skin at the bridge of her nose. 'It's possible. But she doesn't really know what happened with Austin – she wasn't even there. She's pretending to know more than she does.'

'That can be dangerous,' Dara said.

'It was actually Vanessa who found him.' Eabha looked at Dara again, the strain evident in her face, a tightening across her forehead and around her eyes. 'All Miriam knows about that is what Vanessa told her.'

'Is there *anything* else she might know? Any details that might hurt you and Austin.'

'I don't know – I mean, I can't think of anything in particular, but I just can't shake the idea that she's trying to hurt us.'

Dara flinched at her use of 'us'. How deeply were their fates now intertwined?

'It was backstage on the opening night of the production,' Eabha continued quietly. 'He was behaving strangely for days before that – nothing we could pin down, but he was on edge, quick to anger. He was in recovery at the time – trying to get clean – and I didn't know if his odd behaviour was just his body responding to sobriety or . . . or something else. The pressure did funny things to all of us.' Eabha was naturally pale but she now looked thoroughly exsanguinated. 'But then . . . on opening night . . . Austin just seemed to lose track of himself completely. He thought he was back at the Bodkin School, screaming about Cillian, about me.' She paused, turning to look at Dara again. 'He tried to climb out a window – Vanessa had to stop him from falling. I wasn't there . . . I wasn't there to help him. I only saw him after the ambulance came and dragged him off to hospital.'

She was on her feet, the butterflies taking flight around her. 'I opened us up to this danger – I know that. His mental state is so fragile.' She brushed a strand of hair out of her eyes, wandering slowly into the kitchen again. 'I know it's my fault, but there's nothing I can do about it now. I just have to make peace with that.'

Dara watched her retreat, a sickening feeling in her stomach. She wanted suddenly to go somewhere – anywhere – to get out of this house, to flee the situation entirely, to be anonymous again, to be back home where she belonged, by the sea in Beara.

Instead, she sat alone in Eabha's garden, feeling terribly stuck, as if she were tied to the chair under her, arms and legs bound with cord. She didn't move for a long time, watching the sun glint through the branches of the apple tree, thinking of Eabha, thinking of Austin, thinking of the past with its hand around their ankles, pulling them back again and again, pulling them under.

* * *

Sam met Dara at the canal that afternoon, dumping his bike down next to hers on the grass. With the afternoon's rehearsal cancelled while Eabha met with Miriam, Dara had texted him to see if he wanted to meet and work on their lines. That was what her text said, at least, but they both knew she wanted to clear the air.

Since Dara told him she would be moving into number 74, Sam had been dancing around her, responding briefly and politely when necessary, but mostly keeping his thoughts to himself and maintaining a new distance from her. It had been bothering Dara more than she cared to admit, occupying her thoughts in those vulnerable moments before sleep came to offer release, worries crowding into the silent space her mind was preparing for dreams. By agreeing to meet, it seemed possible – just possible – that Sam was softening towards her again, willing to forgive Dara the great sin of having trusted Eabha.

They sat together on the dock at Portobello Harbour, legs kicking down towards the canal, where waterlilies were growing through a layer of algae, in between the empty cans of Heineken and Grolsch bobbing on the surface of the water. She hadn't yet worked up the nerve to clear the air of tension and instead sat frozen next to Sam, watching as the pages of her script blew gently in the wind. He wanted to work on the scene just before

Austin's first confrontation with Cillian, the first flash of violence between them, the first spilling of blood.

Austin: What happened to your arms? Eabha ... what are those bruises?

Eabha: It's nothing, Austin. Just leave it, OK? (*She snatches her arm away from him, pushing her sleeves down*)

Austin: They're like fingerprints. Did he do this? Did Cillian hurt you again?

Eabha: Please, Austin. I'm asking you to just leave it, OK?

Austin: If he hurt you, I swear to God, I'll kill him. I'll fucking kill him.

Austin strides away from her, anger filling each step.

Eabha: Where are you going? Austin? Austin, don't hurt him. Please!

Austin (*furious*): You're not to see him again. Do you hear me? This has to stop.

Eabha: Listen to me — please. Just stop for a second! I'll deal with this. I don't need you protecting me, Austin!

Austin: It looks to me like you do! I'm not going to wait around for something worse to happen. He threw stones at you, Eabha — look at the gash over your eye. Now, you're covered in bruises. Do you think I'm going to do nothing? (*His voice breaks*) I'm all you have ... and you're all I have too!

Eabha: Just ... just don't hurt him, Austin.

```
At least we have each other ... Cillian has
no one.
```

'Whew!' Dara said as she lowered her script, a smile lighting her face. 'You're really starting to sound like him now. You've perfected Austin's growl.'

Sam bowed his head. 'Why, thank you. Let's hope it doesn't rub off permanently,' he said, watching a swan float by, turning her long neck briefly to regard them, hopeful for bread they hadn't brought with them. 'You know, I actually like this scene. It's the one time I get my character's motivation – I mean, I'd beat the living shit out of Cillian if he did that to you.'

She was surprised by the conviction in his voice and even more surprised by the hopeful, upward slope it brought to her lip. He still cared.

Her smile grew bolder. 'You want to keep reading?' she asked.

'Not really,' he replied, leaning backwards on the wooden dock. He watched her, as if assessing her, while he scratched at the stubble spread across his neck and chin. 'Tell me – how's the new gaff?'

'It's grand,' Dara said, adjusting the belt of her linen jumpsuit. 'Oisín stayed over last night . . . I ran into him making a quick exit this morning.'

Sam threw his head back, laughing loudly. 'Caught red-handed.' He shook his head. 'You know he was giving out stink that you moved in?'

'Was he?'

'Yeah . . . Am I the only one who doesn't want to live with Eabha?'

'I guess so. You don't fancy her? Not even a little?'

'She's not my type.'

'No? What's your type then?'

'Don't do this, Dara . . . don't be all coy with me.'

'Don't do what?' She smiled. 'I don't know what you're talking about.'

'Yeah, you do.' He slid closer to her; she could feel a sudden nervousness in him. 'Dara, what are we doing?'

'What do you mean?'

'You know what I mean . . . you know *exactly* what I mean. It's been there from the start, but then you moved into the house and it . . . I don't know, it just really bothered me. I was so annoyed at you. Like, I was fuming! And I was thinking about that, you know? I was thinking about *why* I was so angry about it.' He looked at her. 'You know why, don't you?'

'Because you don't like Eabha?'

'No – it's because I like *you*, Dara.' He reached for her face, pausing briefly before he pressed his lips against her lips. She felt her mouth open, her mind melting away, worries fleeing with it, as if they had slipped out through her ear and were now floating away on the water in front of her.

'I wasn't expecting that,' she said, pulling her hair behind her ear.

'Yes, you were.'

'No, I mean . . . it's just . . . I didn't know if we would . . . if we would . . . just because, well, it makes things messy,' Dara said, tripping over her words as she spoke. She was nervous, embarrassingly so.

He pulled her towards him and she lay her cheek flat against his chest, letting the warmth of his skin coat her face, letting his presence reassure her. 'I wasn't going to do anything until after the play,' he said. 'It just seemed like too much.'

'Yeah, I mean . . . I felt the same way,' Dara admitted. 'But then you changed your mind?'

'I guess so,' he said and kissed her again. 'And you changed yours?'

'What's a little more chaos?' Dara said, then laughed, swinging her legs again, the tip of her shoes catching the surface of the canal, sending ripples across the water. 'So, is that the plan? We'll just see what happens?'

'There's no plan, Dara – I don't want a plan.' His arm was around her shoulder. 'As soon as we start putting this into words, it'll start to die.' He lifted a strand of black hair out of her eyes. 'All we'll see are the reasons we shouldn't and I don't want to think about them right now.'

'Me neither,' Dara agreed, but it was easier said than done, already battling herself not to overthink the moment, not to let her restless mind ruin it.

On the dock next to her, the breeze was stirring the pages of her script; she reached for it, in case it blew into the water, her eye catching on a line.

Eabha: I took a leap of faith with Cillian.
I thought he might cure the sadness in me.
But now I'm falling ... falling into a great
chasm and there's nobody to catch me.

There she was again, invading the moment, making it about her, Eabha's voice echoing through Dara's mind.

She closed her script decisively, sticking it into her backpack where it could do no further harm. Her head rested against Sam's shoulder and she tried her best to inhabit the present, a moment of peace.

'Looks like rain is coming,' Sam said, pointing up at the dark clouds gathering behind the copper dome of the church in Rathmines. 'Should we go?'

Dara agreed, rain on the air as she climbed onto her bike again.

Sam kissed her goodbye at Portobello Bridge, taking off down Camden Street, while she turned in the opposite direction, back towards Leinster Road. The rain started at the corner of Rathmines Road, bouncing off the asphalt around her, her hair quickly drenched, her skin sticking to the linen of her jumpsuit. By the time she reached number 74, a rumble of thunder was sounding, electricity humming in the air around her. She could almost feel it inside her, as if buried beneath the skin.

Chapter Thirteen

A loud clanging of the brass door knocker – a lion's head –
against the pale pink door announced Austin's presence on
Leinster Road the following day. He entered the house with
his hands in the pockets of his corduroy trousers, something
in his demeanour making Dara feel nervous, some change in
frequency disturbing the air around him.

The others were waiting in the attic, but Austin stalled, hovering at the bottom of the stairs, fiddling with the ornaments on
the sideboard.

'I heard you moved in here?' he said, reaching for a jade statu-
ette standing next to the brass lamp. 'With my sister?'

Dara watched him turn it absently in his hands, a trio of
monkeys: see no evil, speak no evil, hear no evil. 'Yeah, she's
letting me stay for a while, until I get myself sorted with another
place.'

'Why would she do that?' She could feel his suspicion, like an
itch on her skin.

Dara swallowed. 'I don't know – I guess she wants to help
me.'

He considered this for a long moment. 'Does she?' He wasn't
looking for an answer. 'Is it getting to her at all? All this cancelling her shit?'

'I don't know, really. She seems OK.' Dara looked at him, meeting his steady, unknowable gaze. 'She worries about you.'

He ignored this, standing in front of the window, through which he looked out at the road beyond. 'They're watching me. Did she tell you that? They probably followed me here this morning. They're waiting to catch me out.'

Dara looked down at her hands. This didn't seem likely; there hadn't been any new photographs of Austin in the papers – or, in fact, any of the other cast so far. It was just the occasional photo of Eabha walking serenely in and out of the Gate Theatre.

'That must be difficult,' Dara said, choosing her words carefully. 'Austin, are you doing OK? You must be under a lot of pressure.'

A deep frown line formed immediately between his eyebrows. 'Why would you care?'

Dara met his frown with one of her own. 'Because somebody should.'

He laughed at that, but Dara didn't flinch. His guilt was an open question, the very air around him drumming with suspicion, with the possibility of murder, and yet she felt this growing responsibility towards him. She couldn't say why. Maybe playing Eabha for twelve hours a day was starting to rub off on her?

Austin was looking down towards the Berber rug under his feet now, saying nothing.

'Will we head up?' Dara said gently.

He gave a curt nod and, when he spoke, his voice was softer. 'What scene are you working on today?'

'Same scene again – the one down at the lake,' she replied, watching his reaction.

'You mean Cillian's violent assault on my sister,' he muttered, his voice gruff as they climbed the stairs up to the attic. 'Or is she still blaming the mushrooms?'

* * *

There was a certain weariness in Dara as she entered the rehearsal room. The initial convenience of living and working in the same house was quickly fading, cabin fever setting in, the air growing stale, each day feeling very much like the last. At night, her dreams brought her to Beara, the sea air kissing her face, the ocean roaring in her ears. But when she woke, it was to the sound of cars on the road outside, or Wagner playing in Eabha's room while she dressed for the day: something from *Tristan and Isolde* or maybe *Tannhäuser*, always mournful.

Dara sat down by the window, while Austin and Oisín sat together, side by side – Austin and Cillian, together again in an attic. She glanced at Oisín to see if he felt it too – the strangeness of seeing them like that – but his expression was blank, his chain caught between his teeth, his eyes watching Eabha, waiting. Sam was uncharacteristically late and hadn't provided an explanation.

The morning light, shining in through the window, caught on the dust in the air. Dara watched it dance around Oisín's outstretched body, its movements matching his languid posture. They were the same age, but he seemed younger.

She glanced at Eabha, wondering if Oisín had any idea what he was doing, if he could see he was no match for her. A golden boy, untested by life, primed for a fall.

'Shall we get started?' Eabha said. 'Or should we wait for Sam?'

'Where is he?' Oisín asked, adjusting the beige cap that sat backwards over his head. With a grin, he looked at Dara and added: 'Maybe you know . . .'

'No!' she replied, a little too quickly. 'No . . . why would I know?!'

'It doesn't matter,' Eabha said. 'I'm sure he'll show up. Let's just start.'

With her left hand, she was playing with one of three gold lockets around her neck. With her right, she held her phone. It was buzzing incessantly: a string of emails from the production team at the Gate. She gave a sigh, throwing it onto the settee next to her.

'Geoffrey Goode is chasing some big names to attend our opening night,' she said, referring to the Director of the Gate Theatre. Dara had only ever seen him from a distance: a short, stocky man, with a shock of silver hair who wore red, square-framed glasses and had a taste for cravats. 'I was wondering if the arts community would abandon me, but it seems there remain some people with a backbone in this world . . . Geoffrey is telling everyone he meets that Richard Butler's campaign of harassment is an attempt to stifle artistic expression.' Eabha laughed. 'He's whipping up a crowd of supporters – no better man. He thinks we can get a good show of support on opening night.'

'That's good news,' Dara said. 'So the petition isn't scaring them away?'

'It seems not,' Eabha replied, her smile almost gleeful. 'I was worried they'd shaft me, but Geoffrey says we're on the front line, defending the arts.'

Dara was quite sure neither her mother nor her Aunty Sheila would find it a convincing argument, but then, they weren't the audience. They weren't the people who would pay for seats, fill the auditorium, and then mutter to each other over bubbles at the interval about how cancel culture was eroding free thought.

'Will we get started then?' Eabha suggested. She looked to her brother. 'Maybe, since we have Austin here, we could focus on the final act instead?' Her phone was still vibrating relentlessly next to her; she ignored it, arranging her turquoise skirt so that it fell prettily around her.

Next to Oisín, Austin sniffed. 'Hang on a minute – are we going to talk about all this shit online? The *Justice for Cillian* campaign . . . what are you going to do about it? They're talking about an investigation now, Eabha. Some local TD in Clare is after writing to the Taoiseach. They have his letter up online.'

'What's there to talk about? The Gate's PR team are drafting a statement in case we need it. Geoffrey is working hard on a positive spin. The troops are rallying behind us. The show will go on! What more do you want?' Eabha looked at each of them in turn, assessing their expressions, searching for warning signs, for the stealthy advance of her greatest enemy: their doubt.

Dara gulped some water, avoiding her gaze.

'Look, none of this is unexpected, OK?' Eabha added. 'They did something similar the last time.'

'Eabha, would you stop?' Austin said, his voice rising. 'It's very different this time. A public inquiry would—'

'A public inquiry has nothing to do with the play.' Her hands lifted into the air, as if borne on a gale of frustration. 'Let's just focus on the play, all right? We can talk about the rest later, Austin. Christ, we need to get this right and we're nowhere – nowhere!'

Dara wondered if they were separable anymore for Austin: the play and his reality. She watched him, his shoulders hunched over, staring venomously at his sister, his acquiescence a fragile thing.

Eabha let the air out of her lungs, her fingers tapping against her forehead. 'I promise you, there's nothing to worry about, Austin. It's all in hand.' Her eyes flashed to Dara. 'Have you tried to reach Sam?'

'He hasn't answered my texts yet,' Dara said. His absence was concerning her. It wasn't like him to miss a rehearsal.

'Trouble in paradise,' Oisín muttered. There was an unkindness in his voice that Dara didn't understand. Why did he care? What difference did it make to Oisín now he had Eabha?

'Well, do you want to fill in, Austin?' Eabha said, a quizzical expression on her face as she looked at her brother. 'Sam's part is small in this scene so you won't have to do much.'

To their surprise, Austin didn't hesitate, reaching for the script Eabha held towards him. 'All right,' he said, clearing his throat. 'I can play the villain.'

* * *

It was the most gruelling day of rehearsals Dara endured. With Sam remaining absent, Austin stayed for the full day, committing to his part at an almost feverish pitch, reading the lines on the page as if delivering divine truth, his eyes gazing into Dara's as if he were trying to burrow a hole through her skull and into her brain.

There was one scene in particular that made her skin tingle, the play suddenly blazing with reality, fiction melting into fact, past into present. It was the scene where Eabha first turned to Austin for help.

SCENE: *An empty classroom, an Irish grammar lesson still scrawled on the whiteboard behind them.* **Austin** *sits on a desk, swinging his legs. Enter* **Eabha***.*

Austin: You're late ... everything OK?
Eabha *(closing the door behind her quietly)*: Yeah. Yeah ... I'm fine.
Austin: Your text gave me a fright.

Eabha: I'm almost certain it was him, Austin
... He was standing outside my window,
shining a light through the glass. But when
I looked out, there was nothing. Why is he
doing this to me? Why would he try to scare
me like this? (*She runs her hand through her
hair in agitation, scratching angrily at her
scalp*)

Austin: He's a weirdo, that's why.

Eabha: I just don't understand ... I don't
know what he wants from me. (*A sob escapes*)
What should I do?! I don't know what to do! I
feel like ... like I'll never get away from
him.

Austin: You will ... I'm here for you. I'll
always be here for you.

Eabha didn't give them a break, not until their mouths were
dry, perspiration slipping down their backs, coating their hands,
filling the creases snaking across their palms. They didn't stop
until Dara had felt the intensity of Austin's presence, the mon-
strous demands of a close relationship with him. Not until Dara
knew – *really* knew – how it felt to be Austin's sister.

By the time she escaped from the attic late that evening, it felt
as if Austin and Eabha had, together, drained the life out of her.
In her bedroom, she lay on the white sheets and breathed deeply
until the fierce edge of her tiredness gradually blunted.

Picking up her phone, she sent another text to Sam.

Dara Gaffney (8:34pm): Where have you been?! I had to do
our scenes with Austin! I may never recover. D x

It was an hour before Sam texted back.

Sam Demir (9.21pm): Oh shit, Dara – sorry. Was it that bad?

Dara Gaffney (9.25pm): It was worse than you're imagining. I don't think he's well, Sam. I'm getting really worried. Seriously – where were you?! I can't do this alone!!

Sam Demir (9.32pm): Sorry, D! x

Dara Gaffney (9.33pm): Are you going to tell me where you were?!

Sam didn't reply.

* * *

Dara had an appointment for a costume fitting the following morning at the Gate. Cycling through the city, she felt lighter the further she got from Leinster Road, the sun warm on her upturned face. She sailed by Trinity College, over the river, past the statue of Daniel O'Connell, and up the boulevard to the theatre on Parnell Square, arriving just after nine.

As she arrived, her eyes scanned the footpath for photographers, but there were none visible in the crowd milling at the busy traffic lights. She locked her bike to a nearby pole and headed quickly in through the main door, glad to have escaped the penetrating stare of a camera lens.

The fitting was straightforward – Dara could almost fit the sixth-year uniform the costume department had ordered from the Bodkin School – but her stomach clenched with fright as she caught her reflection in the mirror. Her dark hair flowing over her shoulders, the tips brushing the school crest. There was no denying it now. She was Eabha.

Word of Dara's presence at the theatre must have spread because as she was unlocking her bike again after the fitting, a woman sprang forward from the crowd moving along the foot-path, calling her name.

'Dara Gaffney? Can I have a quick word?' Her hair was scraped back from her face, her hands shoved into the pockets of her leather jacket. Dara had never seen her before.

Startled, her fingers paused, the keys to her bike lock rattling in her hand. 'Sorry? Do I know you? Wh-what's this about?'

'My name is Linda O'Rowe. I've been trying to speak with you for a number of weeks now. I'm sorry to stop you like this, but it's important.' Her voice was very professional, almost official, but it was no less jarring.

The bicycle lock shook in Dara's hand as she pulled it open.

'I wanted to ask you a few questions about the de Laceys. If you had a minute?'

For a moment, Dara hesitated, the urge to free herself of the murky association with Eabha and Austin rising with the frantic beating of her heart. She could just get it off her chest – right there, in that moment – and tell Linda that she was just an actor, just a young actor who couldn't pass up this job. Not someone who needed to be questioned in the national media, not some-one worth speaking to at all.

Dara looked back at the theatre, wondering if this was how Vanessa Devin had felt when she first betrayed Eabha and started talking to the press. She pulled her bike free from the lamp post, the thought of Vanessa calming her again. She did not want that fate – on the wrong side of Eabha, her career in tatters before it had really begun.

'Dara, I know you're afraid to talk to me, but you're making a mistake.'

She wheeled her bike away down the busy footpath, waiting while a tram passed by, its bell sounding.

'People are going to think you're part of this – I *know* you're not. I know you're an innocent party in all of this. Let me tell your side, Dara.'

Dara threw her leg over the bike and mounted the saddle. 'How did you know I was here?' she said, glancing back at Linda who was still following behind her.

'What?' Linda said, surprised by the question.

'Did someone tell you I was here?' She pushed her hair out of her face, running through who it might have been, trying to remember the names of the costume team who had taken her measurements.

Linda ignored her question. 'This happened before, Dara. You should know – I was there the first time. I saw what happened to the cast. She pulled them apart, Dara. Don't let her do that to you!'

She had to shout her final words at Dara's back as she cycled furiously away.

A cold wind lashed her face as she made her way down O'Connell Street again, an anger stirring her blood, while, next to her, some pigeons rose skyward, coming to rest on the granite pediment of the General Post Office opposite. She was growing tired of the assumption – implicit in every warning – that she was walking doe-eyed into some kind of trap, as if she were a puppet on a string.

She pushed her hair off her face again, pedalling until the sweat was gathering in her armpits, until her breath was burning in her chest, until she turned down a now-familiar street, coming to a stop at number 74 Leinster Road.

Home.

Chapter Fourteen

Condensation was dripping down the windows, a jazz band playing in the living room for the guests dressed in white, as per Eabha's invitations. The house was filled with actors, producers, directors, some faces Dara knew personally, but most she only recognised from films and television. In the study, she spotted Geoffrey Goode holding court with a group of young actors lying in a semicircle around him, bodies sprawled across Eabha's parquet floor. In the living room, a man with a top hat had found a bottle of crème de menthe on Eabha's bar cart and was pouring it into the open mouths of the crowd cheering around him.

With just twenty days left to opening night, a party had been arranged at short notice at the house. In the face of public disquiet, it was a show of strength, a vote of confidence from Eabha's own community, even if the rest of the world was against her. It proved that, despite the raging controversy, Eabha could still pull a crowd.

Dara was searching for Sam. Since that kiss on the dock, he had pulled away from her again, drifting into single-word text messages. She still didn't know why he had missed rehearsal and his refusal to speak about it made her distrustful. Had she done something wrong? Was it just cold feet? Or had he thought better of mixing the personal with the professional? Four glasses of champagne had emboldened her to find out, pushing her way through the perspiring kitchen and out to the garden beyond.

The night air cooled her face. She held her champagne flute against her cheeks and breathed. Her feet were sore in the metallic heels she had borrowed from Eabha; she slipped them off and let her bare feet rest on the grass.

'You all right, Dara?'

Startled, she turned her head. Sam had taken one of the wrought-iron chairs onto the grass beneath the apple tree, where he sat in the dark rolling a cigarette on his knee.

'Jesus, Sam, you nearly scared the life out of me,' Dara said, walking towards him. 'I've been looking everywhere for you.'

'It's only me – no monsters out here,' he said. 'You want to sit down?' He pointed to the chair under him.

'No, you're grand. Stay where you are,' Dara said, settling herself on the grass instead. Her white sheath dress bunched up above her knees. It was another item borrowed from Eabha's wardrobe, bearing a label far outside the scope of her buying power. She took a sip of champagne. 'Are you hiding out here?'

Sam glanced up. 'Just needed some air.'

Following his gaze, Dara looked skyward, the stars blurring slightly, her vision swimming, though she could just about see Orion's Belt glimmering through the black. She took another sip of her drink. It made her feel light, as if the champagne were carbonating her blood, lifting her a few inches off the grass.

'Is everything OK, Sam?' she said. 'Why are you out here alone?'

Behind them, a crashing sound came from the house, followed by disparate whooping and cheering from the crowd inside.

Sam made a face. 'I just don't know why she's doing this – this party. It's a real fuck you to Richard Butler. Don't you think?'

'I don't think it's meant that way,' Dara said. 'I think she just needed to have a little fun, you know? She likes to feel a crowd behind her.'

'She's sending a message,' Sam muttered. 'It's a show of force. How is Richard supposed to feel about all this? You know, he's holding candlelight vigils outside the Bodkin School? And she's up here partying with every Z-list celebrity in Dublin.'

'There are a couple of A-listers too,' Dara replied, but Sam didn't laugh. She sighed, trying to summon the nerve to ask him what she really wanted to know, but the thought was making her feel a little nauseous. If he regretted kissing her, did she really want to hear him say it? 'Have you seen Oisín?' she asked instead. 'He was going to get us some drinks, but then he disappeared.'

Sam sat back in his chair, puffing on his cigarette, and pointed up at the roof of the house. A small square of light shone out from the eaves. 'He's up there . . . with *her*.'

'Of course he is,' Dara said. 'Wherever Eabha goes, her shadow follows.' She looked up at the attic window, across which a shadow had just passed. 'I don't get it . . . they're so different. I mean, what does she see in him?' Dara's eyes were on the window, waiting for Eabha to come into view.

'Why do you care, Dara?'

It was a fair question. Why *did* she care? She could feel it growing in her, building day after day, this hold that Eabha had on her. It wasn't just gratitude. It wasn't a romantic interest either – at least, she didn't think so. It was more like an impulse towards imposture. Eabha had this way of stirring in Dara a desire to be like her, even – could she admit it to herself? – to *be* her, at least in some ways. Not in the unending intensity, the ravenous hunger for attention, but in all the ways that Eabha could beguile and fascinate, in the quiet ferocity with which she lived, her Midas touch gilding the world around her.

Dara looked down again, her champagne-soaked mind returning her to the words of the play.

> **Cillian:** I don't know what you've done to me,
> Eabha. It's like you're in my head now and I
> can't think of anything else. I can't imagine
> a world without you. I don't want to — I
> won't!

Her attention snapped back to Sam. 'You don't like Eabha – I get it, Sam. But I need to know . . . is that why you've been avoiding me again? Is it something I did?'

Inside the house, somebody was trying to wrestle a tuba from one of the musicians, forcing a flurry of discordant notes from the instrument.

'No, of course not.' Sam rose from the chair, coming to sit on the grass in front of her, gathering her into his arms. 'No – God, sorry, Dara. I'm not avoiding you . . . I've just had a lot on my mind.'

'Because you know, after that day at the dock—'

'Yeah, I know . . .' He sighed, his head rolling back on his spine, his face angling towards the stars. 'I'm sorry . . . it's not you. It's just a *lot*, you know?'

'Yeah,' she said, stretching forward until her face was leaning against his shoulder. 'I know . . . I know it is.' She looked up at him. 'Where were you the other day, Sam? The day you missed rehearsals?'

He pulled another cloud of smoke into his lungs, his eyes watching her. 'Why – are you suspicious of me, Dara?'

'No – I just . . . You're the one who insists on honesty, Sam. So, I don't understand why you won't tell me where you were?'

He looked at her steadily for a moment, considering whether or not to speak. 'Honestly, I couldn't face it . . . I couldn't face them.'

'Why? What does that mean?'

He sniffed, looking slightly miserable now. A revelation of some kind was hovering on his lips. She wished he would just say it, tension running through her muscles and into her bones.

'I learned some things about Eabha and her brother that disturbed me,' he said quietly, twirling his cigarette between his fingers, watching the swirling shape the smoke made in the cool night air.

Dara's eyes widened. 'What? What are you talking about?'

'Well – just between us – I had a conversation with Richard Butler and I needed time to think about what he told me.'

Dara took a sharp intake of air into her lungs. 'Jesus – Sam! Are you serious? What are you playing at?! Why would you talk to him?'

'Because he *asked* me to talk to him. Didn't you get his letter?'

Dara's expression melted from shock to confusion. 'No . . . what letter?'

'Oisín got one too. It came to the theatre for us. Maybe Eabha intercepted yours. Oisín probably told her about it – I mean, of course he would.'

'Eabha wouldn't do that.'

'Stop, Dara . . . come on. You know she would.'

Dara took a breath. 'Does she know you were talking to him? To Richard? Did you check with her?'

'Of course not – and she's not going to find out about it.'

'She might!'

'It was just a phone call, just a friendly chat. What was I supposed to do? Ignore a heartbroken father grieving for his son?'

'Yes! I mean . . . no, but . . . you know we can't talk to him.'

Sam paused, his mouth briefly a straight, tight line until it loosened and seemed to escape his control. 'You're not a little bit curious? You don't want to know why Richard was writing to us?'

'Let me guess, he wants us to quit the play and sell Eabha down the river?'

'Well, yeah – but it was more than just that. He wants the other side of the story told. He wants to fill the blanks about the night Cillian died.'

'But we *know* what happened the night Cillian died!'

'Dara, come on, not even Eabha says the play is the full truth.'

Her eyes flashed to the attic window, as if seeking her out, but there was still nobody visible.

'Do you want to know what Richard told me?'

She didn't know if she did.

'He said Cillian wasn't at all the way Eabha paints him in the play. He was a quiet kid, kept to himself. Never gave the teachers a moment's hassle. They never got any calls from the school about him sneaking out – and there were never any visits from his brother Fergal. Fergal wasn't even in Ireland at the time. He had fucked off to the South of Spain.'

Dara felt her stomach flip. She swallowed hard. 'No, that can't be right . . . the attic, the mushrooms, the goat skull . . . that was all Cillian. And we know from Austin that they were about to expel him over the drug-taking.'

'Well, according to Richard Butler, that was all *Austin*. It was his attic lair, his sneaking out at night, his goat skull, his drugs. He was the one dragging Cillian astray.'

'Stop, Sam! I don't believe it. And I can't believe you do either! Can't you see what he's doing? Can't you see why Richard would lie?'

Sam watched the upset his words had caused her and shook his head slowly. 'Jesus . . . Dara. You're just as bad as Oisín, aren't you?' There was a sudden scorn in his voice.

Her cheeks stung, as if he had reached out through the darkness and slapped her. 'What is that supposed to mean?'

'You're living with her. You've given up your job at the boutique, right?'

Dara gave a curt nod, Sam's cigarette smoke provoking a flare of nostrils.

'You've stopped auditioning for other roles. What are you going to do when this is over? Have you thought about it? This is how she wants you to be, Dara. Tied to her. Defending her. Under her thumb.'

'Sam, it's not like that! You don't know what you're talking about.'

He picked himself up from the grass, sitting down on his chair again, his limbs hanging limp, like a marionette at rest. 'Fine – you know what? – grand, whatever. It's your life, Dara. You can choose to trust Eabha if you want. But you should think about what you're doing. I mean it . . . you should give it some serious thought.'

Dara drained the last of her champagne. 'I don't know why you're being like this. I thought you liked me, Sam. But you're going behind our backs now – you're talking to the man who wants all our work to be for nothing.'

Sam looked up. 'I'm just not prepared to get caught up in Eabha's mess, Dara. I'm protecting myself – and you should too.'

'Honestly, Sam . . . I'm surprised at you.' She scrambled to her feet a little inelegantly. 'I don't know what you think Eabha's done to you, but you've just betrayed *all* of us. I thought you cared about the play . . . about me. But you only care about yourself.'

'Dara? Dara, come back,' Sam called after her as she marched back towards the house. But she didn't turn around, her heart racing, the blood thumping in her ears, her hand brushing off the lavender bush as she passed it.

A wave of heat hit her as she stepped inside, followed by a burst of music. There was an arm around her, a voice cheering in her ear, someone holding a champagne magnum to her lips. She pushed it away, kept her head down and made for the stairs. The man with the top hat was blocking the way, a long, sweeping peacock feather dangling from it. He tried to pull her into a dance; she dodged him, feeling a hand suddenly close around her arm. Irritated, she wrenched herself free, turning briefly to see who was impeding her progress. Her heart stopped in her chest.

Long dark hair flowing down to rest just above the curve of her spine, her face pale, her jaw square. She was taller too, more solid, and she bore herself with a certainty that Eabha lacked.

Vanessa Devin.

'It's Dara Gaffney, isn't it?' They were caught in a crush of bodies, jostling in the hallway, the portrait gallery now askew on the walls, the de Lacey family less intimidating when crooked. Dara winced as someone stood on her foot. 'I'm Vanessa – I'm the first Eabha!' She was smiling, her teeth sparkling with an unnatural perfection.

'Yeah, eh . . . hello,' Dara said, moving gradually towards the open door where some air might reach her lungs. Someone was laughing next to her, the shrieking sound ringing in her ears. 'Does Eabha know you're here?' She didn't know what else to say, an awful shyness crawling over her suddenly.

'No . . . well, I mean, I heard about the party and I thought I'd come along and try to talk to her. She's a hard woman to track down.'

A frown crossed Dara's face. If Eabha was proving difficult to find, it was because she didn't want to be found. Why would she? What could a conversation with Vanessa possibly achieve?

'Do you want to go outside for a minute? To chat?' Vanessa said, her face hopeful. 'I can't hear a thing in here.'

Dara nodded. She was in no mood after her conversation with Sam, but her curiosity wouldn't let her miss this opportunity. She pushed her way onto the steps outside, with Vanessa following behind her.

A small group of people were talking quietly under the cherry blossom tree. She couldn't see what they were doing in the darkness, but they didn't seem to want any attention, which suited her fine. She sat down on the steps, the stone cold against her skin.

'I came to see Eabha, but I was actually hoping I might run into you here,' Vanessa said. She gave a laugh. 'I've wanted to meet you.'

'Really?' Dara said, brow wrinkling again. 'I'm not sure I'm worth the trouble!'

'You're the girl who got the role everyone wanted . . . everyone's curious about you.' Her lips were thinner when she smiled, almost disappearing inside her mouth. She was older than Dara by about a decade or so, but she looked largely unchanged from the photos Dara had seen online of the debut production. 'I heard you're a modest one.'

'Oh really? And who has been talking about me?' Dara said, her tone combative. 'Was it Miriam?' She felt a sudden tightening in her stomach but didn't voice the thought causing it: was it Sam?

'No, it was just, you know, on the grapevine.' Another smile. Her voice was distinctively low and a little raspy. 'I heard they're trying to get the play pulled . . . can't say I'm that surprised, but that's intense, even by Eabha's standards. Are you worried?!'

Dara was silent for a moment. 'Not really. The Gate is standing behind us. Geoffrey Goode is here tonight so . . .'

'Yeah, I saw Geoffrey. But you know he'll bow to pressure if it goes that way? Geoffrey isn't going to risk the Gate's reputation for Eabha de Lacey. She's paying you, right? Like, you're getting paid up weekly for rehearsals? Because I had to insist on it last time.'

Dara still hadn't spoken up about the payment issue. She didn't want to make a fuss, especially when Eabha wasn't charging her for rent, utilities or any of her meals. 'They're not going to pull the play,' she said. 'Half the run is already sold out and every big name in the industry is going.'

Vanessa snorted at that. 'Right – because they all want a front-row seat for the drama.' She turned towards Dara. 'A little advice – be prepared in case they cancel it. It nearly happened the first time. It could easily happen now.'

Fear was now mixing with the champagne in her stomach and Dara felt, again, a little nauseous. There was very little stopping Geoffrey Goode from walking away from the whole production and then she would have nothing to show for all the weeks of work and stress. Nothing. There were still twenty days left for it all to go wrong, twenty days left for the worst to happen.

Subdued, she watched a man break away from the group under the cherry blossom tree, slipping past them up the stairs and into the house. He pointedly didn't look at them as he approached the steps, but, before he could disappear inside, his eyes stole their way, as if unable to help himself. Dara frowned: something about his nervous air made her doubt he had an invitation. She wondered briefly if she should intervene, but Vanessa pulled her thoughts away.

'So, how is it anyway?' she asked. 'Working with Eabha?'

Dara took a breath. 'It's great,' she said, defiant. 'I've never worked with anyone so dedicated.'

She felt the need to put Vanessa in her place, to assert herself, but she was finding it difficult to know how to react to Vanessa. Her deep inhabitation of herself was off-putting, her beauty intimidating. She seemed nothing like the portrait of a washed-up actress that Eabha had painted.

'Yeah, I guess she was pretty dedicated – but she's always on edge, right?' Vanessa laughed, though she hadn't said anything funny.

'It was her first play,' Dara countered. 'She was young. And it's such a personal work. I'm sure it was very difficult for her.'

'So, it's different now? *She's* different?'

Dara felt disinclined to reply. She shook her hair out from behind her ear, letting it fall across her face so that Vanessa wouldn't have such a clear view of her reactions.

Vanessa leaned back on the steps, her fingers fidgeting with her sleeves. 'I really need to talk to her but there are *so* many people here . . . Do you know where she is?'

Dara shook her head. 'Why do you want to talk to her anyway?' Her hand was on her face, pulling her hair back.

Vanessa's voice dropped. 'Has Eabha told you our dirty little history?'

'No . . . I mean, she said you were leaking information to the press,' Dara said.

Vanessa sighed. 'She's still saying that about me?'

'Isn't it true?'

'I was tricked by a journalist. I thought it was off record – I didn't realise she was going to print what I said.' She gave a sad laugh, but Dara felt no sympathy for Vanessa. 'You know she blacklisted us? Me, Nick and Oliver.'

'I heard that,' Dara said, provoked again. 'Does she really have that kind of influence?'

'Absolutely. The theatre world is a small one – just look around you. They're all here,' Vanessa replied, trying again to catch Dara's eye through the strands of her hair. 'She told everyone in the industry that me, Nick and Oliver couldn't be trusted and they took her word for it.'

'Then why are you here, Vanessa? You show up uninvited to see someone who blacklisted you?'

'I'm trying to repair things.'

'It's a funny way to go about it,' Dara replied darkly.

Vanessa watched her silently for a moment. 'Dara, I know how it feels to be where you are right now – I remember it. On the rise, all eyes on you, but believe me, one wrong step and you're suddenly in the dark. Out in the cold. And you know why?'

'Because this business is a bitch?'

Vanessa shook her head. 'Because Eabha made *sure* we failed. The higher she rose, the lower we fell.' She looked at Dara again, trying to draw her in, though Dara's gaze was elusive. 'Let me tell you what happened to us and maybe then you'll understand that I'm not out to get you?' She ignored the low snort of disbelief from Dara. 'Everyone in the business at the time knew Nick O'Mahony was in recovery, but Eabha actively encouraged him to embrace his appetites. She enabled his worst instincts, telling him he needed to loosen up to understand Cillian, praising him for it. He told me Austin gave him some magic mushrooms, said they'd help him with his performance.'

Another wave of nausea rose in Dara: this was horribly familiar and entirely plausible.

'Nick was out of it, slurring his words right through the play. The audience thought it was part of the performance – Cillian careening across the stage, volatile, unpredictable – but we knew the truth. He was a gentle guy, except when he was drinking. And I don't know if he ever sobered up during that time, or if the play was just one big bender. Either way, he never came back from it. I lost contact with him years ago, but Oliver says he sees him sometimes around the city, lost to himself.'

'And that's Eabha's fault?' Dara muttered, though she had to admit that it sounded credible. At the back of her mind was a suspicion – a whisper of an idea – that Eabha was encouraging Oisín's affections to bring him closer and closer to her, closer to Cillian.

'Then there's Oliver,' Vanessa continued, pretending she hadn't heard Dara's remark. 'He was besotted with Eabha, right from the beginning. She was much younger than him and she seemed like the more innocent of the two. But she had him on a string – we just didn't see it until it was too late. They were inseparable, but he was clearly into her more than she was into him. It meant she got a great performance out of him, but, when she started winning all the awards, when the play went international, she didn't need him anymore. She could have just broken it off and left it there, but that's never Eabha's style. She wanted to be properly rid of him so she started spreading rumours that he was difficult to work with, unstable, possessive – where have you heard that before? – and Oliver couldn't get another role. Eventually, he gave up. He works in sound design now.'

Dara swallowed hard, thinking of Oisín, the way he fixated on Eabha. She thought of the little looks Eabha would give him, her hand always drifting over his chest, his back, his cheek, reminding him that she was present, that her attention was there to be won.

'And you, Vanessa?' Dara said, eyes dead as she stared at her. 'How did Eabha ruin your life then?'

'Oh, well, my great sin against Eabha – Our Lady of Perpetual Sorrows – was drawing too much attention to her brother. I was there when Austin had his breakdown on opening night – did you know about that?'

'I did . . . Eabha told me.'

'Well, then you know I saw him lose his mind,' Vanessa said, aware Dara was hanging on her every word, no matter how hard she was trying to hide it. 'I found Austin trying to throw himself through a window, saying over and over that he was sorry. It was like he thought he was back at the Bodkin School, back in the attic.' She paused. 'I helped to restrain him while they called 999. I was there when they packed him into an ambulance.' She paused. 'You know where Eabha was? Still at the afterparty, Oliver on her arm. I was the one who noticed Austin was missing. I went back to find him. She was too busy basking in the limelight.' Vanessa shook her head. 'And, you know, Eabha just wanted to keep it all secret. She told me not to say anything about it to anyone. But I told her I wasn't going to be part of her web of lies. I didn't tell any journalists – I wouldn't do that – but I wasn't going to keep something like that a secret either. Austin needed help and Eabha was just hiding him away.'

'She's just protecting him,' Dara said. 'She's scared that people will say Austin's breakdown is proof he killed Cillian – a guilty mind. A psychotic episode isn't proof of anything but a sick man, but you know what people would say about it if they knew. They'd twist it.'

Vanessa looked at her closely. 'Dara, I don't think you know what happened that night. I don't know what Eabha has told you, but the things he said were . . .' She paused. 'Austin basically confessed to me. I mean, not in so many words but—'

Dara's eyes were on the cherry blossom tree, tracing the branches, their coiled shapes like a great entanglement of fingers and arms. 'He was out of his mind.' Her voice was quiet but urgent, as if to convince herself of what she said.

'That doesn't mean it was untrue.' Vanessa sat forward again, following Dara's gaze towards the tree. There were still a couple of people standing under it, though they were quieter now, almost hidden in their dark clothing.

Dara squinted. 'Is that . . . is that a camera?'

'Where?' Vanessa said, but before Dara could point out the dark lens – only barely visible between the branches – a commotion behind them drew their attention towards the door.

Sam was shouting at the man Dara had seen entering the house earlier, shoving him backwards through the door. 'Get out of here! Get the fuck out before I break that phone over your head.'

'What's happening, Sam?' Dara said, as she and Vanessa scrambled out of the way. The man stumbled down the steps behind them, his hands in front of his chest defensively.

'This guy was inside filming people on his phone,' Sam said, his chest puffed out, the muscles of his arms tensed and ready for confrontation. 'Going to sell it to the papers for a quick quid, weren't you?'

'Calm down, all right? I'm just doing my job,' the photographer said, moving cautiously away from Sam, who looked angrier than Dara had ever seen him before. There was something uncharacteristically menacing about him and it took a moment for her to place who he reminded her of – with a jolt, she realised it was Austin.

Behind them, there was a rustling sound from the cherry blossom tree, two more photographers appearing from beneath it, visible now in the light cast out from the house.

'Jesus,' Dara said, her hand reaching instinctively for Sam. 'Sam, there's more of them. Should we call the police?'

'No police,' Sam replied, 'we'll deal with this ourselves.' A group had formed behind him – party guests shouting drunkenly at the photographers to clear off, though they were already running away down the path. Sam followed after them, two actors Dara recognised from her time at the Wilde Academy running behind him.

Turning back towards the house, Dara tried to pick out Eabha and Oisín from the crowd of faces, but they were nowhere to be seen.

Vanessa was standing at her elbow. 'They never would have dared do that ten years ago,' she said. 'They must be getting some serious cash for the footage.'

Dara glanced at her, irritated that she was still here and hadn't cleared off with the other trespassers. 'Don't you think it's time you left, Vanessa? If Eabha wants to talk to you, she will.'

Vanessa pulled her leather jacket tighter around her, watching as the group behind them retreated back into the house. Somewhere inside, they could hear peals of laughter as someone popped another champagne bottle, the music loud again.

'Look, I didn't come here for a fight,' Vanessa said. Her voice was quieter, less strident after the interruption. 'Really . . . I didn't.' She gave Dara a sad smile. 'Just remember, if you find yourself on the wrong side of Eabha, I'll be there waiting for you.'

Sam was walking back through the gate. He looked as if he were in command of the situation, but Dara knew him well enough to see that he was rattled.

She turned to Vanessa. 'You know, everyone talks such shit about Eabha, but she's only ever been kind to me. She's only ever been decent.'

There was an undercurrent of nastiness in her voice as Vanessa replied: 'I know how it feels . . . she takes you by the hand and makes you feel like the world is turning for you. But when she drops you again – believe me – you've never felt so alone.' She walked down the steps, pausing at the bottom. 'Eabha has a long list of causalities – Cillian was only her first.'

Sam's chest was heaving as he reached them, trying to catch his breath as he looked from Vanessa to Dara. 'What's going on here?'

'Nothing – I'm just leaving,' Vanessa said tightly, her dark hair swinging behind her as she headed for Leinster Road. 'Bye, Dara. And . . . good luck.'

They watched her leave, disappearing quickly from view, into the gloom of the orange street lights on Leinster Road.

'What was that about?' Sam asked, turning to Dara, who folded her arms, standing close beside him.

'Vanessa Devin decided to drop in on Eabha.'

'Why would she do that?'

'I don't know. I don't trust her . . . Are the photographers gone?' Dara asked.

'I think so,' Sam replied. He looked at Dara, his hands now gripping her arms. 'Dara . . . I'm sorry . . . I'm so sorry about earlier. It's just . . . I can't relax anymore. I don't feel like myself. I can't shake this anxious feeling.'

'I know,' she said. 'I feel it too. And I'm sorry, Sam. I don't want us to fight.'

'Me neither,' he said gently. 'We need each other if we're going to get through this . . . this madness.'

He reached down then and kissed her. She let her shoulders drop, the tension easing from her while he held her in his arms. It was delicate, breakable – this thing between them – but they stood on the steps together anyway, looking up to the stars again.

Dara's emotions were in a tumult, but, for once, she didn't interrogate herself, letting her mind float away towards the wisps of dark cloud hanging in the sky over the city, out to the great expanse of space, heading in the direction of Orion's Belt.

Chapter Fifteen

Dara had just fallen asleep on her bed when a loud bang over-head woke her. She sat up immediately at the sound, ears strain-ing to hear. Muffled voices overhead in the attic, then a shout. She couldn't hear what was said, but there was a desperation in Eabha's voice that made Dara leap to her feet. She crossed the room, reaching for the door handle and wrenching it open. She was on the attic stairs when she ran headlong into Oisín.

'What are you doing?!' he said, holding her back.

'Is Eabha OK? I heard shouting.' The attic door was shut behind him.

Oisín had a grip on her upper arm, his fingers pressing into her skin a little too firmly. 'She's OK ... she just needs to be alone.'

'What's wrong? What happened to her?' Dara said, pulling herself free of his grip. There was no sound from the attic now.

'Calm down, Dara,' Oisín replied. 'Eabha is fine. I'll explain what happened if you come with me.'

'Why won't you let me talk to her?!'

'She's on the phone! She's talking to Austin. That's who she wants right now. She wants Austin.' He was pulling her back towards her bedroom and she had little choice but to follow him.

Oisín switched on the overhead light, the sudden glare

causing her to blink several times, feeling dazed. Her head was pounding, tiredness condensing in her right temple.

'Austin's on his way over,' Oisín said, sitting down on the edge of the bed she had so quickly vacated. His hands rested on his thighs, his mouth slightly open. 'Something happened to her . . . I . . . I don't really know what. She just . . . she freaked out.'

Dara could see now that he was upset. She took a robe from the hook behind the door, pulling it tightly around her as she sat down on the bed next to him. 'I don't understand what you're saying . . . what exactly happened up there, Oisín?'

He shook his head. 'I . . . I don't know, Dara. I think I hurt her somehow.'

She could almost feel Cillian's hands grasping at her, a line from the script threading through her thoughts.

Eabha: My arms are covered in bruises, Cillian, because you *keep* hurting me. My face is still swollen from the stones you threw at me. (*She pulls her sleeves up, her arms red where he has pulled at her*) You did it again tonight. Do you even realise you're doing it?
Cillian (*expectorating as he speaks*): I didn't mean to — you're making me out like I'm . . . like I'm some kind of violent woman beater . . . Please, Eabha, don't be like this. Don't push me away!

'Start at the beginning. What exactly did you do?'

'I didn't *do* anything! We were . . . we were just on the settee and, you know, I was kissing her and—'

'You were on the settee together?'

'Yes.'

'Just kissing?'

'Yes . . . well, no – Jesus, Dara, do you want a fucking diagram?' He stood up, his hands grasping at his hair as he walked to the window. 'She was into it, I swear she was, but then something happened . . . maybe I did something wrong . . . I don't know . . . like, she was . . . she was there with me and then she was gone somewhere else. Screaming, pushing me off her like I was attacking her. I wasn't, Dara, you have to believe me.'

She could picture them together. Eabha pale in the moonlight, Oisín lying on top of her, his chest pressing down on her, his arms holding her to him. She knew how that felt from their rehearsals together: the scene at the clearing in the trees.

'Maybe she was thinking of Cillian?' She heard herself say it before she had thought it through – before considering how that might make Oisín feel. But he didn't react, staring down at the Turkish rug beneath his feet.

Eabha stands in a clearing in the trees, wearing her school uniform, waiting for Cillian to arrive. There's a picnic at her feet, some sandwiches wrapped in tinfoil, a bottle of water. She's agitated, pacing, wringing her hands.

Eabha (to audience): When we talk about love, how do we know we're experiencing the same thing? What if one person's act of love is another's act of obsession? What if love isn't one thing at all? What if love can't be separated from other emotions – lust, jealousy, fear, even hatred? Nothing exists in a vacuum, safe from the influence of other emotions, safe from our selfish needs, our fears, our passions. (She pauses, stands

in the centre of the stage, as a spotlight
*descends. Enter **Cillian** from stage right. He*
stops next to her, reaches for her jumper,
pulling it over her head) Cillian asked me
to prove that I loved him. When I told him
I wasn't ready, he said that meant I didn't
love him. *(**Cillian** unbuttons **Eabha's** shirt and*
slips it off her body) So, I stand here for a
long time, convincing myself that it's no big
deal. That I *am* ready to give myself to him,
that I love him. *(**Cillian** unzips her skirt*
and it falls to her ankles) Cillian says this
is love, but what does love mean to Cillian?
(Pause) What does love mean to me? I wasn't
ready. He knew that: he knew I wasn't ready.
But he took what he wanted anyway.

* * *

Austin arrived at the house, his footsteps heavy on the stairs, and disappeared quickly into the attic, which he didn't leave again for several hours. The house was empty of people now, but they had left a mess in their wake, evidence of their presence everywhere, invaders from an outside world.

Dara and Oisín picked their way to the kitchen, stepping around dirty glasses and forgotten shoes, a bejewelled bra, an elaborate headdress of white feathers. They sat down at the kitchen island to wait until Eabha and Austin emerged from the attic again, both of them tired, insides gripped with a dull ache of fear. Dara laid her head on the marble in front of her, using her arm as a pillow, one eye closed, the other watching Oisín sleepily. He seemed deeply shaken by the night's events. His arms were folded in front of his chest, his chain in his mouth, his hand running compulsively through his hair. Back and forth, back and forth.

'I don't know why this happened,' he said, looking down at Dara through his long lashes. Dara wondered how many women had fallen for that particular angle of Oisín's head, for the vulnerability in his eyes. 'I met Eabha on the attic stairs and she looked so . . . so *sad*. Lonely, despite all the people at her party, in her home.'

'I think she throws these parties to feel more visible . . . I'm not sure they work,' Dara replied, her mouth half-pressed against her arm still, too tired to raise her head.

'She was talking to me about her parents . . .' Oisín added. 'I think that's what started it.'

Wearily, Dara rubbed her eyes and stood up with some reluctance. The kitchen was a state, the smell of various alcohol spillages rising through her nose and into her head. 'She's been melancholic lately. She talks a lot about the past. I'm not sure she spends much time in the present anymore.' She reached for the dirty glasses from the table, slotting them into the dishwasher. Oisín helped, seemingly glad to have something to do.

'I just wanted to cheer her up a little, so she wouldn't be so alone, but then she was . . . she was screaming at me . . .' His words trailed away.

Stacking some empty bottles next to the back door, Dara shrugged. 'She has so much going on with the play. I'm sure all of that was on her mind, Oisín. Whatever happened, it probably wasn't anything you did.'

Oisín said nothing, wrapping his arms tighter around his body. In the silence, they could hear Austin's heavy step on the stairs again.

As soon as he entered the room, Oisín's face lit up with a bewildered anxiety. 'How is Eabha? Is she OK?'

Austin closed the door quietly behind him. He cracked a window open, the fresh air pouring in to sit on top of the staleness, doing little to make any of them feel better. First light was breaking at the edge of the sky. *Banú an lae*, her mother called it: the whitening of the day.

'She'll be all right. She's sleeping now.'

'Did I do something wrong?' Oisín asked.

'No,' Austin said, his expression relaxing. 'She's sorry you saw all of that. She's embarrassed . . . she didn't mean to scare you.'

'But . . . *what* happened? We were fine one moment and the next, she was, like, having a fit or something?'

Austin walked to one of the cabinets and took a glass from the shelf, holding it under the tap. He filled it halfway and then took two large gulps in close succession. 'It was a panic attack . . . they happen to her sometimes. I don't want to speak for her, but you . . . you triggered a painful memory.'

'I . . . But how . . . how did I do that?!'

'You'd have to ask her yourself. I don't really know.'

Dara rubbed her temples, a pain radiating outwards through her skin to her fingertips. Questions were coming to her lips so quickly that she had to slow them and consider them in case she blurted them out in one go. 'Does this happen a lot? . . . With Eabha, I mean.'

'No, not exactly. Not usually like this.' Austin was holding the glass very steady in his hand. It seemed unnatural to Dara, as if he were using it as a prop. This was something Dara had noticed before, the way Austin would curate his movements, as if he were an alien creature trying to approximate the actions of a person.

'What is it usually like? When this happens?' she said.

Austin took a sip of his water. 'It's hard to describe, but it's like you're caught on a loop. There are certain things that happen in your life that you never forget.' He looked Oisín square in the eye. 'They repeat on you, like acid rising up your gullet.'

Oisín looked at him blankly. 'I don't understand what I did to make that happen.'

Austin laid the glass down on the countertop, where it made a clanging sound. 'It's not about you,' he said. 'The mind is its own place.'

Oisín ran his hand down his face. 'Should I . . . go up and talk to her?'

'Not right now,' Austin said. 'She needs to sleep.' He scratched at the bun at the back of his head, pulled too tight against his scalp. 'Have you ever experienced a trauma? Either of you?' Austin only asked questions when he already knew the answer.

'No . . .' Oisín said, his voice hesitant. Dara just shook her head.

'You're fine one moment and then, the next moment, you've lost all control. You're caught on a riptide. It's worse if you fight it, so you have to let it carry you. When you're ready, you swim parallel to shore. That's what Eabha will do, and then she'll be fine again.'

Oisín looked miserable. 'I didn't mean to do that . . . I didn't mean to trigger her.'

Austin's eyes were blank and unseeing as he spoke, shining marbles in his skull. 'There was one day at the Bodkin . . . she disappeared with Cillian for a few hours and when she came back, there were bruises all over her arms.'

Dara caught Oisín's eye, each of them recognising what was happening. A seal had broken, a vault door opening, just a crack, truth slipping through.

'Eabha tried to convince me it was a hockey injury, with this . . . this fear . . . in her eyes. But I already knew it was Cillian.

He would pull at her, always in this jokey way. It was like he wanted to keep her on edge, a little scared of him, so she would stay in line, so she wouldn't leave. I knew that – I had seen it with my own eyes. I'd seen him pelt her with stones when he took those mushrooms. That day was when it changed. Something had broken inside her.'

Dara's breath felt too loud. She wanted to hold it in her lungs in case she might break the spell and draw Austin away from this moment of candour.

'Eabha begged me not to confront him. She was terrified of what he would do, but her fear only convinced me that I *had* to do something. I had to protect her. I was so angry – I couldn't even hear her properly, the blood thundering in my ears.' The calm expression on his face was disconcerting. He spoke in an emotionless monotone. 'It wasn't just that he had hurt my sister . . . it was that Cillian *fucking* Butler felt entitled to touch her at all. I mean, for fuck sake, she was *sixteen* . . .' Austin's voice broke suddenly. He took a breath, collecting himself again. 'And I hadn't protected her. I wasn't there for her. If something had happened – if I had lost her – I don't know what I would have done. What was my purpose if not looking after her?'

Austin let out a loud exhalation of breath, running both hands over his eyes and through his long hair, which came free and hung around his face. He looked first at Dara, then Oisín. Neither of them moved, afraid to disturb this rare moment of revelation, afraid they might frighten the words back into his mouth.

'So, when I found Cillian, I threw a fist at his face, and then another, and another. I sent blood pouring from his lip and his eye. I only stopped when he was on the concrete. I only stopped when the teachers pulled me away. I'd do it again if I could . . . in a heartbeat, I'd do it again . . .' Austin tried to calm his breathing, but they could see that his mind was now a storm. 'He sent me a letter . . .'

Dara, immediately nervous, glanced at Oisín, then back to Austin. 'Who? Who sent you a letter?'

'Richard Butler,' Austin replied. 'Richard Butler sent me a letter.' His eyes were unfocused, looking out the window, away from them. 'He told me I should confess what I did. He said it would make me feel better, let me sleep better at night. And you know what? I'm tempted. If it would get them off my back, I'd confess to anything. It's been fifteen years.' When he turned towards them again, his face was anguished. 'Fifteen fucking years . . . and they still can't leave me be.' Dara could barely look at him. 'I can't . . . I really can't take it anymore.'

Abruptly, he turned from them and left the room, without another word.

In the stunned silence he left behind, Dara looked to Oisín. 'What should we do? Should we go after him?' she said, but the front door slammed shut before he could even reply. An engine sounded, confirming Austin's decisive exit.

'I think he's gone,' Oisín said. 'Thank Christ.'

This was the way Austin seemed to manage his anger, extricating himself as soon as it flared. Better, perhaps, than if he stayed around and showed them what a full outburst really looked like.

A shadow was hanging over Oisín now, all his usual energy gone from him. 'Are you all right?' Dara asked.

He shook his head. 'No, I need to . . . I need to get home. I need some space from all this.'

She envied him his ability to leave, watching him through the dining-room window as he climbed into a taxi and escaped the mess, whisked away down Leinster Road in a matter of minutes. She would have liked to walk out after him, leaving the door flapping on its hinges, leaving Eabha alone to deal with her own demons.

Instead, she made her way upstairs to bed, tiredness sitting on her like a weight on her chest, an iron ball at her ankle. Upstairs, she paused at Eabha's bedroom door and listened for a sound, but the room gave only silence. The floorboards of the old house creaked as she walked on to her bedroom, shutting the door behind her, climbing under the duvet, telling herself that everything was all right, even as she knew it was starting to come apart.

There were three weeks left.

Chapter Sixteen

Eabha didn't say much to Dara about what had happened with Oisín, except to confirm what Austin had described. She said it felt as if Oisín had pressed down on a circle of bruised skin. A sharp shock of pain, one memory triggering another, one thought linking inexorably to the next, taking her out of the moment and throwing her forcefully back to another life, another moment in time, one she had fought hard to forget. The trauma followed a familiar pattern, like a path beaten through brambles, carrying her towards memories dark and putrid.

Listening to her, Dara thought of Sam, what he had said about Richard Butler's theory of the night his son had died, his description of Cillian as the manipulated and Austin as the manipulator. Where was Eabha in that story?

Despite everyone's advice, Eabha was still refusing to talk to the media and the tabloids had taken it upon themselves to fill the gaps left by her silence. Two different tabloids had printed footage from the party online. The footage itself had been edited to hide people's identities, but the camera panned slowly over the champagne bottles, the art on the walls, the high ceilings and the chandeliers. They published the footage side by side with photos of Richard Butler and his supporters holding candles at Cillian's grave, portraying Eabha as decadent, uncaring and shameless in the face of Richard's grief. The two photographers who had been waiting to snap photos of guests coming and going through the front door had not managed to capture any well-known faces, which was the only comfort. Geoffrey Goode might have reconsidered his position if his photograph had found its way into the *Sun*.

Eabha's lawyer moved in fast, threatening an immediate injunction, and the photos were taken down quickly. But the damage was done. Screenshots were circulating on Richard Butler's *Justice for Cillian* social media pages, inflaming public opinion against the play again.

To Dara's surprise, it only served to push Eabha and Oisín closer. He began to spend more and more time around the house, staying late for dinner after rehearsals, finding jobs for himself here and there, and then, in time, taking his place at the breakfast table as a semi-permanent guest.

Observing them together, Dara couldn't shake the sense that they didn't quite fit. It seemed like a conscious decision Eabha was making to have Oisín occupy this place in her life, but Dara couldn't understand why.

The question still remained unanswered when, with sixteen days left to opening night, Oisín unexpectedly moved into the house too.

'I'm sure you won't mind another housemate, Dara, will you? It's just since he's spending so much time around here anyway, it just . . . makes sense,' Eabha said, her hand aloft, waving it breezily from the wrist. 'It'll be fun – the three of us together!'

The atmosphere felt different with Oisín around. The air felt thicker, its scent cloying. He was always watching Eabha, as if for signs of distress or flickering panic. It was uncomfortable to be around them, but Dara wasn't in a position to object – the topic of rent had still not been broached – so she stayed quiet, smiling pleasantly, and pretending that she didn't mind. Not one bit; not at all.

* * *

As soon as she could escape, Dara took a walk down to Rathmines village so she could complain over the phone to her sister instead.

'How has it been so far?' Rhona said. 'Living with her?'

'It's both exciting and completely mad. She listens to Wagner, eats boiled eggs like they're apples, and sings to her plants so they'll flower, but then there's this darkness too. She carries it around with her, like a vortex, sucking you in the closer you get.'

'And are you getting too close?'

'Maybe . . . I don't know.'

There was a silence. 'Oisín moving in seems very sudden, especially after what happened between them. Have they even talked about that properly?'

'I assume so? They must have . . . but it's almost like she's trying to prove that everything's fine. You know? Like, she's glossing over what happened to convince us that things are completely normal between them.'

'You can just say it, Dara . . . it's fucking weird.'

It brought a smile to Dara's face. 'Will you come visit?' she asked, suddenly missing her sister intensely, the normality she brought, the sense that Dara's feet were on solid ground.

'Into that madhouse? No thanks . . .'

'Please! I could use some space from it all.'

'Then come home? Come to Beara?'

She couldn't imagine returning to Beara in her current state of mind, feeling a mild nausea at the idea. It was too alien now, requiring too much contortion of self. She would have to shed

Eabha from herself completely, Gaffney family life not a way of being she could slip into so easily anymore.

'I can't – there's no time,' she said vaguely.

Rhona was silent again for a moment. 'Think about it, will you? Mam and Dad are dying to see you.'

'I know, but—' Dara sighed. A silence, lengthening. 'They keeping asking me about the play and . . . you know, all the *Justice for Cillian* stuff. It's stressing them out and I don't know what to do about it.' If the play *was* cancelled, at least her parents would feel some relief.

'I saw the photos . . . the ones from the party.'

'Yeah, they looked pretty bad.'

'Does it bother you? The coverage?' Rhona asked. 'It seems to be getting worse.'

'It bothers me when they drag me and Sam into articles about Cillian's death,' Dara said. 'It makes me feel like we're guilty by association, even though we have nothing to do with any of that.'

The vitriol was increasing since the footage from the party circulated. Dara had switched her social media accounts to private that morning to stop the strangers inundating her posts with comments.

'*Liar!*'

'*You're covering up a murder!*'

'*How do you sleep at night?*'

'*Enjoy jail, bitch.*'

They were only words, but they rattled her, the idea that strangers could hate her enough to direct such bile at her. She had, until now, felt somewhat immunised from Richard Butler's campaign – she wasn't its main target – but the controversy had taken a darker turn now, beyond anything she had expected.

'Do you think they'll cancel the play?' Rhona asked. 'After all this?'

Vanessa had seemed to think it could happen and it was starting to seem like more and more of a possibility.

Dara took a breath. 'Maybe – honestly, I don't know.'

'And would that be such a bad thing?'

Dara didn't answer. After everything she had been through, the prospect of the play cancelling felt like a catastrophe.

She let out a long sigh. 'Listen, I actually have to go, Rhona . . .'

'Oh – OK, so.'

'Sorry, I'll . . . I'll talk to you later. OK?'

She hung up abruptly, cutting Rhona off just as she was about to reply, but Dara didn't even notice. She was too wound up now, the clash of emotions producing ill-defined anger, which she chose to direct at Oisín: his presence in the house, his shoes next to the couch, his jacket hanging from the hatstand, his muffled voice sounding from Eabha's bedroom, his docile laugh. Always laughing.

She walked on, past a group of people shouting raucously as they made their way towards the pub nearby, their good spirits seeming to mock her gloom. She was walking with no destination in mind, until she stopped dead in front of the bus stop. Her heart was thudding against her ribcage, her own face staring back at her.

It was the first time she had seen the posters for the play: The Truth Will Out in large letters around her face.

It was the oddest experience to look at her own face and see Eabha in it. Dara as Eabha, so convincing that the line distinguishing one from the other was vanishing more by the day. She was the face of it now, the face they would hold responsible when the truth remained out of reach.

* * *

Rehearsals continued that afternoon in the attic and, though Oisín was physically present, his mind was completely absent. He was out of it, his eyes drawn constantly to the attic window, as if the sunlight glinting through the glass were calling out to him. Sam and Dara watched him silently, waiting for his thoughts to return to the script in his hand, but they never did.

'He's on something,' Sam whispered in Dara's ear.

'Probably those magic mushrooms,' she replied, glancing at Eabha, who was frowning down at her script.

'Oisín? Oisín, it's your line?' Eabha said, growing impatient. 'Honestly, I don't know where your head is today.'

He fumbled with his script, blinking his eyes several times as he searched for the right line on the paper in front of him. Dara pointed it out for him, watching his eyes struggling to focus on the page.

'Do you want some water?' she asked.

'No, I have it now,' he said, clearing his throat.

```
Cillian: I don't understand why you're doing
this — I really don't think you're being fair!
Eabha (wipes at her tears with an angry
hand): Fair? You don't stop when I tell you
you're hurting me. Do you think that's fair?
You don't listen. And that scares me. I don't
want to be around that. It's too much. I don't
have the energy for it, Cillian. I lost my
parents, and it still takes all my strength
to wake up every morning and get dressed and
go to class. I don't have the strength to
carry you with me through all of this. I just
... I just can't.
```

Cillian: I knew you were going to bring up your parents! The two of you think you're the only ones with a sad little story. You have no idea. You have no *fucking* idea!

Austin: There's no need for this—

Cillian *(bellowing)*: Shut the fuck up! Seriously, shut the fuck up! This is between me and her. *(He takes another angry drink from his bottle of vodka)* Why do you always get in the way, Austin? Everywhere we turn, there you are. Telling her I'm not good enough for her!

Eabha: You say you love me, Cillian, but you hurt me. Look at me! Look what you did. *(She rolls up her sleeve to show him the bruises on her arms, red welts on her skin.)* You did this to me!

Cillian: I didn't *mean* to ... I promise, I would never hurt you.

Eabha: How am I supposed to trust you? How can I trust a word you say when you keep doing this to me?

Cillian: Because you have to ... because I don't want to live without you in my life ... I won't, Eabha ... I can't.

'OK,' Eabha said, clapping her hands excitedly. 'Wow. That was ... I have chills. I mean, that's ... that's exactly the right energy, Oisín. You're just like him. The way you're holding yourself, the loose limbs, the slight slur of your words. You're him ... you're Cillian.'

'Really?' Oisín said, his face lit up with a bashful gratitude at her praise.

'Yes, really,' Eabha replied, smiling as he threw his arms around her, lifting her from her feet. 'OK, put me down now! That's enough.'

Watching them, Dara felt a dread creep over her. She turned to Sam, who couldn't hide the worry on his face. 'I guess Austin was right about the mushrooms,' she said, her voice low. 'Cillian has been resurrected.'

Sam nodded. 'That's what worries me.'

At the foot of the settee, Eabha's phone vibrated against the wooden floor. She reached down for it. Surprise lit her face briefly. 'It's Austin. I have to take this,' she said, hurrying out the door. 'You three read on. I'll catch up.'

Oisín was at the window again, watching the light dancing in front of his eyes as time slowed down around him.

'Will we read on ourselves and leave him to it?' Dara asked, nodding towards an oblivious Oisín.

Sam shook his head. 'This is ridiculous. We don't have time for this shit.' But he picked up his script anyway, skipping ahead through the pages. 'Will we do the scene just before they go to the attic?'

Dara nodded. 'Yes,' she said. 'The scene where it all starts to unravel.'

Sam flashed a dark look towards Oisín, standing at the attic window. 'Seems fitting.'

Eabha: I don't know what to do! What can I do, Austin? How do I stop him?

Austin: You said you didn't want my help — remember?

Eabha: I know, I ... I was wrong. I can't do this alone!

Austin: Where is he?

Eabha: I told him to meet me in the attic.
He's waiting for me there. I think he knows
why ... He knows I'm going to tell him it's
over. And I'm afraid, Austin. I'm afraid of
what he might do.

Austin: He's going to leave you alone, once
and for all — that's what he'll do.

Eabha: What does that mean— Wait, Austin.
What are you going to do to him? You're not
going to hurt him again?

Austin *(hesitates, looking back at his
sister):* I'm going to do what I have to. This
time, he'll listen. You're not going to face
him alone.

Eabha: Austin, I—

Austin turns away as ***Eabha's*** *voice catches in
her throat, the gratitude unspoken.*

Austin: Come on ... let's go meet Cillian.
We'll face him together. We'll put an end to
this.

Dara looked at Oisín, lowering her script. 'Sam? What's he
looking at? He's teetering at the window. Is he OK?'

Sam walked to the windowsill, a hand on Oisín's arm. 'Are
you all right?'

Oisín didn't reply, but Sam's eye caught on something moving
in the garden below.

'Oh, shit!' he said, jumping backwards.

'What is it?' Dara said, alarmed.

Sam's hand was on his chest. 'It's Austin. He's in the garden.'

A chill ran through Dara. She took three steps towards Sam,

leaning around him to see what he was looking at. Sure enough, Austin was standing at the bottom of the garden, next to the apple tree, muttering to himself, though they couldn't hear a word he said.

'What's he doing?!' Dara said. 'Why isn't he moving?'

'He's not really here,' Oisín said, suddenly breaking his silence. 'He's somewhere else.'

Down in the garden, they watched as Eabha appeared through the dining-room doors, taking slow, deliberate steps across the grass, her hands visible in front of her chest, as if to show him that she was no threat. Dara remembered something Eabha had said once about Cillian – that he was just like the wild goats he chased across the Burren – and she wondered, now, if Eabha had been talking about Cillian at all.

At the apple tree, Eabha reached a hand towards her brother. He flinched as she made contact, then whirled away, saying something they couldn't hear.

'Austin?' Eabha shouted, as he hurried away from her, her voice sounding dimly through the glass of the attic window. 'Austin?! Wait! Let me help you!'

He broke into a run, slipping around the side of the house and out through the open gate. In the back garden, they watched Eabha drop to her knees, her head buried on her lap, her body shaking with soundless, heaving sobs.

Chapter Seventeen

It was no surprise to Dara when Eabha announced the following morning that she was cancelling the day's rehearsals. The reason she gave was that a break would do them good, especially while the heatwave continued to bathe Dublin in sunshine. They would spend the day, instead, by the sea at Dollymount Strand. "We need to get out of the attic," Eabha said. "That's what's wrong."

'What about Austin?' Dara asked gently. Eabha hadn't yet mentioned his strange appearance in the garden yesterday. It was beginning to seem like maybe she never would.

Eabha's eyes were round and almost startled by Dara's question. 'He'll meet us there too,' she said, smiling tightly. 'He'll meet us at the beach. It's what he needs. A little sea air.'

Dara felt a frown stretch across her face, confusion descending, but she said nothing more about it. It seemed that Richard Butler's letter was the final straw, draining Austin of the last of his strength. And it seemed that Eabha had no idea what to do about it.

The days seemed to dwindle at an ever faster pace, as if they were a liquid leaking through her fingers. Fifteen days to opening night.

* * *

Eabha drove the cast from Leinster Road in her Ford Cortina, Nico playing on the old stereo as they drove. She sang along, extending one hand out the open window, the other on the steering wheel, while Oisín sat in the passenger street, his expression unreadable behind dark glasses. In the back, a picnic basket sat between Dara and Sam, sliding occasionally across the leather seats to knock against their legs. It contained some towels, a change of clothes for Eabha, a picnic of salads and sparkling pink lemonade.

Glancing across towards Sam, Dara watched the light shining in through the window, lighting up one side of his face, reaching her hand across the seats to hold his. Through the window behind him, Dublin Bay spread out like a silver puddle in the sunshine, the sea calm, a passenger ferry slicing through the water as it made its way to Dublin Port.

Eabha steered the car across the wooden bridge towards Dollymount Strand, sand dunes rising across the nature reserve, stretching towards the headland of Howth to Dara's left. To her right, the Poolbeg chimneys rose on the other side of the bay, red and white stripes glimmering in the sunlight, and behind them, the gentle profile of the Dublin Mountains cushioned the city below.

'Dara, grab the basket, will you?' Eabha said, switching the engine off. They had found a parking spot near the yellow bathing shelters, into which Eabha quickly disappeared. Dara reached for the basket and followed after her, leaving Oisín and Sam to shuffle off towards the men's shelter, a little further down. They had chosen a quiet morning for a dip, the sea almost empty of other swimmers.

Eabha pulled her dress over her head, her pale skin like a mirror held to the sunlight. Dara looked away, towards her feet, while Eabha unhooked her bra and set it down with her dress on top of the basket.

'I'm thinking about ending things with Oisín.'

Dara looked up again so quickly she nearly hurt her neck. 'What?! But he has literally just moved in . . . what happened?'

Eabha made a face. 'Nothing happened. Don't look at me like that – I know, it's going to seem fickle, isn't it?' She slid her underwear down her legs to her ankles, standing in front of Dara without a hint of embarrassment.

Dara stood up, slipping her shoes off, trying to avoid looking at Eabha. It wasn't her naked body that bothered her, it was the way she was weaponising it, demanding Dara's attention, demanding to be seen.

'Well, yes,' she said, shimmying out of her jeans awkwardly. She was already wearing a one-piece swimming suit under her clothes. 'Does he have any idea you're thinking like this?'

'He knows I'm not interested in anything serious, if that's what you mean.'

'But he's living with you!' she said. 'I just – I don't understand how you could change your mind so fast?' She slipped her T-shirt off and dumped it next to her jeans, spotting another swimmer in the water, their red cap bobbing on the surface of the waves.

'It's not that I've changed my mind,' Eabha replied, reaching for her bikini. 'I just don't think we're on the same page . . . I told him I don't have time for anything serious.'

There came the sound of splashing and, to their left, Oisín paddled into view, a big smile on his face now, his eyes still hidden behind sunglasses.

'Are you getting in?' he shouted, his voice carrying across the water.

Dara watched him, feeling suddenly deeply sorry for him. It was always going to end like this.

'I'm just changing!' Eabha called back to him, while Dara pulled her hair into a bun on her head.

Sam was swimming very purposefully, moving expertly through the water, dunking his head under occasionally, then lying spreadeagled on top of the waves.

'Just get in like that!' Oisín called.

'You'd like that, you perve,' Eabha replied, giggling in a way that Dara found embarrassing. Eabha needed Oisín to want her, even as she was in the process of rejecting him. It felt wrong, Dara's face hot and red as she rooted in the basket for the sun cream, squeezing too much onto her arm.

'Could you put some of that on my back?' Eabha asked, nodding at the great excess of sun cream coating Dara's hands like mayonnaise. She held her hair over her head expectantly and presented her back to Dara. Slowly and thoughtfully, Dara spread the cream over Eabha's skin. This close, she could see the soft hair of her neck and back, the raised freckle on her right shoulder, the red straplines from the bra she had worn that morning.

'When are you going to tell him?' Dara asked. 'He needs to know.'

'I don't know,' Eabha said, a half-laugh emerging through her nostrils. 'There's no rush. It's just that I can't give him what he wants right now.'

It sounded familiar, one of her lines sounding in Dara's ears.

Eabha: This isn't right, Cillian. It's too much. And I just can't do it. I just can't be what you want me to be. *(Her face is wet; she hasn't noticed she's crying)* I'm sorry ... I am so sorry.

Eabha was watching Oisín in the water. 'I'm not sure I should do it before the play. It's just, he's doing so well lately . . . I mean, he's really inhabiting the character. Would it be *really* bad to wait?'

Dara answered immediately. 'Yes. It would be a lie, Eabha.'

'I know, yes . . . But—'

'You need to tell him soon,' Dara said again, her hands moving further down Eabha's back, forming concentric shapes as they brushed over her skin.

Eabha's tone was a little frostier as she replied. 'Look, it's not like I haven't been telling him how I feel.' She picked up her sandals and placed them next to the basket. 'I've been telling him to slow down, to give me space . . . he just refuses to take it in. One minute he's storming away from me; the next he's in tears, asking me not to shut him out. It's exhausting.'

'I think he . . .' Dara felt she owed Oisín a little loyalty, but wasn't sure how she could best phrase matters. 'You know he *really* likes you?'

'He does,' Eabha said, the coldness still present in her voice and in the set of her jaw, 'and that's the trouble.' She fixed the straps of her bikini so they sat more comfortably against her skin. 'Will we get in the water then?'

Hand in hand, they made their way down the stone steps towards the sea, slippery towards the bottom. Eabha gripped Dara tighter as she stepped onto the seaweed-coated rocks, shrieking at the cold. Dara didn't shriek: she didn't cry out at all as the cold engulfed her body, staying beneath the water for as long as she could bear, letting the sound of the outside world recede as the icy water jolted her awake, a defibrillator to her chest.

When she rose to the surface again in search of air, there was someone standing on the path next to the bathing shelter, staring at her. With the water in her eyes, she couldn't see him clearly at first. Only gradually could she make out Austin.

Eabha and Oisín were giggling somewhere behind her, locked in each other's arms. It was difficult to watch the duplicity. Was it just attention Eabha craved? Didn't she get enough?

Sam was swimming back towards dry land. Dara did the same, her legs kicking, driving her into shallower water until she felt the steps beneath her feet once more. She was shaking violently with the cold as the water dwindled to her knees, then her ankles. Her wet hair, plastered against her skin, formed black curlicues on her shoulders.

'Where are you going?' Eabha called, but she didn't bother to reply.

With a towel wrapped around her shivering body, Dara joined Austin on the footpath, leaning against the metal railing which separated walkers from the seaweed-strewn rocks. Despite the heat, he was wearing a blue shirt and his usual corduroy trousers, tucked into thick leather boots.

'You don't want to get in?' she said as she reached him.

He didn't answer her, watching as Oisín splashed Eabha, who gave another cry and dunked him under the water. 'So that's still happening then?'

Dara wrapped her towel tighter, watching Eabha half-laughing and half-screaming in the water next to Oisín. 'For the moment.'

Austin gave a curt nod of his head. 'I wasn't sure which of you it would be this time.'

'Oisín won her over pretty early,' Dara replied, blinking some saltwater out of her eyes. 'It was Oliver last time?'

'It was.' He stuck his hands in his pockets. 'For a while.'

'Does it bother you?' Dara asked. A scurry of movement on the rocks near her feet drew her attention. Maybe a crab, maybe a rat.

Austin rubbed his nose and shifted his weight from one foot

to the other. 'She doesn't understand her effect on people. She draws people in, makes them feel special, then panics when they get too close.'

Austin's hands on the railing next to her were large, the veins protruding slightly from the skin. Her eyes travelled up to his face. He seemed better today, calmer.

'The day we went to the lake . . . the day they took the mushrooms, I couldn't stand watching them together, so I went to find kindling for the fire. When I got back, her face was dripping blood – dark red, matting in her hair, spilling down her cheek.' Dara closed her eyes and tried to imagine how that would have felt. 'Eabha was so out of it that she wasn't defending herself from Cillian. She was just standing there in shock, arms at her sides.' A trickle of cold water was dripping down Dara's face from her wet hair. She imagined the drops turning warm, viscous and red, the smell of blood coming to her nostrils. 'Cillian freaked when he saw me, ran into the water again, wet up to his knees, while I tried to stop the blood pouring out of my sister's head with my school jumper.' Austin gave a harsh, bitter laugh. 'He said it was a bad trip. It was the mushrooms. And I believed him at the time.'

Sam was approaching, a towel over his shoulders, water dripping down his legs and darkening the concrete path under his feet. On the rocks, a heron was standing very still, staring down at the waves like a Greek philosopher.

'Has she seen the *Independent* yet?' Austin asked as Sam reached them, his eyes still on his sister, who was climbing out of the water.

'I don't think so,' Dara said. She hadn't seen it either, feeling her mood immediately plummet; it was never good news.

Austin reached into his back pocket, retrieving a rolled-up newspaper. He held it up so they could see the large photo of

Vanessa Devin. She was demure in a long floral dress, a pensive expression on her face, gazing over her shoulder at the camera.

'Now we know why she showed up at the party,' Sam said, contempt in his voice. 'She was doing her research for a tell-all.'

Eabha, hand in hand with Oisín, had reached them, a bright yellow towel wrapped around her. Teeth chattering, she looked from one worried face to the other. 'What is it?'

Austin handed her the newspaper and her damp fingers closed around it, her expression switching immediately, anger engulfing her. She read silently, with Sam, Dara and Oisín craning to read over her shoulder.

The article was titled *'My Time with Eabha de Lacey'* and told, in extraordinary detail, the story of the first production, Vanessa's fraught relationship with Eabha and, worst of all, Austin's breakdown.

'I can't believe she has done this,' Dara said. She knew Vanessa had been angling at something that night at the party, trying to cause a rift between her and Eabha, to plant doubt in Dara's mind. She looked at Eabha, who had turned quite ghostly, and felt her stomach lurch inside her with guilt. The truth was, Vanessa had nearly succeeded – nearly. She thought back frantically to their conversation, hoping she hadn't said anything to Vanessa that could be used against Eabha.

'*Why* is she doing this?' Sam asked. 'What does Vanessa have to gain? Is it just revenge?'

'She needs the coverage,' Oisín spat, taking the newspaper from Eabha's hand. 'Life support for her career.'

Eabha hadn't spoken yet. She was looking at her brother, communicating something to him that Dara couldn't understand, a language she didn't speak.

But she could guess: Vanessa had a lot to say about Austin's breakdown.

Austin was never a stable character. You feel it the moment you meet him. He's a big guy and he has this intimidating presence. He makes you feel as if you're in danger. But on opening night, it was much worse. Austin was out of his mind. It was like his guilt was pushing him to the edge of his sanity. I probably shouldn't say, but it made me wonder if it was his guilty conscience.

'It's disgraceful!' Dara said. 'Is there anything you can do about this? Maybe your lawyer could—'

'What's the point?' Eabha said. 'It's done now. If I turn to lawyers, they'll just say I'm trying to shut down our critics again.'

'Vanessa has been talking to Richard,' Sam observed. 'I'd bet on it.'

Dara looked at him sharply. It seemed unwise that Sam, of all people, would mention conversations people might be having with Richard Butler, but nobody else seemed to notice.

'The thing is,' Eabha said slowly, 'I didn't even put most of Cillian's bad behaviour in the play. I was trying to spare his family the public humiliation of the truth. What a mistake that was.' She looked to Austin, who took a step towards her, his hand on her elbow, as if to keep her upright. 'He would talk about hurting himself if I ever left him. If I was late meeting him after class, he'd accuse me of cheating on him. He was completely erratic, dangerously so – and everyone knew that. That was why they shunned him. But you won't see any of that in the play. I couldn't do that to his family, to their memory of him.' Her eyes had glazed over, staring into a past only visible to her.

Dara took the newspaper from Oisín and, ignoring his protestations, threw it into the nearest bin. 'That's where it belongs,' she said forcefully. 'We can't let it affect us. That's what she wants.' Next to Oisín, Eabha gave a small, grateful smile.

Wrapping her towel more tightly around her, Dara turned

towards Austin, watching a shadow come sweeping over his face again. Nobody else seemed to notice, but Dara was watching, in slow motion, the change creeping over him, as if a weather front had broken suddenly, rain hammering down on him. And then, while she watched, Austin slipped away from them without a word, walking towards the rocks, his boots carrying him towards the water.

Transfixed, Dara stared after him, watching his arms stretch into the air around him, his lungs inflating like sacks of air, before he let a long and anguished scream erupt from his chest, filling the sea air around them, sending the birds into flight and Dara's heart into her mouth. Before their eyes, Austin was coming undone, the last threads about to snap. They were watching it happen in slow motion.

Dara reached for Sam's hand and held it tightly in her own, drops of seawater from her hair snaking icily down her spine. She shivered.

Two weeks left.

Chapter Eighteen

Their routine was changing, their world opening up from the house at Leinster Road to include the theatre on Cavendish Row. With two weeks left, the Gate Theatre had been made available to Eabha and the cast for technical rehearsals on-site. Work was nearly complete on both the set build and the lighting. The final touches were being made to the costumes. All eyes were now turning to the actors.

The night before their first technical rehearsal at the theatre, Dara found Oisín slumped over on the dining-room table in a puddle of drool. When she woke him up and suggested bed, he left the house instead, muttering something about meeting friends. That morning, hours before they were due at the Gate Theatre, Dara had found him curled up asleep on the steps outside. She'd helped him up to Eabha's bedroom, where he flopped across her bed, dead to the world, leaving Dara to stand over him wondering how such a mess could possibly pull it together for their first performance in just fourteen days.

Leaving Eabha to deal with Oisín, Dara decided to walk alone to the theatre. She needed the time to reclaim a small part of her mind from Eabha's colonising force and Oisín's chaotic energy. The theatre would be a welcome change from the stifling atmosphere at Leinster Road, from Eabha and Oisín with their exhausting bouts of overt adoration, quickly followed by a sudden cooling, or, worse, an outright fight.

'I'm sorry, Eabha,' Oisín would say later, in a fit of repentance, angling his face so that his eyes were full and round and boyish. 'I was upset. Forgive me.'

And Eabha would. Time and again. She still hadn't let him out of his misery, still determined to wait, for the sake of the play – or so she said – but Dara suspected that he suited Eabha better like this.

The bells were tolling the hour as Dara passed Christ Church Cathedral, the sound competing with the screeching seagulls circling high above the nearby river. On the corner of Parliament Street, she stopped for a coffee, pausing at the door of the café to fix the lid on her reusable cup. Her eyes squinted up towards the grey-pillared majesty of City Hall opposite, behind which the sun was shining, the rays pouring over the top of the pillars and down to the street below, sunlight falling like cascading water. Her shoulders were hovering halfway to her ears; she let go, letting her body relax, the beauty of the morning giving a brief sense of peace, a calm descending.

Crossing the Liffey, Dara paused on Grattan Bridge to take a photo of the sunlight dancing on the river, resting her coffee on the ornate lamp with its cast-iron seahorse standing next to her. The tide was full and the river was high, a briny smell wafting through the air. She sent the photo to Rhona: *Dublin misses you, sis xx*

It was at the top of Capel Street that Dara spotted the poster of herself, pasted on the bright blue scaffolding around a derelict site. They had sprung up around the city, her face pasted on walls and bus stops, on the side of buses and at train stations. But this one was different, stopping her dead in her tracks.

Across her face, in thick black marker, was the word '**Killers**'.

It was easier to dismiss the online abuse – screens creating both a distance and a sense of unreality – but the shock of this real-life statement sent her reeling. Some stranger, somewhere, thought this of her. They were so sure of it that they had taken a marker and written it across her face. Was it just one lone defacer, or was this evidence of the general public sentiment? Was she complicit, guilty, condemned?

Dara walked on down Parnell Street as quickly as she could, avoiding the eyes of passers-by – feeling in their empty gaze a great judgement – until, at last, she saw the stone facade of the Gate Theatre.

Rushing forward towards the entrance, she almost didn't see the photographer. He had been waiting for her, stepping immediately towards her when she came into view, his camera click-click-clicking millimetres from her face.

'Smile for me, Dara,' he shouted. 'Do you want to give a comment?'

'Leave me alone!'

She stumbled forward, head down, shoulders hunched, adrenaline coursing through her body now.

'Dara, did they do it?'

Her hand was in front of her face, trying to block his view.

'Are they guilty, Dara?'

She pushed the stage door open.

'Dara? Did they do it, Dara? Dara? Did they murder Cillian Butler?'

* * *

Sam was already standing on the stage with his script in his hand as Dara arrived, out of breath, her heart pounding still. 'There you are,' he said as she entered the wings, pulling her backpack off and dropping it at her feet.

It was supposed to be a moment of triumph – her first time standing on the stage at the Gate as a principal actor – but instead, she was shaking, disturbed, the photographer's voice still in her ear.

Seeing the look on her face, Sam stepped towards her, frowning. 'Dara, is everything OK? You're shaking.'

'Yeah,' she said, blinking several times, as if to force the fear out through her eyes. 'I'm fine. Just . . . there was a photographer outside . . . hassling me.'

'Shit – I should have warned you,' Sam said. 'He caught me outside too . . . I thought he had cleared off, but he must have come back.'

She pulled her hair free from her hairband so that it fell down her back like her character, trying to order her thoughts again, before her mind dragged her back to the photographer's barking voice, his rabid questions to which there seemed no answer, the mystery of Cillian's death.

'It's getting worse,' Dara said faintly. 'The attention . . . I saw a poster on my way here. Someone had written "killers" across my face.'

Sam pulled her into a hug. 'Dara, I . . . I'm sorry.'

She waited for him to say something else – something comforting, something to absolve her, maybe even some practical suggestion or solution, some way out of all this – but Sam had nothing. He held her in silence, until her breathing had calmed, until the trembling had left her body again.

'It's fine,' she said with effort. 'I'll be all right.'

She stepped away from him, wandering the stage, taking in the set that was nearly complete. The western turret of the Bodkin School had been recreated in the corner, a set of wooden steps leading up to it which were unseen from the audience's view. The attic window was lit from behind – the window through which

Oisín would fall at the end of the play – so that wherever you sat in the auditorium, the eye was drawn upwards to that fateful square of light.

A door slammed, Eabha and Oisín approaching the stage through the stalls. Dara could tell already that Eabha was unsettled; she could feel it in the deliberateness of her movements, the tightness with which she cleared her throat as she stepped onto the stage. She felt herself seize up too, as if Eabha were infecting her with contagious stress, bits of it leaking from her body, carried through the air of the auditorium, and in through Dara's lungs with each breath she took.

'Morning, everyone,' Eabha said curtly, resting her leather satchel on a chair and rooting through it for her notebook. She had arranged for a chair to be placed at the front of stage left so that she would be up there with them for rehearsals, watching every slight shift of emotion through their bodies.

Somehow Oisín seemed worse that morning. Even before he took to the stage as Cillian, there was a restlessness in him that day. He was vibrating with it – a need for attention, for love – and since Eabha was withholding from him, he turned his sights on Dara and Sam instead.

'So what's going on with you two?' he said, coming to stand between them, his hands on Dara's shoulders until she shrugged them off again. 'You're getting very cosy, aren't you?'

His eyes were hidden behind sunglasses, his hair unwashed, his shirt still dirty from the day before. Stale alcohol sat on his breath.

Irritated, Dara looked to Sam. 'I found him at the front door this morning.' She folded her arms. 'Where were you last night, Oisín?'

Oisín grinned at her, letting his sunglasses slide down his

nose and gazing at her over the top of the round frames. 'Why? Do you miss me when I'm gone?'

'Oh yeah,' Dara said. 'It tears me up inside.'

'Hear that, Sam? Does that make you jealous?'

'Give over, will you?' Sam said. 'We're here to work – just focus on that for once!'

'Someone's tetchy,' Oisín replied, a look of pure innocence on his face. 'More and more like Austin every day, aren't you?' He glanced at Dara. 'Only, that would mean you fancy your sister.'

'That's enough, Oisín,' Eabha said, scribbling in her note-book, the nib of her fountain pen scratching at the page. She must have been feeling the pressure more than anyone, weeks of endless work taking their toll on her.

Oisín ignored her. 'But then everyone fancies Eabha – right, Dara?'

Dara looked down at her feet, the white fabric of her Con-verse stained by the grass of Eabha's lawn. Eabha's tactic was to ignore him; Dara would try to do the same and bite her tongue.

'If this is a Cillian impression, you're overdoing it now,' Sam said, watching Oisín shuffling around the stage, as if looking for something he could kick, something he could break. 'It's getting a bit hammy.'

Oisín laughed, something contemptuous in the sound. 'There it is . . . that Austin energy. You going to lose your cool with me, Sam? You want to take a swing at my face?'

Dara reached for Sam's arm, her fingers pressing into the muscle that had already clenched. 'Don't react,' she mumbled. 'That's what he wants.'

A sigh came from stage left and Eabha pointedly shut her notebook, reaching into the satchel at her feet for her lipstick and slowly applying it with the help of a compact mirror. They waited, the stage falling silent, but for the sound of Oisín's directionless pacing.

'All right,' Eabha said, her lips now red. 'Will we begin the rehearsal?' Her eyes flicked to Oisín. 'And you? Are you ready to join us?'

Dara reached for her script again, watching Oisín from the corner of her eye as he poked about the set.

'Ready and waiting,' he replied, taking a seat on the wooden steps leading up to the attic.

'Do you think we could talk about the ending today?' Sam said, rubbing his eyes with a knuckle. 'I mean, are you happy with it, Eabha?'

A familiar edge came to her features. She moved her satchel off the chair and sat down, setting her feet apart on the floor as if to brace for impact. 'Why . . . what's your problem with the ending, Sam?'

Sam looked briefly to Dara, but she was watching the stage lights dancing with the moonstone gems hanging from Eabha's ears. He took a couple of steps towards Eabha. 'I just . . . I don't know, Eabha, the ending just isn't working for me.'

'How is that, Sam?' Her head was tilted at a curious angle, her expression very serious, but the strength of her hostility had not yet sunk in, so Sam pressed on.

'It's just . . . I don't understand the bit where . . . Well, why do you turn the audience's attention away from the window in the moment of Cillian's death? Why give the spotlight to Dara – to yourself, I suppose – when you could show us what actually happened?' He was waving his script now. 'Wouldn't that be better for Austin? If Austin didn't do it, why not just *show* us that?'

Eabha's eyes narrowed on his face while she allowed a silence to develop, his words echoing in the space between them. He fidgeted, waiting for a response which seemed like it might not come.

On her feet again, she turned away, towards Oisín, towards the attic window at the back of the stage.

'Can't you see . . .' She paused. 'Can't you see that it doesn't matter? What Austin did or didn't do doesn't matter. The end result is the same whatever happens with Austin – Cillian dies. Nothing changes that.'

'But it does,' Sam persisted. 'It changes the nature of his death.'

'It changes *nothing*. The play is about so much more than the moment of Cillian's death. It's about who he was before he died and all the many things that led him to be in that attic, standing in front of that window. No *one* thing caused Cillian to fall out that window. Can't you see? He was in the attic that night because he wanted to see me. He wanted to see me because I couldn't say no to him. I couldn't say no and he took advantage of that. Austin was there because I asked him to come with me. Can't you see? Can't you see that the moment of his death is *nothing* without the story of what brought us all to be there?'

'It all matters,' Sam said, a stubborn set to his jaw. 'But the way Cillian dies also matters.'

Eabha threw her hands in the air. 'Then you don't understand . . .'

Dara took a deep breath. The auditorium was large and empty but somehow the theatre felt crowded, as if unseen spectators were already watching from the seats.

'I disagree,' Sam replied, his voice sharp. 'Think of it from Austin's perspective—'

'It's not about whether you agree! I don't *care* if you agree,' Eabha said, snapping suddenly. A ripple of fright spread from Dara to Oisín and then Sam. 'You just have to do what I'm paying you for and read my fucking script!' Her face had turned first pale, now red, and she leaned on the back of the seat in front of her, as if to recover from the outburst, the strength of which seemed to surprise her as much as the cast. 'This isn't a democratic process, Sam. We're not writing this story together. It's *my* story. My name on the posters! My name on the fucking awards!'

Standing on the stage, a vertiginous feeling was spreading over Dara, the ground undulating under her. Sam looked bewildered, the weight of Eabha's anger not justified by his opinions on the ending, and not caused by it either.

Dara looked down at her script, the scene in question looking back at her.

> *Darkness falls,* **Eabha** *walks to the centre of the stage, a single white light shining down on her. Behind her in the attic,* **Austin** *and* **Cillian** *are entangled, moving in slow motion towards the window, shrouded in darkness.*

'The writing is the writing,' Eabha said, sitting down again on the chair, one leg crossing over the other. 'Decisions on direction are mine to make. And as for Austin's perspective . . . I can *assure* you, Sam, I know my brother better than you. I know what he needs.' This thought seemed to spur her further into anger, the power of it convulsing her features. 'You've no right to assume anything about me, OK? You've no *business* involving yourself in that. You just play the part, Sam. You just read the fucking lines.'

Dara watched Sam's expression, hoping he would drop it now, allowing Eabha to pull back from the brink of her anger with some dignity intact. Sam seemed to be contemplating his next words, hesitating. She shut her eyes and wished for peace.

'The thing is, Eabha—' When he spoke, his voice was very calm. 'At least I'm thinking about what happened to Cillian that night. You don't seem to care about it at all.'

Dara's breath was caught in her lungs, as if the air were frozen in place, as if it might shatter at any moment.

'Oh really? Is that why you spoke to Richard Butler behind my back?' Eabha said quietly.

Surprise crossed Sam's face before his eyes flashed to Dara, an accusation in them, burning through her. She took an unconscious step backwards.

'Yes,' Eabha said, 'I know all about that – and it wasn't Dara who told me, so stop looking at her like that.' Dara, whose heart had juddered inside her at the sudden look of betrayal on Sam's face, felt a rush of relief to be summarily cleared of suspicion. 'Miriam told me. She was delighted to share your little secret with me. She found out from Richard himself. Apparently, he's been ringing around, looking for weak links in the people close to me. It turns out . . . that's you, Sam.'

Sam rubbed at his face, the fire immediately gone from his voice, just as a flush of heat rose in his cheeks. 'He just rang me, Eabha. I talked to him . . . please don't make a big thing about this.'

'It's up to you whether this becomes a big thing. But ask yourself – how can I trust your opinion on my ending when you're talking behind my back to the man trying to put me and my brother in jail? How does that make sense for me?'

'It wasn't like that,' Sam said, unnerved. Dara could feel his panic now. Though his pride wouldn't let him admit it, he needed this role as much as she did. And even as a part of her wanted to reach out and place a supportive hand on his shoulder, another part could taste the betrayal Eabha felt, burning her tongue.

'It wasn't like that?' Eabha repeated slowly, the anger straining to escape her body. Dara could see it crawling across her face, tightening the muscles around her eyes and mouth.

'No—'

'But, didn't Richard tell you that Cillian was an angel and Austin was the villain all along?'

'He told me how *he* sees those things,' Sam said, fidgeting with the fabric of his shirtsleeves, gathered up at his elbows. Oisín was shuffling about next to him, muttering under his breath, though nobody could catch what he was saying.

'And what about you, Sam?' Eabha asked. 'How do *you* see things?'

Sam rubbed the back of his curly head. 'I don't know, Eabha, because the lights go down and you hide the moment from us. You promise the truth, then you leave it to us to fill the blanks. You can't turn around and get upset when people come to conclusions that don't suit you.'

'He fell!' Eabha said, her voice rising to a shout. 'He fell through the window.' She pointed up at the set, her finger shaking. 'He threw a bottle at me, the shards spraying across the room, into my hair, into my scalp. They had to pull glass out of my head with tweezers, Sam! Did Richard Butler tell you that? Were those the actions of his poor little Cillian? Austin protected me! He only ever *protects* me! And he has paid with his life for it.' Dara felt each word strike her, as if there were a thousand shards of glass pressing into the back of her head. 'This play – that moment – is our chance to reclaim our lives and tell *our* story, but people like Richard Butler, Vanessa Devin, and *you*, Sam – you won't let us!'

Sam was very still, his eyes unblinking while he listened. 'If this was the grand plan for escaping the past, Eabha, it wasn't a very good one.' He didn't wait to hear her reply or to gauge her reaction, grabbing his bag from the floor as he jumped off the stage and exited to the empty lobby outside.

Dara's instinct was to follow, but Eabha called out firmly: 'Let him go! We don't need him.'

She stopped at once, rooted to the spot, torn between them. When she turned back towards the stage, Eabha was standing next to Oisín, her fingers gripping his shoulder. The gesture was possessive and, noticing Dara's eyes on her, Eabha let her hand drop to her side again, her expression changing quite suddenly from anger to concern. Oisín's face was blank behind the dark glasses.

'I'm sorry about all that with Sam.' She took a couple of steps away from Oisín, wrapping her arms protectively around her own body instead. The sudden change in Eabha, the immediate evaporation of her fury, left Dara reeling. 'Sam just has a way of getting under my skin . . . I shouldn't have . . . I'm just . . . I'm just so tired.'

Dara turned away. No wonder she was tired; she was carrying such latent rage in her body, hidden behind a veneer that seemed to crack more and more with each passing day.

'Sam was out of line with that Richard Butler shit,' Oisín said, the words coming automatically to his mouth. 'You were right to call him out, Eabha.'

Feeling herself bristle, Dara wondered when this hostility towards Sam had become so strong in Oisín. Was it reserved for Sam or did he feel the same way about her?

'I don't think he means to sound as . . . as . . . as confrontational as he does.' Dara felt the need to mount a defence, but with Eabha staring at her, it came out limp. Sam's scepticism was entrenched and consistent, though not well-defined. It tended to manifest itself in scattered, largely incoherent bursts of dissent.

'I don't mind his disrespect,' Eabha replied quietly. 'I mind his distrust and I mind that he's starting to believe Richard Butler instead of me.'

Her head fell into her hands, her voice catching at the end. Instinctively, Dara stepped forward to comfort her, but, before she could, Oisín had pulled Eabha towards him instead, whispering that it was all right, that he was there, that she was fine. Dara watched and felt a weight form in her stomach. How had it come to this? When had the dynamic between them become so toxic? And where did that leave her? Division was spreading, sides forming, and no time left for resolution.

Eabha's eyes were shut, her head resting against Oisín's shoulder, so that they didn't notice Dara slip away, didn't hear the door shut behind her, didn't sense her absence at all until it was complete.

* * *

On Cavendish Row, double-decker buses were rumbling past, cyclists sliding downhill in the direction of the river. At the traffic lights, pedestrians waited to cross the busy road and, though she searched their faces to find him, to spot the familiar warmth of his brown eyes, Sam was nowhere to be seen.

She was too late. He was long gone.

Dara was about to go back into the theatre when a sharp tug on the sleeve of her lilac cardigan sent her head whipping around. 'You're Dara Gaffney.'

Her heart was racing. 'You're Cillian's dad.'

Richard Butler was shorter than he looked in photographs, and older. His eyes were piercing blue, shot through with streaks of blood from vessels ruptured by age. They were eyes that knew the scratch of sleepless nights, the insatiable welling of tears. 'I've been trying to reach you, Dara.' There was a tremor in his hand. 'Did you get my letter?'

'No . . . no, I . . . I haven't seen any letter.'

Sam was right; Eabha must have intercepted it from the theatre.

Richard reached into the inside pocket of his coat. He couldn't have been as old as he seemed, but even from a cursory glance, it was clear he was in ill health. There was an infirmity to his movements, his body aged by the weight of tragedy.

'I thought that might be the case.' Richard drew out an envelope, handing it to her. 'Please read it.' His hand, clasped around hers, felt leathery. 'That's all I ask – just read it. Just hear what I have to say.'

She nodded her head, the lump in her throat preventing speech. His pain radiated from him; she could feel it seeping in through her porous skin.

He didn't wait for Dara to recover words, walking away there and then, leaving her alone on the steps of the theatre, his back stooped as he headed towards the nearby Garden of Remembrance, in which stood a monument to the children of Lir, another grieving father.

Watching Richard leave, Dara's breath poured from her mouth, her eye catching on the poster fixed to the wall beside her as she turned back towards the safety of the Gate. In large letters, a declaration to the world: '**THE TRUTH WILL OUT**'.

She looked down at the envelope in her hand. Just a few days ago, she had been so angry with Sam for talking to Richard Butler, but it felt different when confronted with the reality, outside the bounds of the house on Leinster Road, outside the boundaries of a script.

Dara sat down on the steps, her heart rate still elevated. Taking a moment to centre herself, she let her breath slow and her heart calm, then drew the letter out of its envelope. Richard had written it by hand, his cursive a little shaky. She read it slowly, so as not to miss a word.

The loss of Cillian destroyed me and my wife. Not only had our youngest son died, but we had no answers about how it could possibly have happened. A young, healthy, happy boy doesn't just die. Yet, at every turn, we were blocked from finding out what had really happened to him. Nobody would help. They told us Austin and Eabha de Lacey were minors and were protected by the law. That meant silence. It meant dead-end after dead-end. We accepted this at the time – what choice had we? – until Eabha de Lacey wrote a play about our son, about his death. Suddenly, here was the story of his last moments – supposedly the truth (ha!) – on a stage for all the world to see. We were expected to sit in the theatre like everyone else, waiting to see what she was going to say about him. She didn't talk to us about it. Neither did Austin. Not a word since Cillian's funeral from the two people who saw him last. How could I forgive that?

Dara felt as if there were a hand around her stomach, squeezing it to paste. She thought of the photo of Cillian that Richard always held in his interviews, the one all over Google Images. His lopsided grin, his fringe hanging down over his eyes, his teeth clamped in braces, a metal bar piercing his eyebrow. So much pain and suffering, all caused by that one split second in an attic, that momentary loss of control.

Since my wife died, I spend much of my time thinking of the past and of what happened to my son. I am asking for answers. I am asking for respect. Will you support my call for the play to be cancelled? Dara, will you join my campaign for an independent public inquiry so we can finally know the truth? Don't I deserve the truth? I do not blame you for what happened to Cillian, but I need you to do what is right now. Do the right thing, Dara.

The letter continued, just like Sam had described, telling a story of a boy who was nothing like the Cillian of the play, the character Eabha presented to the world. As she read, Dara felt suddenly dizzy again, as if the ground were giving way under her feet, as if she were floating free of her body, rising towards the clouds.

Looking from the letter to the footpath in front of her, she tried to steady herself, watching the ordinary march of life. Parents pushing babies in prams, the old woman wheeling a trolley bag full of groceries behind her, the man with his terrier on the way to the corner shop – it all felt unreal.

She blinked, trying to stitch herself back into the world, to draw a line between fact and fiction again. There was the possibility of escaping this, renouncing Eabha publicly, walking away, hand in hand with Sam, just as Richard said.

Shoving the letter into the back pocket of her jeans, she placed her hand on her chest, feeling within her ribcage the unmet urge to run away, to jump on the nearest bus and let it carry her somewhere else – anywhere but here.

Richard told a good story, but it had been filtered through the memory of a grieving father, polished to a shine over the course of a thousand hours spent thinking of Cillian's death. That was the trouble with memory. It changed constantly, an iridescent substance in sunlight: made, unmade and remade over the years. Within the confines of subjective experience, the past was a story told to make the present feel purposeful, the suffering worth it.

Dara watched the passers-by, the buses, the traffic rolling past, the pigeons cooing at her feet, the seagulls floating on the air currents overhead. It all felt so ordinary, but she was an aberration in the midst of it, made alien by her choices, by the play, by Eabha.

With a sigh, she looked at the poster again, her own sad eyes staring back at her. She imagined taking a marker from her pocket and scrawling a single word on her forehead.

KILLER.

Chapter Nineteen

After dinner the following evening, Eabha slipped out of the house to meet Sam at Portobello Bridge. They took a walk together to clear the air, strolling the canal bank in search of a pragmatic peace. Mutual understanding was too much to ask for, but so long as the play was going ahead, Sam would play the role of Austin, and that required them to stow differences and work together fruitfully. There were ten days left to opening night, which meant ten days of tolerating each other until the opening of the play created a momentum of its own to carry them through.

When Eabha and Sam returned to the house after their peace talks, they both seemed in better form, even managing to smile as they entered the living room. Eabha walked straight over to Oisín, who was sitting cross-legged at the record player, her hand ruffling his hair as if he were a house cat. He was playing Nina Simone, her voice sounding through the speaker, begging a lover not to leave her.

Ne me quitte pas, il fault oublier.

Sam filled the space on the couch next to Dara, his body easing into the cushions, the couch sinking to accommodate him.

'Hey,' she said quietly. 'I'm glad you're back.'

'Me too,' he replied, squeezing her knee.

'Everything OK now?'

Sam's eyes were watchful on Eabha at the other side of the room. 'About as good as it's going to get.' He moved to the window, pushed it open halfway, and sat down on the ledge to smoke a cigarette. Behind him, the evening sky was a wash of pale yellow.

'I've been thinking a lot about what you said, Sam.' Eabha wandered slowly through the room to join him at the window. 'I can't stop thinking about the ending.'

Dara, who had been feeling a niggling urge to yawn, stifled it again and sat up a little straighter to listen. On the rug next to the record player, Oisín was hugging his knees, watching Eabha ravenously.

Sam offered Eabha a cigarette, which she took, pulling her hair out of the way as he lit it for her. Her eyes were locked on his, her red lips puckered around the cigarette. Dara watched his reaction, curious to know if he might fall for this provocation, but his expression didn't change. She smiled to herself. The odds had been so firmly stacked against Sam – son of an immigrant kebab shop owner – that none of Eabha's tricks worked on him. He wouldn't easily cede the ground that had been so hard-won.

The music drifted past Dara, through the window, and out to the garden beyond, dispersing into the darkening sky.

Eabha inhaled some smoke, watching Sam thoughtfully as she did so. 'It keeps shifting in my mind . . . the memory. I can see it happening about a dozen different ways. Sometimes Cillian trips and falls. Sometimes he jumps. Sometimes . . .' She swallowed. 'Sometimes Austin pushes him. Sometimes I push him too.' Her face was angled away from them, eyes following the spiralling dance of smoke and air. 'I can see the different versions clear as day in my mind, as if they all happened. Weird, right?'

'Maybe they did happen . . . in different timelines, different worlds,' Sam said, his face obscured behind a cloud of smoke, before brown eyes peered through again.

Eabha pondered what he said for a while, her face heavy. 'Maybe . . . who really knows? The trouble is, I think maybe I've forgotten which world this is. I've forgotten which version happened here.' She gave a small laugh. 'Silly, isn't it?' Her fingers pulled at the skin of her arm, as if picking at a scab that wasn't there. 'I don't know if it's the passage of time or it's the way I tell it in the play – you know, the ambiguity. Maybe I've told that version of the story so often that I can't remember the truth of it anymore.'

'Maybe the truth is never clear,' Oisín muttered from the floor. 'Maybe time always makes things muddy.'

'I've been reading about the fallibility of memory,' Eabha continued. 'Decayed retention – that's what they call it. We don't remember the way we think we do, like a camera recording the events precisely as they happened. We lose bits and pieces over time, the details falling into a haze, and then when we call up the memory again, we reconstruct it. But it's never the same. And yet . . . and yet, it can feel so very real.'

Dara reached for her wine glass on the coffee table, taking a drink. 'If memories are a huge part of how we see ourselves but we forget them and then recreate them the wrong way, does that mean that our whole picture of ourselves is wrong?'

'Who are we except what we say we are,' Eabha replied with a muted laugh. 'There's a line Austin always quotes from one of his books on Eastern thought. Goes something like, "our life is shaped by our mind; we become what we think".' Eabha's eyes were glassy again. 'There's something to it, I think.'

She reached out the window and ran her cigarette along the brick of the exterior wall until the glow faded from red to grey, a small flurry of ash gathering on the window ledge beneath.

'That reminds me, I need to call him,' she said, driving her fingers into the corner of her eyes, where the tiredness gathered.

'Is he all right?' Sam asked, a softness creeping into his voice, to Dara's surprise. A tenderness, almost brotherly.

Eabha waved a hand in the air, the gesture a little helpless. 'Not really. Celia sent me a worrying text. Austin attacked a neighbour this morning. Gave the man quite a fright! He mistook him for a photographer – Austin's just *obsessed* with the idea they're following him. Celia managed to calm him down before anyone rang the police but . . . what if he does it again when we're not there to help him?' She wandered to the door. 'It was a mistake to make him part of this. I need to keep him from the play, from all of you. I hope you'll understand. It's . . . it's too much for him.' Her hand gripped the door, her knuckles white against the wood. 'This was how it happened before. He was fine . . . until he wasn't.' The door shut behind her, the sound of her footsteps on the stairs following.

Oisín shook his head, reaching for the bottle of whiskey on the table next to him. 'I can't keep up with her,' he said, helping himself to another generous serving. 'One minute she's talking about not really remembering if her brother fucking *murdered* someone, then she's suddenly all worried about him?! Doesn't she know we're up to our eyes in this with her? Doesn't she know we're fucked if she's lying?'

The anger in him surprised Dara, though she could understand it. She had been wondering when Oisín's tolerance for Eabha's lukewarm affection would run out and, with it, his patience for her obfuscation.

He took another gulp from his glass of whiskey, his anger making his leg twitch.

'She doesn't mean to question what happened in a literal

sense,' Dara said. 'I think she just likes to mess about with the idea of truth and fiction . . . the blending of fact and story.'

Oisín ran his hand through his hair, chewing his chain with his teeth. 'We become what we think . . . that's an interesting one. If I think I'm an innocent man, do I become innocent? If I think I'm Cillian, do I become Cillian?'

Sam finished his cigarette and closed the window carefully, coming to sit next to Dara again. 'There isn't a big a difference between madness and reality when it comes down to it. We just draw a line and try to stay on the right side of it.'

'Where does that leave Austin?' Oisín said.

'Teetering,' Dara replied.

'There's a clear line between a person being pushed out a window, falling through it, or jumping out of it,' Oisín muttered, picking at the frayed denim at the knee of his ripped jeans.

'You're determined to be literal about this,' Sam said, with good humour. Dara wondered when they had switched roles, when Sam had become Eabha's defender and Oisín her interrogator.

'You know Eabha's feelings about Cillian are complicated,' she said. 'I think she struggles with the idea that she could have prevented it – like, maybe if she hadn't brought Austin to the attic that night. On some level, Cillian will always be her first love – she'll always care – and maybe she feels guilty about what happened, even if she knows she shouldn't.'

'I doubt it,' Oisín replied, with a snort. 'Guilt isn't something she seems to feel. She told me once it's a superfluous emotion.'

'She didn't mean that,' Dara said. 'You take her too seriously.'

'And you don't take her seriously enough.'

There was a silence between them, broken only by Nina's voice from the record player. It made Dara think of another line from the play.

Cillian: I can't just stop loving you — I
can't control it! I'm sick with it. It's taken
over my mind. All I want is to be near you.
Every moment. Can't you see what you've done
to me? Look at me! You can't just send me
away and think that I'll stop caring ...
can't you see that I will always love you? No
matter what, no matter where you go. I can't
help myself, Eabha. Look what you've done to
me!

Oisín took another gulp of his drink, seeming to struggle with himself for a moment until he gave in and spoke his mind. His voice was a mumble, eyes on Dara. 'I feel like I'm competing with you for Eabha's attention.'

'What are you talking about?' Dara said, unnerved by the harsh expression on his face, by his unblinking stare.

'She talks about you all the time, always asking me how you were reacting to things she said at rehearsals, or how you're feeling about her. She doesn't care what I think.'

Dara felt the heat rise in her cheeks. 'Of course she cares what you think. Really, Oisín, I don't know what you're talking about.'

Briefly, he watched her, as if trying to decide something, before losing his patience and rising to his feet. 'I think you do.' He placed his empty glass down on the table. 'Look, I have to go meet some friends. If Eabha asks – which she won't – tell her I've gone out.'

He was out the front door before Dara could say anything further, slamming it behind him.

Sam looked to Dara, his face troubled. 'I don't know how you live here ... with the two of them, like this.'

'It's a little claustrophobic,' Dara conceded. She sat back on the couch and let Sam wrap an arm around her, resting her head against his chest, just beneath his chin.

'Promise me you'll look after yourself?' he said. 'I don't want to see you get sucked into all this.'

'I'll try my best.' She looked up at him again. 'I was afraid you were going to walk out on us, Sam.'

'Honestly, I thought about it for a while,' he replied, 'but it's too late for that – I might as well see it out. If this play is going to happen, it'll happen with me in it.' His breath was on her cheek, reaching down to kiss her. 'And how could I leave you on your own?'

His chest rose and fell beneath her cheek, his heart beating against her ear, and she didn't think of Richard Butler's letter, or the *Justice for Cillian* posts online, or the photographs of her in the newspaper, or her mother's worried texts, or Austin's spiralling paranoia, or Oisín's mounting jealousy.

She let her breath rise and fall with Sam's and tried to concentrate on the moment, on the brush of his fingers through her hair and the warmth of his lips against her lips, pushing the rest from her mind, focusing on the present, leaving the past and the future to be what they would be.

* * *

Dara didn't hear Oisín return to Leinster Road that night and he was missing from rehearsals the following morning. Eabha noted his absence briefly, but wanted to press on without him.

Eabha: Put down that bottle, Cillian. Please – just put it down! You're going to hurt someone.

Cillian ignores her, his anger turning on

Austin who stares, his eyes dead, his hands hanging by his sides, waiting.

Cillian: Are you jealous, Austin? Is that what it is? Do you want Eabha for yourself? Because that's fucked up.

Austin's eyes flash helplessly to Eabha. The idea of her walking away scares him, the idea that there's nothing really binding them anymore, now that their parents are dead, their family broken. He can't stand the idea of an empty world in which he is alone. But Eabha isn't looking at him; she is walking slowly towards Cillian.

Eabha: Cillian, stop! I'm begging you. It doesn't have to be like this.
Austin: Eabha, get away from him!

Eabha ignores Austin's warnings, reaching out to take the vodka bottle from Cillian's hand.

Eabha: You don't have to do this to yourself. Please ... stop this, please.

Eabha's hand is on Cillian's wrist briefly, before Cillian wrestles free from her, flinging the broken bottle at the wall behind her, against which it smashes, sending a wave of broken glass into the air. Eabha screams and, for a moment, they freeze where they're standing, Cillian looking down at Eabha, the expression on his face wretched.

* * *

Rehearsals ended early – they could only do so much without Oisín – which frustrated Dara hugely. They weren't ready to meet an audience, not ready for the eyes of the world to descend on them. How much worse it would be if the play were to flop – after all the fuss, all the abuse online. Time was ebbing away and Oisín was nowhere to be seen.

Sam caught Dara by the elbow as she left the dressing room, his voice low, his face close to hers. 'Are you all right heading home with Eabha? If you need space from the house, you can stay with me. You might have to stay on the couch . . . my mam is traditional.' He was sheepish, almost shy.

She rose onto the balls of her feet and reached up to kiss him. 'I'm grand, Sam. You don't need to worry.'

He wasn't convinced, only reluctantly letting her go so she could slip her arms through the sleeves of her denim jacket. 'I got a call from another reporter,' he said. 'They want to know how I feel about playing a killer. Just goading me into saying something quotable, you know?'

Impatience rippled across Dara's forehead. 'What did you say to them?'

'Nothing . . . like we agreed,' Sam replied, 'but there are more journalists interested now.' His hand was on her elbow again. 'They're going to figure out that Oisín is our weak point. The way he's behaving? He could turn on Eabha . . . on all of us. We need to get this under control again.'

Dara didn't want to meet his eye, letting hers drift around his face instead, to his thick eyebrows, to his hairline, where the curls met his sallow skin.

'All right,' she said, when his expression didn't soften. 'I'll talk to Eabha about it. Again.'

* * *

They ate together in the garden that evening, a salad Dara thew together from remnants in the fridge. She hadn't yet raised the topic of Oisín and, specifically, what Eabha intended to do about it.

A text had arrived from her mother, with another photo of her in the newspaper.

> Mam (16.12pm): You look tired? Are you sleeping??? Hope she isn't working you too hard. Mind yourself, love. Call us when you can! Mam x

Dara scanned the article accompanying the photograph, the headline of which seemed to blare out from the screen: *'Justice for Cillian' Campaign Plans Protest for Opening Night of Controversial Play*

'Let them protest,' Eabha said when Dara showed it to her. 'That's their right, same as it's our right to stage this play.'

They sat largely in silence, neither of them in the mood to talk and, by the time they had finished eating, Dara still hadn't asked about Oisín. She couldn't seem to find the words.

While Eabha disappeared inside to replenish their glasses of wine, Dara sat alone with the long shadows in the garden, watching the sinking light play with the clouds over Dublin, until the quiet was upended by the sound of the Tannhäuser Overture booming from the speakers in the living room. Eabha was dancing on the mustard velvet couch, her flowing silver kaftan draped around her small body, eyes shut tightly, waving her arms as if she were conducting an orchestra. Dara wandered inside, watching silently for a moment – not wanting to disturb her – her arm leaning against the door frame, until Eabha's eyes eventually opened, their blue-green colour piquant in the fading light.

'Come dance with me, Dara,' she said, climbing off the couch. Her feet were bare on the circular rug. She held her arms out and Dara filled them, dancing with her, a lilting waltz.

It made Dara feel oddly sad, as if she were carrying Eabha's melancholy for her, but she still felt an urge to preserve the moment, to pin it, like a butterfly, to a board. The transitory nature of their intimacy felt increasingly stark. It wasn't going to last forever: an end was coming.

'My father used to play this song in the car for me and Austin,' Eabha was saying, her voice a little sleepy. 'He would make us wave our arms in the back seat, like conductors. I almost expect you to remember it. Sometimes I forget you haven't always been around.' Her eyes opened, a small smile crossing her lips. 'Isn't that strange?'

'Sometimes I forget too.' It was true; Eabha had invaded Dara's life so thoroughly that it felt as if she had always been there, lurking in the background somewhere.

'I wish you could have met Cillian,' Eabha said. 'I wish you could have known him.'

Dara stopped dancing, feeling the hum of Eabha's anxiety vibrating against her skin. Mention of Cillian made her think of Oisín. 'Any word yet?'

'From Oisín?' Eabha shut her eyes, as if in frustration. 'No – but he'll be back.'

Dara held her right hand in her left, twisting her fingers. This was not a conversation she wanted to have. 'Eabha . . . you need to put an end to this. Once and for all. You need to talk to him.'

Eabha's eyes were searching Dara's, the blue and green colour mingling. 'Where is this coming from, Dara?'

She pushed her hair back off her face. 'It's just – Sam and I were talking and . . . honestly, we're worried. Oisín has been a complete mess the last week and we're nowhere near ready . . . we can't fail!'

Eabha was breathing hard, doubt seeming to quiver in her lip, and it felt as if Dara might have finally managed to open the shell of her mind – just a little, just a hairline fracture through her defences.

But just as the first crack appeared, Eabha pulled away again.

She leaped onto the couch as the music reached a crescendo, sweeping her hands around her, one final rousing musical surge. 'I don't want to talk about this, Dara,' she said, shouting above the music. 'I just want to dance.' Her arms swept around her, light catching on the silver of her kaftan.

'Eabha, come on . . . talk to me? You can't keep the world out forever. Eventually, you have to talk.'

Eabha's eyes were shut, her attention turned inward, and nothing Dara could say would bring her back to the present, back to reality. Always dancing with the truth, always trying to spin away from it.

'Dance with me, Dara!' Eabha said again. 'Forget the play!' Her breath was rising and falling quickly as she spoke. 'Forget everything else and just dance with me!' She stopped suddenly, before Dara could reply, the smile falling quickly from her face to the floor at her feet. 'Oisín,' she said, stepping a little awkwardly off the couch and onto the ground once more, all the effervescence now gone from her body.

He was standing at the door watching them together, his expression dazed, his lips curled into a nasty smile.

'Where have you been?' Eabha said, walking towards him as Dara switched the music off. The silence felt abrupt and totalising.

For a moment it seemed that Oisín would collapse into her arms as usual, accepting what little affection Eabha cared to give him, but before she reached him, he turned away, walking quickly out the door without another word.

'What's wrong with him now?' Dara asked. He was at the front door already. They could hear the hinges squeak, a flurry of wind entering the hallway, knocking over a photo frame on the glass sideboard.

'Isn't it obvious?' Eabha said, hurrying towards the door after him. 'He's jealous and angry and trying to hurt me. This is what they always do. They punish me when I don't give them what they want.'

'And what do they want?'

'Attention, control, power. Always power.'

Dara thought about Oisín, about what he wanted. None of those words seemed to apply to him. She thought next of Cillian.

Cillian: I loved you! I really did.

From the hallway, Eabha's voice sounded. 'It's always the same.' She paused. 'These boys are always the same.'

* * *

When Eabha returned to the house much later, Dara was waiting for her, sitting on the bottom step of the stairs. 'Did you do it? Did you talk to Oisín?'

'Yes – are you satisfied?!' Her expression was grave, tiredness in the cracks and pores of her face. 'It's over. I told him we're done.'

'How did he take it?'

'How do you think? He's not coming back here tonight. Honestly, I don't know when we'll see him again. I knew it was a mistake to do this now. I *knew* it.' She didn't wait for a reply, pushing past Dara as she hurried up the stairs, locking the door of her bedroom behind her.

Dara reached for her phone to send Sam the news.

Dara Gaffney (23:03pm): Eabha and Oisín are finally over. O just stormed out and I don't think he's coming back this time.

From Eabha's bedroom, Wagner's prelude to *Lohengrin* sounded. Dara shut her eyes for a moment and listened, until a text from Sam vibrated in her hand.

Sam Demir (23:07pm): I can't say I'm surprised. But if he doesn't show up, we're done.

It would be the perfect way to hurt Eabha. To destroy the play, now as the end approached.

Dara Gaffney (23:13pm): He'll show up. I know he will.

Sam Demir (23:14pm): No, I'm serious Dara. I think we're really in trouble.

Dara Gaffney (23:17pm): I'm not listening to you!!!

Sam Demir (23:18pm): Dara – seriously! You need to prepare for this. The play is dead.

Chapter Twenty

Of all the different challenges the production had faced, Oisín's absence was the most dangerous. When they tried to contact him, he would only answer to confirm that he was fine and to tell them to leave him alone.

If he was trying to punish Eabha for rejecting him, it was working. She wasn't sleeping: Dara could hear her footsteps on the floorboards at night, creeping downstairs, and sometimes to the garden, where she stood in the middle of the lawn, staring up at the stars, as if waiting for them to speak to her. From her bedroom window, Dara thought she heard, on occasion, Eabha whispering into the night air and wondered which of her many ghosts were listening and which answered her, stepping out from the dark of the shrubbery, goat skull in hand.

* * *

They tried their best to hide Oisín's absence from the Gate's production team for fear of triggering a panic. Geoffrey Goode had taken to emerging from his office at various times during the day, hovering at the back of the set while they worked, or standing with the sound technicians, keeping a watchful eye on progress.

'He's a little jittery,' Eabha explained. 'All this talk of protestors outside the theatre has Geoffrey spooked. So long as ticket sales are healthy, we'll be OK. But Geoffrey has his limits. We need Oisín to show his face . . . wherever he is.'

When he returned abruptly after two days away, it was quite suddenly after breakfast. Dara was just out of the shower when she heard the front door slam shut, followed by heavy steps on the stairs.

Pausing outside the bathroom, she clutched her towel to her chest as Oisín appeared, as if summoned by force of their wishing, at the top of the stairs.

'Where have you been?' Dara said, startled at the sight of him. His hair was unwashed, his T-shirt dirty, but his two-day absence was otherwise unevidenced.

'Ah, you know, here and there,' he said vaguely. 'Why . . .? Did you worry about me?'

Dara pushed her wet hair out of her eyes. 'You've missed so many rehearsals. Eabha is freaking out.'

'Good,' he said. 'Good to know she has human emotions.'

He was standing too close, his behaviour confusing her. There was some calculation occurring in his mind, some decision being made. She clutched her towel a little tighter, aware there was only a thin layer of cotton shielding her from him.

'What about you, Dara? Were you worried about me too?'

She squirmed slightly, trying to take a step backward, to create some additional space between them. His pupils were dilated; she wondered what he had been taking.

'Where have you been, Oisín?' she said again, ignoring his question and the creeping sensation it sent across her skin. Why was he making her so nervous?

'That's a secret,' Oisín replied before, to her surprise, leaning in towards her face and catching a handful of her wet hair in his fist as he slowly, firmly kissed her cheek. It wasn't an affectionate peck – there was something aggressive about it, the gesture leaving her frozen at the doorway while Oisín made his way to Eabha's bedroom. The door slammed shut behind him.

Rattled, Dara hurried into her bedroom and turned the key in the door, before pressing her ear against the wall to listen to their muffled voices in the room next door. It was a shock to think it, but she wasn't entirely sure that Eabha was safe on her own with Oisín, not in his current state. Her fingers traced the skin of her cheek where he had kissed her, the thought of it sending a bolt of anger through her.

Through the wall, Eabha's voice sounded strained, urgency in it, while Oisín either didn't reply at all or said something impatient, provoking another weary response from Eabha. Dara couldn't make out the words, but she could hear the sound of drawers and cupboards opening and shutting. Oisín must have been gathering his belongings, preparing for an exit.

She almost envied him his new-found independence from Eabha, but something about it felt wrong. It wasn't so much a return to self as a doubling down, a strategy. To what end, Dara wasn't sure. But something had come loose in Oisín. He was floundering and he seemed determined to drag them down with him.

* * *

They left the house together, a deeply uneasy trio, cycling towards the theatre for the day's rehearsal. Oisín sang loudly to himself as he led the convoy of cyclists, seemingly unaware of the double-decker bus to his right, or the taxi that almost pulled out in front of him at the junction of George's Street, or the pedestrian he nearly flattened as he sailed merrily through College Green.

'He's out of it,' Dara said to Eabha, shouting over the noise of traffic as Oisín cycled on through the red traffic light next to the old parliament building on Westmoreland Street.

While they waited at the lights, Eabha turned back towards Dara. 'I know . . . he was incoherent at the house,' she said. 'I don't know how we're going to get through the day with him like this.'

Dara wondered if he was still taking mushrooms. He must have got his hands on more. 'Better hope Geoffrey Goode doesn't drop in on us today.'

'Stop – I can't deal with that right now,' Eabha said. 'I've spent my life dancing around one male ego after another. Someday soon, it'll be the end of me.'

Next to them, the lights turned from red to green, the line of traffic to their right roaring into life. They pushed off from the kerb, pressing hard on the pedals, following the road down which Oisín had long since disappeared.

As they approached the theatre, down the wide boulevard of O'Connell Street, a nervousness was creeping over Dara. There was a small band of people congregating on the footpath at the statue of Charles Stewart Parnell, carrying a large banner. She squinted – trying to read the text from a distance – feeling suddenly nauseous as the words became clear: *Justice 4 Cillian – Stop the Lies*.

It was just as the newspapers had predicted, a handful of protestors gathering outside the theatre. They were a ragtag crowd, some carrying tricolour flags and some carrying posters scrawled with seemingly unconnected messages about other popular conspiracy theories: something about pylons and the fluoridation of drinking water.

'Take a left,' Eabha called over her shoulder to Dara. 'We'll go in the side door – and keep your head down!'

Dara's hands were beginning to shake as she followed Eabha

across the road and in through the gates of the small car park, reserved for staff of the neighbouring maternity hospital.

They had almost made it to the stage door unobserved before a woman spotted Eabha, shrieking suddenly: 'It's her! It's Eabha de Lacey! Shame! *Shame* on you! You're a liar! A killer!'

They dismounted swiftly, wheeling their bikes towards the theatre, while the shouts rose behind them. The stage door swung open as they reached it. Sam, who had been keeping watch for them, held it while they hurried inside.

The door slammed shut, the cries and shouts of protestors replaced by the sound of their own heavy breathing.

Dara looked at Eabha. She seemed unnaturally calm, as if the pressure rising around them were nothing out of the ordinary, as if everything wasn't spiralling out of their control.

'I'll talk to Geoffrey about this,' she said, a band of angry protestors reduced to another item on her to-do list. 'We need to get a cordon set up.' She left her bike propped against the wall and disappeared upstairs to the director's office.

Sam turned to Dara, her face very pale. 'Are you all right?'

She nodded, leaning into his chest. 'Where's Oisín? Did he get here OK?'

'Yes, he's changing into his costume,' Sam replied, his fingers running through her hair. 'He seems a little . . . off.'

'He took something,' Dara said, walking in the direction of the dressing room, which had been set up for their use. 'I don't know what, but it's probably more of those mushrooms Austin gave him.'

Sam followed her, a long groan sounding from his throat. 'It never ends, does it?'

Dara didn't answer, pushing the door open to find Oisín at his dressing table, trying and failing to knot his tie, the Bodkin crest beneath his thumb.

Oisín laughed when he saw Dara. 'So, you made it through that crowd of pricks outside, did you?'

'Just about.' She watched him struggle with control of his fingers, taking the tie from his hands and knotting it herself. 'Are you going to be able for this rehearsal, Oisín? You've buttoned your shirt wrong.'

He looked down, laughing again, a helpless, almost childish, look on his face. 'Yes,' he insisted. 'I'm fine.'

'What did you take, Oisín?' Sam asked, impatient with him. He was standing with his back to the door, in case anyone tried to come into the room and disturb his interrogation.

Oisín's finger tapped his nose. 'Can't say. It's a secret.'

Dara finished the tie, fingers moving down to fix his buttons for him, his eyes vacant as he watched her. 'Why did you do that?' she muttered. 'We're days away from opening to an audience, Oisín. We're nowhere near ready!'

'Drink some water at least,' Sam said, handing him a bottle.

Oisín took it, spilling more water onto this chest than into his mouth. When he had swallowed a few mouthfuls, Sam sat down on one of the dressing tables, his feet on the chair in front of him, his arms folded across his chest. 'Where were you? Come on – we deserve to know.'

Dara took her costume from the rail next to the door, slipping behind the dressing screen to change.

'Not that it's any of your business,' Oisín said, 'but I went to see Austin.'

Her neck craning around the screen, Dara glanced at Sam, catching the lightning streak of anger cross his face. 'And did he give you more of those magic mushrooms?'

'He might have.'

'Fuck's sake, Oisín.'

'What?'

'You can't fucking disappear and then arrive back off your tits.'

'I can do what I want, Sam,' Oisín said, growing agitated. 'Stop fucking hassling me about it – all right?!'

'Sam—' Dara warned, voice sharp. 'Don't. He's not . . . This isn't the time.' She slipped into the grey skirt of the Bodkin School uniform, pulling the jumper over her head. 'Drink some more water, Oisín.'

He took another drink, not that it would do much good.

'Why did you go to see Austin?' Dara called from behind the screen, pulling one sock up to her knee, then another.

'I thought he might . . .' Oisín said, seeming to lose his train of thought briefly. He lay down on the carpeted floor, watching the lights overhead.

'Thought he might?' Dara prompted, a little impatient.

'I thought he might help me understand.'

'Understand what?' Dara said. 'Cillian?'

'Eabha.'

'And did he?' Sam asked, but Oisín didn't answer, his hair falling across his face, his eyes drooping, until finally they closed, his breathing slow and heavy.

Dara's head appeared around the screen again, her eyes meeting Sam's. 'He can't rehearse like this,' she said, eyes on Oisín, who had curled into a ball next to his dressing table, falling slowly into sleep.

Sam nodded. 'No . . . he needs to sleep it off.' He paused at the door, holding his hand out towards her. 'You coming? We better let Eabha know.'

* * *

It felt as if the outside world were a distant place, a muffled sound, only dimly heard. Under siege, they couldn't leave the theatre until some plan was in place to deal with the crowd outside.

Geoffrey and Eabha were still in his office, on the phone with the police trying to come to a solution. Dara knocked on the door, drawing Eabha out to the hallway, where she and Sam told her about Oisín's condition.

'We'll just delay the rehearsal,' Eabha said, in hushed tones. 'We'll blame the protestors . . . do you think he'll be awake by the afternoon?'

'I don't know,' Dara said. 'We'll have to wait and see.'

'This is . . . This can't go wrong,' Eabha said, her hand resting against the teal wall, on which hung portraits of various plays that had been staged at the Gate through the years. 'I can't keep this from Geoffrey much longer. He'll want a contingency plan if we can't get Oisín onto that stage.'

Dara's eyes wandered over the portraits on the wall behind Eabha's head, faces she recognised – Orson Welles, Michael Gambon – who began their careers on the same stage she would soon inhabit. Would she join them on this wall? Or would she soon join Austin and Eabha in ignominy?

'It'll be grand,' Sam said, interrupting her thoughts. 'Let me and Dara manage Oisín if you and Geoffrey can deal with the protestors.'

Dara frowned; Oisín would not easily be managed.

Eabha's shoulders sagged and she gave one brief nod. 'All right. I'm relying on you both.' Before disappearing into Geoffrey's office again, she glanced back at Dara, blue-green eyes sparkling with the threat of tears. 'We can't fail,' she said, her voice catching. 'I won't fail.'

The door shut and she was gone.

* * *

With nothing else to do but wait for Oisín to return to a lucid state, Dara and Sam took themselves into the auditorium, where they sat reading lines, watching the technicians adjusting the lighting for different scenes, casting shadows across the rocks and hills, across the spectral trees. Every so often, the sound team would send a wind howling through the speakers and the hair would prickle on the back of Dara's neck.

At lunchtime, they checked on Oisín again, by which point he was almost sober, waking at the sound of the door opening.

Rubbing his eyes, he sat up, bones creaking stiffly into a stretch. 'What time is it?' He was still a little spaced, unsteady on his feet as he tried to stand.

'It's nearly half one,' Sam said. 'Time to rise and shine, buddy.'

He went to the coffee machine to fetch Oisín a double espresso, while Dara summoned Eabha down from Geoffrey's office. She had been locked in with him all morning, as if it were a war room, from which they were directing a grand defence of artistic freedom. Eabha seemed relieved at the interruption when Dara knocked on the door, telling Geoffrey to call her if he needed her again. But as she followed Dara down the stairs, her steps were heavy, boots thudding against the old floorboards, her worry a weight she dragged behind her.

Arriving at the dressing room, Eabha made no comment at all about Oisín's incapacitation that morning, instead smiling determinedly at all of them.

'Right, are we ready to get started?' The beads on her wrists shook as she clapped her hands together. 'Geoffrey and I spoke with the police and we have a plan now for opening night. There will be a police presence which, when you think about it, just sort of adds to the—' She paused, choosing her words. '—The *mystique*.'

Dara glanced dubiously at Sam, whose eyebrow flickered upward.

'As for you, Oisín,' Eabha said on an exhalation of breath, fidgeting with the frilled cuffs of her white shirt. 'I hope we can depend on you to behave yourself now?'

He stretched his arms into the air, running his hands through his hair. It was darker now – he must have dyed it during the two days of his absence – so that he now resembled more closely the photograph of Cillian from the *Justice for Cillian* campaign.

'Would I let you down, Eabha?' he said, his boyish charm less charming when he weaponised it. But Eabha merely smiled.

'Let's go,' she said, leading the way to the wings.

* * *

The afternoon's rehearsal was Oisín's best ever performance. After days of broken momentum, nobody was prepared for Oisín to inhabit his character with an emotional resonance that, finally, felt authentic. He was changed, as if something had finally clicked into place inside him.

During their scenes together, Dara felt newly moved. As he held her in his arms, he looked into her eyes in a way he hadn't before, with a curiosity and interest that had been entirely absent before. When he kissed her, Dara felt for the first time as if he really meant it, as if he were Cillian and she were Eabha.

On the grounds of the Bodkin, brought to life on the stage, Oisín's hand reached for her:

```
Cillian: Being around you ... it's like ...
you make me feel like ...
Eabha: Like what?
Cillian: Like ... like maybe everything
doesn't have to be bad. It's like ... I don't
```

know ... like good things can happen ... you
know?
Eabha: I make you feel hopeful?
Cillian: Yes ... I guess that's it ... hope.
Eabha: Things will get better for you,
Cillian. It won't always be like this. You
won't always need me to make you see that.
Cillian (*laughing*): See, when you say shit
like that ... you make me feel like it could
be true, like maybe it's possible that life
can be good. (*He reaches for her hand again*)
I ... I love you, Eabha.
Eabha: You do?
Cillian: Yes ... I do. And you love me too?

*Eabha hesitates, then reaches forward and
kisses him.*

Eabha: You know I do.

They weren't forcing a chemistry anymore. Finally, here at the
end, it was really there: a connection.

From the side of the stage, Sam and Eabha looked on, and
Dara thought she caught – did she imagine it? – a twinge of
jealousy crossing their faces as she drew away from Oisín
again.

'Well . . .' Eabha said, her heels clacking loudly as she walked
towards them. 'That was ... well, honestly, I could cry! Well
done!' Her hands were on Dara's shoulders, her eyes gazing at
the crest of the Bodkin School on her chest. 'God – look at you
... it's like I'm looking in a mirror.'

Dara returned her smile, but she found the thought alarming.
It was becoming more difficult to shed Eabha from her mind.

As she changed out of her costume in the dressing room, it felt as if Eabha were sticking to her skin – dry, itchy patches covering her arms and her face. She scratched at them with her fingernails.

'Are you heading straight home?' Sam asked as Dara emerged from behind the dressing screen in her jeans and Vans, back to herself.

'I don't know really . . . I guess so.'

'I thought maybe we could grab a drink first?' he said, his smile coaxing her lips upward until she was smiling back at him.

'That sounds like just what I need,' she replied, exhaling. 'Count me in.'

'Are you two going drinking?' Oisín asked, entering the dressing room behind Sam. There was a whisper of wildness in his eyes still as he pulled his tie free from his neck and tossed it onto his dressing table.

'Why?' Sam said, tension filling his shoulders. 'You want to come?'

'Well now that you've invited me, I suppose I will,' Oisín replied, a grin spreading across his face. 'Are you inviting Eabha?'

'Wasn't going to,' Sam said, hands in his pockets, fingers fiddling with the box of cigarettes visible through his jeans.

'Great,' Oisín said quickly. 'Better without her. It'll be like the beginning again. Just the three of us.'

But it didn't feel like a beginning. Dara's eye caught on her reflection before she followed Sam and Oisín out of the dressing room. Face pale, hair dark, eyes mournful. It very much felt like an end.

She switched the light off, her fingers rubbing unconsciously at her forehead, across which the ghost of an accusation crept.

* * *

The police had cleared the protestors from the front of the theatre and the footpath was now empty of judgement as Dara, Sam and Oisín stepped outside. With the protestors showing up at the theatre, Austin's behaviour seemed less and less like paranoia. Dara could feel it herself: fear at the edges of her thoughts, tickling the back of her neck, a slight prickling sensation under her skin.

When they reached the pub, Sam began peppering Oisín with the questions that had been nagging at him all day. 'Should we be worried about Austin's state of mind?' he asked, leaning back in his chair, one leg folded over the other. 'Another breakdown is a realistic possibility.'

There were dark rings under Oisín's eyes, his skin carrying an unhealthy shine.

Dara took a breath, shifting in her seat. 'And you, Oisín? Should we be worried about you?'

He cast a glance her way, through the hair flopping down over his eyes.

She persisted. 'What was that all about this morning? What did you take?'

He shrugged, the bravado gone from him, like wind from a sail. 'I might have got the dose wrong,' he said, raising a pint to his lips. They watched the beer drain from his glass. 'Mushrooms, the same type Cillian was on the night he died.'

'For Christ's sake, Oisín, you need to stop this!' Dara said, rolling her eyes. 'I mean it – if you keep fucking up like this, Eabha is going to murder you.'

'Like Cillian?' Oisín said, his eyes lit with a strange mischief.

'No – I mean . . . you know what I mean,' Dara replied, flustered, but Oisín just shrugged.

'She doesn't care what I do.'

'I think she'll care about this,' Sam muttered.

'You're wrong about that,' Oisín retorted. 'She doesn't care about anyone but herself. We're all just props to her, just necessary means to an end. She'll drop us all as soon as it suits her, just like the last cast. Wait and see.' He shook his head, looking down at the table in front of him. 'And you can't say we weren't warned.'

Cillian's words rose in Dara's mind.

Cillian: She won't talk to me now ... I don't know what she told you, Austin, but I would never hurt her on purpose — never! I couldn't live with myself if I hurt her ... But she won't even *look* at me. She's so cold. It's like ... it's like it was all a lie ... like she never loved me at all.

Oisín was chewing on his chain, unable to keep his leg still. 'You know, I asked Austin why she can't just walk away from the play – why she can't let Cillian go.'

Dara sat up straighter. 'And? Did he have an answer?'

Oisín's laugh was wretched. 'He said he thinks she's drawn to broken men who cling to her.'

Dara exchanged a quick look with Sam. 'You know that's not you, Oisín, right?' She reached forward, a hand on his shoulder, and when he looked at her, he seemed so unsure of himself that she was taken aback. He was so confident when they first met – *just* on the right side of arrogant – now here he was, deflated, as if Eabha had stuck a pin in him.

He looked away from them again, drawing himself up straight in an effort to project a more defiant front, though they were unconvinced.

'Yeah, like, I know all that,' he said, puffing out his chest, 'but, the thing is, Austin ... he's – I don't know – it's like he's coming apart.' He reached for his pint again. 'He kept talking about the Bodkin. About the three of them, three lost kids rambling through the empty hills. All they had was each other, isolated from the outside world, and it made me think about the last few weeks . . . you know, the three of us with Eabha. Making us rehearse in that attic. Making the play our whole lives. It's like she was intentionally trying to raise the stakes, to build the pressure, until we were changed by it.'

Dara shut her eyes. She didn't want to think about all that – not right now, not before they had limped over the finishing line, onto the stage, into the bright lights of a glowing future.

'That year they spent at the Bodkin, Austin said it felt like walking a thin line between life and death, as if he could swerve slightly into death, just for the hell of it. Not that he wanted to die, but that it didn't seem like a distant possibility either. It was just there, before their eyes, the constant presence of death.' Oisín's foot was jittering against the leg of his chair, making the table vibrate and the liquid wobble in their glasses. 'When you feel that sort of boundlessness – a world without structure or rules – reality becomes unfixed. You're floating.' Dara felt a slight shudder down her spine. She had felt for weeks as if her mind had come loose from her body, as if she walked on cloud. 'Austin said they all felt it, but Cillian felt it especially. He had been miserable for so long that, when Eabha walked into his life, he thought he had found an escape at last.' Oisín sniffed. 'But she only brought him death.'

Dara swallowed, pressing down the lump in her throat. 'I suppose he did escape,' she said, quietly, 'in the end.'

'He nearly took Eabha with him. Austin said the play doesn't really show what happened that night. He said he thought Cillian might kill her – but they can't say that publicly without admitting to a motive.'

Sam was watching the jerkiness of Oisín's movements, the vacuity of his stare. He exchanged another look with Dara, but she was staring at Oisín fixedly, hanging on every word.

'Did you ask him?' she said, hunger in her voice. 'Did you ask Austin what really happened? How Cillian died?'

Sitting back in his chair, Oisín smiled again. 'He dodged the question. He just said that Cillian was a drowning boy, clinging to Eabha to stay afloat and pushing her head under the water in the process. At a certain point, Eabha wriggled free and then there was nothing holding Cillian up anymore.'

Dara looked away, a sigh escaping down through her nostrils. She rubbed her forehead again. 'Do you think they'll ever give a straight answer?'

'You already know the answer to that,' Sam said. 'You just don't want to accept it.'

* * *

Oisín drank four pints in the time it took Dara to drink one and then, as they left the pub together, refused to be dissuaded when they told him he was too drunk to cycle home.

'Maybe he should come home with me?' Sam said. 'The mood he's in? I don't think he should go back to Leinster Road with you.'

'All his stuff is at the house,' Dara said. 'He wants to get it.'

Sam watched nervously while Oisín clambered onto his bike, one foot on the kerb, the other on a pedal. 'This is a mistake . . . maybe I should come with you or something?' he mumbled to Dara, so Oisín wouldn't hear.

'What good would it do? I'll just follow behind him and try to keep him out of danger,' she replied. 'He won't let us get a taxi for him.'

Sam had a face like thunder. 'I shouldn't have suggested a

drink. I didn't think he would hear me. Honestly, I thought we could . . . we could spend some time together, the two of us.' He pulled her closer to him. 'But that's clearly not going to happen any time soon.'

Dara glanced over at Oisín, who was calling her name. She reached out, her hand on Sam's cheek. 'There will be time for us. Things are so complicated already and—'

'Yeah,' he said, cutting her off – a little abruptly, she thought. 'I know all that. I'm not trying to . . . to rush things.' He took a half-step backwards, his eyes skirting around her face. 'Listen, just be careful, all right? They're holding another vigil tonight at the gates of the Bodkin School. I wouldn't be surprised if some of those protestors show up at Eabha's house.'

A small sigh slipped out between Dara's lips. 'Really? They couldn't take the night off?' Her fingers brushed her eyebrow.

'I don't know for sure – I just . . . I just heard about it from someone.'

'Someone?! . . . Who?'

'You don't know them.'

Why was he avoiding her eye? 'Who told you, Sam?'

'What does it matter?'

'Is it a secret or something?'

'No – just . . .' He turned away. 'Linda O'Rowe called me.'

'Sam!' Dara said, suddenly worried. 'You can't talk to her!'

'It's not a big deal,' Sam replied. 'I . . . just . . . Sometimes she . . . she gives me information. It's all off the record – I don't say anything they could use against Eabha!'

'*Shit*, Sam . . .' Dara said, her hand travelling slowly down her face. 'I really wish you wouldn't—'

'Don't worry, Dara . . . I know what I'm doing. There's nothing to worry about, OK?' Sam said, gripping her arms, but suspicion was rippling through her.

From the footpath, Oisín called again. 'Daraaaaaa. D a r a. Come ooooon. Let's go!'

'I'm just following a little advice I got about dealing with the press in this kind of situation. You feed them crumbs to keep them onside.' His hands were on her arms still. 'Don't be angry at me.'

'Who gave you that advice?' Why did she suspect it was Miriam?

He looked away again, towards the street light overhead, its deadening orange glow lighting his face. 'Does it matter?'

'I'm going to fucking leave without you!' Oisín shouted, at the end of his patience.

Dara waved at him again. 'I'm coming – just hang on!' Her fingers gripped the handles of her bike. 'I have to go.' She shook her head, casting one last, annoyed look in his direction. 'Stop talking to journalists, Sam.'

'Don't forget what I said about the protestors,' he replied, watching her wheel her bike towards Oisín. 'And text me when you're home safe.'

'Don't worry,' Oisín called over. 'I'll take good care of her.'

'Goodnight, Sam,' Dara said, leaving him alone on the footpath behind them, hands hanging limp by his sides, watching their backs as they cycled away.

* * *

To Dara's relief, Oisín had sobered up significantly by the time they reached the other side of town and, as they neared South Richmond Street, he signalled at her to pull over.

'Chips?' he said, on the footpath outside the Bernard Shaw pub.

Famished, Dara agreed immediately, propping her bike against a nearby lamp post.

Oisín bought the chips, carrying them out to the kerb, where they sat together to eat them, Dara's eyes drifting occasionally to the street art on the wall opposite. Large white letters, filling the grey gable wall: DON'T BE AFRAID. She turned them over in her mind, as if it were a message meant just for her. *Don't be afraid, Dara. Don't be afraid.*

The vinegar wafted up her nose as she ate, the vapours dislodging some of her worry so that she gradually began to relax in Oisín's company. A group of pigeons were eyeing her up; she tossed them some scraps to keep them friendly.

'This is nice,' Oisín said, and Dara laughed out loud at the unlikeliness of it. She could feel the dirt from the street rising up through her jeans. Even at a distance, the pigeons seemed liable to spread some kind of disease and there was a small group of men having a lively argument outside the Bernard Shaw. Something about someone's girlfriend, or was it their mother?

'Are you sure you're OK, Oisín?' Dara said. 'If you want to talk about it – you know, what happened with Eabha – I'm . . . I'm here.'

Oisín sniffed, turning to look at her quizzically. 'You really want me to believe you care.'

'I do care,' she replied, looking out at the road, down which taxi after taxi was passing, passengers bound for the nightclubs of Harcourt Street around the corner. It was Friday night: she had almost forgotten. One week left. The pressure of the play made each day feel indistinguishable. 'I think she was wrong, for what it's worth.' She turned to look at him. 'You deserved better than that.'

He looked down at his chips, touched one a couple of times, then seemed to lose his appetite, placing the paper bag down on the kerb next to him. 'You won't tell her about the mushrooms, will you?' he said. 'You won't tell her that Austin gave them to me? I promised him. She thinks he's clean as a whistle.'

'Don't you think she should know?' Dara said, wiping the salt and vinegar from her hands as best she could. 'If his mental state is so fragile—'

'Just do me this favour, Dara? Please? I need to know there's *someone* I can trust in all of this.'

She recognised the feeling, her thoughts flicking to Sam.

'All right, Oisín. Fine . . . I'll keep your secret.' She watched his fingers playing absently with his chain again. They were so close to the end. She just had to keep him from blowing everything to hell. 'I won't say anything to Eabha. You don't need to worry about me.'

'Thank you,' he said, his smile warm now, and when she turned towards him again, he was doggedly watching her.

'What?!' she said, suddenly embarrassed. 'Why are you looking at me? Is there something on my face?'

'You're beautiful,' he replied, and then, before she could react, he reached out, cupped the back of her head with his hand and kissed her. His lips were as salty as hers and she was so surprised to find him kissing her that she immediately pulled away, almost falling over as she did so. The last of her chips fell out of the grease-soaked brown bag and the patient pigeons had their reward.

Dara's hands were shaking slightly – with fright or indignation, she didn't know, her body soaked with adrenaline, the feeling making her a little nauseous. 'What the *fuck*, Oisín?!'

Oisín was laughing. 'Sorry . . . sorry, I shouldn't have done that. I just . . . It just felt different today at rehearsals.' He reached for her hair, gathering the strands between his finger. Quietly, he said: 'Eabha's right. You look so like her now.'

A thought was creeping up from the back of her mind, a fear she had been trying to ignore. She felt it again, the sense that she was not herself anymore, as if a great inhabitation of her mind and body were happening, carried out by a character on a page.

Oisín was on his feet, holding his hand towards her. 'Will we go?'

She let him help her to her feet, scrunching the chip bag into a ball which she deposited in the nearby bin. One more week to opening night: one more week to keep Oisín from imploding.

They collected their bikes from the lamp post; Oisín steadied the back of hers while Dara climbed onto the saddle.

'Ready?' he said. He was so much calmer now, as if he hadn't, moments before, tried to stick his tongue down her throat.

Cycling behind him for the last few minutes of the journey back to Leinster Road, the confusion that had hung over her all day deepened. Dara watched the back of his head. Oisín was unravelling – what would happen when the final knot came undone?

Don't be afraid, she whispered to herself. *Don't be afraid.*

* * *

The house was dark as they pulled up in front of it. No protesters had materialised, despite the tip-off Sam received from Linda. Eabha wasn't home yet, her Ford Cortina absent from the driveway. Dara was relieved to find that she would not be immediately confronted by her. Her thoughts were still in disarray, her confusion over Oisín still painted on her face: she didn't need Eabha questioning why.

As she walked up the steps and opened the front door, she was apprehensive of what Oisín might do next. She would have to fix up a spare bedroom for him, find some fresh sheets, and get him into a bed of his own without further incident. She should text Eabha too – a warning. He's here: your inconvenience won't simply disappear from your life.

But she needn't have worried; the destructive urge had left Oisín for the night, a calm descending over him now. 'I'm going to head off, OK? I don't want to see Eabha again tonight.'

'Oh?' Dara said, one foot in the dark hallway. 'But your stuff? Don't you need it? Where are you going to stay?'

'I'll figure it out,' he replied, pushing his mess of hair so that it all flopped to the right. 'Honestly, I can't bring myself to walk into that house right now. Don't worry about me. You've done enough of that for one night, Dara.'

In the gloom of the front garden, she couldn't tell if he were smiling, but she thought she could see the glint of moonlight on teeth.

'Goodnight,' he called, throwing his leg over his bike again. Within a matter of seconds, he was gone, silence filling the street once more.

Across the road, a single light shone in an upstairs bedroom, and a flash of movement at the gate suggested the presence of a prowling fox.

Dara locked the door behind her and headed for the kitchen.

First, she sent a rushed text to Sam to confirm that they had made it home alive. He replied with a smiling emoji, a thumbs up and a love heart.

Next, Dara scrolled through her contacts for her sister's name and hit the call button.

It took two tries before she answered.

'Hello?' Rhona was a little hoarse, as if Dara had woken her. She hadn't even considered the time, but the clock on the kitchen wall showed it was nearly midnight.

'Rhona, sorry it's late but I . . . I need to talk to you.'

'Everything OK?!'

'Yeah, it's fine . . . but, Rhona, I need your advice. I don't know what to do . . .'

'About what?'

'About Oisín. He just . . . he *kissed* me, Rhona . . . earlier tonight.'

'What? Why?!' Rhona sounded vaguely annoyed. 'You serious?'

'Yep.'

'Jesus . . . What's he playing at?'

'I don't know,' she replied, trying to calm her heart. 'It's weird, isn't it? I mean, I'm not overreacting?'

'You've never mentioned anything between the two of you before, but maybe there was . . .?'

'No,' Dara said emphatically. 'Honestly, there was never anything until today. He's been obsessed with Eabha this whole time.'

Rhona was silent for a moment. 'What do you think he's up to? Do you think he's using you to mess with Eabha?'

Of course he was; why was she so slow to see it? She felt a shiver run through her. 'He said I look like her now. Maybe he's just . . . he's trying to come between us?' The longer the idea sat with her, the more sense it seemed to make.

'Between you and Sam?' Rhona queried.

'What? No . . .' She could feel her anger grow. 'Between me and Eabha.'

In the battle between them for Eabha's affection, she was now the last competitor on the field: the victor. Was this Oisín's revenge? She had been kind to him – concerned, understanding. She had promised to keep his secrets.

'Right . . . I see,' Rhona said. Dara didn't hear the worry in her voice.

'I'm fuming, Rhona.' She was pacing now; five steps to the window, five back. 'Should I talk to Eabha about it?'

'No!' Rhona said immediately. 'Absolutely not. Why would you do that?'

'I don't know,' Dara replied, her arms in the air. 'Shouldn't she know he's trying to mess with us?'

'But you don't know that for sure, Dara.'

'I do.'

'I'm just saying, you can't be *certain*. And if that's what he's trying to do, then it will just upset Eabha if you tell her. What's the point of that? I'd keep my mouth shut if I were you.'

'But, Rhona, what if she finds out about it? What if he tells her? She'll think I was keeping a secret from her.' The idea made her face grow hot. She should have stopped him. When he first kissed her cheek that morning: she should have seen this coming. She let the air empty from her lungs, trying to calm herself. She didn't want to react as Eabha would, seeing betrayal at every turn. 'I don't know, Rhona. I feel like my head's going to explode. It's too much.'

She walked to the window. The lights inside the kitchen were reflected against the dark glass like a mirror. For a moment she was looking at herself, but then her eyes seemed to perceive something else in her features, as if Eabha's face were transposed over her own, the two blending together until she wasn't sure where she ended and Eabha began.

'You can always leave, Dara. You can always walk away.'

She could have laughed at that. After all this? After everything they had been through?

Behind her, the kitchen door opened. Dara turned at the sound and saw Eabha's face take on an expression of surprise as she switched on the light. 'Oh, Dara, you scared me half to death . . .' Her hand was on her chest. She gave a little laugh as the fright left her. 'What are you doing standing in the dark?'

Dara turned away from the window again, leaning heavily

against the nearest kitchen counter. She knew already what she was going to do. 'Rhona, Eabha's just home so I have to go, OK?'

'Don't tell her, Dara. Trust me. No good will come of it.'

'I have to go.'

'All right . . . Take my advice, Dara. Bye.'

She put her phone down on the counter. 'Sorry about that. I was talking to Rhona.'

Eabha placed her leather satchel on the table, kicking her sandals off her feet wearily. 'And how is she? Everything OK?'

Dara ran her hand through her hair, catching the front section between her fingers. She stared down at the ends. 'Rhona's fine.' She let her hair go and then looked up at Eabha. 'There's something I have to tell you.'

Chapter Twenty-One

A small group of six protestors showed up at the house early the following morning, huddled beneath umbrellas. They weren't chanting or making much noise at all, standing on the footpath as if it were an ordinary place to congregate, as if it were part of their usual routine.

It had rained all night, spongy clouds dumping their water to the thirsty ground. The air was cooler after the washout, summer beginning its slow fade, petals shedding, leaves slipping free from branches.

At the bathroom window, Dara pushed back the blind, rubbing her eyes at the sight of the group outside – drizzle sliding down the *Justice for Cillian* banner – a weary sigh of resignation escaping her lips. She took a photo of them and sent a text to Sam.

Dara Gaffney (8.03am): You were right. Look who showed up!

Sam rang her immediately. 'Dara – everything OK over there?'

'Yeah . . . yeah, they're just standing out there. They're not even doing anything.'

'You should call the police.'

'Yeah, I suppose I should. I don't know if Eabha has seen them yet.'

'Do you want me to come over?'

'No, don't. It'll only make things worse if they see you. We'll get the police to clear them off.'

There was a silence, then a long sigh. 'Just . . . be careful, will you? I don't like this . . . it doesn't feel safe.'

'I'm fine, Sam. Don't worry about me.' She was smiling as she said it; it gave her a modest thrill to know that he cared. But a memory, floating up to the front of her mind, made her pause: Oisín on the kerb next to her, his salty lips on hers. 'Sam . . . something weird happened with Oisín last night.'

'Oh? Why am I not surprised?'

'He kissed me.'

There was a silence.

'It just happened out of nowhere. You know he's been in such weird form lately and I think the drink just . . . I don't know . . . honestly, it was very strange . . . Sam? Are you still there?'

'Yeah, I'm just . . . confused.'

'I think he's trying to make Eabha jealous.'

Sam's laugh was harsh. 'Right . . . as if she'll care.' He sighed down the phone. 'I'm sorry he did that to you.'

Dara hesitated. 'You're not annoyed at me?'

'Of course not. I knew I should have gone back to the house with you. I could feel something brewing in him.' He sighed. 'I tell you what, though. I'd like to punch Oisín in the fucking face.'

'Who does that remind you of?'

'Ha, yeah . . .'

The fight had happened three days before Cillian died, on the day Austin saw the bruises on his sister's arm, the day he had gone looking for Cillian, looking to put a stop to it once and for all.

*The stage lights dim, **Austin** and **Cillian**
freeze in place. **Cillian** is on the ground,
with **Austin** reaching over him, gripping
Cillian by his jumper, fist poised and ready
to land another blow. **Eabha** steps into the
middle of the stage, a spotlight descending
on her, **Austin** and **Cillian** fading into shadow.*

Eabha: None of the students who were there
that day questioned why Austin and Cillian
were fighting. They just stood there cheering
Austin on, taunting Cillian as each blow
landed. They won't admit to it later. They
won't acknowledge that they stoked the anger
in my brother, fuelling his fists with a
righteous anger — because Cillian deserved
it, didn't he? He was the outcast and we
reserve our human cruelty for them.

*She turns towards **Austin** and **Cillian**, briefly
lit again, still frozen in place.*

Eabha: Here is my brother, behaving just as
you expect him to — violent, hateful. But I
haven't shown you the others, egging him on.
I haven't named them here, the ones who will
soon point at Austin and call him a killer.
They had seen blood spilled, staining the
pavement — Cillian's blood. What more did
they need to know? And so when the police
come and questions are asked, a ready answer
sits on their lips. They have their villain.
Here he is.

'I better go deal with this protest,' Dara said, her mind snapping back to the present. 'Knowing our luck, Austin will show up any minute and make his fight with Cillian seem like child's play.'

'Yeah,' Sam replied, then hesitated. 'Look, eh, thanks for telling me . . . about Oisín.' He sounded nervous; she had never heard Sam nervous before.

Another smile broke across her face. 'Of course. We're in this together, Sam. No matter what.'

* * *

Eabha was on the phone in the kitchen when Dara descended the stairs. In her pink robe with the feathers, her hair wrapped in a towel on top of her head, she was speaking live on RTÉ radio to veteran broadcaster, Ciarán Quinn. Dara could hear him through the speaker on the phone. She waved seeing Dara, placing a finger briefly against her lips. Soundlessly, Dara closed the door behind her.

'I fully appreciate people's rights to protest, Ciarán – I do. I believe strongly in the rights of free expression and speech, but they're at my front door right now, as we speak, trying to intimidate me into silence.'

'They're at your *home*, is it, Eabha?'

'That's right, Ciarán.'

'Are you safe there, Eabha? Are the police on their way?'

'Yes, they're on their way, but, honestly, I don't know if I'm safe right now, Ciarán. We have been harassed for weeks now – and I understand completely why people are upset. I understand why Richard Butler is looking for answers. I want to say now, publicly and definitively, that my family and I fully support a public inquiry.'

This was news. A change, sudden and resolute. Eabha had never raised the idea before and Dara had just assumed it would be the last thing she would want. Did Austin know? Was he a part of this decision? Her face was turned towards the window, down which the rain slid in snaking trails.

She turned around. 'If an inquiry is what will give Cillian's father peace, then we will gladly support his call. I have always valued the truth, Ciarán. It is a huge part of my values as a person.'

Dara watched Eabha's face. Was there a smile? Was it lurking there between her words? A strategic, knowing decision to twist the narrative once again, giving her audience what they wanted? She sat down on one of the stools at the kitchen island. It was dastardly but brilliant. The perfect chess move.

'So you're publicly confirming this? Because you haven't said this before? Why the silence from you until now, Eabha?' Ciarán asked. 'Why the change of heart?'

Eabha laughed: a light, tinkling sound. 'I was waiting to give you an exclusive, Ciarán.' She laughed again. 'No, but seriously, there's no change of heart involved – I was hoping we could talk privately to Richard first. I didn't want it to play out in public like this, but I haven't been able to reach him . . . I don't know why.'

Dara knew this to be a lie. Richard's face rose before her eyes, the stoop of his back as he shuffled away from her, away from the theatre, his letter in her hands.

'The problem, Ciarán,' Eabha continued, 'is that the tactics used here are highly regrettable. Attacking an artistic work is not the right way to establish fact. It is censorship – pure and simple – and I felt that I had to defend myself, as an artist, from this attempt to silence me. I've been so honoured to have the whole theatre community behind me on this.'

'Well, Eabha de Lacey, thanks for updating us on what has been a fascinating story. We'll let you go and see to the incident at your home this morning, but we're very glad to have heard from you on the *Ciarán Quinn Show* and the very best of luck with the revival of your classic play *The Truth Will Out*.'

'Great to speak with you, Ciarán.' She hung up, turning to Dara, euphoric. 'Well, that went well – very well, actually! Better than I expected.'

Dara ran her hand over her face. 'I . . . I don't get it. Since when are you supporting a public inquiry?!'

'Since Geoffrey and I spoke yesterday. It's just the best way to end this protest once and for all. It's outliving its usefulness now.' She reached for the bunch of grapes in a bowl on the counter, popping one in her mouth, her face lit with an excited glow. 'It's one thing having the papers talk about us, but it's another to actually face serious pressure to cancel the play. And with the protestors showing up, it was all getting too disruptive.'

'But won't an inquiry hurt you? And Austin?'

Eabha looked at her levelly, her smile fading slightly. 'Of course not. We have nothing to hide. There's nothing an inquiry could do to us because there's no evidence to look at, no witnesses except me and Austin. All they can do is call some former pupils into a room and ask them about a schoolboy fight they witnessed years ago. That sort of baseless rumour and distortion has been hurting us for the past fifteen years – maybe an inquiry would end it. Maybe it would be good for us. Richard Butler might regret it yet, when people hear what Cillian was really like.'

She sounded so confident that it was difficult to doubt her, but Dara was thinking of Austin. He would break under cross-examination, the very moment the past met the present and the truth was coaxed from its sleeping place.

A siren was sounding dimly from the front of the house, the police arriving to remove the few rain-sodden protestors from the public footpath.

They walked to the dining room, watching through the window as the police spoke with the organiser, a thin man in a long overcoat and a flat cap. The blue flashing lights from the police car poured into the room, reflected on the chandelier and on the blank space of wall, where an Arthur de Lacey painting used to hang.

'Get them out of here,' Eabha muttered, her eyes on the protestors. 'Bastards.'

Dara glanced her way but didn't comment. There was still a stiffness in the air between them after Dara's confession the night before. She thought about confronting it, thought better of it, then changed her mind again and said: 'Eabha, are things OK between us? You know, because of Oisín—'

'We're fine,' Eabha said, turning to look at her, expression stern. 'You did the right thing telling me.'

Why, then, were her eyes so cold? Why was the blue-green iris dead?

'But Oisín . . . is there anything we can do about him?' Dara asked, holding Eabha's eye, until she gave a sad smile, walking away from the window towards the dining-room table that had sat unused for weeks now. There had been no family lunches since Dara moved in. They had drifted into the background – Austin and Celia – just as Dara, Oisín and Sam took centre stage.

'You know I can't do anything with Oisín that might set him off,' Eabha replied, adjusting the candlesticks so that they stood in a straight line beneath the chandelier. 'We can't have him disappearing again, not this close to opening night. You know he can't cope with rejection – like every man I've ever known.'

Dara pulled at the sleeve of her pyjama top, thinking briefly of Sam. He had been so gracious when she told him what happened with Oisín. There wasn't a hint of blame, jealousy or possession. Maybe Austin was right. Maybe Eabha appealed to broken people, to those trying hard to hide their wounds. Sam was immune to Eabha's charms, but Oisín clung to her; Oisín whose mother had left him, Oisín who needed so badly to be loved. Just like Cillian.

'So, what am I supposed to do now?' Dara searched Eabha's face for answers. 'Like, how should I behave with him? What if he tries to kiss me again?'

Eabha stood up straight, smiling serenely. 'Just do what I do,' she said. 'You know how to do that – you've been learning all this time, right?' An elegant eyebrow rose, like a streak of black ink against the white of her pale face. 'Ignore him. He'll stop when he sees he's not going to get the attention he wants. Just like those protestors outside.'

Eabha squeezed Dara's shoulder on her way out of the room, leaving her alone to watch the protestors rolling up their banners, before gradually shuffling off down Leinster Road. They hadn't spotted her in the window, but every so often one of them would point at the house, and then laughter would sound. Dara didn't feel Eabha's optimism: people who think they're not being heard tend to shout a little louder.

* * *

The physical presence of protestors outside Eabha's home had stimulated sympathy for her, as had her articulate and – many said – generous interview on the *Ciarán Quinn Show*. Now that they were cooperating with the idea of a public inquiry into

Cillian's death, the campaign against her play seemed dispro-
portionate, even censorious. Opinion was dividing, the feeling
spreading that the public condemnation of the de Laceys had
gone too far. Posts online began calling for balance, insisting
on innocence until guilt was proven, and suggesting that while
Richard Butler was well-intentioned – how could anybody doubt
that – he was also a grieving father and not to be entirely trusted.

It probably helped that the photographs flooding the newspapers over the past week were now carefully curated. Geoffrey
and Eabha were working to shift the narrative by shifting the
imagery. There were moody magazine spreads of her standing in
a ball gown among the deer in the Phoenix Park, or walking in a
petrol-blue velvet suit along Sandymount Strand. It gave her the
right look to appeal to the right kind of people: the theatregoers,
the chattering classes.

This swaying of public opinion brought a new energy to the
final days before their opening performance. Eabha was in buoyant mood, her good humour contagious, so that the rehearsals
ran smoothly, despite Oisín's best efforts to upset progress.

* * *

The course of their final days of tech rehearsal became determined entirely by whether or not Oisín had taken mushrooms.
On the final Monday, his eyes were shot with blood and Dara
could tell that he had not slept, the psilocybin still draining out
of his body. On Tuesday, it seemed to have an active hold on
him, loosening him further from the bonds of his own person-
ality to romp around the theatre in character as Cillian. His
behaviour was increasingly unpredictable, even volatile, but then
so was Cillian. Dara wasn't sure if Eabha knew what was driving
it – these transformations of his – but if she did, she hid it well,
behind a perfect veneer of aloof calm.

On Wednesday afternoon, as they returned from lunch, they found Oisín leaning off the top turret of the Bodkin School, while, from the wings, the set designer roared up at him that she wouldn't be responsible if he fell and broke his neck. Unfazed, Oisín just smiled at her. He only climbed down again after delicate, but determined, cajoling from Eabha.

Eabha's response was to continue her policy of appeasement. Her single-minded focus was the success of the production and, though he was wild and erratic, the moment rehearsals began, Oisín would simply transform. The switch would happen so suddenly and so perfectly that Dara deemed his new-found capacity to come to life as Cillian nothing short of stunning. In those final scenes, he really was Cillian, screaming at her to love him.

Cillian *(holding his hand towards Eabha)*: Why are you standing so far away from me? Come here, will you? Come over here to me ...

Eabha doesn't move at his command, so Cillian takes several quick steps towards her, grabbing her roughly by the arm and pulling her towards the window. She cries out in pain, trying to free herself from his grip, but he's too riled up to care that he's hurting her.

Eabha *(pained)*: Let me go, Cillian

Enter Austin at the top of the attic stairs.

Austin: Let her go, Cillian.

Austin's sudden appearance gives Cillian a jolt, his grip loosening enough to allow

Eabha to pull her arm free. She moves several paces away from Cillian, towards Austin, who steps forward to put his body between his sister and his friend.

Cillian: What's going on here? *(His eyes move from Austin to Eabha)* What's all this? Is this some kind of ambush? Seriously, what are you doing here, Austin?

Austin: We need to talk to you.

Cillian *(looking pointedly at Eabha):* We?

Austin: She asked me to come, Cillian ... because she's scared of you.

Cillian: Is that right? Why are you letting your brother speak for you, Eabha? Aren't you able to speak to me yourself?

Eabha: I've been trying to, but you haven't been listening. You don't listen to me. I thought you might listen to him.

Eabha feels a little light-headed, as if she isn't entirely within her own body, as if some core elements of her are leaking away.

Cillian: I don't listen to you? *(He walks around her slowly)* Well, I'm listening now. What is it you want to say?

But by the time rehearsals ended on Wednesday, Eabha finally cracked. She was packing up her bag when she let out a sudden scream, lifting something out of her satchel. It dropped quickly from her hand, landing with a thud before rolling a short distance from her feet, behind the curtain at the very edge of the stage. For a moment, Eabha didn't move, transfixed, a look of horror on her face. And without uttering a word, she turned and walked at pace through the wings to the stage door. It banged decisively behind her as she left the theatre.

Cautiously, Dara advanced on whatever had fallen behind the curtain, kicking at it with her foot as she drew the red velvet material out of the way, so they could see what had caused Eabha to take such a fright.

'It's the goat skull,' she said, recognising it immediately. Dara bent down to pick it up from the floor, brandishing it in front of her face as she turned to confront Oisín. 'Is this your idea of a joke?'

He was laughing, bent over, with two hands on his knees, the blood pouring into his head so that his face was quite red, a vein on his forehead now prominent.

'Stop laughing! I mean it. It's not funny, Oisín!'

He didn't seem to agree, Dara's anger only encouraging him. She looked to Sam, who gave a helpless shrug and said nothing. He took a packet of tobacco out of his pocket and began to roll a cigarette, keeping his fingers busy, as if to control the flare of his temper.

'Enough now, Oisín. You've gone too far this time,' Dara said, heading outside to find Eabha. She was standing just outside the door, her back against the stone wall, her eyes turned upwards to the oxidised copper dome of the Rotunda Hospital opposite.

'You all right?' Dara asked, leaning against the wall next to Eabha. 'Oisín's just trying to get a rise out of you.'

'I know,' Eabha replied, her hand passing through her hair. 'I'm not worried about Oisín. The skull just . . . it just gets to me. It makes me think of that night . . . and my brother, he's . . .' She let the air out of her lungs. 'He's not doing great.' Dara watched a muscle near Eabha's jaw tense. 'We're doing our best for him, trying to keep him from the press coverage, but he's . . .' She didn't finish the sentence.

Dara could imagine him, bent over the newspapers, his hair coming loose from the topknot, that awful look in his eye, the intensity of it. 'It's good he has you looking after him,' she said. 'He needs you.'

'We need each other,' Eabha replied. 'It's symbiosis. He manages my little panic attacks and I manage his.' She gave a shrug. 'I know some therapist would say it isn't healthy, but it works for us. It keeps us going.'

Dara looked down at her feet, her ankle rotating in the black deck shoe she was wearing – part of her costume. She had learned that theirs was a relationship hostile to external questioning: it made sense to Eabha and Austin, and that was enough.

'My family is up in Dublin for the play,' she said, changing the topic instead. She hadn't been sure that they would come, not while the *Justice for Cillian* campaign was raging, though Rhona insisted that their presence was never in doubt. Her parents' suspicion of Eabha and Austin had not abated, nor their instinctive dislike of Eabha – they had heard her interview on the radio and declared her 'a bit smug' – but it only served to strengthen their resolve to be there for Dara on opening night.

'That's good,' Eabha said, her voice a little limp. 'It's nice your parents could come. I like to imagine mine, sitting somewhere in the auditorium. Proud of me.'

'They'd be very proud of you, I'm sure.'

'Probably. They were good parents. I didn't appreciate that while they were alive.' She turned to Dara, leaning her head against the wall. 'I'd love to meet them, the people who made our Dara.'

Dara smiled and gave a half-nod, but had no intention of bringing her family anywhere near the house on Leinster Road. Not until after a successful opening night. Not until she knew it was safe, whenever that would be.

Chapter Twenty-Two

It was the final rehearsal. The stage set, the moon shining down from the rigging on the newly constructed Bodkin School and the karst bedrock of the Burren spreading around it. As they took to the stage for the final run-through, they could feel the clints and grykes beneath their feet and, on their lips, they tasted salt. Together, they stood in Cillian's hidden attic and recreated the final moments of his life.

Austin: Calm down, Cillian. There's no need for any of this—
Cillian *(bellowing)*: Shut the fuck up! Seriously, shut the fuck up! This is between me and Eabha. Why do you always get in the way, Austin? Everywhere we turn, there you are ... telling her I'm not good enough for her!
Eabha *(sobbing)*: Cillian, please ... please, stop.

Eabha *is shaking. The back of her head feels wet. She runs her hand through it, feeling a sticky substance — blood from the scratches she's only now beginning to feel. Glass*

shards are biting into her scalp, glass from
*the bottle **Cillian** smashed against the wall*
beside her.

Eabha: Austin ... *(She holds her bloodied*
hand towards her brother) Austin, I'm
bleeding.

Austin *sees her blood-covered fingers and is*
momentarily dazed, his ears ringing as the
anger rises, a wave of it slowly engulfing him.
*He advances towards **Cillian**, about to give*
***Cillian** the beating he started days before,*
*thoroughly enraged. Next to him, **Eabha's** hand*
is on his arm, trying to stop the violence
*about to erupt between them. She holds **Austin***
*back long enough for **Cillian** to grab another*
glass bottle. It's in his hand.

Eabha *(spotting the danger)*: Austin, watch
out!

***Cillian** smashes the bottle against the wall*
next to the window, the broken shards like a
*mouth reaching out for **Austin**.*

Eabha *(screaming)*: Cillian — no!

*She lets **Austin** go, the fabric of his school*
jumper slipping free from her fingers as he
*advances now on **Cillian**.*

By the time they finished, Eabha was in a state of excited exhaustion. She hugged each of them in turn, the sweat of their bodies transferring to her linen dress. Dara pushed her hair off her face, the strands of her fringe wet, wondering how she would have the energy to survive the full run, night after night, producing the emotion required to tell that story to audience after audience.

Eabha's arms were around her again. 'You look flattened,' she said. 'But, Dara, I knew you could do it – I *knew* you could! And you did. You are the perfect Eabha.'

Dara smiled, her breath still coming a little fast. 'Better than Vanessa Devin?'

'Much! There's no comparison,' Eabha replied, laughing. 'I hope she comes to see you some night. I hope the whole cast shows up. They'd *die* with envy. You are all—' She looked around at each of them, beaming. 'You're all magnificent.'

Dara shook her limbs out, a restless energy in her bones. 'I feel like I need to dance off the day or something.'

'Well, why don't we?' Eabha said. 'I left some of Geoffrey's champagne in the dressing room for us. He has a crate of it in his office for the after-party tomorrow, but why wait?'

'Isn't that tempting fate?' Sam said.

'It's not a celebration . . .' Eabha replied. 'I just think it would be good for all of us to blow off some steam.'

'I'm game,' Oisín agreed at once, marching towards the dressing room.

'Of course *you* would be,' Sam said, following behind him. 'You've been blowing off steam for weeks now, right Oisín?'

Oisín didn't answer. He had already found the stash of bottles Eabha had left under Dara's dressing table, unpeeling the foil from one. 'Should we make a party of this? Call in the crew?'

'No,' Eabha said quickly. 'No party! It's just a little drink for the cast. Don't get carried away, Oisín.'

'What about Austin?' Oisín asked, with an insincerity that struck Dara as cruel. 'Why not invite Austin in? You've cut him out so suddenly, Eabha. I thought he was part of the team?'

Oisín worked on the cork until it popped into this hand with a modest fizzing sound.

'Why don't we just leave Austin out of this, Oisín,' Eabha said stiffly, handing him one of the stack of paper cups she had taken from behind the bar in the lobby.

'Is it because he's losing his mind again?' Oisín persisted, sensing a weakness in Eabha's defences.

'That's enough, Oisín,' Dara said forcefully. 'Leave it alone.'

Oisín stared at her for a moment, as if surprised by the strength of her intervention, then decided not to mount a challenge; at least, not immediately. He filled four cups, waiting while the fizz rose and then fell, refilling each again until the liquid was licking the brim.

'A toast,' he said, raising a cup into the air, 'to surviving the curse of *The Truth Will Out*.'

Dara raised her cup to meet his and took a drink. 'Bit early for that,' she said, only half-joking. 'You just jinxed us, Oisín.'

He winked at her as he took a long, slow drink. 'Why? Is there something we should be worried about, Dara?'

'Nope,' she said quickly. 'Not that I know of.'

He was leaning back against the dressing table, his head turned at an angle, his chain visible beneath the white shirt he was wearing. They hadn't yet changed out of their costumes.

'Are you sure, Dara? There's really nothing on your mind?'

Her heart was starting to beat faster now, her mind cycling through his possible meanings. Was it the kiss? She looked at Sam. He already knew about that. There was nothing to fear there.

'I don't know what you're getting at,' she said, her voice uneasy.

Eabha chose to intervene. 'I'll put on some music!' she said. 'Any requests?'

'Nothing depressing,' Sam said while she plugged her phone into the speaker on the nearest dressing table, choosing a *Pixies* album.

Eabha was swaying slightly side to side, taking furtive sips from her paper cup, trying to break the tension forming around Oisín and Dara. She reached for Dara's hand, pulling her towards her, so that they stood face to face.

'Dance with me, my little alter ego,' she said.

Reluctantly, Dara moved her hips a little, her weight shifting slightly from side to side. This close to Eabha, she could feel the heat of her skin, the beat of her heart, the tips of her fingers pressed against Dara's back.

'Yeah, obey your director, Dara,' Oisín said, his voice suddenly bitter. He finished his drink and poured himself another. Sam downed his too, holding his cup out for more. Already, Dara could feel the jubilant mood souring.

Eabha was resting her head on Dara's shoulder, her slight body pressed against Dara's so that she could feel her hipbones against her leg. Watching them dance, Oisín sulked silently for a moment, then shuffled closer to Sam.

'Me and Dara had a little flirtation . . . a little kiss. Did she tell you about that?'

Dara glanced over – so this was the card Oisín was going to play – but the look on Sam's face was derisory. 'I heard you were drunk and all over her, yeah. Not sure I'd be telling people about that,' he replied. 'Is that how you get all your women, Oisín? Not really something to brag about.'

Oisín gave a chuckle at that. 'So, she told you?' He looked at Eabha and Dara together again, a curl coming to his lip. 'There was a real moment between us, whatever she's telling you now.'

Dara turned towards him, watching him contemplate his next move. She was about to object when she felt Eabha stiffen in her arms, her voice at her ear. 'Don't react,' she whispered, her breath tickling Dara's skin. 'It's what he wants.'

From the corner of her eye, Dara watched Sam's reaction as Oisín leaned closer to him again. 'She fancies me, you know,' Oisín said. Sam swallowed, his face carefully blank. 'Think she fancies Eabha more, though.'

Oisín had hit his mark, anger rising in Sam so suddenly that it must have been there all along, hovering just below the surface. 'Oisín, why don't you shut up and cool off a bit, OK?' he said, his teeth gritted. 'We're all sick of your bullshit.'

Eabha had stopped dancing, her arms falling limp at her sides. Dara's breath felt shallow, as if her chest were too full with fear to let the oxygen in.

'All right – calm down, Sam,' Oisín said, raising his hands, as if to surrender. 'I'm only messing around.' He smiled at Eabha and Dara. 'But maybe I do need to relax a little.' He reached into his pocket, pulling out a small plastic bag. 'Anyone for a little mushroom?'

'Put them away,' Dara said, her eyes on the bag, while Oisín pulled out a couple of small mushrooms, layering them onto the palm of his hand. 'Oisín! Put them away right now.'

'You can blame your brother for this,' Oisín said, staring coldly at Eabha. 'He was the one who gave them to me.'

'Tomorrow is opening night,' Eabha said, her voice jumpy. 'You don't know how those things will hit you.'

'Don't worry, Eabha,' Oisín replied. 'I've been educating myself – I know what I'm about.' He lifted the mushrooms to his mouth and tossed them in, chewing vigorously, his mouth full.

'Jesus, Oisín, stop! Spit it out.' Sam's arms were on his shoulders, shaking Oisín violently. 'Stop this! You've made your point. You've annoyed everyone now. So you can fucking stop.'

Oisín ignored him, chewing with ever more vigour, spitefully sucking into his soul the mind-bending effects of the mushrooms. They watched him – helpless – and Dara felt Eabha weaken next to her, as if her body couldn't hold itself upright anymore.

'Oisín,' she said weakly, '*please*, spit them out. I'm begging you.'

'You remember trying these, don't you, Eabha? Made you feel light as a bird – remember? The day at the lake? You could feel that way again. Go on, take one.' He was holding the bag towards her; she tried to snatch it from him, but he was too quick. 'Ah, don't be like that, Eabha. Don't take everything so seriously.' His face turned, his expression suddenly savage. 'Isn't that what you told me once? Remember that? Remember when I told you I loved you? You told me I don't know what love is . . . I kept trying to figure out *why* you were pulling away from me . . . thought maybe you had your eye on someone else. Does Sam know you're into Dara?'

Eabha's face took on that harsh edge which Dara knew came before a burst of sudden, icy ferocity. An acoustic version of 'Wave of Mutilation' was playing from the speaker on the table. Nobody spoke. Faintly, they could hear the sound of hammer on nail coming from the stage, final touches being made to the set. Dara felt her body seize in anticipation of Eabha's reaction, but, to her surprise, it didn't come.

Instead, her face slowly melted into an indulgent smile.

'You know what? Have fun, Oisín. Whatever you're doing with the mushrooms, it's none of my business. Just as what I do with my life is none of yours.' She reached for her cup again and took a drink, almost casually, almost convincingly.

But Oisín wasn't finished.

'You know, I've realised something about Cillian,' he shouted. 'After all this time, I actually get him. He's not all that different from me, really. You used him, just like you used me. You let him fall in love with you. You lied to him – pretended you loved him too. But you, Eabha, have never loved anyone but yourself.'

Cillian's final line rose in Dara's head. She could hear it echoing in her ears as she watched pain contorting Oisín's features.

Cillian: Jesus Christ, Eabha. I loved you! I
really did.

Oisín's eyes fell on her next. 'She doesn't love you either, Dara. She doesn't even love her brother. This grotesque play of hers – she doesn't care what it does to him.'

'Stop it,' Eabha shouted, clenching the paper cup in her hand so hard that the champagne spilled all over the floor. 'We're not doing this! Oisín, you've made your point. You've had your little scene. We all need to leave now. We need to go home before . . . before this gets out of hand. The show is opening *tomorrow*. It's time this stopped – this has to stop.'

Oisín looked at her and his eyes were so blank they were almost voids. 'I'm not going to stop, Eabha. I won't stop until people know who you really are. Everyone's favourite little playwright – Eabha de Lacey. Fuck me, you managed to convince people you're the real deal, didn't you? But you're a liar. A fraud. You suck everything into your orbit and then you devour it. Cillian knew that. Didn't he? He saw what you were doing to him. And he wasn't going to take that from you. Was he? Is that why he's dead now, Eabha? Is that why? Did you do it? Did you kill him?'

There it was. Now, at the last, after weeks of trying, Oisín had punched her straight in the gut, sending her reeling backwards into a dark attic, back to a small space in which stood a lonely boy who said he loved her.

Eabha's eyes fell to her feet and Dara watched them glaze over, her mind transported back to the Bodkin School, to the moment her life had changed irrevocably. Defeat was sweeping through Eabha's body, robbing her of the last of her strength.

In the middle of Dara's chest, a knot was forming. She looked at Eabha, feeling the panic rise in her, wondering if they would need to call Austin. Was this one of those times when she needed him? If it was, the timing couldn't be worse.

Sam placed a firm hand on Oisín's shoulder. 'It's time to go, Oisín. Those mushrooms you just took are going to hit you hard and you're not going to want to be out here barking abuse at people when they do.'

Oisín reached for the champagne bottle. 'You know, you really changed your tune about Eabha. Was it Dara that did that to you, Sam? I bet it was. She has that innocent look about her – those big eyes of hers – but she has you under her thumb now. She has Eabha too, by the look of it.' Danger played in Oisín's smile. 'But, Sam, you were right about Eabha when you said she was fake. I guess I just didn't see it at the time.'

'Dara,' Eabha said quietly. 'Can we leave now? I . . . I can't deal with this.'

'Yeah,' Dara replied. 'I'll get us a taxi.' She glanced at Sam. 'Can you – I don't know – get him home or something?'

Oisín was finishing the last of the champagne from the bottle, his head thrown back, his throat open.

Sam nodded. 'I'm not letting him out of my sight,' he said. 'I'll make sure he shows up tomorrow.'

Oisín wiped his mouth with the back of his hand. 'I'm not going fucking anywhere with you.' Sam had a firm hand under Oisín's shoulder, his superior physicality obvious as they stood side by side. Oisín seemed, by comparison, reduced.

'You've done enough damage for one night,' Sam said. 'You're coming back to mine and I'm going to drag you here tomorrow if I have to.'

Dara's face was a portrait of worry. 'You're sure, Sam? You can manage him?'

'I'm not a fucking child who has to be *managed*,' Oisín interjected, but was entirely ignored.

Sam gave her a weak smile. 'Yeah,' he said. 'It'll be grand. You two go on home. Get some sleep. We'll see you tomorrow.'

They flagged a taxi on the road outside, the driver perplexed as Dara climbed into the back with Eabha, still in her Bodkin school uniform. As the engine roared into life, Eabha slumped across the car, resting her head against the window opposite, through which a waxing gibbous moon was shining over Dublin.

Dara watched the tears rolling down Eabha's face, words from the script rising in her mind again.

Eabha: I can't do this, Cillian. I can't be around you anymore. I know you're in pain — I *know* you are — but this isn't right. It's too much. And I just can't do it. I just can't. I'm sorry ... I am so sorry.

Dara turned away and gazed out the window, fear prickling at the edges of her thoughts. Next to her, Eabha reached for her phone, selecting a number and raising the speaker to her ear. She was silent while the phone rang.

'... Austin? Austin, it's me.'

Chapter Twenty-Three

Sleep must have come eventually. The process of waking felt as if she had been under ether. Sitting up in the bed, Dara blinked several times, rubbed her eyes, and then remembered, with a thundering jolt, that the play was opening for an audience that night.

When she checked her phone, there were texts from her mother and Rhona – wishing her luck – and one from Sam, sent late the night before.

> Sam Demir (00:03am): I brought O to mine for the night. He has been hallucinating since you left. If he's like this tomorrow, we're fucked.

She dialled his number; he answered quickly. 'Dara?'

'Hey! How are things over there? How is Oisín now?'

'He's grand, actually. He woke up a few minutes ago and said he was ravenous! My Mam made him a fry . . . he's eating it now.'

'Well . . . didn't he land on his feet?'

'I know . . . she's giving him the full VIP treatment.' He paused. 'He'll be all right for tonight – I think. But Jesus . . . this play has his head fucked.'

'I know the feeling.'

'Ha, yeah. Me too.' Sam sniffed. 'But like, he was muttering in his sleep. I think they were lines from the play . . . I'm worried about him, Dara.'

'Speaking of people to worry about, Austin came over last night.'

'Oh?'

'Yeah . . . Eabha rang him from the taxi and, of course, he dropped everything for her – came running.'

'Of course.' Another pause. 'And is he . . . is he all right in the head or . . .?'

'I don't know. I went straight to bed when we got in and I haven't left my room yet.' She was looking at her costume, thrown over the armchair in the corner. The costume department would flip when they found it missing from the rail. She shut her eyes. She needed to stay focused on the performance. Everything else could wait – Oisín, Austin, even Sam. Once they made it through opening night, they could pick up the pieces again. 'What time are you heading to the theatre?' she asked.

'Early enough, just to be sure nothing goes wrong with Oisín.'

'Good plan.'

'I'll see you in there?'

'Yeah.' She paused. 'Are you nervous, Sam?'

'Bricking it.'

'Oh . . . good. I'm not alone.'

'Never alone, Dara.'

'See you later, Sam.'

* * *

Austin was in the dining room when Dara arrived downstairs, standing at the window, a cup of coffee in his hand, gazing out at the road in search of photographers. But Leinster Road was empty that morning.

Watching him twitching at the curtains, muttering occasionally to himself, Dara felt alarm crawling over her slowly. 'You're still here,' she said from the door.

He looked around and, for a moment, she wondered if he recognised her, but then his expression cleared and, with it, his throat as he coughed and said: 'Yep. Still here.'

Dara leaned against the door frame, one socked foot pressed against the opposite ankle. 'How is Eabha?'

'Better,' he replied. 'She'll be down in a few minutes if you're looking for her. She's just taking a shower.'

Dara nodded, walking further into the room. There was nothing physical about Austin that suggested anything was amiss, but her senses were heightened all the same, as if, on some non-cognitive level, her body sensed his fragility.

'I heard Oisín was bold last night,' Austin said drily.

'It was the mushrooms you gave him,' Dara replied, before she could think better of it. She could feel her irritation with him, hovering in the space between her words.

Austin felt it too. 'He asked for my help. He was . . . he was struggling.' Dara's expression hadn't changed, so Austin sighed and then continued: 'He showed up on my doorstep, like some lost dog. What was I supposed to do?'

Dara avoided his eye, keeping her voice very steady, betraying no emotion. 'It was good of you to take him in.'

'I shouldn't have given him the mushrooms.'

She looked up. 'Why did you?'

Austin turned towards the window, casting his eye out to the road again. 'People think I pushed Cillian out that window, but Cillian was out of his mind in the attic. He was hallucinating up there, seeing things. The mushrooms did that to him. And, when Eabha tried to confront him, they made something snap inside him. What happened was an accident, Dara – just a stupid, meaningless accident.'

He was getting worked up now, his right hand clenching and unclenching, the coffee trembling in his left. Dara bit the inside of her lip. This was a mistake. She shouldn't have spoken to him at all. She should have said hello and continued on to the kitchen. But something in her still wanted to know.

'All right,' she said carefully. 'I believe you, Austin.'

He laughed then, a horrible barking sound. 'No, you don't. Not really,' he said. 'Nobody does.' He lumbered past her, to the door. 'Someday, it won't matter. Someday, people will stop caring . . . and this story will finally fucking die.'

* * *

While she ate breakfast alone in the kitchen, Dara thought about what Austin had just said and pondered the idea of the past as a state of mind, instead of a place where human feet could go. The past was still present only because the story of Cillian's death still mattered to people. If Eabha had allowed it to fade, if Richard Butler had accepted the coroner's finding of accidental death, Cillian's name would be remembered only by those who had loved him, the night of his death fading into the vast forgotten soup of collective human experience. Instead, here she was, about to tell the story yet again for a new audience, keeping the past present, giving old ghosts life.

Eleven hours left to opening.

* * *

Eabha left the house shortly after Austin, a collection of papers in her arms as her footsteps sounded on the floorboards of the hall-way. She had drawn her hair into a severe bun and was wearing a deep emerald velvet kimono with her amber ring and the three lockets she liked to wear around her neck. Dara had seen her open them only once, when Eabha thought she wasn't watching. There was a different photo in each. The first two contained a man and a woman – Máire and Eamonn de Lacey – but she hadn't seen the third, left to wonder who sat next to her heart.

'See you at the theatre, Dara. Are you sure I can't give you a lift?' Eabha called from the doorway.

'You go ahead,' Dara replied. 'I'd like the walk. I'll see you in a bit.' She held the door open while Eabha walked to the Cortina, throwing her handbag and papers onto the passenger seat.

'Let me know if Oisín gives Sam any trouble,' Eabha said, climbing into the driver's seat. 'God, he *better* make it to the theatre.'

'He will – Sam's on it,' Dara said, as the car door slammed. She waved Eabha off, then went back upstairs, heading for the bathroom when her eye caught on the poster hanging on the wall of Eabha's bedroom. She usually kept the door firmly shut, but it was now slightly ajar and Dara could just see Eabha's face as it had appeared to her on the walls at the Wilde Academy.

The original poster.

The Abbey Theatre Proudly Presents
A new play by Eabha de Lacey

THE TRUTH WILL OUT

Starring
Vanessa Devin, Oliver Fiennes,
and Nicolas O'Mahony

On the bed in front of her, a photo album lay open. Dara took a step towards it, spotting Austin's teenage face and, next to him,

Eabha with her long, black hair. The third person was Cillian, standing outside the Bodkin School, staring unsmilingly at the camera, near the spot where he would soon die.

Dara reached for the album, laying it on her lap as she sat down on Eabha's bed to flick through it. Photo after photo of Cillian, of Eabha, of Austin, on the grounds of the Bodkin, wandering across the Burren, or in the attic of the western turret. She gazed down at the frightened way Eabha held her body, the lost expression on Austin's face, the anger blazing in Cillian's eyes.

Eabha standing by the lake in the clearing where they took the mushrooms.

Eabha under the tree with the nook where Cillian left the note telling her he loved her.

Eabha in the attic, sitting by the window, through which Cillian would fall to his death.

* * *

The police had moved the protestors to the footpath near the Rotunda Hospital so they couldn't block the audience arriving at the front door of the Gate Theatre. They looked less intimidating cordoned off behind a railing.

A camera crew stood in a huddle near the stage door, hoping to catch the actors arriving for the performance. Richard Butler was at the Bodkin School in Clare for another vigil, more cameras surrounding him, while he held a candle in one hand and a photo of Cillian in the other. Eabha said he was spending more time down there now than he ever had while Cillian was alive. Dara wasn't sure it mattered: a neglectful father could still miss his dead son.

Oisín was sombre all afternoon as they ran through lines for a final time. He took the sandwich Dara bought for him at the deli around the corner and drank the water she suggested, like a feral cat allowing himself to be briefly domesticated for the sake of an easy meal. When she was sure he wasn't going to cause any trouble, she left him alone while she conferred with the costume department about the mess that was her costume. She'd had to pack it into a bag for the walk across the city and it was now thoroughly crumpled. After a little fretting and tutting, they steamed it for her and delivered it back to the rail again, just in time for the final preparation before their stage call.

As she undressed behind the screen, her skin was alive with nerves, insects crawling through her nervous system. Her family had texted to say they were on their way into town.

'How was Austin this morning?' Sam asked, while she tucked her shirt into the skirt and reached for the jumper.

'Not good,' Dara replied. 'He's erratic – fine one moment, then he seems to disappear into some other part of his mind.' She looked up, struggling with the zip on her skirt. 'Eabha doesn't seem too worried.'

'That's no proof of anything,' Sam said.

Dara caught sight of herself in the mirror over Sam's shoulder and paused. It wasn't just a physical resemblance to Eabha now, it was something else too. She could feel it in herself: a hunger, a biting thirst. She wanted to be seen, to be known – the face in the mirror wanted it, the woman looking back at her no longer the Dara who had left Beara on a wing and a prayer, hoping to build a career in Dublin. She had been transformed by Eabha's Midas touch, turned to gold, flecks of it visible in the eyes shining back at her.

She turned to Sam again. 'It's going to be fine, Sam,' she said. For the first time, she believed herself. 'It's all going to be fine – I can feel it.'

A slow smile spread across Sam's face, lifting his features. 'If you say so, Dara.'

She reached forward and kissed him, resolutely and without hesitation.

Slipping past him, she took a seat at the dressing table to do her make-up. There was a bouquet of flowers wrapped in plastic next to the mirror: roses from her family. She glanced at the card again.

We are so proud of you. Mam, Dad and Rhona x

Brushing pale powder across her face, she traced her cheekbones with some blush and tried to inhabit the moment. Opening night of her debut and the auditorium was filling with an audience there to see her, an audience she would soon transport to a windblown corner of the Burren.

She took a deep breath. Somewhere in the wings, Eabha de Lacey would be watching, and she – Dara Gaffney from Beara – would make her smile, would make her proud.

Eabha was at the door, smiling at her now. 'There she is . . .' Her hands gripped the back of Dara's chair. 'Our leading lady!'

'How's the crowd out there?' Dara asked.

'The auditorium is filling up – and the rain is driving the protestors away!' Eabha's laugh was mocking, but her smile slackened as her eyes fell next on Oisín.

'How are you feeling, Oisín – or should I say Cillian?'

He said something slightly incomprehensible in response so she stepped closer to him.

'I didn't hear you. I asked how you're feeling?'

'Like you fucking care.' His shoulder met hers on his way out the door, and Dara saw the flash of pain as Eabha's hand grasped at her upper arm. The door slammed shut behind Oisín.

Fear, like a shadow, passed over Dara's face. 'He's going to be OK to perform, right?' she said, watching Eabha teetering slightly in her heels before taking the seat Oisín had just vacated.

'Let's hope so,' she replied. 'We don't have a choice.'

Sam was playing with his tie. 'The show must go on.'

'How's Austin?' Dara asked. 'I haven't seen him since this morning.'

Passing a hand over her eyes, Eabha sat down opposite Dara. 'Austin is . . . fine. He wanted to come tonight and, honestly, I couldn't say no to him.' She saw the look that passed between Dara and Sam. 'I know what you're thinking. Frankly, I don't want him here either . . . I can't relax knowing he's here. But I couldn't physically restrain him, could I?'

'Is he here right now?' Sam asked.

'He said he was going out for coffee, but I wouldn't be surprised if he's going out to taunt the protestors . . .'

'Is that a good idea?!' Sam said, looking at her through the mirror. 'The cameras might catch him.'

'What can I do?' Eabha asked, one leg crossed elegantly over the other. 'I can hardly lock him in a room.'

'Might be an idea,' Sam replied. He flicked his gelled fringe out of his eyes. 'Is he – I don't mean to be rude, but – he is mentally *stable*, right?'

'He's fine, Sam,' Eabha said, rising to her feet. 'I don't know why, but it's like whatever storm was brewing in his head has passed in the night.'

Dara met Sam's eye; neither of them believed her.

At the door, Eabha glanced back over her shoulder at both of them. Sam and Dara – Austin and Eabha – in their school uniforms. 'Break a leg tonight . . . I'll see you in the wings.'

* * *

The audience was filling the auditorium, the sound rumbling onto the stage and into the dark of the wings. Dara stood next to Sam, his hand in hers, her skin humming, her stomach clenched, a trickle of sweat running down her back. Across the stage, they could see the white of Oisín's shirt, his face cast in darkness. There was no curtain, the stage open to the audience, the western turret standing at the rear left, a gnarled hawthorn, contorted by an Atlantic gale, standing next to it in a shadow cast by the lighting.

The lights were growing dim, the sound technicians summoning a howling gale while the final few people were taking their seats. Dara breathed in and out slowly. Lost in the dark of the crowd, her family would be watching – producers, directors, and casting agents too.

On his way to take his seat, Geoffrey Goode had stopped backstage and taken her hand in both of his, squeezing the blood from her fingers: 'This is the start for you, Dara Gaffney. Get this right and I can see a shining future for you, my girl!'

Outside the theatre, a crowd stood calling them killers, and outside a school in Clare, a father grieved the death of his son.

Dara looked at Sam – by her side, just as he promised – then she reached over and kissed him, feeling her bones drain of their marrow, her feet rising from the ground. She was untethered, but she wasn't afraid of it anymore.

Emergency exits were identified; the audience were instructed to turn their phones to silent. The last gasp of reality, the final layer peeling back to reveal a past that was hiding there all along.

Briefly she glanced across the stage, where Eabha stood next to Oisín, then took a breath, stepping out from the shadows and into the light.

* * *

The silence of the dark auditorium fed the actors, stripping back the walls, the ceiling, and the stage under them. They were alone – Eabha, Austin and Cillian – trudging through marshy ground, across a barren landscape, chasing the ghost of a wild mountain goat.

Oisín's anger at Eabha made his performance smoulder. With his hands gripping her arms, his lips gasping at her lips, his eyes reaching into her heart, Dara felt entirely lost to herself. She was sixteen years of age, orphaned, wandering free through a frightening world of new possibility. She was Eabha, both attracted to and repelled by the wildness in Cillian and the safe harbour of Austin. She was Eabha, standing in front of a room of strangers, baring her soul, waiting for judgement.

Oisín was lost too. She could see it in his eyes, in the desperation in his voice, in the way he clung to her body. Eabha had broken him and it was Cillian who stepped forward now to fill the gaps.

* * *

It was dizzying to step off the stage for the interval, coaxing themselves back into their bodies so they could walk the short distance to the dressing room. Dara found that she couldn't speak. Her mind was a blank, as if her thoughts had been washed clean away. The performance was going well – better than they could have hoped. She looked to Sam, who just smiled, taking a seat at his dressing table rolling a cigarette.

Oisín was in the corner of the dressing room, muttering quietly to himself. Dara didn't want to disturb him, leaving the spell unbroken so he could carry Cillian with him, back onto the stage for the second act.

In the mirror, her face glowed, sweat coating her forehead and spilling down her cheeks. She dabbed at it with a tissue and a brush heavy with powder, watching as Sam rose to his feet, cigarette hanging from his mouth.

'I'm going out for a quick smoke,' he said, slipping out through the door. 'I'll meet you back out there.'

Alone with Oisín, Dara glanced his way while she fixed her make-up for the finale. He was fiddling with his tie, then his hair, then the chain he still wore around his neck, a last piece of himself.

She had turned away from him, rooting in her make-up bag, when quite suddenly, Oisín stood up. He took two quick steps towards her, pushing her chair around until she faced him. She jumped as he reached for her face, holding her head between his hands. 'Jesus Christ, Eabha,' his said, his eyes wild. 'I loved you! I really did.'

Oisín left the dressing room without another word and Dara didn't see him again as she made her way to the wings for her five-minute call. Still shaken, she listened while the audience took their seats again – the chatter of voices, the shuffling sound they made as they advanced down the rows, knocking against knees and stepping on toes. There was still no sign of Sam.

From the black hole of the wings opposite, Oisín stood in his Bodkin uniform, dishevelled now, just like his character, his tie undone, his shirt untucked, his hair plastered down over his eyes. A terrible smile twisted his face; she couldn't bear to look at it. Even from across the stage, she could feel the abandon in him, the destructive impulse asserting itself again, danger brewing, a successful opening night slipping through her fingers. Dara couldn't shake the sense that he was planning something.

Turning towards the wings behind her, she looked for Sam again, but only the crew looked back; the set designer, the stage manager, two stage technicians. She needed to tell Sam, to warn him – of what, she wasn't sure yet. She looked again at Oisín and felt a cold dread flood over her.

There was a presence next to her. Sam's hand slipped into hers. His breath smelled of smoke.

'Where have you been?!'

'Sorry . . . did I cut it a bit fine?!'

'Sam, I need to tell you—'

'We're on,' Sam hissed, letting her hand go as he walked into the light and took his place on the stage.

She took a breath, her heart racing as she stepped out of herself and into Eabha once more, the gaping mouth of the auditorium opening to her as she entered the scene.

* * *

The critics described Oisín's performance that night as transformative, giving a complexity to the character of Cillian not seen even in the debut run. It was a performance nobody in the theatre would forget, Dara least of all.

As they progressed through the scenes, the trouble seemed to have passed and she began to relax.

He had frightened her in the dressing room, but standing with him on the stage – in front of their friends and family, strangers and critics – she felt how Eabha must have felt all those years ago, no longer able to separate herself from the scene. He kissed her and she kissed back, not as she had in the rehearsal room, but with the full strength of a feeling that wasn't her own. Sam couldn't have known these secret thoughts, and yet, as they reached the fight scene, his rage felt real, his punches landing so close to Oisín's face, as if his arms were struggling to restrain the anger in him, righteous and deadly.

Reaching the final scene in the attic of the western turret, there were audience members already crying, knowing what was about to happen, knowing death waited for Cillian. Right on cue, the glass smashed behind Dara's head and she cried out to Sam while Oisín screamed at her to love him, speaking again the words he had said to her just moments before in the dressing room. The stage went dark as they reached the finale, frozen together in the attic, frozen together in time – Cillian and Austin – in a state of paralysis.

*Darkness falls, **Eabha** walks to the centre of the stage, a single white light shining on her. Behind her, **Austin** and **Cillian** are entangled, moving in slow motion, shrouded in darkness.*

Dara descended the stairs, the spotlight lighting up her face. Behind her, while she delivered the final words of the play, she could hear a slight scuffle, muttered words, laboured breathing.

Eabha *(to audience):* There are moments in time that change the course of our lives, inflection points that we return to, seeking answers, alternate choices we might have made, different paths we could have taken, a shift in perspective that might alter the past and create a new truth for us to live by. This is the moment I would change, but my mind is a prison and the past is my jailer. I'm stuck with the consequences of this moment. I watch the scene again and again, turning it over in my mind, seeking answers, watching for clues lurking in the darkness, a map to show me a way forward. I wonder who I would be if Cillian were alive, if his

feet had not failed him, if gravity had not
abandoned him, if death had passed him by. I
try to tell the story differently, to move the
details around in my mind and see if that
changes it, but the past proves inescapable.
I can tell you a story, spin you a yarn, but
Cillian remains cold in his grave. The truth
is not coy. It is not hiding from me, from
you. It is not here on this stage. It's gone
from my mind. I let it fall out the window,
tumbling to the ground with Cillian, dying
with him on the cold, hard concrete. I can't
change that. (*She pauses, eyes passing over
the audience*)

'The past remains the past,' Dara said. 'The truth a mystery, and this story just a story.' She paused, her eyes passing slowly over the darkness in which her audience sat, all watching her, their attention entirely hers. 'Make of it what you will. The rest is silence.'

* * *

The lights were doused, a sudden black engulfing the stage, as a loud crack sounded behind Dara. Three hundred feet hit the floor, three hundred hands clapping, her own heart beating inside her ribcage like a bird frantic for escape. A triumphant smile lit up Dara's face as she caught her breath, thinking of the protestors outside, the journalists, the critical voices on the radio, Richard Butler, Vanessa Devin, her parents, her Aunty Sheila, her neighbours back home in Beara, all of them wrong to doubt her, just as she was wrong – utterly wrong – to doubt herself.

But into this exultant moment cut a sudden scream. It sliced through her thoughts, the kind of anguished cry she had never heard before and would never forget. She turned around. Eabha had appeared from the wings, staring down at the crumpled body in the middle of the stage, a pool of blood spilling out from the broken skull.

They say everything slows down, the moments seeming to stretch, time becoming an elasticated substance. A slow-motion descent, the glass shards frozen briefly as the falling body reaches upwards for the solid ground from which it has just been separated. Gravity, the great betrayer; death its accomplice.

Oisín lay dead on the stage, while applause thundered from the audience.

The lights came on for the curtain call, but the actors were not lining up to take a bow. From the attic window, Sam stared down in shock and disbelief, just as Austin had all those years before. At the front of the stage, Dara was rooted to the floor as if nails had been driven through her feet. Slowly, a creeping realisation spread from the actors, to the crew, to the audience, the applause petering out, a ripple of shock spreading from the stage to the back of the auditorium.

Dara's thoughts were blank, her body trembling, her mind refusing to accept what her eyes could see. She couldn't process what was happening around her, didn't notice the stage manager ringing for an ambulance, didn't see the front-of-house staff directing the audience as quickly as possible out of the auditorium, didn't hear her own parents shouting her name, didn't see Rhona trying to get to her before she was blocked by a staff member. She didn't notice Sam's arm around her, didn't see Austin leave the theatre quietly by the stage door. She didn't look at Eabha kneeling over Oisín's body, the warmth seeping from him by the moment. She saw only the blank expression on his face, only the unnatural way his body lay, contorted painfully.

She saw Cillian lying dead on the ground outside the Bodkin School, saw Austin and Eabha staring down at him from the broken attic window, and saw that the past had repeated itself, reaching out to grab them and hold them. Puppets on a string. They were captive to it and bound by it, and it was that realisation which sent a gurgling cry racing up from the pit of her stomach, snaking up her throat and exploding out through her mouth. Sam's arms were around her but she could hardly feel him, her knees weakening under her, her ears ringing, her vision crackling.

* * *

The paramedics arrived quickly and tried some basic CPR, though they knew it was futile. As they placed his body on a stretcher, already Oisín looked entirely different. Not himself, not quite human anymore, his eyes closed, his mouth hanging open.

Dara still couldn't move, shivering on the spot where her performance had ended, even after they had carried Oisín out to the waiting ambulance. It was then that she spotted it at the edge of the stage. It must have rolled away from Oisín when he fell, but it was visible now.

Cillian's goat skull. Still in one piece.

Epilogue

Beara Peninsula, West Cork

When she thought back to those days during the months and years that followed, the memories never appeared as Dara would have expected. It was as if a veil were covering her eyes, as if her mind were protecting her from the pain of it, trying to coax her to forget. Danger lay in the remembering, the past filled with unanswerable questions, with consuming regret.

The funeral occurred and Oisín was placed in the ground. The police had quietly ruled out the possibility of foul play. The toxicology report confirmed the presence of psilocybin in his blood and they had formed a theory around it: Oisín had lost control in some way, lost his sense of space and time, stepping out of himself and off the set, crashing to the stage floor. He must have taken some mushrooms during the interval, though nobody had seen it happen. Dara was the last person who saw him before Act Two began. But after he spoke his final lines to her, with his hands grabbing at her face, he had left her alone in the dressing room. He could have taken more mushrooms then, either alone or with someone else. But if anyone had seen him after Dara, they certainly didn't want it known.

Sam, who had been standing on the set with Oisín when he fell, had no explanation to offer when the police interviewed him. He told Dara afterwards that it felt as if they were asking him to describe something that had happened to someone else, or to speak a language he didn't know.

'Mr Demir, we need you to tell us, in your own words and to the best of your knowledge, what occurred on the attic set before Oisín Langford fell.'

'I . . . I don't know. I mean, it was so dark – I couldn't see anything. He was standing beside me and . . . and . . . and then he fell. He just – I don't know how – but he just fell.'

'You're sure he fell?'

'Well, how else could it have happened?'

'He could have been pushed.'

'No – I didn't do that! Why would I do that?!'

'Was there anyone else on the set with you?'

'No – I . . . I don't, I don't think so.'

'You don't think?'

'I didn't see anyone. It was pitch black up there. All I could see was Dara on the stage.'

'He could have jumped.'

'There's no way he'd do that.'

'He fell headfirst, the full weight of his body coming down on his spinal column. A dead weight.'

'Jesus . . .'

'It was almost as if he were diving into water. It was almost deliberate.'

'I . . . But why would he . . . why would he do that?'

'The pathologist said if he had tried to cushion his fall, he might have survived.'

'I don't know anything about that.'

'Why did he consume the mushrooms?'

'He was . . . it was for his character work. That's what he said. To become more like Cillian.'

'Was he under any form of emotional distress?'

A pause. 'Aren't we all?'

'Specifically, Mr Demir, are you aware of any reason why Oisín Langford may have been upset?'

Another pause. 'Yes.'

'Why was he upset?'

'She messed him about . . . he didn't know why. He thought he was in love with her, but it was more like . . . like obsession, like an illness.'

'You're talking about Eabha de Lacey?'

'Yes.'

* * *

The simplest explanation fit best – Oisín's fall was a tragic accident – and yet it didn't quite sit easy with Dara. Standing by the graveside with Sam, she listened to the low hum of sobbing from Oisín's family and friends while the coffin was slowly lowered. They were standing back a little, aware that the other mourners were casting furtive glances their way, at the two people who had been on the stage with him when he died. Was she imagining a whiff of suspicion? Was there a question in their eyes when they swung around to look at her? Was it there in whispered exchanges, in knowing glances?

Dara leaned closer to Sam, her cheek resting against his chest. She was still struggling to make sense of what had happened, to understand why they were standing in this cemetery instead of the theatre. There were pathways in her mind, bringing her back again and again to that moment, to the spotlight, to the crack of his skull, to the roar of applause. *The rest is silence.*

'I thought I heard him say something, up in the attic.' She looked up at Sam. 'Did he? Did Oisín say something before he fell?'

He looked tired, sleepless nights gathering under his eyes.

Cigarette smoke drifted from his mouth on an exhalation. 'Yeah, he did. Oisín said, 'What are you doing here, Austin?' I guess they were his last words.'

'Austin was there?!' Dara said, lashes flicking as she blinked rapidly.

'No,' Sam said. 'No, it's a line from the play. He was talking about . . . he was talking about *me* . . . right?'

Across from them, standing near the family, they could see Eabha leaning towards Celia, dressed all in black, sunglasses hiding her eyes.

Austin had not come to the funeral.

'You're sure, Sam? You're sure Oisín was talking about you?'

Dara watched him raise his cigarette again, letting the smoke fill his mouth briefly.

'Yeah,' he said, though he sounded less and less sure of himself now. 'Yes – I . . . like, who else could he have meant? You've been spending too much time in your head, Dara.'

Dara was watching Eabha again, Celia's arm wrapped around hers, a small space between them and the rest of the crowd, as if everyone else were keeping them at a distance. She couldn't blame them; Eabha seemed utterly cursed.

'He's sick – Austin, I mean. That's why he's not here,' she said. 'Did I tell you that?'

'Yeah . . . you said he's an in-patient at St John of God's,' Sam said. 'The shock of Oisín dying triggered another episode?'

'Yeah,' Dara said. 'That's what Eabha told me. She said she found him back at the house . . . in the attic.'

She was looking at Eabha again; Sam leaned towards her. 'What is it, Dara? Your face . . . you look so suspicious.'

'Do I?' she said, though her expression didn't change. 'You know, I keep trying to piece together that night . . . to remember all the details and I can't seem to get it straight . . . but there's this . . . *feeling*. It shifts when I try to pin it down, as if I'm reaching out to grab at fog.'

'I don't know what you mean,' Sam said, pulling her closer to him. 'What sort of feeling?'

'Just . . . this sense that he was there . . . Austin. I didn't see him . . . I mean, I *couldn't* have seen – I was looking at the audience – but . . .'

'He wasn't there, Dara. I would have seen him.'

Dara looked down at the gravel at her feet, falling silent. With the tip of her shoe, she kicked at the loose stones, listening to them crunch, a chalky film forming on the black leather.

Oisín's mother said a final few words, throwing a white rose onto his coffin, a handful of earth following after it. She thought of Richard Butler – seeing again his sharp blue eyes that day outside the theatre – and pitied Oisín's family, now experiencing the same fate.

What are you doing here, Austin?

The words kept sounding in Dara's mind, rippling through the pool of suspicion in her stomach. She couldn't seem to shake it. Eabha was raising a white tissue to her face, dabbing at tears, and Dara could see, clearly, the lost girl standing at her parents' graveside, or at the broken attic window. Now, here she was again. Another graveside.

This time, Oisín's turn.

* * *

With the play cancelled, there was nothing keeping Dara in Dublin and her mother's insistence that she should come home felt like reason enough to make a swift escape from the house on Leinster Road. It had felt funereal in the days since Oisín's death, the air dead, the silence stifling. She left as soon as she could, insisting to Eabha that she would be back. She didn't know yet if that were true.

On the Beara Peninsula, at the edge of the world, Dara walked along the headlands until her feet were red and raw, until her throat was parched and she was too tired to think, too tired to give any thought at all to the people she had left behind in Dublin and the one who lay beneath soil.

Rhona knew better than to ask her about Oisín, so they spent their days talking of nothing of consequence, or not talking at all. She had adopted her father's penchant for silence, sitting passively at the dinner table, speaking only when spoken to and only when there was something to be said. She found it restful, seeking out her father's company, where she could sit and let the world pass by, without feeling the need to interfere and shape its passage in some way. For the first time in her life, she understood her father a little. She didn't mind her mother's fussing. She dyed her hair blonde again and cut it short. Sadness lingered in the tips of the hair: she wanted rid of it.

* * *

Sam phoned her every evening to see how she was, though they tried to avoid discussions of Oisín or what had happened. Instead, they spoke about the weather changing, the nights drawing in, the swallows lining the telephone poles. They spoke about the new production Sam was working on, the auditions he was going for, the trip he was planning to Turkey with his father. Dara would sit in her childhood bedroom while she listened to Sam speaking of life back in Dublin, the walls still covered in old concert tickets, photos from school, and from her first production of *Salome* at the Wilde Academy, her old self beaming out at her.

She was in Beara nearly three weeks when Sam broached the

subject of her return. 'Have you thought about what you're going to do?' he said. 'Is it too soon to ask?'

She closed her eyes, listening to the low strum of his voice down the line. 'You can ask, but I don't have an answer.'

'You left in such a hurry . . . are you planning to come back to Dublin?' he said, then stammered slightly. 'I'd . . . I'd really like to . . . to see you again soon, Dara.'

She pulled her hair back behind her ears, a flush rising through her. 'I'd like to see you too, Sam.'

'It doesn't have to be in Dublin.'

'Where else would I go?'

Sam was silent for a moment. 'We could go literally any-where else. If you wanted to, we could leave this behind – go to London, let some time pass, and then nobody would remem-ber that we were there, that we were on the stage when Oisín Langford died. Nobody will think of Eabha de Lacey when they hear our names. They won't know we were ever mixed up in any of this.'

'I'm . . . I'm not going to do that, Sam. I'm not going to run away and hide.' She heard him sigh into the phone, her eyes on her own face in the mirror, out of place now, as if she didn't belong in her own bedroom anymore.

'Why not?' he said. 'Look, for your own sake, Dara, think about it? If you come back to Dublin, back to Eabha, you might never escape this. You'll always be living in the shadow of it.'

Dara's heart was thumping, her voice lost somewhere in her chest. She had only just made a start in Dublin. Why should this be the end of all that? Why should she be the one to leave? There was nothing for her anywhere else, except the bottom rung of the ladder. Again.

A dark thought surfaced: they knew her now. Dara Gaffney's name would not be soon forgotten.

'Think about it, Dara? Will you?' Sam's voice was beseeching. She found it unnerving. '. . . Dara? Please?'

'I'll think about it, Sam.'

'Good . . . that's good. I'm glad to hear that. Really glad.'

Dara didn't reply, lying back on her bed, listening as the worry in his voice gave way to a lethargic hope.

'They're careless people, Dara – Eabha and Austin – don't be the one left cleaning up their mess.'

* * *

On her way to bed that night, Rhona knocked on her sister's bedroom door. Dara had spent most of the past week alone in her room, taking some of her meals back with her, emerging only for cups of tea or an occasional shower. They were giving her space, letting her grieve as she needed to grieve, but now the isolation was lengthening and deepening, just as the night was gaining pace on the day, the summer falling to autumn.

'Come in,' Dara called from inside the room at the sound of Rhona's knocking.

She entered, her eyes taking in the state of the room: dirty plates lying on the floor and on top of the dresser, laundry in small piles across the carpet. Papers were strewn all around the bed, across which Dara lay, her bare feet dangling in the air above her.

'Have you made a decision yet?' Rhona asked, picking her way through the room. 'Are you going back to Dublin?'

Turning over, Dara rested her head on her hand, her lips forming an ambivalent expression. 'Probably. Can't see any other way forward. I'm not going to stay in Beara for the rest of my life.'

Rhona nodded, gathering the scattered pages into her hands so she could sit down on the edge of the bed. 'You won't go back to her, will you? Back to Eabha?' She placed the pages on her lap, ordering them together into a pile.

'I haven't decided yet. Sam says I shouldn't. He says she'll only draw me back in.'

'Sam's right.'

'It might be different this time – I know her better than Sam does, better than you.'

'But you don't need her, Dara. You can make your own path.'

Dara wasn't listening, a notepad open in front of her, her pen flowing across it.

'You haven't mentioned him in a while . . . Oisín.'

'Haven't I? It feels like I think of nothing else.' Her legs were still kicking the air, her focus still on her page, pushing Oisín's face from the front of her mind, where he liked to linger. 'I'm trying to figure out if he was up there when he fell . . .'

'Who? If who was there?'

'Austin – I heard something behind me . . . a commotion of some kind . . . but it's just like Eabha said . . . the memory shifts and changes. It slips through my fingers.'

Rhona was silent for a moment. 'Wouldn't Sam have noticed? Wouldn't he have seen Austin?'

'Not necessarily. Not in the dark.' She paused her writing, her eyes staring momentarily at nothing, at the past.

Rhona tugged on her leg, as if to remind her of her presence. 'There's no point thinking too much about it, Dara,' she said. 'It'll only drag you back into that whole mess. It won't do you any good.'

Dara didn't reply, her attention on her notebook.

Rhona sighed, eyes on the back of Dara's head, her blonde hair gathered over one shoulder, but Dara was in a world of her own.

The pages on Rhona's lap rustled. She held them up to her eyes, trying to read her sister's rushed handwriting. 'What's . . . what's all this, Dara?'

Dara sat up on the bed, her pen still poised in her hand. 'Don't read it!' She snatched the pages out of Rhona's hands. 'It's not ready yet.'

'But, Dara,' Rhona said, concern growing. 'What is it?'

Dara thought once more of Eabha, the girl in the photos outside the Bodkin School, dark hair billowing around her. Next to her, Austin and Cillian. A face in the window of an attic. She thought of Oisín, standing at the door, watching Eabha dance to the sound of the Tannhäuser Overture, his face contorted in the pain of betrayal. She thought of his skull broken on the stage floor. Broken people, broken hearts, broken bones.

'It's . . . the truth,' Dara paused, a slow smile spreading across her face, 'as I remember it.'

'What are you talking about? I don't know what you mean?'

'I'm going to do what Eabha couldn't. I'm going to tell people the truth, Rhona. I'm going to find out what really happened and I'm going to tell the real story.'

Rhona's shoulders sank, her expression drooping, just as an exuberance was sweeping over Dara, swallowing her whole. 'Dara, I don't think that's a good idea. You're making the same mistake – you're doing the same thing she did.'

Dara wasn't listening. She could see it, right before her eyes, actors on a stage, an audience staring up at them, while she stood in the wings, watching, waiting, until the final moment came, the final word uttered, the audience on their feet, applause rising, filling the theatre.

'Dara? Dara, can we talk about this?'

She could see it so clearly that it was as if it had happened already, as if it had all been leading to this point. The words already assembling, filling page after page, the story practically telling itself.

'So that's what you've been doing in here? I thought you were moving past all of this, Dara – past her.'

'It's not about her anymore, Rhona.'

Rhona's hand was on Dara's shoulder, gripping her tightly. 'Then what's this about? Why would you do this, Dara?'

'Don't you see, Rhona?' The words came quickly to her, because she had heard them before. They were Eabha's words. 'The past isn't fixed. It's a story we tell. And if I don't tell this story, who will? Someone else will own the past, someone else will control it.' Dara's eyes were unseeing, her ears unhearing. 'So, I have to do it, Rhona. I have to tell the story of what happened – to Oisín, to Sam, to me.' Hope was expanding through her, a chance to set things right, to set the past free, to let it recede into shadow again, to let it rest in silence, maybe even in peace. 'I'm going to do it, Rhona. I'm going to write it. It'll be different this time.' She looked at her sister and smiled. 'This time, the truth will out.'

CURTAIN.

Acknowledgements

This book was written during the pandemic, at a peculiar time of shared isolation and loneliness. During those difficult days, the support and love I received from friends and family was so greatly appreciated and kept me going.

Thank you to early readers who were so encouraging of this story, Molly Joyce, Hannah Lowry O'Reilly, Emily Turner, Aimee O'Hanlon and Hugh O'Connor. Thank you to my editor, Charlotte Mursell, whose ambition for this story far exceeded my own, and to the team at Orion Fiction for all your help. Thank you to Hayley Steed – I can't imagine going through the publication process without you! Both your steadfast support and your keen editorial eye are deeply appreciated. Thank you to Dan Colley, for casting your expert eye over the theatrical details and giving me such valuable advice.

Thank you to my parents, who have been reading my work since I was a child (some might think it should be better by now!). I'm forever indebted to my father for the lifetime of loyalty and love he packed into my first 30 years. In the months before he died, we spoke frequently about our writing projects and I have greatly missed his wisdom and his company through the writing of this book. Without the steadfast support of my father, I think it's quite likely I would have sunk beneath the weight of my inner critic long ago. Though he isn't here to say it anymore, I remind myself daily of the kind words he would have spoken and the love he felt for me. I try every day to be worthy of it. He was the most wonderful man.

To my mother, who has read everything I have ever written since the days I wrote in crayon, thank you from the bottom of my heart. Your strength and grace are guiding lights to me and I can still remember you teaching me to persevere with my stories, even when I was too young to know the word. It was an invaluable lesson for a young writer! For everything you do for me, thank you.

Finally, to David, who was locked away in an apartment with me and these characters for months, I can never express to you the depth of my gratitude. Your love is the making of me. It is your belief in me which gives me the courage to pursue the things that seem beyond my reach. It is your support which allows me to keep trying. You are the truest friend and I love you, always.

Credits

Rosemary Hennigan and Orion Fiction would like to thank everyone at Orion who worked on the publication of *The Truth Will Out* in the UK.

Editorial
Charlotte Mursell
Sanah Ahmed

Copyeditor
Jade Craddock

Proofreader
Sally Partington

Audio
Paul Stark
Jake Alderson

Contracts
Anne Goddard
Humayra Ahmed
Ellie Bowker

Design
Tomás Almeida
Joanna Ridley
Nick May

Editorial Management
Charlie Panayiotou
Jane Hughes
Bartley Shaw
Tamara Morriss

Finance
Jasdip Nandra
Afeera Ahmed
Elizabeth Beaumont
Sue Baker

Marketing
Helena Fouracre

Production
Ruth Sharvell

Publicity
Alex Layt

Operations
Jo Jacobs
Sharon Willis

Sales
Jen Wilson
Esther Waters
Victoria Laws
Rachael Hum
Anna Egelstaff
Frances Doyle
Georgina Cutler